BOSOM PALS

An omnibus edition
SWITCHBACK
FAST AND LOOSE
A BITE OF THE APPLE

BOSOM PALS

An omnibus edition

SWITCHBACK
FAST AND LOOSE
A BITE OF THE APPLE

GUILD PUBLISHING
LONDON

SWITCHBACK

'Identical twins are, so to speak, the "same individual of whom two copies have been printed".'

Larousse Science of Life.

Joan Rostand and Andrée Tétry

For my sister Sally

One

Blossom Tree opened her eyes. It wasn't light yet, but she had been rudely awakened (an apt description, she thought) by her husband's heavy erection twitching between her warm buttocks. Nosing its way in like a determined torpedo.

'Bugger me!' she exclaimed crossly. 'I don't know about that!' And sliding over to face him she took his tool in her hand. The firm touch seemed to satisfy the taut, questing flesh; by the time Blossom had drifted to sleep once again, her handful had subsided to nothing.

Meanwhile, some 290 miles away in London, Blossom's twin, June Day, was awakening too. But in quite different circumstances. The man sleeping beside her was a stranger as far as she could tell. She felt cautiously. Circumcised. Nothing much to write home about, neither dressing to left nor to right, but centrally and in the perpendicular – Christ – suddenly there was *heaps* to write home about! She abruptly ceased her sly reconnaissance, having no wish to disturb her bed companion; not before she had had the chance to get her bearings and at least establish where the hell she was. She wasn't at home, that was for sure. This wasn't her bedroom, nor was it one that she had been in before. Yet there were certain similarities to others that she had known, belonging to those of her married lovers.

This man beside her was married. She could tell in the thin light leaking through the thick curtains that this was a family man. The evidence was there; in the nightgown and negligée strewn over the chair and his pyjamas nearby on the carpet; in the extended width of the fitted wardrobes, one openly displaying a costly row of fur coats

7

beyond a plethora of pearled and sequined party wear. This wife was obviously one who enjoyed getting out on the town. Was that where she was now, still whooping it up, but about to arrive back unexpectedly?

June shut her eyes tightly and tugged at her thick fringe. Hell! Hadn't she meant to give this sort of thing up! But last night at Television Tower, events had run away with themselves, ending in a wonderfully boozy blur. Hospitality had been unduly generous with the spirits. She was more used to the frugality of the BBC. Her head ached, but only slightly, not half as much as she deserved. But she was suffering from a terrible thirst and a vague, though not yet troublesome, urge to empty her bladder.

She blinked several times at the bedside table. Someone thoughtful, herself(?), had put down a tall glass of water. She seized it gratefully and drained the whole lot in one gulp, realising too late that it was her vodka and tonic from last night. Instantly drunk, she fell back on her pillow into a state of appalled semi-consciousness. Then mercifully sank into a deep sleep.

When she awoke again it was with a feeling of abandoned gaiety. Rather naughty, yet thrilling recollections of the night before had infiltrated her fleeting dreams. Smudged images surfaced of herself in the centre of an admiring circle of men (consisting in the main of her television colleagues) gradually thinning out to make way for their superiors. Of course, the king-pin would be the programme producer. It was the producer whom June had finally nailed last night, deliberately enchanting him with a stream of light anecdotes, accompanied by occasional smouldering looks geared to lead his thoughts along the same lewd path as her own. She had been fancying this one for months. And then she'd blown it . . . She stretched in the bed, luxuriating in the comfort of the quality linen sheets and the firm base to the hard sprung mattress. Sleeping around and around as she did (as she often delighted in telling people whom she had only just met) made one as much a connoisseur of cribs and couches, as of cocks. She would go on to confide that her favourite was her married sister's four-poster, which was covered in black fur and had sheets of slippery black satin. But this was simply an arbitrary piece of additional

8

information imparted solely so that she would then be asked, as she unfailingly was: 'So you have a married sister – is she anything like you?' Then she would be able to say that she was one of twins. She never felt right until people knew.

Experience told her that this particular mattress belonged to somebody who had a bad back. She had awakened on quite a few of these orthopaedic mattresses of late and could vouch that they gave a damn sight better night's sleep. Not that she was a sufferer, her spine had so far never played her up – touch wood.

Her fingers contacted the smooth veneered surface of the carved bedside table, brushing the empty glass against what she now saw to be a framed photograph of a family. She stared at its focal point, at the pater familias, posing so proudly surrounded by his children. All of them young adults, one even holding a small baby, presumably a grandchild. Yes, that's who she had fucked! The father of them all. This face that as recently as six months ago had been plastered all over the press. The Director General of Universal Television, newly appointed – this very family snap was the one they had run in the *Guardian*. June permitted herself a small self-congratulatory smirk. It wasn't every day a girl landed as big a fish as this, though it was a shame to have had to forego the sexy producer.

A slight stirring behind reminded her that all was not yet over. The Director General appeared in favour of making his presence felt. He was speaking. He was murmuring, murmuring one word softly: 'Cynthia.' June bristled, but not for long, her good humour was such that she was able to forgive the inaccuracy. The poor man was muddling her up with his missus. Next to the family snap stood another photograph, a heavily retouched studio shot of an anaemic blonde whose particular brand of bloodlessness suggested aristocratic forebears. 'Darling – Cynthia', was scrawled across the spray of orchids. Cynthia was without doubt the absent wife.

She turned around carefully; it wouldn't do to move too fast. The Director General was a person of a certain age – not ancient exactly, yet in those hazardous years the heart could, as like as not, do very funny things. The sudden shock of discovering that he was not in bed with his wife might well trigger off an alarming and highly embarrassing set of circumstances. It had happened to June once before. She had found it very frightening, although secretly admitted to a gruesome fascination – she had never heard the death-rattle before. And it was many, many months before she felt sufficiently detached to be able to relate the experience with her customary wit. Of course by the time she had 'perfected' it with several titillating embellishments, the tale did become one of her more hilarious. And she enjoyed the piquancy of dining out on a corpse.

Shit! Now he had seen her – now he'd seen who she wasn't!

Mere inches away from her nose, June was being regarded by a pair of moist, bloodshot brown eyes. The expression was one of puzzled suspicion. She felt as if she'd seduced a St Bernard.

'Good morning,' she said brightly.

The gentle beast blinked, then uttered a low groan sounding more like a bronchial bark; this led to a heaving convulsion of coughing. The bed shook. The brown eyes spun in pivoted frenzy midst an alarming complexion of stretched pores and strained veins. The ham-fists which had lain lightly clasped about her body were now clenched, making mince-meat of her breasts.

'Ah-ha, here we go!' June spoke out loud, voicing her instant and spiralling concern. 'Come on, old boy – enough of all that –' She gripped his hands hard over her swiftly shredding mammaries; and in an ill-conceived attempt to distract him from his bodily paroxysm, she went childishly boss-eyed and stuck her tongue out in his face. It didn't work. Worse, the fierce complexion deepened to a bluish puce. Quite obviously, lack of respect was not much appreciated. Added to which, there now appeared to be a hectic activity down below; the substantial limbs of the Director General were threshing beneath the quilt like a hefty combine-harvester. In two ticks and a tear they'd be buried in feathers, June thought wildly. Babes-in-the-bed, but with a gaping disparity in age. She felt herself to be too young to relish a downy grave. Clearly, direct action was needed to relieve this poor bugger's agitation.

10

At a certain personal risk to her lush, lissom flesh she lowered herself in the bed and with her capable lips applied the principle of the leech to his parts.

Blossom prepared breakfast, it didn't take long. Her children, Pip and Willow, were away with friends for half-term. She thought about them briefly. 'Little sods,' she said, and grinned. Then she went to the bottom of the stairs and plucked an offensively unmelodious chord on the strings of a free-standing gold harp, before returning to dish up the kippers.

The harp was typical of Blossom's rather theatrical style in decor. Though neither she nor her husband, Randolph, were at all musically inclined they possessed, apart from the harp which nobody could play, various decorative instruments including a most striking grand piano which was lacquered a scarlet vibrant enough to dominate any normal domestic interior – but not Blossom's of course. Here it simply merged in the exultant riot of colours; in the vivid pink and crimson of the Mexican rugs on the painted tangerine floor; the brilliant sunshine yellow of the vast dining table – one of Blossom's favourite possessions, the *plastic* table. Purchased in Paris and shipped over to Puddlemouth with immense difficulty and expense, she had claimed it as her tenth wedding anniversary present. The morning it arrived she had let Randolph fuck her on it – free. It was the first time for three years that she hadn't charged.

Upstairs in the spartan austerity of his study Randolph Tree sat reading the *Times Literary Supplement*. He was pondering on an aphorism of Karl Kraus, selected by a Professor Zohn in his recently published *Half-Truths & One-And-A-Half Truths*: 'Life is an effort that deserves a better cause.' Randolph Tree was rather irritated; he wished he'd written it. Added to which he felt unusually hungry. He was used to getting up at six and not breakfasting until Blossom arose, but today found him with a keen edge to his appetite. Perhaps the pervasive smell of kippers had something to do with it. In any event, on hearing his wife's hideous twanging he rose with alacrity. The harp always made him smile; it so exemplified Blossom's beguiling absurdity. Like herself it was

11

an example of impressive grace and beauty, at the same time capable of a discordant note. It was the contrast which led to excitement.

Randolph paused to consider this whilst collecting his reading matter, every single daily newspaper, the *TLS* and the *New Statesman*. And, because she had so pleasured him last night, he had treated Blossom to the new *Vogue*, *Harper's*, *Cosmopolitan*, and *Men Only*. He bet himself that she would choose to look through the *Men Only* first. He heard her shouting to him now.

'Randy – Randy! Come on, you bugger, your kippers are getting cold!' And for good measure she ran what sounded like a fish-slice across the entire surface of the harp-strings. Randolph Tree ran down the stairs, whistling to the diminishing reverberations.

June was late for work, which meant no breakfast again – a fact which didn't worry her unduly. Last night (not to mention her bed-time vodka this morning), she'd drunk enough calories to last for a fortnight. It wouldn't harm her to cut out food for a bit; the television camera mercilessly magnified every ounce. She was naturally greedy, like Blossom – that was the trouble. They were both forced to discipline themselves, Blossom just as much as June, in order to keep old Randy happy – which was bloody well worth doing, any girl would have agreed on that! June considered her brother-in-law to be one of the most edible men she had ever had; if Blossom hadn't married him she would have done so herself. They had decided that at the time, she and Blossom. It was simply that Blossom had got pregnant first. There had never ever been any hard feelings.

June considered the day ahead. As far as she could tell there was no knowing when she might expect to be sitting down to the approximation of a square meal – sometime after midnight if she managed to get back from Dublin in time. In between now and then, it would be a series of snatched beers and unappetising sandwiches with the sound and camera crew. Not scotch eggs, they always made her fart – a fact which generally embarrassed the interviewee more than herself. Though not necessarily this one. Today's subject was the Irish poet, Connor McConnors who, despite having one foot in the grave, managed to maintain the rumbustious image that had taken a lifetime to cultivate. June couldn't imagine that he'd be thrown off his eloquent balance by the olfactory and audible effects of inner wind.

But before all that started, before she was even due for the final run-through with the director, she had to attend the Female Conference at Media House. At least two extended series on the role of women in society were in the pipeline and the choice of a presenter had yet to be decided. June knew through her agent that she was in the running.

Life was hectic these days, there was no doubt about that. But there was no one to blame; no one and nothing, except her own driving ambition and an inexhaustible appetite for work that made it impossible to say 'no' to new projects. And since she had turned free-lance and left BBC2, where she had irregularly presented the late-night Arts Spot ('irregularly' resulting from the up-and-down nature of her affair with the director), the work had come flooding in. She had appointed an agent, her first surprisingly. Until then it genuinely had not occurred to her that her work, that television, might take over her life. She had supposed that like Blossom she would get married and have children. Viewing it now, in hindsight, that was how she imagined that she and Tiny (the director) would end up – married. Well, married, but both having what they could on the side – the whole set-up a constant and bitter battle to preserve their separate and positive identities, just as they'd been for seven years.

'Bastard!' June swore at the smudged mascara beneath her eye. The desk downstairs had chosen to ring at the least propitious moment. The taxi firm couldn't get a cab to her in under twenty minutes, which would put her bang in the middle of the rush-hour.

'Bastard!' She swore again. It was going to be one of those days. The start of it for Christ's sake was enough of a clue that the gods were seeing fit to exercise their sense of humour at her expense. She had suffered a head-on collision with Cynthia, the blanched wife of the Director General. Whilst June was scurrying away down the stairs from his plush apartment, Cynthia had been furtively sidling up. Both parties, their respective evening attire wildly unsuitable to the hour, had had their eyes firmly fixed on their feet in case of awkward and embarrassing confrontation.

The glitter of Cynthia's sequined dress had stamped itself on June's dazzled retina before she'd had the chance to fully register the woman within. Head bent, elbows flying in the attitude of attack, June had swerved around the curve of the carpeted staircase at the speed of a soccer international, with no possibility whatsoever of last-minute withdrawal.

Collision was unavoidable; skull cracked against skull.

'Fucking hell!' The strangled expletive from the flailing sequined shape, now slithering swiftly back to base on ground floor, surprised June into a fleeting understanding of what had taken place. The voice so exactly fitted the face in the photograph – high and horsey but with the gritty huskiness of too much gin and cigarettes. The fine wife of the Director General had also been out on the toot!

June had cautiously proceeded in the wake of the poor woman to find her in a state of distressed disarray at the bottom of the stairs, displaying a great area of gusset. June left her whimpering on all fours, autocratically refusing further offers of help.

The memory of the grotesque sight made June wince as she ruefully explored the tender lump above her forehead. 'That's how you'll end up one day, the way you're going on my girl,' she addressed herself in the mirror. 'Arseholed before eight on all fours in some foyer, but without even a husband awaiting you upstairs.'

The telephone rang again. This time she welcomed the shrill intrusion. The image of her future had fleetingly depressed her. For a bleak second she had felt as lost as she had done in those disorientated months after she had finally split up with Tiny. But it surprised more than disturbed her. It proved that her single state harboured a vulnerability that fought shy of facing the future. This she chose to reject, if not violently then with conviction. In the short time that she had been living alone the most important principle she had learned was that it was not only easier but wiser to live in the present. She optimistically approached each separate day with that in mind. It

14

wasn't that she had any feelings of dread for unforeseeable events — indeed her nature was not inclined toward pessimism — it was more that with Tiny she seemed to have spent so much more time *planning*. Always '*when* we go to such-and-such', or 'we *will* try and do that one day'. Never anything *now*, no immediacy. But that was Tiny's trouble. Now that she was on her own she wasted no precious time on these prevarications. She neither lived in the past or the future, the present offered enough excitement.

She rose to her feet and swung around to answer the telephone, catching sight of herself in the long mirror. It was a fetching reflection, but she viewed herself with the lack of vanity usual to any professional whose appearance is part and parcel of their work. She leaned forward, frowning slightly. To the untutored eye all would have seemed above criticism. The flaming red hair (the previous spring a caramel brown) swung smoothly to her shoulders in a straight, silky cut; the long fringe skimming the darkened thickness of eye-lashes. One glowing hair had become trapped between two intertwined lashes and was now actually resting on the sensitive rim of the upper lid and in danger of grazing along the white of the eye. Skilfully, June removed it just in time, narrowing her startlingly green eyes in order to do so. They slanted from her reflection in the mirror. She looked assured and efficient, intelligent and alert. She gave the appearance of being capable and in control, the sort of person able to restore calm to chaos. It was this quality on which her growing reputation was based — an air of relaxed, yet informed tranquillity was rare enough, but in the frenetic world of television it was exceptional. June was, it was generally agreed by those in the know, a girl with a most promising future. (Even at this very moment the Director General was wracking his brains to remember her surname. Before the morning was out he would have put his secretary on the job and made a note in his diary for a luncheon date.) And yet there was something extra, wild and wilful sensuality that lurked behind the shining grape-green of the eyes. On meeting her, strangers had admitted to finding her blazing gaze somewhat disturbing, not knowing that it was many years ago that both

15

Blossom and June had learnt to make use of their remarkable cats' eyes. Hadn't they practised in secret on each other? Not that June ever used her eyes in that special way when she was actually on the television screen. She didn't want to alienate any part of the viewing public, and those sort of looks were specifically meant for men she wished to seduce. It aroused a positive dislike towards her from women. Her sexuality was, from a professional standpoint, something best kept in check. She enjoyed the private reputation of being a much sought after girl, given to distributing her favours where and when her desires dictated. Or, as in the case of last night, when the drink decided – she would not have, if sober, behaved in such an abandoned fashion. After all the Director General was a force unto himself, pursuing a markedly brutal and unpopular policy of hiring and firing in his latest administration. Added to which he was not noted in any way as being a ladies' man. It was the drink, and the snide challenge of the sexy producer that she 'wouldn't stand a chance there', that had made her behave so recklessly. But on the small screens of the nation June showed not a sign of any of these goings-on. As far as Mr and Mrs Average Viewer went she was suitable to be welcomed into the family home. Just sexy enough for the husbands to think privately that they wouldn't mind slipping her a length; just friendly enough for the wives to think how nice she would be to have as a pal. And just attractive and fashionable enough for teenage daughters to write in and ask where she had her hair done, and what colour eye-shadow she used. Her public image bore little relation to her private self.

Blossom on the other hand, since she had no public image, suffered very little from this need for camouflage. Her natural flamboyance was reflected in everything around her, not only her furniture and fittings, but even the spot in which she had decided that they should live. Slap-bang in the middle of Puddlemouth's most spectacular surfing beach, theirs being one of the few remaining fishermen's residences midst a complex of crumbling lofts rented out as artists' studios. There was a small inadequate beach café, two monstrously ugly blocks of recently built

16

balconied flats, and a scattering of tiny over-priced, bed-and-breakfast hotels which were only open in the season.

But upon that short, secluded beach stormed the Atlantic Ocean, hurtling its waves against the suppliant sands in a furious effort, so it always thrillingly seemed to Blossom, to reach and demolish the entire line of habitations. As if the mere presence of these frail man-made buildings was an affront to the strength and elemental force of the sea. The noise of the breakers was overwhelming. Indeed when Blossom opened the sliding glass doors onto the verandah the sound made normal conversation impossible. Only at low tide did the threat of the waves recede to a safe though mutinous distance, like a dangerous animal kept barely at bay. Blossom thrived on the continual excitement of the sea. It, more than anything, had been her reason for coming to live in Cornwall. And it happily coincided with Randolph's need for isolation, his wish to be right away from the seduction of the city. But he would have been able to find mental peace as easily in the green depths of the countryside. Blossom felt she might honestly die if she were to be deprived of the daily drama of the sea.

She stood now at the sliding door staring down at the beach below. This communal floor was the first floor of the house; this was where the open-plan kitchen led onto the dining area, which in turn spread through to the family sitting-room. The sea-facing wall of each floor had been ripped out and replaced with sliding glass doors, all except Randolph's floor at the top of the house which had been converted into his study. He had deliberately obliterated his view, had instructed the architect who had undertaken the conversion to build a false wall over the existing windows, and remove a major part of the roof instead. This then had become his daytime light source. But more than that, it had become his only view. A view of the sky, as variable in its way as Blossom's beloved view of the sea. A blank canvas of clouds suspended over his head, sometimes static and solid, sometimes foaming and free, but forever on the move. Never one day the same. And at night a total change, as if somebody had substituted a completely different painting, transformed by the light of the moon and the stars. Visiting academics who voyaged this far to converse with Randolph Tree seemed always surprised at the sight of the sky-view, immediately jumping to the mistaken conclusion that it betrayed a deep interest in astrology.

Descending the stairs, whistling, Randolph Tree passed the marital bedroom. The door was open. Before closing it he popped his head around, looked quickly into the room and smiled. He was still smiling when he reached Blossom one floor down. But when he saw exactly what she had chosen to wear whilst serving his breakfast he broke into satisfied laughter.

Blossom's love of dressing up was a source of pleasure to them both. Whilst June by the nature of her work was forced to practise restraint over her appearance, Blossom was encouraged by her husband to do the opposite. He thought of June now as he approached the delectable curve of his wife's bare, sunburnt thigh, gleaming against the frilled edge of the tiny white apron. It struck him as odd (whilst relishing the shape of Blossom's rich pubic mound, discernible beneath the fine organza) that for the past few mornings running he had not overheard the twins having one of their animated and seemingly interminable phone conversations. This *was* unusual. Some days they contrived to talk not just in the morning, but in the evening too; he tried hard to resist the crass urge to tot up just how much this recent lack of communication was saving him on the telephone bill.

He had learned a long time ago to accept this unparalleled affinity between the two girls. They were, after all, not just twins but *identical* twins. Monozygotic (identical), rather than merely dizygotic (fraternal). Monozygotic being identical and developed from a *single* egg, as opposed to dizygotic being fraternal, developed from *two* eggs and held to be as separate in their origin as normal brothers and sisters. Randolph had read all the relevant research material within days of meeting Blossom, but he was still unprepared for the uncanny shock of coming face to face with her double.

Both were left-handed. Their hair whorls were identical, each swirling clockwise at the crown of their heads, instead of anti-clockwise. Their palm patterns and finger-

18

prints, their dental irregularities, their complexions, their eye colour – even to the pigment pattern of the iris – all these were exactly the same.

It was unnerving, that couldn't be denied.

But Blossom had warned him that it would be, she had completely understood his child-like consternation. She had smiled, and had humoured him from his sudden feeling of chilling uncertainty. He didn't like the idea of there being two of her, he wanted there to be one. And he wanted all of that one to be all for himself. But it was impossible. Now, even now, almost twelve years later he still found it difficult to come to terms with just the simple fact that for as long as they all continued to live the girls would continue to be closer to each other than he could ever hope to be with Blossom. She was his wife and more precious to him, almost, than his work. And yet their rich and harmonious intimacy would never transcend the intense bonds which existed between the twins.

Even the fact of Blossom's pregnancy, the pregnancy that had led directly to their marriage, had first been divulged to June. At the time he had resented that bitterly, choosing to see it as a betrayal. But over the years he had learned perforce to forgive and understand. As Blossom had tried to explain whenever he had expressed pain at being second friend and confidante instead of first, it just wasn't like that. He was getting it all wrong. When she shared secrets with June it wasn't like sharing, not like it was with him. When she talked to June it was like talking to herself. A form of 'self-reference' was how she put it. And then she'd comfort him, hold him close to her, enveloping them both with her womanly warmth.

'We were made for each other, you and I.' That's what she'd say. 'This marriage will go on forever.'

And yet, until he had met Blossom, Randolph Tree had honestly never contemplated marriage. Marriage had not seemed to fit in with his plans for the future. He had had many affairs and in almost every case the girls had fallen desperately in love with him and in several cases had even been driven to propose marriage. But Randolph had always fought shy of the notion. Sex was no problem, he was a very attractive man and had always adored women. But his work, his writing, was the most important thing in his life.

He was twenty-eight when he met Blossom, and was about to publish his first book, *The Other Meaning*, a philosophical treatise. His publishers were confident that *The Other Meaning* would capture a world-wide cult readership, at the same time exciting sufficient critical acclaim to assure its commercial success. But no one was more surprised than Randolph Tree when that was what did happen. His economic situation altered, so it seemed, almost overnight. He was free from financial pressure to pursue that which was closest to his heart (apart from darling Blossom). He could give up teaching and spend the rest of his life in study. The study of original thought. And, unless he wished to do so, he need never write another word again.

At the time of his first meeting with his youthful future wife however, his reputation was still unfounded. The occasion was part of the inaugural festivities of the South West Summer Adult Education Symposium. An informal dance was being held, with an extended bar-licence. Randolph Tree was already pleasantly tight. He was a tutor at the Symposium, Blossom was a student from the local Training College. It had been her mesmerising eyes that he had noticed first of all. That and the inviting challenge of her impudent cleavage.

He had said so, in that order. 'You have very seductive eyes and superb bloody breasts – I compliment you on both!' They had stared at each other without speaking.

Then he'd lost her. She had been claimed by a steady stream of men demanding to dance, and he had been left behind in the slip-stream of her lustful admirers. 'Well, that's that,' he had sworn silently to himself. 'You should have known better than to have gone for the belle of the bloody ball.' And he was shocked by the sharp sense of loss.

But she had returned to him.

She returned at the moment that he was taking to the floor for the third time running with a thin and handsome, though slightly haggard, brunette. She reminded him in certain lights of Audrey Hepburn, a film star he had always desired. And indeed he was discovering under fairly discreet and localised pressure that this girl's hard, wiry body was not half bad. Though he had not thought of a way to reveal that the series of lectures on Creative Writing, that she was so looking forward to, concluded with his own withering attack on such writing. He had thought to call critical attention to its gross irrelevance and self-indulgence, pinning the whole thing on Samuel Beckett, but with a massive swipe on the way to James Joyce.

'Of course Joyce is the boy . . .' The brunette was saying. Randolph ran his hand casually between her sharp shoulder blades to check whether or not she was wearing a brassiere. He nodded, she was. 'Ah, Joyce! He is the one all right . . .'

Blossom was standing before him, behind the brunette. 'This is a Ladies' Excuse Me, so excuse me,' she said, tapping sharply on the shoulder of the other girl.

'It most certainly is no such thing!' the brunette began indignantly. 'I definitely heard no such announcement . . .'

'You've heard it now.' Blossom interrupted smiling and kicked savagely at the other's shin. Randolph's fleeting and final impression of his former dancing partner was one of snarling feminine defeat softened only by a wan expression of wincing pain. Blossom was a girl who snatched what she wanted.

Taking her in his arms that first time in the Summer School dance, nine Newcastle Brown Ales pressing on his bladder and conscious of a host of hot jealous eyes upon them, Randolph Tree nevertheless sustained an instant erection. Blossom remarked upon it immediately, but he was to learn pretty soon that this was her way.

'You've got a cock-rise! Oh, goody!' Her candour took him by surprise. 'What's your name?' She spoke with a lilting rush of words.

'It's Randolph Tree,' he answered somewhat stiffly, finding it difficult to concentrate on speech.

'Randy – that's ripe –' She laughed out loud, her head thrown back. He could see extra depths in her cleavage, and to his annoyance was aware that most of the other males around them were straining for a similar view.

They had barely been dancing a few minutes, but he badly needed, for all sorts of reasons, to get outside as soon as possible. He deftly steered Blossom between the leering faces towards the nearest exit. The one he was aiming for he had checked earlier with the brunette in mind. It led directly to the lawned grounds of the establishment, and thence to the leafy perimeter. Though all *he* had honestly intended for that evening, after a pee, was to fondle and kiss. But they had both been carried away by the raw and combustible nature of her passion. It was no surprise when she missed her first period.

'You were trying to bugger me last night.' Blossom undulated towards the breakfast table, her naked breasts breaking free from the restricting bib of the flimsy pinafore. She was wearing perilously high heels which forced her to walk with her shoulders thrown back and her torso arched in an extremely tantalising pose. Randolph could feel the back of his throat tighten up and a distant ache descend to his balls.

'This isn't fair,' he protested.

Blossom stopped moving immediately and looked disappointed. 'Bloody hell, I thought you'd like it – the children aren't here. I was going to make a day of it. We could even go for the record if you're up to it.'

Randolph collapsed into a chair and held his hands over his ears, giving a short, strangled groan. 'Don't say these things, you get me over-excited, then your kippers will give me hiccups. Why not hold on till I've eaten – I mean, keep on walking, I like all that. But keep your mouth shut. Just parade. Don't mention buggery.'

Blossom dimpled, then twirled around slowly. She was not eating breakfast today, she'd decided to cut it out for a whole month (she must remember to tell June that when she spoke to her later, though these days it was getting harder and harder to find her in). 'Your kippers are in the oven.' She presented herself to him in profile, provocatively, with one hand on the curve of her hip. 'I take it I'm allowed to talk if it's about your breakfast?' She approached his chair without waiting for a reply. If he raised his head a little higher he would be able to take a sly bite from the nearside of her luscious breast. Straining further he would be in the delightful position of demolishing the nipple itself . . .

He ground his front teeth together in pleasurable anticipation. 'Get a move on, woman,' he growled. 'I'm bloody starving.'

22

Blossom flounced past, breasts bouncing, tossing her shoulder-length bob. This summer she and June were wearing their hair in exactly the same shade and style, though they had chosen to do so quite independently, just as before that they had both decided to go caramel brown. Only the colour of her pubic hair, a dark, bosky brown, betrayed the truth; that she wasn't a natural redhead.

Randolph studied her openly whilst sipping his orange juice. 'You're not wearing any knickers,' he observed.

'Do you object?' she said coyly. She had now reached the Aga oven and had to be careful of her state of near nudity against its hot surface. Last time she'd served his breakfast in similarly scant clothing she'd splashed her stomach with scalding Scott's Porridge Oats. There was still a nasty little scar in her navel.

'Yes, I think I do, to tell you the truth.' Randolph poured his black coffee calmly, fully aware that his mild criticism would not go down well.

He was correct. She straightened up, the orange oven-mittens on her hands ready to remove his cooked kippers. But he enjoyed the straightening-up process very much indeed, this way he would be getting it twice over. It afforded him a fine view of taut and stretched buttocks; at one moment arched in a high haunch, and the next relaxed and plumped into a pair of firmly filled pillows. In his opinion the gluteus maximus was the most spellbinding muscle in the whole of the human body. He was fortunate that Blossom was possessed of a particularly splendid illustration of this. Her scrumptious bum was a never-ending pleasure to him. He couldn't imagine now what it must be like to make love to an empty-arsed woman, to a girl whose posterior resembled an unfilled paper bag. Though, of course, in the past he had slept with all sorts, those included and they had never disappointed him then – as far as he could remember. Randolph's view of the female reflected his humanitarian principles – so he liked to think. He strongly deplored men who categorised women in terms of their desirability; distinguishing in a disparaging way between the young and the old, or those less blessed with good looks than others. His own tastes were Catholic. All woman were a delight to him, a constant mystery and a continuing excitement. It was just that for him Blossom embodied them all – he worshipped at the shrine of her femininity.

'You mean you would rather have knickers *as well* as the suspenders and stockings?' Blossom's glacial green eyes registered her displeasure. She was still standing with her back to him, speaking over her shoulder. Her legs were set wide apart, one supporting her weight, the other, angled away, was bent at the knee for the best balance. The slender shape of each limb was further emphasised by the heavy seam which climbed like a strong pencil-line up the length of her stockings – her tart's stockings, sheer and silky, and sinfully black. With one long sluttish ladder on the inside of the left leg. Randolph could just see its twisted top stretching over her tanned thigh. A sly sensation of tickling had started inside the tip of his prick; he resisted the natural urge to touch himself, with some effort. Standing the way she was, on her high suede stilletto heels, she reminded him of something. A pin-up of the '40s. A Vargas girl, or the currently resurrected wartime photo of Betty Grable, the one prisoners of war used to wank over. (Or did the Red Cross humanely send out saltpetre to subdue the sex urge of all those poor devils?). It was the combination and contrast of the harsh slick line of the black satin suspender belt outlining the curve of her hips, and the frothiness of the white apron almost concealing it. The result was a graphic delight, though of course the girl inside helped. She exuded what was now an out-dated word, much in use in the era of those particular pin-ups; she exuded a great deal of 'oomph'.

But Randolph still felt that knickers were needed. 'A G-string. That's what you want with that outfit.' He put his head on one side. 'A black one with silky tassels at the crotch. You've got one of those, you used it on Easter Sunday when the kids went to All Saints Sunday School for tea. What were you – a Finnish stripper or something?'

Blossom spun round indignantly. 'A what? A Finnish stripper? I bloody well wasn't! I was a Mother Superior who by mistake had been sent some "erotic underwear to turn your husband on" by a mail order firm. It was meant to be in the outer Hebrides; she'd sent for Thermal underwear for the harsh winter months. What on earth put Finland in your mind?'

24

'The weather conditions I expect.' Randolph rubbed his chin. 'Oh yes, I remember the Mother Superior. She was *very* good, you should do her again –'

Blossom sniffed huffily. 'It's not my practice to repeat myself – that's the whole point of the thing I should have thought, that you never have the same one again.'

'Your rule. Not mine. I actually do have some favourites that I would very much enjoy having again. It would make it much easier for you.'

Blossom crossed one long lissom leg over the other and laughed forgivingly. 'I rather enjoy the challenge,' she purred seductively. 'Shall I go now and put on my knickers . . .'

The Female Conference was very jolly, June found to her surprise. It was an invited audience of about 250 women, much larger than she had expected. And although there was a leading panel of ten on the platform there was a responsive participation from the rest of the hall. Individuals would freely stand and state their views, interruptions were welcomed, if not actively encouraged. The whole thing had a refreshingly lively feel to it, even the aggressively militant feminists were showing a rare sense of humour. One of them, a short, plump lady-wrestler with blonde hair and black roots had just made them all laugh a moment ago. She'd given an articulate account of how she had recently re-met the husband of years before, with whom she had led a miserable existence as a battered wife. Drunk and unaware of his ex-wife's new career he had made a vicious lunge at her in a Stepney pub. He was now residing in the Rehabilitation Wing of the hospital at Stoke Mandeville, a centre for the permanently disabled.

June was seated between a wry, witty barrister, who she suspected was gay, and a homely little woman with a wart on her nose who spoke with an incomprehensible Scottish accent. So incomprehensible was it that when she rose to her feet and spoke for fifteen minutes total silence ensued, which seemed to indicate that not a single person present had understood a word of what she had said. Until a fellow Scotswoman at the back had given a rousing, 'Hear, hear!' followed by a positive storm of applause.

'My rough guess is that she was going on about North

25

Sea oil,' whispered the witty barrister to June. 'I understand that she's a Member of Parliament, a Nationalist I shouldn't be surprised.'

June didn't speak because she was worried about time and was forced to leave in the middle of a most interesting paper, being read by a member of the panel on stage. The woman, a well-known gynaecologist, was explaining the revolutionary replacement of the womb in puberty in such a way as to banish menstruation and the menopause for good and all. She had already been enthusiastically questioned by an excited posse of expensively clad girls, who claimed matter-of-factly to be prostitutes. June would have liked to have heard more but had already cut it a bit fine for getting to the air terminal on time. The witty barrister passed her telephone number and whispered that she must get in touch, pressing her hand suggestively as she did so. June made her apologies to the rest of the row for having to make them stand and eventually made her escape.

Many people smiled at her on her way out, several mouthing 'hello'. They were all complete strangers who thought that they knew her simply because her face was familiar. It was becoming more familiar the busier she became. Only a year ago it would have been perfectly possible to walk around and lead her life in almost complete anonymity. The Late Show had had small and limited audiences, mainly intellectuals. But this situation was altering as her television appearances increased on the various channels; and, too, her recent programmes had had a far wider appeal. She was gradually becoming known to the public – whether she liked it or not.

Outside June tried hailing a taxi, to her relief one drew up immediately. The driver recognised her. 'I seen you on the telly,' he said pushily. 'Never forget a face. Now don't tell me – let me guess what it was you was on – it was with some old bloke talking about something. Was it Panorama? Or was it Nationwide? It was one of them sort of programmes, wasn't it – I know you, you're one of them brainy type of birds. All that women's lib sort of balls – now tell me if I'm right . . .' The conversation lasted one-sidedly all the way to the air terminal and for the first time June thought she detected a note of aggression directed at her – it wasn't a pleasant feeling. She caught a glimpse of what some of her better known colleagues had to put up with.

To her relief she found that she was the first to arrive. No one else had shown up, this suited her admirably. It gave her time to check how she looked in the Ladies. She had a small make-up bag, the one she took with her on these outside locations, and now was as good a time as any to adjust to a more exaggerated camera complexion. She began brushing a rich russet shadow beneath her clearly defined cheekbones, holding her head high to judge the effect from the harsh artificial lighting, turning her chin left and then right. The lavatory attendant was a swarthy, handsome Asian dressed in layers of screaming nylon garments, clashing lime with petunia, combining the ethnic harem trousers of the east with a mundane knitted cardigan of the west, in a drab fawn. She scowled with apparent loathing at June's friendly smile. And who could blame her, June thought, swabbing up and pulling chains all day long; her view of Great Britain was contained in this neon-lit landscape of porcelain wash-basins, liquid soap, rolled paper and lavatory bowls. The woman's smouldering eyes burned up the distance between them. She was mopping the floors of the furthest line of cubicles, using a large metal bucket and a long-handled mop for the job. Between each application of sudsy water, she slowly and methodically squeezed out the mop in the special fitment at the top of the pail, until it was dry enough to soak up more moisture. It seemed to June to be a uniquely dispiriting occupation and she was sure that the woman was doing it all wrong. According to the commercials she watched on the box, soapy suds were the old-fashioned way, taking twice as long to dry and leaving messy smears. Weren't sponges meant to be the thing now?

June was hazy about the actual practicalities of domesticity. She left that sort of thing to Blossom, a paragon of all those womanly virtues. But then Blossom loved her home, she cherished her possessions, her vast and colourful collection of china, of objets d'art, of odd furniture and exotic fittings. Blossom would not like or trust anyone other than herself to clean and take care of them. She delighted in her environment and was forever searching

27

for further embellishments. June preferred to travel light. Even when she'd been with Tiny it had been his flat that they had shared and he was responsible for providing the cleaner. On the many occasions of their split-ups she had simply stayed with various friends. She had intended to find a place of her own all the time; but somehow it just hadn't happened. Finally she had ended up where she was now at Flowers, a small and cosy hotel around the corner from the Portobello Road – as a permanent guest. Permanent guests were *not* required to do housework.

June looked at her watch, the woman's gaze brought her back to reality. She felt suddenly self-conscious, keenly aware of the difference between their situations in life, and as she casually dropped the coin in the saucer placed for tips it seemed to add insult to injury. The final gesture in gracious condescension. She left, feeling relieved and it only occurred to her much later that she might well have been paranoiac. The simple reason for the woman's fierce attention was perhaps that she had merely seen June on television, and lacked the necessary vocabulary to communicate this. Her burning glances quite probably held no hostility at all, it was just that the sight of immigrants employed in inferior occupations always made June feel defensively guilty.

Stepping out into the lobby of the busy air terminal, concerned now that the airport coach was due to leave in five minutes and there was still no sign of either the crew or the director, June was startled to hear her name on the Tannoy. She hurried over to the reception desk and was told there was a message, an urgent call which they would transfer to one of the phone booths. It was the director in a state of panic, unusual even for him. Connor McConnors the Irish poet, was dead! Killed in an explosion on the outskirts of Dublin.

'A bomb!' June's brain raced.

'Apparently not. A domestic accident, a trivial thing, a faulty gas-stove that he'd hung onto for years. You know he lived in absolute squalor –' The director's high voice reached a new hysterical pitch. 'Wouldn't you just bloody credit it – I've been trying to pin this old bugger down long enough to get a programme on him for the past three sodding years, and then this has to happen! It means that

28

the BBC has stolen a march on us again, the only television record in existence is that interview on Monitor – and that was done almost nineteen years ago –'

June remained silent. The man was steadily losing control. She had seen him like this before. Though he had done some absolutely brilliant programmes, his sensitivity was now thought to be getting the better of him. He drank a lot when under pressure. June couldn't be certain but right now he seemed to have had a few. His words were slurring, and his reaction was becoming more emotional by the minute.

'So the schedule, I take it, is cancelled for today?' She spoke calmly as if completely unaffected by the tragic news or the last minute alteration to their plans. The crew were booked after all, it didn't necessarily mean that she wouldn't be working with them on something else.

'What's that?' The director was screaming now, tears were not far off. June was forced to hold the receiver some distance from her ear. She sighed softly, feeling suddenly weary. The events of last night and a hovering hangover were beginning to take their toll. She found herself praying that she wouldn't have to work this afternoon after all. It would be the first break that she would have had in weeks.

'I said –' she began.

'What's that?' The director was screaming again, but this time she felt that he was addressing someone else, the rest of the office presumably. 'Darling,' (now he was talking to her), 'could you just hang on half-a-mo? I'm just checking this end, it's bloody chaos here as you can imagine – we were planning to slot Connor McConnors in tomorrow night on the second half of Spectrum. Of course, if we'd done him last Friday as I had originally planned – remember you were working for the opposition that day down in Devon so I chose to postpone it till you were free – we would really have had a scoop. That's, of course, if the old bugger had still kicked the bucket today! With my luck he would have gone on forever – hey, hold on, someone has just walked in –' June heard him screaming again. 'Jeremy, or any of you, I've got June Day here on the phone and a camera crew on call – does anybody want her?' June knew without listening what the

29

response to that question would be. 'They all send you their best love, darling,' the director was back, 'but everything is just too disorganised this end – give me a number where we can get hold of you later. We may think of something live in the studio tomorrow – someone's shouting that Woody Allen's in town –' June gave her agent's telephone number and gratefully left the terminal; it looked as if the rest of the day could be hers.

Randolph Tree lay on the kitchen floor near the sink, in a deeply satisfied post-coital sleep. He would lie there for quite some time if Blossom let him, and there was no reason why not for though his flies were wide open there was no fear of draughts. Randolph had to be careful of those; he was a person who caught colds all too easily.

Blossom eased herself off him, gently and with great care. Sometimes the faint 'plop' as his heavy prick emerged from her wet cunt (like a worm from the soil after a shower, she always thought) together with the soft thud as it slithered against his balls was enough to wake him. A shame. He claimed the post-coital slumber to be the best of all sleeps. So far today he had been privileged to enjoy four. Blossom was charging the rather ridiculous rate of a fiver a time, but then her charges had always been arbitrary. In any case Randolph had not been to the bank and it would have been wrong to accept a cheque. The sly and suggestive rustle of notes before the actual perform-ance was all part of the erotic excitement. Indeed, such was the strong association now in her mind between paper money and sexual pleasure that sometimes in shops she'd found herself responding down below just queueing at the cash desk, whilst other housewives paid their bills. Randolph had been particularly interested when she had told him and had pressed her for further details, taking notes in the process. 'At which shops would you say this sensation was strongest? The butcher's, the baker's, the –'

'The candlestick maker's?' Blossom had added, not taking it seriously. But he had persisted, having recently re-read the famous tome by the eighteenth century philosopher, John Locke, *An Essay on Human Understanding* in which the principle of the association of ideas had been pursued. Blossom must think hard and speak honestly –

30

her answers were vitally important, they might form the basis of serious research. They began again.

She had tried with some difficulty to be more specific. As she had pointed out, it wasn't so easy to say exactly *where* the quim had become activated. It might, in all truth, have actually started in the fish market. The marvellously pungent smell of fresh fish could have turned her thoughts in that direction without her realising it. Then again it may have been the warm, womb-like cave of the bakery, along with the phallic french loaves. Or for that matter, if symbolic shapes were going to enter (sic) into it, couldn't Freda's Fruiterer and Greengrocer come (sic) somewhere. (All the cucumbers and bananas, we must try all that again you know!)

Randolph had delightedly noted it all down, but had persisted until he had finally got her to admit that she first became conscious of actual wetness – indeed almost a sensation of *coming* – near the cash counter of Liptons Supermarket in the High Street. Blossom was ashamed that it had taken place in such mundane surroundings, but there was nothing to be done about it. She knew from past dealings with Randolph that in matters of research absolute truth and scrupulous honesty were all-important.

Blossom knelt over the sleeping form and studied her husband's handsome face. 'God, but you're gorgeous,' she said fondly. A small tremor travelled over the sensual mouth, drawing the corners down derisively. Yet Blossom was certain that he couldn't have heard. She glanced down at her clothing, at her unbecoming nightdress and dreary woollen dressing-gown, purchased at a jumble sale in aid of the Lifeboat Appeal. A hair-curler had fallen from her head during the recent seduction scene (she had been playing the part of a frustrated housewife. Randolph was the shy and reluctant plumber, she'd had to use all her wiles to coax him onto the job). The curler had got caught up in the frayed cord of her dressing-gown, so that's what she'd been feeling all through!

Her knees fitted snugly each side of Randolph's hips. Earlier one knee had pinned him masterfully to the floor, despite his half-hearted struggle. She had approached him from behind as he'd bent to examine the plumbing, and had employed brute force to reduce him to the ground. He

31

had given a frightened bleat of protest which she had chosen to ignore, and had mouthed half-formed sentences to register his alarm. She very much enjoyed his simulated panic. All in all it had been a highly successful session. She felt rather pleased with herself, but the question now was whether he would have the stamina to carry on.

She looked at the time (at the precise moment that June was consulting her watch at the air terminal). Randolph would be feeling like something to eat when he woke up. Screwing always gave him a tremendous appetite. Once, she remembered, he had consumed two entire meals in a restaurant they had driven to after bed. One after the other, just like that. The management had given them each a brandy on the house, and Randolph had ordered a further three so that they both got very drunk and behaved rather badly, doing a lot of shouting and passing rude comments about the people at other tables. But the management had still asked them graciously to come again. The bill had come to three times Blossom's weekly housekeeping allowance, but both of them agreed that it had been bloody worth it. In any case they had been celebrating, that day they had broken their own record. They had chalked up nine pokes in twelve hours, starting at six in the morning. One and a half times more than the previous time they'd tackled it, though they had been reluctant to admit that neither the eighth or the ninth were really worth having. Indeed poor Randolph had complained of actual physical pain at the point of so-called orgasm. He'd said the sensation in his bollocks felt as if they were being internally shaved with a very sharp razor. He feared he might have done himself a permanent damage. Blossom suffered nothing other than a slight irritation when passing water, and perhaps a need to do this more often than usual. It was a condition that used to be referred to as Honeymoon Cunt when she was a student. She considered it rather chic to be able to boast of it after two children and twelve years of marriage!

Randolph stirred beneath her but didn't wake up. He looked tired, Blossom thought regretfully. It didn't seem as if they would be going for the elusive ten today. But she wouldn't like to think that at only nine fucks they had reached the peak of their performance. Nine was such an unremarkable sum. Ten sounded just that much more all-roundish. June thought so too, she was always asking, checking up to see if they had managed it yet. She didn't ask Randolph of course, Blossom hadn't ever told him that June knew anything about the record. She had an uneasy feeling that he might mind. Especially since he hadn't yet reached their perpetual goal. It irked him, any failure. And this he saw as a failure, a breakdown in the functioning between body and mind. But he had the wisdom never to have asked if Blossom had told June. He knew how it was between the two of them.

Blossom stood up, she felt stiff. The kitchen floor was hard, if she had thought about it she could have put cushions down. Although it would have been out of place in the erotic scenario. A frustrated housewife, after all, would hardly be likely to line her lair with goose feathers, and Blossom was very keen on a semblance of authenticity. Anyway, the kitchen floor was not the most uncomfortable working surface they had encountered. Not after they fucked in some of the bizarre locations that they had found.

She went over to the phone, which they always took off the hook when they were having a bit. Too often in the past they had suffered from untimely interruptions. Now Blossom returned the receiver to its hook. If Randolph had his way they wouldn't own a telephone at all. He considered it an unwelcome intrusion from the outside world. But Blossom had insisted, the telephone was her medium. She was a natural gossip and enjoyed the daily trading of tit-bits with all her friends. And in any case how else would she be able to talk to June? She thought of June now with a surge of feeling. She thought of how marvellous it would be to see her. Up until the children had been born she and June had always managed to spend at least several weeks of the year together. Either June had come down or else Blossom had gone to London. But that seemed somehow impossible to arrange any more. Though the children were certainly capable of taking care of themselves these days. This weekend they would be camping on the cliffs with their friends for two whole nights with not a single adult in sight, after all they were hardly babies now.

A pile of her clothing lay on the kitchen table, she'd had to change out of it in a hurry for this last one. Now she nimbly slipped out of her dressing-gown and drew the thick flannelette nightdress up over her head.

'Very nice.' Randolph was awake, sitting up with his knees apart and his cock hanging out of his jeans. It was difficult to think of him as being forty in a few months time. She must start planning what to get him for his birthday.

A button had got tangled with one of her hair-curlers, so that she was stuck with the nightdress high in the air over her stretched arms. Her head was half in and half out. 'Bloody hell – can't you help me!' she wailed. Randolph remained where he was on the floor enjoying the view of his wife's wriggling torso. Although she had borne him two children, it would have been difficult to tell. Her body was as firm and as youthful as when they had first met. In her bikini on the beach several summers ago he had still found it impossible to tell the difference between her and June. But she took good care of herself physically.

'What time are we going swimming today?' he said conversationally. 'Have you consulted the tide chart yet?' His cock felt contentedly tender, studying it he could spot a fine, milky sheen drying already to invisibility in places. A combination of their accumulated juices.

'Sod swimming! Come and get me out of here!' Blossom's scarlet face bent down before him, peeping through the neck of her nightie.

'Do you need assistance? What seems to be the trouble?' Randolph ran boldly investigative hands between his wife's thighs, opening the slightly swollen flesh of her labia, and easing a gentle thumb inside.

'Christ! It's pouring wet in here!' he shouted. 'I shall catch a terrible cold – help me!'

Blossom struggled wildly, trying to back away. And squeezing her upper thighs closely together in an unsuccessful effort to shake his thumb out. 'You bastard!' she gasped. 'I shall – I shall, I shall *charge* you for this!!' She peered at him wildly through her restricting garment and her voice took on a note of rising triumph.

'There you are, you see, it's coming up – that'll be two pounds fifty for an incipient erection!'

June had a late lunch with her agent in Soho, around the corner from the office, which was in a small mews off Berwick Market. June had called in to check whether she'd be needed this afternoon or not.

'The answer to that, my darling, is "Non". Ah but – you wait for it – they are wanting you tomorrow at nine-thirty for a studio interview with a surprise guest on Spectrum. Is very, very good for you, little one, I think. That surprise guest is no other than Dame Tiger Oats! Is she not the famous relic of the twenties, yes? That naughty boy, Zachary Ram, 'e say to me on the line that with luck she will expire on the programme! I 'ave the belief that they are doing it live.'

Cherie Pye, June's clever agent, was an exquisite Parisienne who had trained as a ballerina when a child. She was tiny and intense, with large brown eyes and a small compressed mouth. Her coal-black hair fell as far as her waist when she combed it out, but she wore it coiled like a serpent at the nape of her neck during the day, and in the evening piled it on the top of her head like a plate of profiteroles. Only at night in bed was it allowed to hang loose. She had been married three times, was separated from Samson Pye, her present husband, although she talked incessantly of a possible reconciliation. She had endured two heart-breaking miscarriages following four flippant abortions and had been medically advised never to attempt another pregnancy ever again. She was obsessed with small babies, Samson Pye, her clients' careers, casual sexual encounters with unusual partners, and above all she was obsessed with her weight. She smoked and coughed continuously and suffered intermittently from *anorexia nervosa*, having twice brought herself to the brink of death through self-induced starvation.

But despite her (or perhaps because of her) neuroses she was an inspired agent, who pursued her clients' interests with the persistence of a maggot. She had been one of the most highly respected members of her profession, at a time when female agents were relatively few and far between. Her skills were considered to be legendary.

June was keenly aware of how very fortunate she was to be with Cherie Pye, but her professional regard didn't interfere with the affection the two felt for each other. Despite the distance of years they had a great rapport; there was some fifteen years between them, but Cherie was a sophisticated and sensual forty-five with a basic and black sense of humour. Her sheer style appealed to June enormously, she had always thought that was how she would like to be at that age – without the neuroses of course, and all the personal dramas, but then that was simply all part of the Gallic high temperament.

They sat side by side, on show, at Chez Stalky. Cherie insisted on doing so whenever they ate there, so that not only would they both be in a fine position to see who was in the rest of the restaurant, but that the rest of the restaurant should see them.

Stalky, the smiling proprietor, was delighted to welcome them. He manoeuvred his substantial paunch between the occupied chairs in an attempt to greet them as soon as they came in. June suspected that he had always been more than a little in love with Cherie (as was everyone – just a little bit). But no one would have known, his welcoming embrace was equally warm for each of them. 'My two favourite girlfriends!' Heads swivelled. Stalky's thick Glaswegian accent cut through the cultured discourse of chattering diners. June suspected that the reason Cherie always chose to take her to Stalky's was that he enabled her to effect this dramatic entrance. But they did look a stunning pair. Cherie was wearing a silver kid trouser suit more appropriate to a teeny-bopper rock star than a woman of maturing years. Yet on her it seemed to be the height of absolute chic, outrageously alluring, each movement attracting the change of light to its shining surface. Accentuating the extreme slenderness of her small, tight body, so that the gleaming silver appeared to have been sprayed on.

Following this dazzling apparition into the restaurant June couldn't resist a delighted smile. Her position afforded her a view of Cherie's straight triangular back in its short bomber jacket slicked into the waist – 'bum-freezers' they were known in the rag-trade. And they certainly placed the bum on display. June found herself mesmerized by the sinuous roll of Cherie's boyish buttocks before her, so temptingly pinchable. She was sure that Blossom had a gold suit similar to this one, or had at one time around the middle of the '60's. She must have done, Blossom's wardrobe was absolutely amazing; there wasn't any style or period that she hadn't owned since she'd been married to Randolph. June envied her that – Tiny had always frowned on any tendency towards flamboyance. And since then she had stayed on the side of sartorial reserve. But Cherie approved.

'June darling, you are looking – 'ow do we say – absolument in the pink! I like very much what you 'ave on your back today. Is fabulous, that shit colour so close to your face. Tell me what is the place you 'ave bought this dress – I must consider something drab like that for me. Is time, do you not agree, that I start to dress suitable to my position in life? But you know, I spotted this silver suit in a children's boutique on the Kings Road and I simply could not resist it – and the fit, is *merveilleuse, non!*' Cherie sighed and rolled her eyes, patting her flat belly. 'Oh, but I am getting *so* fat! Yes, but I am – don't I know it –'

June frowned at her. 'Don't start all that, for Christ's sake, or I shall walk out right now.'

Cherie coughed protestingly over her freshly lit cigarette, then took another drag, preparing to speak in her own defence. But June beat her to it. 'We are not discussing it today, all right? We both know perfectly well that your end will be brought about by lung cancer and not obesity, and pretty soon by the sound of that cough, Cherie. Have you seen to it lately? It's like being with a barking dog!' June was enjoying herself. She did when admonishing heavy smokers. Having given up the habit over two years ago, and not succumbed since to the ever present temptation, she felt the zealous scorn of the smugly converted. Though there was an element of self-protection in her sanctimonious attack, the strong desire for a cigarette still lurked in her system, surfacing unexpectedly at times like these, in seductive surroundings with a glass of wine in the hand and the spaces between words waiting to be filled. Not that there was much waiting between words with Cherie.

'*Mon dieu*! You are so, so stern today – you are a

miserable bitch! Tell me,' the throaty accent splintered from a stifled cough into a suggestive chuckle, 'what you were up to last night, little one, to place you in this disagreeable frame of mind? I tell you – I 'ave the answer. Stalky!' She summoned him shrilly. 'Stalky! You must come and choose from the menu – my adorable June 'ere is in a bad mood. I think, yes, that she 'as the constipation – you must give her something very kind to open her poor bowels . . .'

By the middle of the lunch June felt pleasantly airborne, but she knew from experience that this was the danger point. Cherie was gaiety itself and had gathered the best of the rest of the restaurant around their table, crashing into the brandy. Her manner of invitation was nothing if not imperious. Since she and June had arrived so late, many tables were already preparing to empty at the time of their spectacular entry. Several lingered out of a mixture of professional interest, natural curiosity and undisguised lust. Chez Stalky was, at lunch-times, frequented primarily by men. Cherie, well aware of the longing glances being levelled at their much cherished table (much cherished because it was permanently vacant in the corner, reserved by Stalky for his special favourites), had made her choice as to whom should be allowed to sit with them. At the moment of decision, following shamelessly brazen scrutiny of the scene, she would snap her fingers in the direction of the eager victim and graciously incline her handsome head. June, regarding the tilt of the long and vulnerable neck, thought how smashing the teen Cherie must have been tip-toeing about in *Swan Lake*. June noticed she had barely eaten a thing. The artichoke she had chosen to start with had eventually been borne away still practically intact. June could guess at the reaction in the kitchen: 'Just look at this sodding artichoke, some joker's been picking away at one or two of these outer leaves! Making sure we can't offer it out again!' And her rare fillet steak lay untouched on its wooden plate, gently leaking a thin trickle of watery blood from a half-hearted attack some time before, when Cherie had actually seemed about to consume something because her fork had made contact with the meat. But then nice Nobs Plater (everyone's favourite news-caster) and Zachary Ram, the mischievous television critic of the weekly magazine *Views*, had presented themselves at the table. There was no eating anything after that. June rather regretted the way that their intimate lunch had escalated into such a high-powered salon. She had been looking forward to relating her misdeeds of the previous night. So far she hadn't had the fun of telling anyone about the Director General. She'd tried Blossom but the line seemed to have been permanently engaged. She knew what that meant – they were obviously on the job, with the phone off the hook. That was why she had actually called into Cherie's office, to see her face and her sly reaction to this latest piece of gossip. She and her agent shared all their sexual secrets.

There was a slight lull in the proceedings, a noted man of letters had just joined the proprietorial inner group closest to Cherie and June. His name was Professor Hamilton Hamilton and although June had seen him many times on the box, and passed him, his scholarly head high in the clouds, along the corridors of Television Tower on the way to the studio, she had never met him before. And yet, repeatedly, he was smiling at her and nodding his head as if in recognition; June could only conclude that because he must have also seen her on the small screen, he genuinely felt that he knew her. And so she smiled back. Of course he was an intimate of Cherie's. ''am-'am, mon cheri!' she had cried on sight, waving both dazzling silver arms in the air. But it had been June to whom his warm and humorous gaze returned, until even Cherie began to notice. She made use of the lull to mention the fact. 'Darling? You 'ave to tell me, *non*, what you think of 'am-'am, as a lover! 'E is a sexy old goat now, but can you believe that I 'ad 'im first time for me as a student at the Sorbonne. 'E was not a professor in those days – far from it. But 'e 'ad a most knowledgeable penis. Now tell me is 'e that man that you were 'aving last night?' Her eyes shone with anticipation.

June shook her head swiftly. 'Believe it or not I don't even know the good Professor Hamilton Hamilton, but,' she lowered her voice, aware that Zachary Ram on her right could play certain havoc with the piece of juicy gossip she was about to impart, 'the person I landed in bed with, believe it or not, was . . . she paused for greater effect and to relish for a moment longer the expression on Cherie's face, 'the person was the Director General of Universal Television himself!' And she sat back to savour her agent's reaction.

It was not the reaction she had expected.

Cherie went white and immediately started eating without stopping. Within moments she had not only demolished her cold, congealed steak, but had ripped two bread rolls into pieces and was busy wolfing them down, whilst viciously shredding at an inoffensive stick of celery and looking wildly round the littered table for something else to get her teeth into. June stared at her with amazement and mounting alarm.

'Jesus!' she whispered. 'Is he one of yours!' Christ – she knew it would be bound to bloody happen one day! Yet up until now their taste in men had never overlapped, which was probably one of the reasons they got on so well. She tried to conjure up what picture she could of the Director General. Of course it wasn't fair to judge a person's appearance and sex appeal, not when they are suffering the distorting spasms of an imminent seizure, or even when (as this morning, thankfully) that person then emerges from near tragedy in a miraculous recovery. But even so June would never have thought that the Director General was Cherie's type. But he obviously was, otherwise why on earth this extraordinary reaction! June could kick herself for the error, but she could see now that perhaps Cherie had at last grown tired of her procession of handsome men and beautiful boys. Samson Pye her beloved, absent, husband wasn't beautiful after all, and certainly not young. In fact the more June thought about it, Samson Pye was in many ways not unlike the Director General – a substantial and influential figure of authority. And June would have been the last to deny the sexual potency of power – wasn't that precisely what she had succumbed to last night? She glanced around discreetly. The bloody fat could be in the fire if Cherie were to have a momentary aberration and spill the beans at this gathering. She had already spilt nice Nobs Plater's large brandy, without his noticing, in a frenzied attempt to reach the leftover Marrons Glacés on the next table. But there appeared to be one of those intellectual discussions of high intent in progress, one about to deteriorate into a free-for-all debate before ending in actual argument. The only person whose eye she did catch was the watchful Professor. She made the point of again exchanging a sweet smile.

It must have been just what he wanted, just what he had been waiting for, the final encouragement.

'Would you mind awfully, old chap,' he leant towards Zachary Ram, 'if I were to ask you to change places with me? In my opinion you have been in the hot seat for too long – only fair to allow somebody else a fair crack of the whip – eh?' Within seconds he was seated at June's side.

Cherie was deep in conversation with a gratified Stalky trying to decide between Crêpes Suzettes on the vast menu, or Soufflé au Grand Marnier. Since the flavour of both would be virtually indistinguishable their discussion was based on the difference in texture. This was a great occasion for Stalky, in all the years that Cherie had eaten at his emporium this was the first time that he had known her show interest in afters. And he was very much a pudding-person himself; though he would have preferred to tempt her to something more original than the choice in question, he didn't dare start rocking the boat now. June sat in dubious silence listening to their animated discourse. She had only once before witnessed Cherie in this manic tuck-munching mood, and that was when the estranged Samson Pye had, at the very last minute, cancelled their plans for a dirty weekend in a place called Worms, near Frankfurt in West Germany. Cherie had been so looking forward to sending back postcards from Worms. But after the eating bout she had spent the next half-hour in the lavatory forcing her fingers to the back of her throat until the entire bumper meal had been vomited away. June felt that old Stalky's delicious dessert would eventually suffer the same shabby fate.

But now Professor Hamilton Hamilton was pressing her hand to his lips and his twinkling eyes were crinkling away like mad at her own. Something lurched in her stomach, a thread of sexual excitement. It was solely to do with the eminence of the man, a repeat of last night, all over again – she was being pulled by the palpable power. And the challenge of course.

'Well, well,' he was whispering with an unaccountable

41

familiarity. June simpered, aware of curious eyes upon them. Professor Hamilton Hamilton had enjoyed the reputation of being a dedicated ladies' man. His choice in the past, before the death of his wife, had always veered between females of distinction. There had been the series of scandalous affairs with well-known women; the articulate wife of the American Ambassador; the svelte singing star of a long-running musical; the fey French novelist who had finally committed suicide in her suite at the Savoy, because he had steadfastly refused to leave his wife. And then his wife had left him, dying of cancer within three weeks of its diagnosis. He was shattered. Some said she was getting her own back.

But since her death he had maintained a very low profile, his illustrious name had been linked with no one at all. (Might June Day prove the exception? That's what the rest of the table were wondering.) He was still holding her hand, he hadn't let it go. June looked down at their lightly laced fingers and inwardly shivered. She was a remarkably attractive girl, she knew that if only by looking at Blossom, but this effortless conquest had taken her by surprise. It wasn't always as *instant* as this.

She cleared her throat self-consciously, have been about to enquire rather pompously whether or not they had actually been introduced in the past. She could, in all honesty, never be positively sure whether she had met strangers before – or even have been to bed with them for that matter. At the arse-holed end of many evenings she was certain that she'd staggered off with many a choice mortal who she'd be hard put to recognise by the cold light of morning. It happened to anyone with half an ounce of oomph – didn't it?

But Professor Hamilton Hamilton had beaten her to it. 'Well, well,' he was murmuring, 'and so we meet again!'

That was it then. June smiled slowly as if reliving the pleasant memory of their meeting. The thing was to coast now, box clever, just picking up clues as to where that meeting may have taken place. But she needn't have bothered – no coasting, no boxing clever, no picking up clues – they were all quite unnecessary. Professor Hamilton Hamilton's following words made that perfectly clear. 'Blossom. Enchanting Blossom – my loving thoughts have never left you . . .'

The pounding blood in her brain deafened June's ears to the rest of the sentence. It was twelve years since the last time this sort of thing had happened; and two weeks later that man had become her brother-in-law! But she hadn't time to ponder on that sweet memory, although her brother-in-law's name had already insinuated itself into the conversation.

'. . . and Randolph – how is the dear chap? I wish we could winkle him away from your splendid Cornish retreat sometime. Only last month his name cropped up at Disciple's Dinner for this year's Hector Fellowship. He's been awarded it several times before and each time he has refused the honour – do you think that he will turn down the Global Prize?'

'The Global Prize!' June knew that Randy (she and Blossom were the only two in the world allowed to call him Randy) divulged little of what he deemed unimportant to Blossom. Did he then consider the Global Prize to be of no value? He must do, since Blossom had not mentioned the smallest thing about it, and if she had known anything – even had she been sworn to utter secrecy – then June would have been put in the picture. 'For *Understanding Understanding*. In my opinion it is the most brilliant paper of its kind – and the genius of the man to have written it all in Babylonian.' Professor Hamilton Hamilton permitted himself a sly, but modest smile. 'Of course I was one of the few in this country who had no reason to wait for the tardy official translation – I read Babylonian as if it were the Beano comic . . .'

June's thoughts raced back to the previous Easter, to the time when Blossom had tried to persuade her to take a break and come down. She remembered that Randy had been cloistered up in his study for months.

'For God's sake do come down – I'm going mad with him, June! He only emerges for a fuck and some food, and he's babbling away in what he claims to be Babylonian – he even answers the phone with it. People are surprised when they see me out shopping in the streets. The rumour was going around that we had let the house to Arabs!'

The obtuse *Understanding Understanding* (a typical Randolph Tree title) was obviously the outcome of that time.

43

But when would Blossom and the Professor have met? June racked her brains for the answer to that. She could only assume that it must have been when she and Tiny had gone on their walking holiday in Snowdonia in a last bid to resolve the difficulties between them. His idea, not hers, she had hated having to hike about with a heavy rucksack concertina-ing her spinal column. Shoulders back, breasts flung forward like the proud prow of a sea-going vessel. It had rained heavily the entire time and her shoes had developed a dispiriting leak. She had missed Blossom dreadfully, Tiny's circuitous route had not allowed for casual telephone conversations. When she returned, a week sooner than intended – leaving Tiny on the water-sodden banks of the River Usk, she and Blossom had spent all of two hours on the phone. But it was still possible that Blossom had forgotten to make mention of the frisky Professor.

One thing was quite certain. The relationship between them had not been as intimate as Professor Hamilton Hamilton would have liked. Blossom, though fencing flirtatiously with her many fanciers, would never have been unfaithful to Randy. Fidelity was one of the absolute rules of their marriage, one of the sound principles of its trusting success.

But the time had come to disclose the crucial information that she was not in fact Blossom.

'Professor – I'm not Blossom.' The Professor's bony knee was busy nudging her own, not unpleasantly. As he smiled his wide mouth revealed quite a decent set of teeth for a man of his age, though of course he had always been a much-quoted vegetarian. June supposed that all those carrots must have kept them going. She felt a bit of a pang, wondering whether, now she turned out to be someone other than Blossom Tree, he would stop ogling her altogether. It could happen. Being Blossom meant being not simply a highly desirable woman, but being the wife of *the* Randolph Tree. An impressive entity to a man of mind such as the Professor. More than once she herself had deliberately engaged the attention of attractive and scholarly men, who until then had shown no interest in her whatsoever, by letting them know that she was the sister-in-law of Randolph Tree. Not only that, but the *twin*

44

sister-in-law . . . Lying in bed later it amused her to know that they were as excited by this knowledge as they were by her body. That they held in their arms the facsimile of that which Randolph Tree held in his, just as if they were worshipping the very same woman.

A sudden slurping sound to the left of her distracted her attention momentarily. June turned at the noise. Stalky and Cherie were sampling their choices and swilling it all down with champagne, that was all.

Since the sexual revelation over the Director General, Cherie and June had not exchanged a single word. But now, seeing June's face, Cherie took the opportunity to nod vigorously with her mouthful. She also gave a very knowing, lewd wink and jerked her free thumb in the direction of the Professor. June was relieved that Cherie appeared to harbour no undue resentment over last night at least. And probably, knowing the volatile and sometimes completely irrational nature of her agent, she might never learn the reason for her unexpected reaction. Now was certainly not the moment to pursue the matter anyhow. June turned her attention back to Professor Hamilton Hamilton.

To her intense disappointment he was preparing to leave. He was signalling a passing waiter and wishing to settle his share of the brandy bottle on the table. He leaned towards June. 'I am so very, very sorry, charming girl – I fear that I have made a ridiculous figure of myself. But you are the image of a ravishing creature I once fell in love with, for a moment I completely forgot myself . . .'

June stared at him. In a moment she was about to lose a man whose name was a household word in this country. Whose writings were read all over the world. Whose reputation would go down in history. She could imagine the fun she'd be able to have with Blossom on the phone, the kudos with colleagues at work, the salacious comparison of notes with Cherie if she managed to pull this one into the net. Also wouldn't it mean that within less than twenty-four hours she would have fried two of the biggest fish in the London pool! She blinked her eyes several times to bring a brighter sheen to their brilliant colour. She licked her lips and drew them back to display her white and perfectly even teeth. She tossed her flaming hair over the slender curve of her shoulder.

And then she went in for the kill.

High tide was due at 16.55, which gave Blossom a good chance to do her weekend shopping first, or at least part of it. She very much enjoyed popping into the shops, seeing who she could see, swapping gossip and chatting. Sometimes she managed to trot out as often as three times in the same afternoon for some culinary item or other. 'I'm back!' She'd laugh gaily, darting into The Stores, Puddlemouth's old-fashioned grocery and off-licence. 'Well, I'll be blessed if she's not back again!' 'She's never back again . . .' 'She is that!' And the genial trio of apple-cheeked Cornish crones behind the counter would chuckle and shake their heads, each covered by the latest beret they'd just crocheted with the Women's Institute to match up with the nicely home-knitted cardigans. 'One day, my girl, you'll go forgettin' your 'ead!' 'That' she will, that she will, that she will!'

Blossom loved it, the attention. She would squirm and dimple like a small child basking in the affectionate admonition of favourite aunties. 'It's as warm as the womb in there,' she had once confided to Randolph on her return. 'Do you suppose that is why I feel the need to keep returning?'

'What a womb without June?' he had answered mockingly. 'You would find that a trifle draughty.'

'You pompous prick. You always take what I say so – so fucking literally.' It was early April and the weather had been glorious for a week, but today it was drizzling. Blossom hoped for the kids' sake that it would clear up for tomorrow, though she knew that even a torrential downpour wouldn't put them off camping now they had decided upon it. 'I'm off out to The Stores,' she shouted up the stairs wondering whether she should have put her rubber mackintosh on before, or after, doing so. With luck Randolph wouldn't have noticed it was raining. If however he had, then he would probably at this precise second be putting two and two together. In which case Blossom could expect him to come pounding down the stairs in a matter of moments. He had never been able to resist the thought of her in her rubber mackintosh.

That would mean a further delay of fifteen minutes!

She hadn't that much time to spare. There was a Jumble Sale in the Chapel, run by Emily Shawl, in aid of the forthcoming Easter outing to Seal Island for the under-fives, and another, scheduled for tomorrow morning, with the Salvation Army. But Blossom, along with the chosen few, had been invited to this afternoon's preview at the Sally Army. Last time their Jumble had yielded a bumper crop of old pinafores, the wrap-around kind, in sprigged William Morris prints. The sort that Libertys would have given their eye-teeth for. The son of Cuthbert and Son, Ironmongery and Haberdashery, a man in his late seventies had discovered the pinafores at the back of his stockroom. He still played the drums for the Salvation Army. Randolph had reason to curse him horribly every Sunday morning when the pious and uniformed holy regiment gathered beneath the bedroom window to blast out their hymns of praise. Sunday morning was the one morning that Randolph had a nice lie-in, it was his only acknowledgement to the official day of rest.

Blossom held her breath. There was no sound at all from upstairs. She was wondering whether Randolph had perhaps taken advantage of this brief respite before swimming to snatch another forty winks. His post-coitals' were all very well in their place, but in her opinion they didn't count as real rest, whatever he said. And at lunch, late though it was, she felt that he was looking somewhat weary. And indeed had remarked upon it. 'You look positively *haggard*, my darling.' She had honestly meant it kindly. She herself felt and looked the opposite as he was quick to point out.

'Yes, well, there's nothing to be done about that – it's the physiological difference between the female and male species –'

She held up her hand with an offensively radiant smile as he was about to reply. 'No, my angel, I don't want to go into it now.'

But a little later, when he tried to stand up and she saw him actually *buckle* at the knees, then she was sorry that she had spoken so briskly.

There was still no sound from his study. Blossom stealthily slid into her rubbery covering. 'Black as death,

47

but as shiny as sin', that's how he had described it when she had first brought the mac home.

'Is sin shiny?' She had been in the mood for a discussion that day.

'It's inviting.'

'That's not the same.'

'Association of ideas – something shiny to a child, to a magpie, that sort of thing . . .'

'I think it should be "black as death, but as shiny as . . ."'

'Spring?' Randolph had smiled. He was keen on spring, he was always grateful that the girls had been born in June and therefore christened that way (June and Blossom to avoid confusion between the two as to which of them was the elder, albeit by a mere twenty minutes). Their names were a continuing reminder to him of his favourite season. Blossom had laughed, she was enjoying herself. She loved the effrontery of pitting her inferior vocabulary against Randolph's. What she appreciated was that he never condescended to her in any way, as a more stupid man may have done. But then he never had. It was one of the many qualities for which she loved him so much.

'I love you,' she had said impulsively.

It was his turn to laugh. 'What about "spring"?' He was very, very stubborn, as well as everything else, but even managed to turn that into an endearing trait in Blossom's eyes.

'Every man likes the smell of his own farts.' She'd changed the subject.

'What has that to do with spring?'

'It's an Icelandic proverb – I found it in your book of aphorisms.'

'So?'

Blossom had kissed him slowly, running her tongue suggestively along the moist rim of his full upper lip, then insinuating the tip of it in between his half-open mouth. 'Black as death, but as shiny as sex – how about that?' she had murmured, unzipping his trousers. Then she had masturbated him daintily with the tips of her fingers (playing the part of a Victorian virgin), until he had shot off all down the front of the brand new mackintosh, clogging up three of the button-holes. It was interesting to note how copiously he had come.

The Salvation Army Jumble was somewhat of a disappointment. Except for one thing – a magnificent collapsible opera hat which when packed lay flat as a plate in its crimson cardboard box, but when banged sharply against the thigh sprang immediately into a grandiose shape. Everyone burst into cackles of glee when Blossom placed it on her head.

'What do you think then?' She tipped it at a more rakish angle.

'S'beautiful, my 'andsome!' 'Aye, aye, 'tis that – you goin' t'wear it at yer own funeral, are yer now!' Young Mrs Tree, though a foreigner – not coming from Cornwall at all – was nevertheless very popular with the locals. She was known as being a bit of a card, and the sort who could take a bit of a leg-pull. Of course her husband was a very clever fellow with his books and suchlike, but young Mrs Tree was the one who got on with everyone. And she was one of twins which turned her into the object of superstitious gossip, added to which she assumed the glamour of reflected glory from the fact of June becoming established as a television personality. 'C'm'ere quick, there is our young Missus Tree on the telly!' 'No, t'aint 'er, 'tis 'er twin. Them's alike as two peas in a pod.' 'Well, I never did – I could've sworn 'twas 'er!' The exchange was a common occurrence.

Blossom bought the opera hat, paying a pound for it to make up for the fact that she hadn't been tempted by anything else. The rest was the usual paraphernalia of matted woollies and garments moth-eaten beyond description, all smelling sourly of mildew. There was one positively hideous crimplene evening dress in a depressing dusty pink, with a raised surface like that of a person suffering from acne. Blossom toyed with it in her mind, as a possible if ever she thought of playing the part of a very plain wall-flower. But she was put off by the heavy under-arm stains, and knew that Randolph would most certainly have been revolted by them too (though of course that would have been all part of the exercise!) Picking her way carefully over the slippery, wet cobbles of Puddlemouth's many narrow alleyways and back passages Blossom looked forward to Emily Shawl's Chapel Jumble as being somewhat superior.

She kept her eyes widely on the ground, it wouldn't do to look up for an instant! Not with the surface of the streets so bespoiled with this much dog-shit! The canine deposits, their abundance and the haphazard manner of their placing, were the continuing disgrace of the otherwise picturesque Puddlemouth. The hordes of summer visitors who descended in the season expressed horror each year at this blatant disregard of hygiene, unaware that the situation in the summer was rather an improvement on the rest of the year. In the summer many of the turds were deposited on the sands, whilst proud and sauntering pet-owners cooed their congratulations. The hazards to packed lunches and picnic spreads, to bare toes and crawling babies, and the scores of half-naked spread-eagled on the beaches, were immeasurably greater. And Emily Shawl was the leading force in the local Anti Dog Shit Campaign. Her very next Jumble was to be held in aid of funds for the recently formed ADSC. They planned to take an entire page to publish all the names on their petition in the local newspaper, the *Puddlemouth Weekly*. The names of Blossom and Randolph Tree were there on the petition rather towards the end since it was listed alphabetically; in fact they had been amongst the very first to sign.

It would have been difficult to have withheld their signature from Emily Shawl, even if their support had not been wholeheartedly behind the scheme. Emily Shawl was a law unto herself, the self-appointed organiser of causes, with enough natural enthusiasm to carry a whole army. 'If'n them Germans 'ad 'ad Emily Shawl on their side we'd 'ave lost the last bloody war – aye, without shadow of doubt!' This was the general opinion. A generous friend but a dangerous enemy. But she and Blossom had always got on.

'Howdy!' Emily's upper class consonants carried clear through the confusion of harrassed bargain hunters in the large Chapel vestry. She had been to RADA, a very long time ago, and still remembered how to throw her voice.

Blossom waved, she was dripping wet and thought about her imminent swim with an inward shudder. But she would do it, of course, and probably enjoy it immensely. Randolph never let a little thing like a simple shower put him off – not when they went in during the winter, even when there was snow on the ground. Being wet all over was much nicer than this damp which was seeping down the back of her neck and up her sleeves, and inside her ankle boots.

'Bitch of a day!' Emily's large and handsome profile swivelled sharply to her left as an avid forager pounced at the bundle of clothing beneath Emily's strong arm. 'Sorry, ducky – these are all spoken for –' She rapped the eager woman's grasping hand and, heedless of the resulting whimper of pain, strode over towards Blossom at the door.

'Managed to save these for you, Blossom – thought they were rather your sort of thing.'

Blossom gasped her appreciation. 'Oh, Em, you are sweet!' It was a continuing source of embarrassment to Blossom that she couldn't be certain (she'd been very drunk at the time), but she *thought* that one New Year's Eve she had confided in Emily. She had told her all about her fantasy roles with Randolph and how much of a stimulus it was to their sex life. It had come out of discussing Emily's days at RADA and her failed career as an actress. Blossom supposed that she must have been after some thespian tips since she was on-stage, for Randolph certainly twice-nightly. With a good chance of a matinée most days. She couldn't be *sure*, but she felt there to be an image stamped on her retina of Emily Shawl's high surprised pencilled eyebrows and her heavily rouged powdered cheeks all bunched together in an expression of camp outrage. The image was memorable because even at the time it had so reminded Blossom of a painting or coloured drawing she had seen of poor Oscar Wilde before his spirit had been broken. Since then she hadn't been able to see the swooping and posturing Emily without connecting the two together.

'How's Pots?' Blossom enquired solicitously, whilst sorting through the clothes. 'Is her cold any better – I haven't seen her for days.' Pots was Emily Shawl's friend and protegé, a pale and sickly young unmarried mother whose baby had just died when they had first come into contact with each other. It was Emily who had revived

51

Pots from her overdose of sleeping tablets, bringing her down to Puddlemouth to live, caring for her with all the devotion of the dedicated, and coaxing some frail interest in life from that barely flickering spirit. Until the gradual metamorphosis had come about. Seeing Pots now, a relatively confident person and qualified infant-school teacher (Emily had financed her further education), it was difficult to believe she was the same creature. True, there was about her a timidity and certain shyness but in her job amongst the tiniest children these qualities were seen to be an advantage. It simply meant that this gentle soul shared the vulnerability of her charges which led to a greater understanding between them. They lived together, Emily and Pots, in The Mermaid's Nest. Emily's thriving Bed and Breakfast business was one of the few of its sort which actually kept open all the year round. Most of them simply operated in the season, between Easter until the end of September. October if the weather held out. Then the small B&B signs would be withdrawn from the windows just as the cafés, the novelty shops, the Amusement Arcade, the Go-Go Boutique and the ice-cream parlour along the sea-front were being shuttered and locked till the following season.

But The Mermaid's Nest wasn't Emily Shawl's sole occupation. Her redoubtable fund of energy would not have been satisfied to be only spent on that. She was also the highly efficient curator of The Puddlemouth Society of Artists (not affiliated in any way with the now largely extinct Puddlemouth Royal Academy of Artists) who had at their inception prided themselves on their modernity and vowed to adhere to their catholic principles. In the cause of Art, all is allowable.

And so it was. For many years freedom of expression reigned supreme – until in the mid-sixties it ran riot.

For one internationally famed fortnight the Puddle-mouth Society of Artists became a cultural mecca for the avant-garde. The media descended. The town-councillors convened. A mixed group of multi-racial students marched nude through the cobbled streets in political protest, culminating in a sexual orgy on the sands in which many of the locals were pleased to participate. *The News of the World* carried it for two issues as its centre spread. Blossom and June, who were only fifteen at the time, were considering running away from home in order to join in. Randolph was there already, it was how he had first become acquainted with Puddlemouth.

And then suddenly it was all over, as if it had never been.

The Puddlemouth Society of Artists had revelled in their hour of glory. For a brief moment they had relished the fame – as had the locals, once they had grown used to being photographed registering mock-horror and disgust. And for some time after there lingered a pronounced sense of anti-climax. But even this proved to be a unifying force consolidating the warmth of the community. Conversations could still be heard between the folk who had lived through those hectic weeks. For some it seemed as if it had only happened yesterday. Emily Shawl had arrived in Puddlemouth at just the right moment to restore a sense of order to the Society of Artists.

'Pots?' she said now, her expression softening. 'Poor little Pots. I have made her stay in bed all this week. Which reminds me – I shall have to go soon and give her some tea. Would you like some? You're very welcome, I made scones this morning. And it's my own strawberry jam from last summer.'

Blossom laughed. 'Sounds delish, but I can't. We're due to go swimming when I get back and I still haven't been to The Stores yet. These things are perfect by the way –' She held up a pair of thick corduroy jodhpurs and a gentleman's morning suit, the jacket complete with tails. Emily knew perfectly well that Blossom never went riding; and the gent's clothing was quite obviously far too small for Randolph. Emily winked. 'I thought they might come in handy for you know what.'

The sea was tumultuous, it was impossible to swim. All Blossom and Randolph could do was stand at the edge and splash around in the surf. More than once Blossom got knocked off her feet by the force of the massive waves and even Randolph lost his balance several times. They clung together, laughing helplessly like children.

'The kids would love this –' Blossom shouted above the roar of the ocean.

'Who?' Randolph yelled back.

53

'The kids –'

'Oh, bugger the kids.' Randolph tightened his grip around her waist. 'I like it without them, don't you?' The wind carried his words off over the cliffs. Blossom hoped in a motherly way that Willow and Pip wouldn't hear, although they were a good twenty-five miles in the other direction. It was only recently that she had begun to feel vaguely guilty about the children in this way. Realising with a pang that she hadn't given them a single thought for hours at an end when they were out at school all day or when they were away. She supposed that it was all part of the gradual process of them growing up and away from herself as a parent, forging their independence and all that sort of thing. And yet it seemed to have happened so quickly. Only yesterday she was changing their nappies and powdering their botties, worrying about them every minute of the day. And waking in the night at the slightest murmur from their cots, mindful of the smallest sign of distress. She was a good mother, she knew that, but it was just that lately she was becoming increasingly aware of her diminishing involvement. She must remember to talk about it to June.

'Have we had enough then?' Randolph was shouting. A fresh avalanche of spray foamed and bubbled around their bodies, an icy inferno. They were the only ones in the water, except for several rubber-suited surfers waiting some distance out for the perfect wave to break. It wouldn't come today, the conditions were bad. These must be inexperienced surfers otherwise they would know that and give up. Blossom didn't recognise any of them as being local boys.

A few amused onlookers had gathered on the sea-wall overlooking the beach. They stood huddled together sharing one umbrella, amazed to see anyone attempting to swim in the rain. They would look even more amazed when they saw Blossom and Randolph climb the short ladder to get back into their house. For some reason people thought it extremely odd that anyone should actually have a home on the beach.

'Race you!' Blossom started running. It wasn't far to go, the distance back to the ladder was about thirty yards. Although it was high tide the sea wasn't as far in today as it had been some weeks back. Then it had almost touched the wall at some points. They had been forced to remove the ladder lest it got swept away by the force of the waves. Randolph caught her up easily and overtook her, loping in long easy strides.

'Is there anything you can't do better than me?' she gasped on reaching the bottom of the ladder. 'It wouldn't have hurt to let me win that one, you cunt!'

He stood aside to let her up first and smacked her wet buttocks as they swayed past his hands.

'Ouch! That will show, it'll go all red!'

'I'll kiss it better.'

Blossom turned towards him. 'If you're not careful,' she said, 'you could be about to beat your own record.'

June reached Flowers just as Mercedes, the manageress of the hotel was leaving.

'Oh great – now I can have your cab –'Mercedes grinned, showing the attractive gap between her two front teeth. The taxi driver blinked at this stunningly exotic new fare, having only moments before given June up as a dead loss. He'd been wanting to show her off to his mates in the pub but she had claimed to have been in too much of a rush this evening. He wondered if he might do a bit better with this black bird.

'You on the telly too, doll?' He hung out of his seat, eyeing the impressive length of Mercedes' legs. 'Look like a dancer to me –'

'Uh, uh – not any more, I'm not. Used to be years ago when I was a kid in Harlem.' Mercedes grinned at June again from behind her huge dark glasses. Their diamante-studded frames glittered against the deep brown of her skin. She was wearing her crinkly hair in many minute plaits, layered closely to the scalp and arranged in a set of circular ridges. It looked as though her head had actually been embroidered with a thickly encrusted pattern of black silk.

'I like your hair, Mercedes.'

'Gee thanks, honey – I only hope it does the trick. Cross fingers – I'm off for an audition. It's for the rape victim in something that's coming to the Royal Court. I think all the black actresses in Great Britain are up for it and the fucking part only calls for one pissy appearance!'

'Charming language!' The taxi driver was anxious to be

55

off. The black bird was obviously out of his league, he could tell without trying. All those poncey actresses were the bleeding same.

June and Mercedes laughed.

'Good luck!' June waved and shouted.

Mercedes stuck her head out of the moving window. 'Masses of messages for you as usual – mostly all guys. Oh, yeah – your sister rang. I spoke to her, she seems kinda keen to have a chat with you sometime –'

That was one of the best things about living in a hotel, there was always someone to take the telephone calls. It seemed to June to be so much friendlier than simply having an impersonal answering service like all the other single people that she knew. And not only that, but it was altogether more cheerful a homecoming to be greeted by someone like Mercedes or one of the other girls on the desk. Rather than the cold silence of an empty flat.

Dimples was on the desk, she was Mercedes' second-in-command, a sweet-faced dumpling of a girl who everybody loved. Everybody, including a famous and married television comedian with whom Dimples had been having an affair for the last three years.

June greeted her now. 'Hello Dimples, I've just seen Mercedes looking fantastic – it only occurs to me – what an odd time to be holding auditions!' She glanced at the old, restored grandfather clock in the hall, beside the giant aspidistra plant. 'It's nearly seven o'clock.'

Dimples nodded and sighed. 'The audition is taking place in the writer's pad out in Islington.'

'Oh, it's one of those is it?'

'Sounds like it. Your sister's rung twice today. Loads of messages. Two party invites. Lucky thing, that's just what I could do with right now – a bloody good party. Thingy flew off to Las Vegas this morning, he won't be back for a month. At least he hasn't taken his missus with him – that I couldn't have bloody stood, the thought of the two of them out there together.'

June clucked sympathetically, taking the sheet of scribbled messages and quickly glancing over the list of written names. She had given up advising Dimples to put an end to the affair, but she still considered it an appalling waste, all the hanging around. It was perfectly obvious that 'Thingy' wasn't ever going to leave his wife and children for poor old Dimples. But she was helplessly in love that was the trouble, no one would have been able to persuade her to do without him. However unsatisfactory the arrangement.

'You could come to this party with me if you'd like to, that's if I decide to go. Loads of blokes there.' June pointed to one of the names.

Dimples eyes widened. 'Oh no – I'm only joking. He's ringing me anyway some time this evening so I'd have to be here. And I promised to hold the fort till Mercedes gets back, and goodness knows how long that's likely to be. But,' she laid her hand on June's and gave it a light squeeze, 'I do appreciate the thought – honestly.'

June gave up. It was useless trying to drag Dimples out, she'd tried before without success. 'Give me a ring in the room if you change your mind,' she said lightly, and turned to mount the stairs. 'Oh, if any calls come for me in the next half hour can you tell them to ring back. I'm just going to have a bath now – but first I must have a word with Blossom. I've rung her twice today as well but the line's been engaged both times.'

'Perhaps it was her trying to get you. You have said that happens quite often with you two.' Dimples and Mercedes were as intrigued as everyone else with the idea of June having an identical twin, and were always longing for Blossom to come up to London so that they could actually see June's double for themselves.

'Either that or she and her sexy husband have been on the job all day – they always take the phone off the hook when they're at it.'

Dimples looked wistful. 'All day! Lucky for some – that's what I say.'

Blossom sounded positively radiant on the telephone. 'You just caught me in time – hold on. I'll go and turn the taps off, I've started running my bath ... There's an opening tonight at the gallery – you know I told you that I'd done the big nude all in yellows and lemons to cheer up that empty wall above the bath –'

'The self-portrait, you mean?' June remembered. She was always surprised that Blossom didn't paint much more than she did. They had always been considered to have artistic talent. And it wasn't as if she hadn't all the time in the world at her disposal, with the children at school all day and Randolph locked away upstairs in his study. She never had been able to understand how on earth Blossom managed to while away the hours between getting up in the morning and going to bed. But then June had always been in a job. This afternoon Cherie had said that she was about to negotiate a contract for the Female series. If all went according to plan this major programme was scheduled to run for six weeks, later this spring, with June as the presenter. It would mark a definite advance in her career. And yet it struck her that she didn't have anyone close enough in her life with whom she could share this exciting news – except Blossom, of course. There would always be Blossom.

'That's the one, the self-portrait.' Blossom laughed infectiously. 'Well, nothing succeeds like success. Everybody loved it. So I did another one – all in bright greens to go above the red Aga in the kitchen. And Randy and Emily Shawl persuaded me to send them both into the Society of Artists, though Pip and Willow made fun and said they would never get past the Hanging Committee. But they did! It's the first time that I've ever been hung!'

June congratulated her warmly, and then told her about the Female series.

'But that's *fabulous*, isn't it! Soon you'll become a household name – like, like Angela Rippon. No honestly you will, it's starting already. I can tell by the number of people who stare at me in the streets. Twice last week women stopped me to say that they had seen me on the telly – which reminds me. What about that Irish poet who was killed today – weren't you going over to interview him? We saw it on News at Six. A bomb explosion.'

'Actually it was his gas-stove.'

'No! Have they converted in Ireland yet?' Blossom sounded genuinely puzzled.

'What's Connor McConnors' exploding gas-stove to do with religion? You've lost me now, Blossom – ah, before I forget . . . I met an ardent admirer of yours at Chez Stalky's today. Professor Hamilton Hamilton.'

Blossom gasped. 'Oh, I think he is absolutely gorgeous, don't you! I meant converted to North Sea Gas. Yes,

Hamilton came down here when Randy was writing *Understanding Understanding* – I was going to send you a copy. The translation is through now, but Randy said not to. It is a fearful bore. He said he wouldn't dream of inflicting it on his nearest and dearest.'

'Oh, but I'd like one, just to show off. Tell him I won't read it. Though, according to Professor Hamilton Hamilton, Randy is to get the Global Prize for it. Is that true? You didn't say.'

They spoke together for almost twenty minutes and would have gone on much longer but Blossom was mindful of the time.

'I'd best go,' she said excitedly. 'I'm cutting it a bit fine. We can't stay all that long at the opening, although it's my hour of glory. There's a darts match out at The Boozer's Bloom – poor old Randy's shitting himself already. He really needs to win tonight, it's getting near to the end of the darts season and he's lost as many as he's won. I think his own score is ten lost, ten won. They're all playing atrociously this year, the whole of The Boozer's Gloom team –'

'It's that old landlord, that old reprobate, that Gascoigne Teate. He casts the kibosh on everything.'

'Mm – terrific pub though – he makes it. And nobody would go if he wasn't there, and the darts night is the best of the week. It's the only night we drive out there now. Randy's working on something new. The rest of the week we just read or sit around watching television. I get the feeling sometimes that I'm really vegetating. What are you up to tonight? Out on a gay social round as usual? I shall be thinking of you dining somewhere very grand with Professor Hamilton Hamilton. Tomorrow night is our night for fish and chips – will you go to bed afterwards? I would if I were you. I must admit I was very tempted when he was down here.' Blossom gave an exaggerated sigh. 'But I worked it out that I had too much to lose – you haven't anything. It must be absolutely marvellous not to be weighed down with conscience, or hampered as I am by sexual loyalty.'

June was shocked. 'That's the first time I've heard you talk like that, Bloss!'

'I know – awful isn't it! It's the thought of you having it

59

off with Professor Hamilton Hamilton – I was just remembering how horny his kisses made me feel . . .'

June lay in her hot bath sipping her cold drink. Glenfiddich on the rocks. It was interesting to note that no sooner had the icy alcohol hit her stomach but that she had the instant urge to empty her bladder. And that her urine as it trickled out seemed as chill as her drink. Yet it surely couldn't be whizzing straight through her system as swiftly as that, could it! She supposed that it was all to do with the temperature of the surrounding water. In the wintry sea, whenever she had accompanied Blossom and Randy on their daily swim, any personal water that she had passed had been a positive blessing of warmth and all too swiftly dispersing comfort. It had become a family joke. 'Quick, swim over here – the water's really warm!' June remembered now that she'd forgotten to ask Blossom if they'd been in today. Sometimes if Randy was working on something new, he preferred not to interrupt it with the swim and they would miss it for weeks on end. Blossom would never go in without him. She rarely did things on her own.

June studied her list of telephone calls and tried to decide what she would choose to do this evening. She had made a vague promise to Cherie Pye that she would look in at an informal gathering which Cherie was giving for another of her clients. A fashion journalist turned novelist who had become so successful that she was forced into being a tax-exile, and was choosing to flee to Dublin. June had met her once and they had, not disliked – but mistrusted each other on sight. Though she was sure that if they had the opportunity to get to know each other better they would probably end up as very good friends. It was not unusual for Cherie's clients to feel like this about each other. They were after all competing for Cherie's invaluable attention, like siblings clamouring for the mother.

But June did not feel drawn to the event. She had already lunched with her agent, leaving to share the Professor's taxi (needing just that little bit longer to effect a sure conquest). There was no way of guessing how Cherie's eating splurge had ended. She could be in an unpredictable mood by tonight. And it was possible to overdo things socially with Cherie, a little of her could go a long way. She was very keen on raising the emotional temperature anyway, and the departure of the celebrated novelist would be larded with enough overtones of hysteria. June mentally crossed out the idea of going.

It was comfortable in the bath. That and the strong measure of Scotch were having an enervating effect upon her. She felt positively soporific now, wonderfully so. And it occurred to her that there was no earthly reason in the world why she should have to go out this evening at all. She would be missed – but not specifically. Not by any one person in particular. It was like that, her life. She was warmly welcomed wherever she went, but the sort of functions she attended didn't depend on her presence. Her circle of male friends were more like intimate strangers. In many cases she had only known them in bed.

Take the invitations for this evening for instance. One was for a private party, an impromptu affair, to follow the midnight screening of *The Wing of the Rat*. This was the latest science/fiction-cum-domestic/horror from the director of *The Snarl of the Dove*, and before that the hugely popular *The Smile of the Suckling Serpent*.

June had met the Czech director up in Scotland, whilst they were on location shooting *The Wing of the Rat*, but had been unable to cope with his sadism in the bedroom of the hotel where they both happened to be staying. He had abandoned her in highly embarrassing circumstances, so that the chambermaid had been forced to find extra help to free her. It had cost a fortune in tips. June hadn't found it in her heart to forgive him. And yet he continued to pursue her. She had inadvertently switched *Screen* on several nights ago (each of the hotel rooms were supplied with a colour television), and had just caught the start of an in-depth profile that was being done on him. The unexpected sight of the short, squat body and the square swarthy face had shocked in her a tremor of sexual excitement. She had forgotten how attractive she had found him. He had replied to the interviewer's questions in the same low, gentle, insidious voice that by the end of their night together she had learned to half dread. But on the television she thought it enormously seductive. Was it worth sexual humiliation however? June felt somewhere that it was like betraying the fight for female emancipation to allow oneself to be brutalised as a sexual object. She and Blossom always disagreed on that point.

The other party invitation (the one that she had suggested taking Dimples to) was being given in Valentine's Club, in Old Bond Street. Given by Valentine himself to celebrate the first birthday of the club. June had met Valentine in the Marbella Club in Spain when she had gone on a mad and mindless weekend with a girl called Amethyst, whose mother owned a villa out there.

Amethyst had been in love with Valentine, and when she had introduced him, June could understand why. He was immensely wealthy, and that appealed to a girl of Amethyst's social pretensions. He would inherit the title of his elder brother, should that brother die – which was more than likely. The brother had always been considered to be educationally sub-normal as a child, who now as a bachelor nearing his forties, had decided to take up motor-racing. His aim was to win the Grand Prix, he had already written off three racing vehicles and narrowly missed running over his own mechanic. But Valentine was altogether different.

When June had seen him first she had the immediate impression that he was a girl. A blonde, sun-tanned beauty with long curly hair drawn back and held with an elastic band at the nape of the neck. The smile had been as shy and as dreamy as a child barely awakened from sleep. Of course, he was stoned out of his mind at the time. And in no time at all so was she. All three of them had spent the night sleeping together, curled in each other's arms on the hot beach. And in the morning Valentine had made love to each of the girls in turn. At the end of it June had fallen a little in love with him herself. But in spite of much pleading and many invitations from Amethyst on their return from Marbella, she had chosen not to repeat the experience. Then she and Amethyst had lost touch with each other, and June had completely forgotten the existence of Valentine. Until one night she had visited Valentine's Club after a party, with a whole crowd of people – not connecting her Valentine with this one – until he had seen her and asked her to dance. She had stayed with him for almost a fortnight before she (so he claimed) broke his heart by deciding to leave him.

By this time he had inherited the title. His brother had killed himself, and wiped out an entire family of peasants and two goats, whilst running in a new racer in Italy. June tried on the title for size. 'Lady June – Lady *June* . . .' She took to mouthing it in the mirror, varying the emphasis on the different syllables. But try as she would she couldn't get it to sound like anything.

'I think it's the June – it's so *ordinary* there's no getting over it. Lady Blossom sounds *much* better. Just think, if I hadn't been dawdling about at the moment of our birth I could have ended up a bloody Lady.' Blossom had been appalled. 'You mean he's actually asked you to marry him, but you only re-met him last night – that was quick work, even for you! And you're thinking of turning him down, him *and* his title, because it doesn't sound right. Look, I'll come up and take your place. I'm not worried by how it sounds. And then at least we'll keep the title in the family.'

But it wasn't the Lady June part that had decided her in the end, she only wished she had more snobbery in her nature which would have made it easier to marry him purely for his title. The trouble really lay with the sort of life he would have expected them both to lead – it just smacked too much of the privileged and lazy lotus-eating. The richness of the diet was more than she could stomach.

It hadn't been altogether easy, leaving him. So feminine in appearance, even though his hair was now very short, he was an instinctive and sensitive lover. He made her feel more goddess-like than any of the others, touching her all the time and kissing those bare parts of her body that were visible to him when she was clothed. Her wrists. Her ears. Her eyelids. The nape of her neck. And her hair, he was always playing with her hair. Being perfectly content to lie beside her for hours twisting it around his long, thin fingers into tiny tendrils. Plaiting it, combing it, coaxing it into exaggerated styles, even washing it when she allowed him to (he was an inept hair-washer, dripping water all over the place).

'Are you a hair-fetishist, do you suppose, Valentine?' she had asked him seriously one day. They had spent all

63

day in bed as they usually did, smoking joints (with June feeling as guilty as hell, being incommunicado from Cherie). Valentine had become so carried away by the sight of the perfect coiffure he had spent hours creating as she lay on her stomach reading a book that he had unexpectedly shot off between her shoulder blades.

'I adore and worship every inch of you,' came his trembling reply.

She had considered it rather an unsatisfactory answer to what was an interesting question.

But even the adoration had palled eventually, the pedestal proving to be a depressingly lonely place. And his sense of her increasing withdrawal only served to heighten the desperation of his passion. She had thought it best to make a clean break.

It was on nights like these, June reflected, that the disadvantages of being single seemed to be most apparent. Nothing would have been more pleasant at this very moment than to have someone else decide for her. Be there ready and waiting as she stepped out of her bath, with a soft fleecy towel to rub down her back. A quick answer to her query over what she should wear, and then the firm statement as to where they would be going. All decisions made with no prevarications. On the other hand . . . there was a late-night Joan Crawford film on the box; she was halfway through the new Patricia Highsmith; she had yet to try on the Italian, stiletto-heeled boots (bought this afternoon) with the rest of her wardrobe – nor had she had a chance to quietly plan out the line of her questions for tomorrow's confrontation with the eccentric Dame Tiger Oats . . .

June ran more hot water, and refilled her glass from the ice container and bottle of Glenfiddich that she had brought into the warm bathroom, for this very purpose. It was one of her very favourite occupations of all – getting gently and slowly completely smashed in the bath. She particularly liked what it inevitably led on to.

She took a strong steady draught of the fiery liquid between her lips and allowed it to rest, for as long as she could stand the burning sensation, upon her tongue. When she swallowed at last, it felt as though the entire inside of her mouth had been anaesthetized. She waited for the desired effect, it didn't take long. Whilst waiting, and still feeling relatively sober, she lathered and shaved both her legs, and carefully under each arm. She performed this slow ritual as if it were an erotic act, using a soft badger brush to produce the necessary profusion of thick, creamy bubbles from her solid, white square of scented soap. She could never remember the exact name of this soap, but had to save the wrapper; and each time she wanted to buy another she would produce the wrapper to show the assistant behind the counter. Always the same shop, a tiny *Parfumerie* off Shaftesbury Avenue, which displayed a prominent range of contraceptives. Once Valentine had accompanied her to the Shop (on one of their rare daylight jaunts), and had insisted on buying her perfume. The assistant, a frail, and friendly Hungarian in his late seventies, had insisted on calling his brother from the inner premises to decide which of their many perfumes would be the right one for the exquisite young lady. Valentine had been enchanted by the intricate ceremony of it all, and even June had felt flattered and beguiled. The perfume decided upon was *Bal à Versailles* worn, so it was claimed, by both the Queen of England (currently reigning) and Elizabeth Taylor. It was the most expensive perfume in the place. Immediately afterwards they had gone to the cinema, to the Curzon. Halfway through the film, one of Polanski's, June had thought that she was going to swoon. The extreme opulence and sinking comfort of the cinema seats, the decadence on the screen and the overwhelming and suffocating new scent had robbed her of all sense of reality. And Valentine was behaving so amorously. He was all over her – people were looking! He claimed the perfume had got under his skin. Since that time she had been very careful and sparing in its application. It was the only perfume she had ever worn that was infallible, it had never yet failed to arouse desire in men. This soap, its scent, had the same effect on her. Though it was quieter and less heady and somehow more private. And now the Scotch was doing its stuff too.

June sat up, her knees wide apart, and leaned between them towards the shower attachment on the shining chrome taps. She made the necessary adjustments to the temperature of the water and ferocity of its volume. And then, sinking languorously back into the luxuriant foam, she directed the strong spray from the shower straight to her clitoris.

This was one of the advantages of being single . . .

Two

Blossom undulated along the deserted road that ran from the remote Maidens Cove over the moors to Puddle-mouth. She was bare but for her bikini. Now and then a solitary vehicle would pass, slowing down to tempt the poor girl with a lift. The summer sun was already setting to the left, staining the sea and the sky with streaks of deepening red whilst retaining its own burning orange. The entire landscape was awash with this blooded reflection, even the blades of grass beneath Blossom's sandalled feet (thank Christ she had hung on to her sandals!). It was as if a celestial crime of violence had been committed, unleashing the floodgates of an unquenchable heavenly gore.

Blossom shivered but strode on, shoulders back in a brave though not convincing show of jauntiness. At the moment her flesh still held the heat of the day, but when the sun finally slunk beneath the line of the blurred horizon, she would quickly become chilled to the bone. She knew that. She knew also that very soon it would begin to get dark. And the darkness on these moors was quite unlike any other. Even those grown men of Cornwall who were noted for their courage, and who were completely familiar with the coves and cliffs around Puddlemouth, even they refused to venture over the moors after a certain hour of the night.

When Blossom and Randolph had first moved to these parts they had rented a small converted barn on the top of the cliffs. A remote and isolated spot which necessitated their owning two cars, one each. Then if one of them broke down or for some reason became delayed, the other person would not be completely abandoned. Blossom above all was deeply grateful for the arrangement, and felt that without it she would not have been able to survive. Her constant dread was that the time would come when, driving her small car over these moors, the engine would fail her, and she would be stranded, petrified in the unknown horrors of the night. Even in the daytime, in the safety of the speeding car, a sparkling blue beach-buggy with both babies strapped safely beside her, gurgling with happiness – even then she was uneasily aware of something unknown. Something dangerous and evil midst all that normality; something destructive. It was a deeply disquieting sensation of being menaced by the metaphysical.

She suddenly stumbled on a small stone, sliding to avoid the tangled roots of the bracken which grew in such malicious profusion. The bleak winds from the sea were so strong that the vegetation stood no chance of reaching any height. Everything grew close to the ground, crouched and crawling. Virulent – that was the word. Such trees as there were bore no leaves at all. They were thorny and black, hunched and bent all in the same direction with their backs to the cliffs. Like a sparse scattering of beckoning dwarfs. Grotesque and frightening.

Blossom was frightened now, conscious that in this situation her vivid imagination was going to be her worst enemy. She should have accepted the lifts that had been offered instead of this ludicrous show of independence. Now she regretted her own stupidity and the suspicions that had prompted her refusals. Surely the possible rape by a fellow human would be preferable to this savagery of the senses . . .

She resolved to take the very next car that came along.

But where was it? One would come in a minute. She had no watch, but she knew perfectly well that the coves and beaches would be empty by now. When she had scrambled away from Maidens Cove there were very few people left.

But one car must come soon, she was confident of that – wasn't she? In the meantime she must stride along, showing a brave face, her best foot forward And above all, concentrate her thoughts on matters of absolute normality. After all whose bloody fault was it that she was in this bizarre situation – she had only herself to blame.

The car, when it came, was long and low, a malevolent black. It crept behind her so noiselessly that she hadn't known it was there until it had passed her and purred to a halt a few yards ahead. But at that point she harboured no misgivings, she was so thankful that it had appeared at all.

She ran forward, her breasts jiggling; the cold had got to them now and both nipples were erect. There was nothing she could do about them except cross her arms over her chest like a self-conscious schoolgirl. Perhaps this man at the wheel would have a car rug with which she could cover herself. It looked the kind of car that would have that sort of luxury.

Ahead of her the door of the heavy vehicle swung silently open. She caught the glimpse of a powerful male wrist upon which was strapped a skin-diver's watch.

She drew level and bent down, a smile of gratitude on her lips.

The malignant moors bore sullen witness to the savage seduction.

'In my opinion you took far too long – I was shivering by the time you drove up! And it was nearly dark, there were bats about – I was getting really scared, you sod!' Blossom beamed delightedly across at her husband.

She lay, reclining across her latest acquisition – a magnificent tiger-skin rug, complete with head. She was attired in a black satin nightdress, side-slit to the waist. Its bodice was composed of inky intricate lace through which her breasts gleamed like luminous eggs. The matching negligée, edged with a froth of maribou feathers, fell nonchalantly about her shoulders, providing a striking

68

frame for the curve of her uncluttered neck, free now of the hair so recently shorn. The new hair colour, a soot black, suited her eyes. It gave her, more than ever, the appearance of a sleek feline, but now with a touch of the witch. A femme fatale, that's what it felt like. The chic cropped dense hair – as if she was wearing a raven's wing, a symbol of black magic above her brow. No other hair colour had made her react to herself quite so strongly. And June had admitted to having the same feelings! Not so strange really – though this time Blossom had hoped for once to surprise her twin.

'I've had my hair done, it's completely different . . .'

'So is mine. I was going to keep it a secret till you next saw me – you'll have quite a shock . . .'

'So will you. Mine's black . . .'

'No! So's mine! Black and very short . . .'

'Short – so is mine . . .'

They had both laughed. There could be no surprise – that was the way it always was.

Randolph was reading, deliberately withholding attention from his wife – the attention which she so eagerly sought. She pouted and put on a little girl voice, pouring herself a fresh glass of champagne and popping another soft-centre in her mouth (Best go easy on these – she'd already exceeded her daily calorie count. But this role demanded a fair amount of self-indulgence. She was playing the part of a tired businessman's plaything).

'You're not listening to your baby.' She wriggled seductively, cupping her breasts, one in each hand, as if offering them on a plate. Randolph sighed heavily and lay down his *Financial Times*. It was a paper that he never normally would have dreamed of glancing at. Blossom had bought it this morning for a touch of authenticity.

He frowned at her, drawing on his thick cigar. (The role was to his liking in this respect – it enabled him to have a bloody good smoke. A rare enough event. He and Blossom had given up eighteen months before.)

'I hardly regard this to be in order.' It had been agreed that this mogul should display a broad streak of pomposity.

'What's that, pet?' Blossom widened her eyes innocently à la Marilyn Monroe. She continued to hold onto her firm jutting breasts, now squeezing them lightly and pressing them to her with the palms of her hands. As she did so, her cleavage deepened in the delicate lace. The swelling overspill threatened to break the cobwebby boundaries. She could see that her mammary mime was having the desired effect by the tautening bulge in his trousers.

'Gradual Expansion? Or,' she pointed, 'Increasing Inflation?' This was the businessman's jargon.

Randolph crossed his legs with a certain discomfort. 'I hardly regard this to be in order.' Along with the pomposity was a tedious tendency towards repetition. He continued unperturbed, as if he were unaffected by the sight of Blossom brazenly scooping both nipples out and trying to squash them towards each other so that they met.

'Look darling – rubbing noses!' She dimpled ingenuously. 'Would you care to? It doesn't hurt, honestly!'

Randolph coughed and cleared his throat of the rushing saliva. 'I hardly regard this to be in order,' he began importantly. 'This reference to the events of the afternoon. It is a question of etiquette. One has no wish to be acquainted with your activities outside this bedroom. Might I suggest that it is more than a trifle indelicate, if not to say painful for me to have to imagine you in the arms of another man.'

Blossom jabbed at an almond cream, it was not her favourite flavour. She was more fortunate with her next choice. Coffee. She grinned happily. 'It was a *hell* of a poke – it took four and a half minutes from entry to orgasm. I timed it on your watch. Woosh, straight in! A completely dry run, no foreplay – I've rather taken to rape lately. Have you noticed we . . .'

Randolph laid his cigar down with an air of resigned exasperation. 'I'm giving up,' he said testily. 'You're not concentrating tonight. Since when have we agreed to start mixing our sexual metaphors? You can't be in two roles at once, this isn't a rehearsal. If you need an interval or a half time you have to announce it . . .'

'Sorry, sorry, sorry, my darling – I must be getting excited, that's what it is!' Blossom writhed seductively over to where he sat and insinuated her arms between his crossed legs, until she had gently prised them apart. Now his erection was such that it formed a third limb, though marginally shorter – and lacking a foot and five toes.

'How do you do,' she said, shaking its head.

Randolph gave a low groan.

She bent her head down towards the pale pink chequered trousers. Cool for summer and drip-dry. Manufactured in the States but actually sold over here in Harrods. 'I love these pants,' she murmured softly. And she began slowly kissing the tip of the visibly outlined glans. Randolph shuddered, unable to control the tiny tear of spunk than he guessed to be leaking from his extremity. The start of the action – for purposes of lubrication.

But it was lost – a mere spit in the ocean of Blossom's saliva. To his alarm it was becoming obvious that his wife's sexual inventiveness was now leading her to actually suck him off *through his togs*!

It must be the material, the brand name of the fabric, that had sown the seed of the idea in her mind. Seersucker. They had made a private joke of it after the Harrods' assistant had praised the practical advantages of Seersucker as summer-wear. But, Jesus, it hadn't crossed Randolph's mind that it might come to this!

He re-lit his cigar and, despite himself, *squirmed*. Blossom, her mouth full of drip-dry, had now engineered her body into such a rum position that she was managing to maintain a permanent contact between her clitoris and his knee-cap. He had best not bend his leg, lest he lose his whole shin and shank. He still remembered the time that Blossom had made vigorous use of his left elbow as a masturbatory aid, and the irrational terror that, starting with that simple joint, his entire body might be sucked into hers. The primitive fear of castration of course – and yet he had never experienced this during fellatio. Even now, climbing closer and closer to climax, with Blossom's strong jaw clamped to his crotch, her teeth worrying his cock like a terrier with a bone, or a bird with a worm, it was still that trapped knee that caused him uneasiness. Even through the puckered material of the Seersucker and despite the fact that the surface of the knee is not ordinarily sensitive to degrees of temperature (tough elbows by contrast, are the testing instruments for the bath-water of a baby), Randolph was nervously aware of the moist warmth of what felt like Blossom's yawning chasm. He could only pray that he wouldn't fall in. Meanwhile Blossom was enjoying herself enormously.

It was true that she was excited. She had been excited all month, ever since it had been arranged that she should take a holiday with June. Tomorrow she would be in London! It was two years since she had last been up, and then only on an overnight stay. Willow had developed the sure symptoms of measles within minutes of Blossom's train leaving the station. It was obvious to everyone that Randolph was incapable of coping with the situation, even though it had been arranged that Emily Shawl's Pots would be taking care of the children in Blossom's absence. This summer they, Pip and Willow, were camping with their friends and family in the Dordogne. They had begged to be allowed to go, even though it meant that they would be away from home for practically their entire school holiday.

'Six weeks! That's how long it means – doesn't it concern you at all that our own flesh and blood can exist quite happily for that long without seeing us?' Blossom had agonised privately to Randolph.

'Certainly not!' he had answered without hesitation. 'It'll be marvellous to see the back of the little sods . . .'

'Randy!' She had reproached him. Why? She couldn't have explained. But she felt that surely, as parents, it was their duty to at least examine how they stood with their children from time to time. Wasn't this about the age when the generation gap would soon start making itself felt? Shouldn't they be preparing themselves for the eventuality of strife and trouble. Or was it foolish to anticipate trouble in this way – thus turning it into a reality. Randolph thought so.

'We'll meet it head-on when it happens, old girl –'

'Don't old girl me.'

'Why not? You're behaving like an old girl. Fusspotting. For want of something to occupy your mind.'

'You patronising turd!'

'It's perfectly true and you know it. Your children are growing up, you feel threatened by their increasing signs of independence. It causes you to question your own identity and consider . . .'

'I know what it causes me . . .'

'Ah, now we're getting somewhere.'

'It causes me to want to hit you hard across the mouth, you pontificating bore . . .'

But her holiday with June had been Randolph's idea. He was not a believer in holidays himself, he didn't see the point of them. 'Tell me,' he would declaim, sweeping his arms about to encompass the raging ocean to his right, and the magnificence of his library on his left. 'Tell me where on holiday I would find these?'

Blossom never bothered to reply, in a way she agreed with him. It was only lately that the idea of a *change* had begun to appeal to her. Perhaps this was what Randolph had been quick to sense though she had certainly not put it into words.

'You should go away and spend some time with June.' That was what he had said. 'The change will do you good.' It would be their first real parting for years and years. The last time had been when he had been invited to address a literary Symposium in Stuttgart. It had been arranged then that Blossom would accompany him, but at the very last moment it had proved impossible. Pip had fallen and broken the bridge of his nose, and though there was no fear of permanent damage or complication at the time, the small boy was nevertheless very shaken. As was Blossom. She couldn't find it in her heart to leave him. It was a bitter disappointment, but it couldn't be helped.

Randolph had taken the opportunity of having a brief and unsatisfactory four-day affair with a woman, whose name he read regularly of late as a contributor to the TLS. Each time it never failed to bring a small jolt of guilt. He had returned more in love with Blossom than ever, and fiercely protective concerning this love. Above all he was determined that she should be spared the painful knowledge of his betrayals. For there had been others at various times, though each had occurred when he was away from home, when he had been at his most vulnerable simply through missing Blossom. And all that each experience had served to do was make him more than ever aware of her worth. But, though he didn't reasonably doubt her forgiveness for a moment, a further wisdom forewarned

73

that the intimacy between them would ultimately suffer if she found out. His marriage was too precious and important to allow that to happen. This made him doubly careful over his indiscretions. In short – he didn't play the irresponsible bloody fool. He was as devious as the next randy bastard.

Or would be – if Blossom allowed there to be anything salvaged from her assiduous syphoning system. Without admitting it to himself he would quite relish the rest when she went up to London to join June tomorrow. It would give him a real chance to devote himself to uninterrupted thought. It could not be denied that Blossom was an ever-present and disturbing distraction. And delightful though that was, he quite looked forward to leading the temporary life of a monk. He must look up under A-abuse, bodily; in his Ecclesiastical section as to which Order took a lenient line on wanking.

Blossom wriggled provocatively. To Randolph's relief, she had abandoned his knee-cap (beneath the drenched trouser-leg) as a means of sexual stimulation. But – now he feared for his lit cigar – she seemed occupied in fresh and possibly more alarming endeavours. He couldn't be sure but she seemed to be stuffing herself, as he had seen her stuff chickens or turkeys for Christmas – what the devil . . .!!

She gave him no time for further conjecture. Before he'd had a chance to restore order to his whirling thoughts, she had completely reversed the direction of her whole body. One minute facing south she was suddenly facing north! How she had managed to do this without once releasing his saliva-saturated crotch and its burgeoning contents from her teeth was a positive miracle. He found time to offer up a small prayer that the whole caboodle hadn't been bitten clean away! And now that fear, primitive and fierce, was proving a galvanising force . . . the ejaculation was here . . . the searing, soaring, spinning had begun . . .

He opened his mouth wide in an animal groan of rapturous pain.

Blossom sank her haunches to his rigid tongue. He came, gagging horribly on a sickly combination of hazelnut-fudge and chocolate crystallized ginger.

Blossom was leaving in the morning on the five o'clock train. 'Christ Almighty, five o'clock in the fucking morning! What

74

sort of train is that!' Randolph drove everywhere in his powerful motor on his rare trips away. It was ages since he'd been on a train. But between them, Blossom and June had decided that she should come by train instead of prevailing on Randolph to drive her up. Or indeed driving that long way herself (on moving into Puddlemouth from their previous isolated habitation on the moors, Blossom had got rid of her beach-buggy. Though not without a twinge of regret for the loss of independence that this meant. She resented having to *ask* for anything of his – however sweetly he responded). As yet the girls had not decided how they were going to spend their time together, or what sort of holiday they would like to have. But if it called for a car, hiring one would be no problem. Both were experienced drivers, with their licences all in order. The only reason that June didn't run a car of her own was that London had become so impossible for parking, and anyway it was just as easy to take taxis.

'What sort of train? The sort that gets me into London as early in the morning as possible. Ten o'clock, that's when it gets to Paddington.'

Blossom had consulted her timetable. 'Actually, no. Ten forty-two, it says here I must give June a ring, I think I've given her the wrong time. She's meeting me, I'll need a hand with all my baggage.'

Randolph had begun to regard the trip with a certain apprehension. He didn't look forward to heaving six very heavy cases at the god-forsaken hour of five in the morning. Although it was perfectly true that he rose earlier than most, he did so because he considered those to be the most valuable contemplative stages of the day. The dawn. That precious and too fleeting metamorphosis of darkness to light, of blindness to sight, of a world cloaked and concealed beneath a blanket of blackness trembling in paler and paler transition to the radiance of the full spectrum of light. It filled him with awe, this birth of the day. It inspired him and lent a sense of pure magic to the following hours.

And now he was to be called upon to hop into the car, check the choke, charge the engine, drive his departing wife to the station, humping her grotesquely heavy suitcases onto the train (endangering his dodgy back in

75

the process) and stand like a dolt waving on the platform till her sweet suntanned face was but a dot in the distance. All the time the dawn would be breaking. Without him.

'I don't expect you to drive me to the station, my darling.'

Good God – could she read every thought in his head!

'I've already arranged with Wally Cronk to pick me up at about four-thirty. He's the best one for the cases. . . .'

'What old Nelson, with his one arm?' Randolph was trying hard not to reveal his intense relief.

'Two. He's got two now. He's had a marvellous contraption fitted. Like a miniature crane – with a lever, for lifting things. And a steel hand at the end of it, it's the very latest thing. Much better than a human hand in his line of business – he was telling me he's made a fortune this summer, with part-time porterage and the car-hire. So you can commune with the dawn undisturbed, and I'd prefer not to have you seeing me off actually. It would make it all too emotional.'

Randolph was moved. God, he loved her!

Blossom lay awake unable to sleep, her mounting excitement meant that every half hour she was having to get up to check her luggage to see that she had packed various things which kept occurring to her over-active brain. At times she felt as though she would explode with the tension. Keep calm, cool it, kid – she kept saying to herself. But it was no use, rational thinking was out of the question. In the end she just lay there awaiting the alarm, cuddling her unconscious husband.

From time to time she kissed him lightly, all over his face, lingering at the relaxed and slightly open lips, but he didn't stir. Nothing would have woken him, not even the alarm. When it went off, at four o'clock, his regular breathing remained unchanged. His sleeping hours ran strictly to habit. Knowing this they had made their passionate and fond farewells before going to bed. Blossom would depart like a thief in the night. Randolph would awake at his usual time to find her gone.

June waited at the barrier on Paddington Station feeling like death. She only wished that people would stop staring at her. Although she was wearing a large pair of dark glasses and a deep-brimmed black hat, beneath which she would have thought it was possible to hide, passers-by apparently still recognised her. Of course they were glancing in the first place, she knew perfectly well, because she looked so bloody stylish. These days she was dressing completely in black and white, from top to toe, not a smattering of colour anywhere. Except on her lips and nails (finger and toe) which were painted a deep shade of coffee, bordering on crimson. They had worked it out together, she and Cyril, the wonderful old pouf who was the designer on her television series.

Her new look, which though admired greatly by Cherie Pye, Mercedes and the girls in Make Up, had been greeted with some reserve by the male director of the series, and by almost all the camera crew. They thought it too strange, even slightly alienating for the public. In their opinion a presenter should be someone with whom the viewers should be able to identify, not someone who looked like Dracula's mother!

But Publicity had disagreed. The three typists and two secretaries had already adopted the look, and adapted it to themselves. June had cropped her hair very short, leaving a very long fringe which sometimes she swept severely to the side like a boy's. And at other times she combed it straight down her forehead almost into her eyes. Or else frivolously curled it into a bubble of curls, like a '50's musical comedy star. Each style suited her rather long, pointed face, pinpointing the drama of the smouldering eyes. And the colour emphasised the neat outline of the head and the chic-ness of the style. And of course she was also very tanned.

June's method of tanning was one she had devised several years before when she had returned from a continental holiday, disappointingly pale. The Italian sun had put in only two appearances throughout her ten-day stay. Rather than risk being the laughing stock of the office, or the object of pity for all her friends – not to mention the permanently sun-tanned Blossom – she thought of a clever deception. Returning half a day sooner than she was expected, she booked a two-hour appointment at the Beauty Salon in South Kensington. There she received their Instant Tan Treatment, consisting of a thorough over-all creaming of tanning lotion applied by a qualified masseuse. She emerged, slightly sweaty (a side effect of the lotion) but with a deep and thoroughly convincing Mediterranean suntan. Then after a leisurely lunch in an out of the way restaurant, where she had a bothersome time with both Cypriot waiters who assumed she was one of their own race, she had returned to the place where she was staying (this was during one of her 'off' times with Tiny), and rang everyone to say, 'Hello – I'm home!'

She had employed the same ruse each summer since then, and this year had even hit on the idea of having herself tanned in the winter – just after Christmas, when her spirits were in need of a quick lift. It was most gratifying to be congratulated in January on her suntan. Everybody just assumed that she had been skiing at some smart winter resort. Even the more casual of her lovers thought this – those that she went several weeks without seeing. She'd been sunning, because she had simply been creamed in the face, neck and hands – the only parts that are bared in the snow. Similarly in the summer she had donned her bikini, so that those bits of her body had remained white.

This year she had decided to adopt a topless tan. She had forgotten to tell Blossom how aroused she had been as the very attractive cockney masseuse had smoothed the slippery cream over her breasts. 'Do you fancy your nipples?' The girl had asked her ingenuously. June would have loved to have asked her, 'Do you?' but she feared that it might be misconstrued, and she didn't want to become known as having lesbian tendencies, not when she visited the Salon so regularly. She had overheard snatches of derogatory gossip about other clients who on the surface appeared the models of propriety and absolute sexual normality. The cutting comments had seemed to her to be unnecessarily censorious and cruel. But this was South Kensington after all. You would have to travel a few miles further in each direction to find the more raffish element in which she found herself more at ease. 'How do you mean – my nipples?' The girl was tweaking them already, holding the entire breast between both hands and employing a firm whirling motion. It was as much as June could do to simply shut her eyes and lie on the sweetly clean-towelled surface of the couch – smiling. Smiling a sensual smile of absorption. She was beginning to feel unforgiveably horny. 'Well, I only ask,' the girl spoke without any trace of self-consciousness. If anything she sounded just a trace too officious for June's liking. 'I only ask because some of our clients prefer not to be touched up here.' She touched June's stiffened nipples with a delicate flip. 'But I can tell that it doesn't worry you at all. Funny thing, that. But then you have all sorts come in here – I couldn't begin to tell you half of it, honestly! Are you married? No, of course you're not. Well, some of the married ladies are amongst the worst, believe you me.' June nodded, trying to control the drowsy and wholly delightful feeling that she was experiencing as a direct result of the girl's finger-tips on her nipples (did nipples go that much browner anyway in the sun? She must remember to check with Blossom, who this year had taken to this topless lark too.) 'You'd think, wouldn't you that they'd be satisfied with their husbands?' The girl paused, pondering on her own considered opinion. Her mind no longer wholly on what she was doing, she had bunched her finger-tips over each of June's nipples and was idly caressing them, using the tentative touch of a safe-breaker. It was becoming unbearable. June could feel her expression slipping into one of hollow-eyed lewdness, with a permanent lopsided grin pasted in place. Despite herself she found that she was crossing her legs. But not for long. The girl snapped back into action. 'Miss Day! Whatever do you think you're doing – the lotion hasn't had time to take on those legs yet! Now I shall have to give them another coat otherwise they'll smear. What on earth could you have been thinking of to do such a thing?' June chose to apologise, rather than confess.

Blossom's train was going to be twenty minutes late due to an unforeseeable delay on the line. June groaned as it was announced, as did others in the small group waiting beside her. One of them, a middle-aged woman with an unflattering henna rinse on her grey hair, turned to June and raised her hands despairingly. But June looked away, refusing to be drawn into any sort of exchange with the woman who had been covertly eyeing her from a distance for the last five minutes or so.

The trouble was that last night the second of the series had been transmitted, which was why June was being recognised this morning. Her face was still fresh on people's minds. Last week, with the first, it had been exactly the same the following day. But even by the weekend the interest had fallen away.

Contrary to how she thought she'd feel she didn't altogether enjoy the continual goggling. There were times, like this morning when feeling as she did, she would have infinitely preferred to be able to move around the world anonymously. She didn't relish the thought of five further weeks of this and worse to come when the series became nationally networked. Then her soul wouldn't be called her own. Already there were small indications that this was about to happen. Yesterday the *Guardian* had rung for an exclusive interview with her. Publicity had been forced to reply that for the moment June Day was giving no interviews at all. It was a pre-arranged policy, a group decision by all participants in the Female Series that they should work as a collective. No one was to receive more acclaim for their part in the proceedings than anyone else – the presenter included. The success of the series was almost wholly due to this magnificent group spirit. And this was to be so until the present screening had been concluded.

But other signs were starting to appear. June's name had appeared twice in the same week in the gossip column of the *Evening Standard*'s Londoners' Diary. Each time her name was linked with different male escorts, Professor Hamilton being one of them. He had been extremely displeased over the others.

Also the beauty editor of *Vogue* had been trying to persuade Publicity that the inclusion of June's photograph in an article on contemporary faces would not violate the no-interview embargo. Similarly with the fashion editor of one of the Sunday colour supplements who wished to do a coverage of June's black and white wardrobe. It all looked like the start of a positive avalanche of personal publicity. June was at a loss to explain her lack of enthusiasm. She could only think that she must be in need, in desperate need of a holiday. That was why she had so welcomed the suggestion from Blossom. She wondered about that. It was the first time that Blossom and Randolph would have willingly been apart – not that their marriage was in any faintest way less than secure ... She wouldn't have minded having a marriage that happy – who would indeed? She thought of her colleagues in Television Towers, not one decent marriage between them. It must be the hours, or the pressure, the constant living on the edge of the nerves. That's what did it. The ceaseless flow of adrenalin. Only last week nice Nobs Plater had complained of chest pains. Rather appalling ones, so he claimed. 'Perhaps you just experienced your first coronary, Plater old chap!' a fellow newscaster had cried with an over-jovial thump between the shoulder blades. The hearty blow had sent the shaky Nobs reeling in the direction of the nearest seat. Onlookers had been secretly appalled by the callousness of the sentiment.

Twenty minutes delay – well, it gave June the chance to buy all the papers and glance through them over a cup of ghastly coffee in the station buffet. She had risen at the last possible moment this morning. She must be sickening for something to feel this weak, this queazy. Perhaps it was the summer 'flu bug that had been flying round the studio floor. It wouldn't make much of a welcome for Blossom, but she honestly felt that she should go back to bed. She was feeling worse by the minute.

She had meant to ring Cherie this morning. They had arranged between them that June would call before eleven. But she hadn't done so. She hadn't felt up to Cherie's particular brand of continental vivacity, not in her present state of health. It wasn't even as if she had been out on the toot last night either. It had been lights out by eleven, she had felt unutterably weary. It had obviously been this bug thing coming on.

Ten more minutes left. June glanced at her watch. There had been an encouraging review of the programme in *The Times*, with a special congratulation for herself. And a typical throwaway line in the *Sun* describing her as 'a tasty TV dish – the sort that any man would like to have on his knees!' There was nothing in the rest of the newspapers so June barely bothered with them. There you are, she caught herself up with a small jolt, you dismiss them as being of no particular interest. Simply because

81

you, or your programme are not in them. Better begin to control the old ego!

But her eyes ached unbearably, and the effort of reading had thoroughly exhausted her. Nine more minutes. She thought of Cherie and how irritated she would be if June didn't ring. There would most certainly be a call put through to Flowers which would be awaiting her return. She may as well get it over with now.

The secretary answered as soon as the switchboard had put her through. 'Hello June – I'm sorry but Cherie hasn't arrived yet, I've been expecting her for the past hour.' Cherie ran a very democratic office, everyone was on christian-name terms. 'But as you probably know,' the secretary lowered her voice, 'she was seeing Samson last night. I should think that must have something to do with her non-appearance, wouldn't you . . .' The tone of her conversation suddenly altered, 'Good morning, Cherie! I have June on the line. She's ringing from Paddington, you remember that she is meeting her twin there this morning. I trust,' June could almost hear the twinkle in the voice, 'I trust that you had a good evening with . . .'

'With that 'orrible 'usband of mine! 'Ow I 'ate 'im! *Mon Dieu*! This time I shall most definitely 'ave to 'ave a divorce – there is no other way. You would please to get my lawyer on the phone for an appointment – this farce has gone quite far enough!'

June held the receiver away from her head, the seconds were slipping away but Cherie's shrill excitable delivery was slicing across her quivering nerve-ends. Her scalp started throbbing with sharp needles of pain, but just in one spot above her left temple. She would have to take a couple of Panadol, much as she loathed tablets, or pills of any kind.

Six more minutes before the train was due to arrive. The pips in the pay-phone would start at any second and June had forgotten to check that she had enough change to continue talking. Cherie must have had a sixth sense. 'Ma petite – you are in a 'orrible coin-box. You give me the number quick and I shall be ringing you back by return. Otherwise those peep-peep-peeps 'ave to cut us off.'

June gave the number, she felt too weak to refuse. Even

bursting with health and absolutely in the pink it would have been difficult to refuse Cherie. And from where she stood she had a clear view of the platform. When Cherie's call came through there were four minutes left.

Four minutes more. Blossom checked her watch. Was there time to pay yet another (surely her fifth) visit to the lavatory? It amazed her that there would be anything left, of any substance, to evacuate from her exhausted bowels. It had become positively embarrassing towards the end of the journey, her constant trek past the same fellow passengers. So much so that she had been forced to alternate the direction of her visits, swaying first to the fore of the train, and then to the rear. Even once, when she imagined there to be raised eyebrows and meaningful glances between a married pair sitting closest to the TOILET – VACANT/ENGAGED sign, she had pretended to be on her way to the buffet car. She had returned after a particularly belly-curdling bout with an undrinkable waxy carton of British Rail tea in her hand. She had a horror of being thought incontinent. There wasn't time. Blossom clenched her teeth and forced herself to gaze on the fleeting suburban landscape whizzing past the window. She had never shared everyone else's scathing view of suburbia. To her there was something solid and deeply comforting in the sight of row upon row of identical homes, backed as they were with their precious little gardens. It fascinated her, the differences ·between these small plots. It proved how creative an animal man was to shape squares and oblongs of immaculate grass until they were as smooth and as evenly green as the surface of a billiard table; to trim hedges, train creepers, to tidy up trees; to impose his intelligence upon the disorderliness of nature; to cultivate vegetables and take care of raw and unripened fruits until they reached rich succulence; and the blooms, the fabulous flowers. Now, at the height of summer Blossom was seeing the flowers at their best. The marigold, the lily, the lilac, the pink; the antirrhinum, the gladiolus, and the spectacular and wholly ravishing rose – all those pistils and stamens, and corolla and calyx! Blossom marvelled at the hours of industry and dedication.

Of course she didn't have a garden, they had never had one, she and Randolph. They preferred the beach and ocean as a back yard. And in the end those took infinitely less of one's time – a garden after all was very time-consuming.

Two minutes to go! Blossom doubled up over a violent spasm of pain in her gut. Good God – she was behaving like an over-excited child. If Pip or Willow had displayed these symptoms she would have been seriously concerned that she had bred a neurotic. But they hadn't a twin. They couldn't possibly know what immeasurable pleasure – no, something much, much stronger and deeper than that, was consuming her now. Now when the minute was here, the actual moment, the split second . . .

Blossom put her head out of the window as the train shuddered to a grinding halt. She opened the door and stepped onto the platform. A flying form rushed towards her. She had time only to glimpse the face, *her* face, her own. *Her* body, *her* hands. It was as if she were embracing *her* self.

'So tell me what's with you and Professor Hamilton Hamilton – I haven't had all the latest on that yet.' Blossom perched on the curve of June's circular bed, preferring it to the canvas director's chair which was the only other seat in the room, apart from the bean-bag, a tough crimson sack intended to mould to the body when sat in. Blossom had two of them at home, now relegated to the children's rooms, as being entirely unsuitable for adult frames. Randolph had thrown his spine out completely one Wednesday night, watching Panorama with a Pimms in one hand and Roget's *Thesaurus* in the other as light reading (during the yawning parts of Panorama). To Blossom's alarm he had been unable to move a muscle at the end except his face and neck which were contorting horribly. It was as if he had become *at one* with the bean bag. Had he been able to stand, the bean-bag looked as though it would rise with him like some obscene livid growth. Doomed to live out his days as a card-carrying hunchback! The tragic yet trite image flashing before her eyes had made Blossom chuckle. Unfortunately Randolph, in his agony, had chosen that precise moment to glance up. It was months before he could find it in himself to forgive what he viewed as her crass derision at the sight of a loved one's distress.

June was in the bed propped up with pillows, a glass of hot honey and whisky held in her mittened hands, her throat muffled in the fluffy comfort of an Angora scarf. She was wearing a voluminous flannelette long sleeved night-gown, once the property of Emily Shawl's deceased maiden aunt. Blossom was playing Mother. She wasn't drinking, she didn't want to get drunk this early in the day. As soon as she had got June nicely settled and tucked up she had planned to sail out on a little shopping spree. She was very taken with June's black and white wardrobe and had thought of doubling up on several of the items for herself.

But first she couldn't resist the opportunity for a gossip. In no time at all June would be asleep – the best thing for this sort of bug. With luck she might be up and about tomorrow, but the rest of today was out of the question. Blossom had swallowed her disappointment. All the way up in the train she had been fantasising over where they would be lunching, which film they'd see, with whom they'd have dinner, which night-club they might end up dancing in . . . She'd been racking her brains, trying to recall where it was that Bianca Jagger was always dancing cheek-to-cheek with different people. And she had touched her own cheek to test its possible pressability (against that of an, as yet un-met, male cheek).

Now she had come to terms with it. In any case her burgeoning maternal instinct had dictated the rest. Her sister, poor love, was decidedly under the weather. Anyway there was plenty of time for all the high-jinks, after all she would be away from home for a fortnight!

June moved her eyes although it pained her to do so, the sockets felt as though they had been filled with wet cement and left to harden. She waved a weak mitten towards the minute balcony beyond the french window, through which the full blast of summer sun shone. The balcony overhung a typical London scene – the conventional communal garden. This was already languidly alive with parked prams and young mothers strolling and smiling indulgently at small toddlers in sandpits. Thank Christ,

that's all over – Blossom found herself thinking – all over
for me. Finished. In the past. She knew that she would
never have another child.

'What is it, angel? Do you want the blinds down? I'll do
it, the light's too strong for your eyes. You'd best get off to
sleep. That's it – snuggle down. We've got masses of time
for a good gossip. Oh, are you sure you don't mind if I
wear your white dress, and borrow that little black peaked
hat? I shall probably buy the patent sandals first, before
going for the clothes, and I'll get a better idea of how they
look together. I've got the list of places. Now you take care
of yourself. If you like I'll come back around lunchtime, to
see how you are . . .'

June shook her head vigorously, an action she immediately regretted. She ached in every single strand of her
short hair. Unbidden tears sprang to her eyes. Blossom
was so sweet and solicitous, it suddenly made her see what
she had been missing – someone to fuss over her at times
like these. Someone who *cared* even when she looked (as
she knew she did now) positively hideous, a disgrace to
the human race. She flapped a feeble mitten gesturing
Blossom to her, catching her sister's hand and pressing it
with her honey-sticky lips. Blossom kept a judicial
distance (it wouldn't do at all to catch this bloody bug –
she had no wish to spend her precious holiday in bed).

'Now my chicken, don't upset yourself, just keep nice
and warm. The thing is to sweat it out. I know with the
kids.'

When Blossom left, June buried her face into the pillow,
sobbing. It was as if someone had turned off the light, or
brutally sliced her in two.

It started happening right away, as soon as Blossom got
into the lift. An American girl with a tangle of bleached
curls and a bare sunburnt midriff, whose neck was
festooned with highly professional looking camera equip-
ment, hailed her. 'Hi there, Junie – we caught your show
last night! You were really something! I tell you when you
caught that guy bawling out that broad – whew, I thought
"sister have you got him nailed"! Yup, just by the fuckin'
balls!' She screwed up her short bobbed nose (a nice job,
whoever had done it) and twisted her clenched fists as

though she was wringing water out of a wet towel. Blossom winced inwardly and felt instant sympathy for the owner of the threatened genitals.

The American girl didn't stop talking until the lift hit the ground floor, so that although Blossom had opened her mouth to explain that it was a case of mistaken identity and that she was not Junie at all, but her identical twin, she was simply not given the chance. 'Well, 'bye Junie – see ya . . .' The girl flung through the small foyer, tossing a passing greeting to the prettily plump little girl at the desk. 'Hi Dimples – now you see to it you have yourself a nice day . . .'

Dimples smiled after the departing bejeaned bottom, before turning back to Blossom. 'Goodness! You've made a quick recovery! Mercedes was telling me you looked like absolute death when you came back from the station with your sister. Where is she now – sleeping off her long journey? I can't wait to see her! Mercedes said that the likeness was – what did she say – was positively, yes that was it, "spinechilling"!' Dimples giggled confidingly and leaned towards Blossom. 'We've had a bet, to tell you the truth. I have bet her a pound that I could tell the difference between the two of you. Mercedes swore to me that she couldn't, not if you were wearing the same clothes.'

Blossom was reluctant to be the cause of Dimples losing a pound, and had already half decided to continue with the deception. After all June would be dead to the world for hours. There was little likelihood of her emerging and spilling the beans. This was the sort of situation which was always happening when they were together, one which Blossom was well used to carrying off with aplomb. She prepared to make her goodbyes, moving towards the potted shoulder-high plant which stood at the front door, when suddenly the small switchboard started buzzing.

Dimples spun round. Blossom waved her hand, she was trying to decide whether to grab the first taxi she saw and go straight to South Molton Street, the first address on June's list of shops, or linger a little along Portobello Road. Though it wasn't a Saturday and therefore there were no stalls for her to browse among, there were plenty of exciting shops and arcades open selling her sort of stuff. It was like being set squarely in Paradise.

The decision was postponed. 'It's for you, June.' Dimples was beckoning, covering the receiver with her short fleshy fingers. How like pigs' trotters they are, Blossom caught herself thinking, I should love to sink my front teeth into those . . .

Dimples nudged her. 'It's Professor Hamilton Hamilton.' She winked. 'He says he's in a callbox so you had better take it here rather than through there where you'd get a little more privacy. I promise I'll block up my ears.' She handed Blossom the telephone and ostentatiously plugged a thumb in each of her ears. Then turned her back. Blossom took the receiver. 'Hello.' She said confidently. 'Professor Hamilton Hamilton?' She must remember to check with June whether she had a pet name for him.

Out in the streets of London Blossom was finding the response of passers-by to be nothing short of amazing. *Everyone* turned around to look at her! It made her feel absolutely *marvellous*! Not of course that she had ever been short of the attention of strangers in her life. As twins she and June had grown used to being stared at, and although singly neither could command that same attention (since nothing could match the curiosity aroused by the sight of duplicate humans), she could always be sure of admiring glances. Certainly from men.

But this was different. Of course the eyes had followed them across Paddington station as the porter had guided them to the taxi-rank. June had looked so chic in her dramatic black and white, with that chocolate biscuit brown on her mouth (which Blossom had borrowed and was now wearing on her own). And she herself had presented a far from conventional picture in her striking poppy-scattered, scarlet satin kimono, with a blazing bunch of artificial flowers, mostly fuschias, secured to the cherry-red scarf around her neck. All, except the scarf, salvaged from the Puddlemouth Amateur Operatic Society's Sale of Goods the previous spring, after their hugely successful production of *Madame Butterfly*. Ouida Pickles of the wool shop had worn this very kimono, splitting it almost in two after the interval, whilst stumbling heavily on stage, three secret Scotches better off. It had taken

Blossom less than an hour and a half to stitch it carefully together again, with no sign of the join. She considered it to be one of her finest bargains (not to mention the sweet Sunday session during which she had played a sexy slant-eyed Madame Butterfly to Randolph's dashing Captain Pickering). Yes, between them they had caused quite a minor stir at the station. And as June had explained on the way to her lovely hotel (which was much, much odder and therefore nicer than Blossom had expected), she, June, had after all been on the box the previous evening. And people always loved recognising celebrities in the flesh.

That's what it was, without a doubt – everyone was mistaking her for June! Well it wasn't so surprising, especially in June's white dress and with June's black hat. It had been amusing to see how sure Dimples had been of her identity. The Professor had been equally convinced. 'I beg of you not to interrupt, just listen carefully. I have a plane to catch. I'm in Scotland. I shall meet you tonight at the Gay Hussar – sorry, my dear, but I shall have to leave you to book the table. I suggest nine o'clock, I shan't be able to make it any sooner. Oh, by the way – I have of course missed you desperately . . .' The sound of pips had smothered the rest of his words before the line had gone completely dead.

Blossom paused at the window to look at herself in the massive baroque mirror occupying the central position in an entire display of different mirrors. There must have been at least sixty separate images of herself. She smiled at them all.

'Looks pretty good to me, missus!' A cocky boy, who couldn't have been much older than Pip, paused then passed on whistling. 'Thank you,' Blossom called after his small swaggering body. A ladies' man already, despite his youth.

But she could see what he meant, turning back to her reflections. This dress was French, fashioned from a small amount of crisp cotton piqué into a shaped halter-neck sheath. The structural engineering enabled her to dispense with her brassiere whilst retaining a succulent, though discreet, amount of cleavage. Smooth brown hills rising from either side of a deep velvety ravine. Her lean strong swimmer's shoulders appeared elegant, even frail, in the cut-away line of the fitted bodice. Blossom raised one elbow, as if to adjust the jaunty peaked cap (the sort worn by umpires at Wimbledon or rather American baseball teams since the peak was decidedly longer). The cap required no adjustment but it had suddenly occurred to Blossom to check on the state of her underarms. There had been no convenient opportunity to shave on the train this morning.

She peered. Not a shadow of stubble in sight.

The sun was climbing in the cloudless sky, Blossom sauntered on in a highly pleasurable state of receptive relaxation. She was keenly aware of that sensation that only cities can give – that at any moment something exciting could happen. The air thrummed with it, with this special expectancy, this vitality, this exuberance and electricity. Perhaps Portobello Road was more alive than most streets and therefore not really representative, but in the mood she was in Blossom felt as high as a steeple. She could have illuminated Piccadilly, have flown over St Pauls, have dived off Putney Bridge and swum all the way to the Port of London with ease.

She suddenly realised that she hadn't had a poke!

Sitting in the taxi on the way to Bond Street (a good choice of shoe shops all around there), Blossom reflected on this fact. She was still reflecting, though her attention had now been diverted by the Marble Arch crowds, when the door of her taxi was unexpectedly wrenched open. The cab had stopped at the lights when Zachary Ram had happened to glance through the window and saw who he took to be June Day. (Rather a coincidence that. Only an hour ago he had been enjoying himself drafting a quite beastly and withering review of June Day's current television series for his column in *Views*. He had not yet forgiven her for granting her favours to that senile old goat Hamilton Hamilton, that lunchtime at Stalky's. He knew perfectly well that he should have moved in for the kill just that little bit sooner. But how was he to know that the famed fornicator was breathing down his neck? The knowledge that it was his own fault made the lost opportunity all the more bitter. The harsh review had been simply a self satisfying case of sour grapes, he would have been the first to admit that. He couldn't deny that he still fancied her to madness and would have given anything to have a crack at her cherry. The bitch!)

'Well, well – if it isn't the girl of the moment!'

To both the driver's and Blossom's alarm this male person had now thrown himself headlong into the taxi, slamming the door behind him and sprawled all over the back seat beside Blossom.

The driver, forced to move forward by the traffic on his tail, called back anxiously, 'Are you all right, Miss Day?' He too had recognised his lovely passenger half-way up Bayswater Road. It would be just his luck to have an accident with some fucking lunatic who got turned on by the sight of someone who'd been on the telly. It wasn't his sort of thing, not at all –hadn't he, four years ago, driven Ursula Andress to London Airport, crying all the way, her mascara streaming straight down into her mouth? One person's grief was the same as the next. When you're dead it doesn't matter who you've been. All he wanted was peace. All he needed now was a piss and a pint in a pub. It was near enough to one o'clock, his knocking-off time. The geyser in the back was answering, in the upper class accent overlaid with bastard cockney that these young public school blokes considered to be the way to speak nowadays.

'Don't worry mate – everything's under control back here.' The patronising little sod turned to the girl (who was staring at him as though she had never set eyes on him in her life before). 'Cheer up, June duckie – you surely don't object to giving an old pal a lift do you? I have been waiting for a sodding cab here for nearly twenty minutes . . .' Zachary Ram's voice fell away. He was staring at her now. Christ – she was sexy! At the sight of her swelling breasts, and the slim suntanned legs (crossed in such a way at the knee that a ripe slice of thigh reverberated against his retina) his trouser-worm twerked. It reared up, stallion-style, separating itself from the sticky nest of his nuts. The inside of this taxi was like an inferno! Beads of perspiration began to form along his upper lip. Lord, how he longed to get his teeth around those luscious tits!

And the wide-eyed way she was looking at him . . . that mouth, slightly open as if in maidenly amazement . . . that tongue. He could see the tongue trembling pinkly between the perfect white teeth. Hadn't he less than two hours ago made some sneering comment about these very teeth in his rough draft? And wasn't he on the way to the *Views'* office at this precise moment in order to polish his final attacking draft and pack it off to press? God-all-fucking-mighty!!! What was wrong with him – had he gone clean around the bend? Or what?

Now the goddess was smiling at him – smiling at *him*! With an expression in those great eyes that he had never had directed towards him from a woman or a girl for all the years he had been fucking (which actually was not that many). It was blinding, that green gaze of hers. The lust pounded along his loins, had he been just several years younger he'd be close to shooting off by now. He could almost swear that he could *smell* her, his nostrils full of her creamy cunt. That pungent mixture of fish (the fruit of the sea) and the ripest of all the rich cheeses . . .

'Whew!' He stretched his short thick legs, suddenly conscious of the fact that if they stood side by side, she would be at least a foot taller. But so what – be at just the right height to clamp his mouth on her mammaries . . . whew, but dare he say it . . . dare he suggest that she and he might . . .

The taxi slowed down and then swung around the sharp swerve of New Bond Street. Shit! She was preparing to get out, he was going to lose her again. He couldn't let her go this time without even getting her telephone number . . .

'Oh. Haven't you got it already?' she had replied to his request. But her tender look of surprise had turned his stomach to liquid. She'd been half out of the cab by this time and had turned to him, one foot already on the kerb. He could see almost up to her pussy from this position and had to gulp hard to restrain himself from stretching his fingers to touch the inside edge of her panties. His spirits and hopes were plummeting each second. The taxi was revving, impatient to be off. She gave him her number, reeling it off without thinking, as if she gave it out three hundred times a day – which she most likely did. He could feel his face setting in lines of utmost despondency.

And then she kissed him.

92

It wasn't quite on the lips, but it was near enough. Realising at that last heart-stopping moment that a kiss was on the way, he had engineered to have his mouth (all of it) at the appropriate place.

She had actually been aiming, he knew, at his cheek.

But arriving at the junction of Fleet Street and Chancery Lane, paying off the taxi, mounting the office stairs towards his working lunch hour; sitting down at his typewriter to reword an entirely new review of June Day's television series – he could still taste her kiss on his tongue.

June was no better and, though she was no worse, Blossom could tell that this was a twenty-four-hour thing. The only way to combat the virulence of the bug was to sweat it out in bed. She ran herself a bathful of hot water, using June's bathroom instead of her own next door in order to make the start of the evening more companionable. June was drowsy and drugged from the combination of cold cures that Blossom saw fit to administer. She was sipping her second hot whisky-and-honey, but not enjoying it as much as she would have done had she been well. Her throat was still sore despite repeated garglings with guaranteed remedies that Blossom had bought in Boots. The hot whisky-and-honey now tasted unpleasantly of Listerine, and far from soothing her throat seemed to be setting it painfully on fire. The only advantage as far as June could tell was that it did heighten her whirling sense of unreality. Today her infrequent waking hours were merely a dreamy extension of the vivid fantasy world she inhabited whilst asleep. She was looking forward to re-entering that world as quickly as possible – as soon as she could groggily urge the ebullient Blossom to hit the road.

It had already been decided between them that Blossom should avail herself of June's dinner invitation from Professor Hamilton Hamilton. The question was, how should she spend her time until then? There were various alternatives – to Blossom's amazement.

'You mean this is how it is every single evening of the week – all these invites to choose from!' she had gasped excitedly.

June had closed her heavy lids, lined as they seemed with sandpaper. The last thing she could bear to think about was the frenzied supply of socialising at her disposal – all that smiling! All that shoulder-hugging, that hand-shaking, that cheek-kissing! That arse-licking! All that absolutely artificial intimacy . . .

She raked through the scattered cards on her bedspread. These were the formal invitations to functions which had been prearranged weeks, even months, before. They had been addressed to her personally at Television Tower and so had been dealt with by the secretary she had been given for the duration of the series. If she went on to make another set of programmes for the same company, then she would be designated a permanent secretary of her own, but the company were trying very hard to sign June up with a five-year contract, a move which Cherie was adamant that they should resist. It certainly would not be worth tying herself up for anything like that long for the sake of having a secretary to handle among other things, her increasingly overwhelming social diary. Even though things seemed to be getting out of hand!

'Blimey!' Blossom was carried away in a schoolgirl delirium. Of course they received invitation cards at home. Scrawled scraps of cardboard, the back of the corn-flake packet, with 'bring a bottle' on the bottom, shoved through the letter-box by Emily Shawl from time to time. Rather awful abstract linocuts, depicting God knows what, beneath a desperate plea to visit somebody's studio . . . 'wine and cheese'. Larger events of this nature (and after all many of their friends were highly respected artists who entertained in most civilised Bohemian style) were simply arranged over the phone. More often than not on the spur of the moment, but certainly with no more than a week's notice. Even so, these get-togethers, these lengthy and boisterous Bacchanalian occasions were rarer than Blossom would have liked. She actually *adored* going out. Dolling herself up. Being admired and behaving in a deliberately (though innocently) flirtatious manner. It was her idea of real enjoyment. She had always regretted the fact that marrying so young and having had the children straight away meant she had missed out on the chance of being a real good-time girl. There was something vacuous in her nature that made her ideal for the role.

But a thought occurred to her now. 'Who am I going as – you or me?' She studied those invitation cards in her hand. A Private View of the Surrealist Artist, Liberty Bean. Dame Tiger Oats, that wonderful old girl that June had interviewed about six months ago, had spoken of Liberty Bean and her work. Blossom would have liked to have seen it tonight. But she was also keen to see the one-act sexual farce at Shepherds Bush (all girls and a bowlful of goldfish), which started at seven-thirty and was all over in an hour. That would give her time to get over to Soho in time to meet the Professor. Similarly she felt drawn to attend the pre-dinner drinks ('trust you will dine too, June dear!') at the Barbican apartment of Hilda Vengeance. The barrister, the gay one, that June had met first at the Female Conference. Apart from Emily Shawl and Pots, Blossom had never really been in a totally lesbian environment. She felt that it might be rather her milieu and she liked the sound of this witty woman lawyer, Hilda Vengeance. At the same time she was reluctant not to put in an appearance at the party being thrown to coincide with the re-release of the Belle Nuddle Albums from the '50s, or the Champagne Reception for Bethlehem Bungalows at the Savoy ('A SNAZZY SARONG SWIMSUIT FOR EACH OF THE LADIES!!') She rather fancied a free Sarong swimsuit as a change from the eternal bikini. The motivation was rather stronger than vanity, she just liked the idea of getting something for nothing.

But these were only a sample of the avenues open to Blossom between now and nine o'clock. With the Professor she knew that she would be perfectly all right. She had met him before and she was able to handle any situation whether she pretended to be her sister, or simply presented herself as who she was. Either way he would be delighted. This was not so with these other functions. If June had been well enough to go to any single one of them, taking Blossom as her twin, the success of the evening would have been assured. If she went on her own, as herself, then it was doubtful whether her first few hours

95

out of the town would be anything more than a miserably damp squib. After all who would want to meet her?

Down in Cornwall this situation didn't arise. There she was known and revered as being the wife of Randolph Tree. She was a respected and admired parent in the community, the mother of Willow and Pip. She was an indulged and highly popular bundle of fun; an amusingly dressed, faintly eccentric, shamelessly sexy, unfailingly attractive and warm animal – who, when on form, could coax the conviction from the chilliest critic that here was a sensational flamboyant beauty.

This evening she felt a little in her magic mood. It had started with that friend of June's, that poor pimply besotted boy in the taxi. The youth that June had denied as being a friend of hers at all.

'But he's an absolute toad!' she had exclaimed when Blossom had given a detailed description of her taxi intruder. 'Everyone *hates* him! He *crucifies* programmes in his ghastly column. And he writes it so well – so viciously, but cleverly, that everyone reads him. You've read him, I'm sure. Zachary Ram. He has taken over as TV critic of *Views*. Randy will know his stuff, he's very much one of the new young bright boys.'

'Zachary Ram – was *that* Zachary Ram. I have read him. So's Randy. He holds him in very high esteem.'

'That's the trouble, everyone does you see. We're all rather dreading what he'll write about the programme. He loathes me, I do know that . . .' June pulled a long painful face.

'I'm sure that he doesn't loathe you.' Blossom gave a girlish giggle. She was feeling not displeased with herself.

'Oh yes he does! I assure you we've barely exchanged more than a few words.'

'He won't loathe you after this morning. This morning you kissed him. He nearly wet himself, little love . . .'

'This morning *I* did what! Blossom – what have you been doing?'

Blossom giggled again with full-throated satisfaction. 'I have been going around kissing television critics leading them to believe that all along it is you. I shouldn't concern yourself for one moment over the *Views* review – I should think that he will write something absolutely smashing.'

Blossom went (as June) to the Belle Nuddle Album launch since it was at Notting Hill Gate and on her way to the girls and goldfish farce at Shepherds Bush. She had settled on these two as being the safest events, with less likelihood of having to commit herself in any form of intense conversation. This was a testing time after all, and she was being thrown in at the deep end of London social life. After ten minutes of the Belle Nuddle launch she could see that there was nothing to worry about at all. All she had to do was stand there with a drink in her hand, a smile on her face and an expression of concentrated listening aimed at whoever was talking to her. No one, absolutely no one, was interested in what *she* had to say. June had warned her, trying to be reassuring that this would be the case. 'They are all much too busy with their own giant egos to be bothered about you and yours. Why do you think I've done so well as an interviewer – only because I am such a bloody good listener. You could do my job, Blossom, just as well as me – no, honestly you could! You go there tonight and see what I mean. Only,' June raised a weak warning wrist, 'Kid, do be careful who you kiss on my behalf . . .'

There would have been plenty to kiss (on her own behalf, bugger June's!) if she had felt so inclined. But Randolph had rung as she had been about to leave, and his dear, sweet voice was still warm in her ears. Even so, she felt dangerously randy. In the distance she could see (she could swear it was him) Rod Stewart. And further along the same side of the crowded room was Paul McCartney with Linda, his wife. She could imagine telling Willow and Pip all about this. Randy wouldn't have been particularly impressed, pop was hardly his scene. Probably the kids wouldn't either, come to think of it. They had idols of their own. She took another drink from the tray being offered to her. The first of the day, well actually this was now the third since she had been here. She glanced at her watch and saw with no real feeling of regret that there was no time left for the girls and goldfish after all. She had been coasting so well here that there had been no such thing as time. Her first hurdle and she'd passed with flying colours!

She told the taxi to wait for her outside the Savoy, she

would be in there no more than five minutes – she promised. June had claimed that was the only sort of appearance she would need to put in at the Bethlehem Bungalows in order to claim her Sarong Swimsuit. 'Honestly Bloss, you won't like it when you get it. I can just imagine what it will be like – absolutely ghastly, all covered in palm trees with a skirt on the crossover and ruching down the side . . .'

But Blossom had been entranced. 'Sort of '40s, do you mean? Oh, Randy will love that – I shall be able to do my Betty Grable number, I've got some marvellous white wedgies already to go with it!' She was determined not to miss the Sarong Swimsuit.

It took less than five minutes. A dazzling blonde receptionist at the entrance to the drawing room of Suite 244 (hired by Bethlehem Bungalows for the evening) was handing out prettily packaged swimsuits to each female arrival. She herself was wearing one, a completely bumless design with simply a string passing between the division of the buttocks to join the three strategically placed postage stamps on the front of the body. The stamps bearing the head of Her Majesty appeared to be made of cleverly printed cotton, but with a form of adhesive backing. Each stayed perfectly in position as the blonde moved, and although the strings looped one to the other and linked round at the back, they were simply a brightly coloured device to lead the eye all over the torso.

'Colour preference, darling?' the blonde gushed at Blossom. Beyond her, in the main mass of the reception Blossom spotted at least three or four other blondes similarly attired. There were many, many men in the room. Beside their sober business suits the blondes' virtually nude bodies looked obscene. Though each girl looked as though she was having a hell of a good time, and presumably was being paid a decent whack on an hourly rate, there was something distinctly depressing about the whole set-up. Seedy. That was the word. Suddenly Blossom felt the urge to get away.

'What shade do you fancy? There's turquoise, those are the ½p stamps. There's blue, those are the 9p; green, they're the 2p.' The blonde's radiant smile rooted Blossom to the spot. She wouldn't be allowed to leave until she had made her choice.

'Great gimmick, isn't it! Sure you can't stop longer for a

nice little drinkie? Can't we tempt you to a glass of the bubbly – no? Shame.'

Blossom stumbled gratefully into the waiting taxi clutching a whole pile of literature on the construction, durability and desirability of Bethlehem Bungalows. A thick folder of pamphlets, expensively illustrated throughout with photographs of building sites in every single stage of development from the laying of foundations to the final stage – to the drinks being served on the completed patio. The girl in the photograph of this idyllic scene was not, Blossom noted, wearing a Sarong Swimsuit, but a perfectly straightforward Marks and Spencer bikini. Blossom recognised the one, there had been hundreds the very same on the beaches of Puddlemouth this summer. Blossom fingered her tiny ribboned envelope containing the tethered stamps. She had chosen turquoise in the end, a favourite colour of Randy's. Well – at least he would enjoy her new swimsuit.

There was just time, if she stayed no longer than twenty minutes, to put in an appearance at the Barbican apartment of Hilda Vengeance. Although June had warned her against pretending to be June. 'In the mood you're in, I can imagine the repercussions. If you go there, you go as yourself – please Bloss . . .'

Blossom had promised faithfully.

But now, driving up to the brooding nest of buildings – so out of character with the rest of the city, Blossom wasn't sure. The trouble was now that she no longer felt like herself. She had grown rather used to being June. To being treated as a successful career girl rather than a Cornish housewife. She didn't wish to admit to her own identity any longer. She no longer felt that it was something of which she could justifiably feel proud. It was the first time in her entire life that this thought had even occurred to her.

'Have I got time do you think,' Blossom consulted the taxi-driver, 'to visit this friend of mine in the Barbican, just for about twenty minutes – then go on to The Sliced Eye Gallery in Soho, for whatever time I have left – so that I could still be at The Gay Hussar restaurant, in Greek Street by nine o'clock?'

'Blimey! You up from the country or summit? Just like

the bleedin' Yanks! They always try and cram in the impossible too . . .'

But it wasn't impossible. Strolling, entranced, through the streets of Soho which lay between The Sliced Eye and The Gay Hussar, Blossom mused on how little the British actually stretched themselves. There she was with three minutes in hand, having done every single thing that she had set out to do (except the girls and the goldfish). And what's more she had so far absolutely sailed through the evening! Well, almost.

There had been one or two sticky moments. On her arrival at Hilda Vengeance's she had been uncertain which of the ladies present was the hostess. She had quite wrongly conjured up the image of a tall, handsome woman with a strong nose, a determined chin and a firm, well-defined set of sculptured lips. Dressed (Blossom couldn't imagine why she thought this) in a man's hacking jacket with a gent's shirt and tie, and a thick Harris tweed skirt above thick ribbed stockings and a pair of hefty brogues.

Not a single person in the ultra-modern setting of the room remotely fitted this description.

Hilda turned out to be a rather short, busty Jewess with a tiny waist, trim ankles and remarkable doe-eyes, reminiscent of Bambi, above a pertly retroussé nose. Her appearance was completely at odds with her personality, which was more American than British. More New York than the City of London. She delivered everything she said in the way that an actress would. One actress in particular sprang to Blossom's mind – Coral Browne (who several years ago had married one of Blossom's favourite screen actors – the velvet-voiced Vincent Price). But the dry irony was close to the wit of Dorothy Parker. To Blossom's great delight she swore like a seaman.

But Hilda's appearance had taken her by surprise – it was so unlike what she had been expecting. June had not given a description of Hilda at any time during their discussion of where Blossom might be calling in this evening. At that time they hadn't thought that there would really be an opportunity to fit Hilda in. Also Blossom had been put off the idea of her promise to go as herself. Why had she (and June) always had such

100

difficulty in sticking to promises – hadn't they at one time promised each other never ever to make another promise, at least to each other . . .

Hilda had been occupied at the other side of the room when Blossom had made her entrance. The first impression Blossom had was of a roomful of perfectly normal-looking females. Middle class women and girls, the usual mixture of jeans, kaftans, straightforward shirtwaisters. Nothing untoward, no big hulks, not a single butch bitch amongst them! Blossom felt ever so slightly let down, though wouldn't have wished to admit it – not to display her bigotted ignorance and preconceptions to the world. But it was perfectly true that deep inside her she had been rather imagining that she was going to walk right into the party and be instantly *raped*. Dumped down in the middle of the proceedings and pleasured by an enormous baby pink dildo. Brutally. With stormy eyed, massive thighed, Amazon girls pressing their hard bodies to hers.

That's how she had imagined it.

She was in the middle of a discussion with a woman gynaecologist and a PT Instructress in the Womens Auxiliary Corps when Hilda Vengeance had first addressed her. 'Well,' Hilda had said, an amused twist to her red lips. 'No special greeting for the hostess yet, I notice!'

Blossom froze. Then she looked around. 'I don't seem to see her around.'

Hilda caught her by the waist and hugged her tightly against the firmly upholstered bosom. 'You're an absolute doll – but don't overdo it! I haven't lost that much. Only a bloody stone. But not fading away quite yet –'. The tricky moment had passed! But at The Sliced Eye Gallery several potentially dangerous situations of a similar nature had occurred. The greatest hazard of being June was the not knowing which amongst these gatherings of strangers were friends and familiars, and which people June had never set eyes on before.

The only way out for Blossom, the only practical solution was just to smile indiscriminately at everyone. It proved to be a wonderful way of meeting people, but it presented the problem that she never got to know anyone's name.

'You two know each other I'm sure.' Blossom lost count

101

of how many times she was forced into this trick as a means of introducing people to each other, without the advantage of knowing the names of either. It was a social device that she had learned to adopt with great success over the years when her memory failed to supply a name to match the familiar face with whom she might have happened to be in conversation. The two persons would wait, gazing first at each other then shaking their heads. 'No, haven't had the pleasure . . .' 'No, can't say we have met . . .' Then they would turn enquiringly toward Blossom, waiting for her to effect proper introductions. To which she would smilingly insist: 'But I could have *sworn* that you had met!' Then, only then would she learn what they were called. 'I'm so-and-so.' 'I'm such-and-such. Nice to meet you.' Etcetera, etcetera.

That got her out of a few spots.

What surprised her most was how few people posed her the real questions that she had been dreading. That is, genuinely serious and searching demands to be told about her work. It was as if, she reflected (now almost at the Gay Hussar), she had already proved herself as an intelligent and capable woman. But more than that – as a *success* in this fiercely competitive stratum of London life. Having done so there was no longer any need to strive to impress. The mere fact of being sufficiently "in" to be invited, that was enough in itself. She was simply yet another in a gathering of celebrities . . . The question now, still undecided in her mind, was who should she be with Professor Hamilton Hamilton? And that question required an immediate answer – she had arrived at the scarlet door of The Gay Hussar. One half-minute late. A woman's prerogative. As soon as she set eyes on the Professor there was no doubt in her mind. She knew without question who she should be.

Three

'Blossom are you busy – I'd like a hand with this –'
Randolph Tree grinned wickedly to himself. He was
standing at the top of the stairs, his erect cock sticking
straight out of his winter-weight combinations (the pale
colour of porridge) and the sturdy corduroy trousers
which he would wear right through till the first signs of
spring.

June was in the middle of making her mincemeat for the
Christmas mincepies, and had just got to the stage of
mixing the shredded suet in with the brown sugar and
spice, the dried fruits, walnuts and chopped apples. She
was looking forward to adding the brandy (and taking a
hefty swig from the bottle). 'Oh, darling – can't it wait,
whatever it is?' she shouted back. 'Only I'm just coming
to the brandy –'

'Bring the brandy with you! This won't take very long, I
promise. I could do it on my own but with your help I'd
make a better job of it.'

'Hold on –' June went to swill her hands at the kitchen
sink.

'I'm holding!' Randolph grasped his shaft like a
truncheon, standing perfectly still like a statue so that this
would be the first sight to greet his wife as she rounded the
bend of the stair. He composed his features into the sort of
noble expression that ruling monarchs or valiant warriors
display on coins. And with the thick dark beard which he
had grown since the summer he actually did look the part.

June hummed as she dried her hands. She loved
Randy's interruptions, but they were becoming so fre-
quent lately that she couldn't imagine how on earth he
managed to get any work of his own done at all.
Yesterday, for instance, he had spent the *entire* day in her

103

company. Not letting her out of his sight for a single second – not even to go to the lavatory. 'I'm insane about the smell of your shit!' he had suddenly announced, sitting on the edge of the black-enamelled bath (a bad mistake of Blossom's – the black bathroom. A bloody nightmare with white talc), watching her strain. And then he'd pleaded, 'Please, please will you let me wipe your botty, Blossom – I promise I'll do it most beautifully.' And he had. As skilfully and as tenderly as a nurse would have done. June had paid him for that as well as for the following poke. They agreed between them that it came under the category of imaginative foreplay.

Before leaving the kitchen area of this the ground floor, June checked the contents of her oven. She had a spiced date crumble pudding in there for Pip and Willow's tea. It had roughly three-quarters of an hour to go, by which time they would be home from school. She was also roasting a half leg of pork in preparation for the cold buffet she would be serving tomorrow evening. There would be about ten guests – no, more than that. All the darts team anyway were coming for a practice session upstairs in Randy's study. (Bloss hadn't believed that when June had told her on the phone. 'But no one is *ever* allowed into the sanctuary, not even me!')

'Oh, *I've* been in there,' June said smugly.

'Bloody good for you too!' Blossom had responded warmly. There was no rivalry between them.

The rind of the boned half-leg of pork had been removed. It lay succulently in a roasting pan at the bottom of the oven, tied into a fat sausage shape, surrounded by the trimmings, the skin cut into strips, and a pig's foot split in two. The added water came halfway up the pan. June had made two rows of incisions along the meat, into which she had pressed chopped fresh herbs and little spikes of garlic, rolled in pepper and salt. The next day, after removing the cooked meat (later this afternoon) and straining the liquid into a bowl, she would carve the cold pork into thin slices. Then she would turn out the jellied stock, chop it finely and arrange around the meat, serving it with a potato salad.

But before that she would have warmed the cockles of their hearts with her hot chestnut cream soup, a recipe she

104

had tried and tested on Emily Shawl only last week. She must remember to make a supply for the deep freeze – or not, there were many other planned dishes in her mind for the deep freeze. It was strange how easily she'd adapted to her new role.

Randy was calling again, he sounded impatient. But she couldn't help it, she simply *had* to take one last look at her seascape. She had put what she considered to be the finishing touches to the tiny canvas just over an hour ago. And so far nobody had seen it but herself. It was very, very good.

She had painted seven of these seascapes in the last nine weeks, taking just over a week to complete each of them. But her plan was to finish a whole set, a full dozen, and then to mount them as one on a large prepared square of backed and reinforced board. It would represent her personal and changing view of the pounding ocean outside her window.

This communal room, the open-plan cooking area at the other end, was where she had chosen to set up her easel. Here at the indoor side of the balcony, an area now strictly forbidden to the rest of the family.

Not that the rest of the family viewed her artistic efforts with anything other than proud and affectionate respect.

'It sort of looks like a bowl of washing-up water, doesn't it?' Pip had said ruminatively about the first painting, his head on one side.

'Oh, thanks very much, son!' June had tugged his short hair.

'No, Mum –' Willow had put loving arms around her waist. 'He doesn't mean it rudely. I know what he means. It's all the swirls. Isn't that the sort of effect that you were after?'

'Yes, it is. You're quite right.' June had smiled to reassure them both. She continued to be astonished at what very clever, kind and considerate children, her sister's children had turned out to be. Of course she had known they were *nice* and she'd known them since birth, it wasn't as if they were strangers. But that was hardly the same as living with them day in and day out – as their mother. Or rather with them believing her to be their mother. In fact the children had been more the cause for

105

doubt in her mind that the life-switch would work, more even than Randolph.

'The kids will *know* though, Blossom, that it's me and not you . . .' This had been at the start of the thrilling laying of their plans. When the idea of the swap was still partly a fantasy in their minds. But even then they had begun to practice as though rehearsing for the eventual reversal of roles.

'How will they *know*? You mean that you think children have some extra-sensory perception as to whether or not someone is their natural mother?' Blossom had snorted rudely through the end of her nose. 'Bollocks! They've researched it with little monkeys – taken the mother away and replaced her with an old bolster wrapped round a hot water bottle. And nobody has been able to tell the difference – honestly, I've seen a programme on television . . .'

June had interrupted. 'Bollocks to you too, Bloss! The facts remain that Pip and Willow are not little monkeys –'

'Ooh, you should see them sometimes!'

June continued '– and nor am I an old bolster with supplied inner warmth. Those two are very bright eleven and twelve-year-olds, who would spot the difference in one second flat. I just know that they would, I'm worried. I'd love to try it for a lark but I don't think I could fool them.'

'You're quite wrong. You could. The reason's quite simple. They're absolutely wrapped up in a complete world of their own – honestly. Do you want a run-down of their day? Well, I shall give it to you – and I promise you that you'll be amazed at how very little we see of each other, the kids and me. We hardly ever eat together, for a start. They have breakfast on their own. I lay it all ready the night before. Cornflakes. Bananas, or apples and oranges. Sliced bread ready for toasting, which they love doing themselves. Butter, or Flora (easier to spread straight from the fridge), honey or jam, milk. Instant coffee, sometimes they prefer teabags. Everything's there. What you don't understand is that they prefer to be self-sufficient. They have their mid-day meal at school. In the evening they tear in, throw down their stomachs whatever happens to be there – I usually just leave cheese

106

or cold chicken, or ham. Something like that, with a bowl of tomatoes and lettuce, celery, radishes – whatever's in season. You'll be going into the winter so they will need something warmer. In which case you leave a shepherds pie in the oven, or a cauliflower cheese, or a steak and kidney pie – just something simple, they don't care. Sometimes I only know that they've been back because the food has gone. Yes, really! They spend the whole time out with their pals, or lolling in front of the television – it's OK, you don't have to put up with them in front of our colour telly. We've bought them a new one of their own which they have on their own floor beneath the rest of the house. I can envisage the day when we shall have to devise a way that they even have their own entrance to the house – knock a hole in the outside wall, something like that. Randy's all for the little buggers having as independent a life as possible from us. He says that apart from the creature comforts of food, warmth and clean clothes all the children need to know is that we are there if and when they need us. And that's about how it is at the moment.'

June had not been convinced. 'What about when they're ill?'

'When they are ill, they just stay in bed. They try it on when they have exams at school. You'll learn to tell the difference. And if you think it's anything serious, you get the doctor round. It's a new one by the way –'

'Has old Wisdom died? You didn't tell me.' June had stared accusingly at Blossom. 'There you are you see – there are all these sort of things that I should obviously know. I would give myself away left, right and centre.'

'Not if we go into everything thoroughly. It's a straightforward research job, no more involved than that. The sort of thing that Espionage is up to all the time.' Blossom had smiled reassuringly and had hugged her sister tight. 'Honestly, baby, your part of it is going to be miles easier than mine. You do at least know my life and all the people in it – it's a pretty small circle, after all. And nothing much happens most of the time.'

June replied nervously. 'But that's just the trouble. It's just in a small intimate set-up like yours that anything untoward is going to be immediately noticed. The very familiarity will make the slightest strangeness on my part seem even odder.'

Blossom had shaken her head most emphatically. 'It's a community of oddities, you know that. Small eccentricities are not only expected but welcomed as tiny diversions with which to pass the day. Half the time people you may have had dinner with the night before will not even greet you in the street – it means they're involved in their work. No more than that. They're bound up in the creative process, just thinking. That's why Randy likes living there so much. He can behave as he chooses and no one regards him with awe. He happens to be a famous philosopher, but so what – in Puddlemouth that's no more special than being a painter or a fisherman. You could return tomorrow as me and behave in any way you like, be completely withdrawn until you felt surer of yourself – even with the kids and with Randy. Everyone would accept it as natural behaviour. They would, honestly. They'd just think that London had had its effect on you, that you were feeling unsettled and that it would take you a little time to acclimatise yourself to being back home.'

This indeed was precisely what had happened. Walking slowly up the stairs now to be confronted (any second) by Randolph's exposed privates, June reflected on the events of the momentous past four months. Momentous to her because the change had been so fundamental, though no more fundamental than it had been for Blossom. The fabulously fortunate thing, they agreed between them, was how successfully they had coped with the switch, themselves. How tragic if one of them had taken to her new life as to the manner born, loving every single minute of it, waking each morning with the secret knowledge that for yet another day she would be who she was not, getting away with it yet again – whilst the other was already bitterly regretting it. And worse, wanting their roles to revert back to normal.

But this had not happened – so far. And if the likelihood appeared to be even remotely looming up in the darkest recesses of the minds of either, it was understood that the dreaded words should be spoken. In truth, neither girl could really believe her good fortune. At the start of the experiment, during those first hazardous weeks in August when the prearranged daily phone calls were quite obviously not enough to cover the incidences of the unexpected, each dreaded that the other might admit to thinking that they had made a mistake. That the joke had gone far enough. That they had had their fun, but now it was time to call it a day. But their mutual reassurances were absolutely genuine, they came jointly and independently to the joyful conclusion that in having changed over at this point in their lives, they were without doubt experiencing the best of both worlds.

'You are *sure* Bloss, you're not regretting it?'

'June, I am *absolutely* sure!'

'You're not . . .' June had hesitated before putting into words what she felt certain to be the case. 'You're not missing Randy too much?' She had held her breath through the small pause before Blossom's reply.

'Missing him – *of course* I'm missing him, silly! But you're there taking good care of him for me so it's all in the family. How are the games going, by the way?'

June had laughed in relief. 'The games? Oh well, we've got a new thing – now I pay him. He does it all. I hardly do anything anymore!' Blossom had been intrigued by this development between her husband and sister. Throughout her entire married life she had always been the one to make the first sexual move, until it would have seemed vaguely obscene had it been the other way around. It wasn't that Randolph had become sexually lazy, but that she enjoyed the ritual of seduction so much. She relished the power to arouse him sexually. It delighted her to feel that she was in control of their games. Although their financial arrangement, whereby she charged him for each intimate act, had originally developed from the amusing idea that this might be a novel way of providing her with the housekeeping money and her dress allowance, this money bond helped the illusion that she was the one who had the upper hand. True, she was an object, but this way an object only available at a certain price. The price being dependent on just how much effort and imagination she chose to throw into each performance. Once, when tired and rather irritable, her periods approaching, she had set an arbitrary figure of 50p on the deal. Her intention being simply to slip down her tights (one leg out was enough) and sprawl back passively on the settee in front of the television. And yet,

109

curiously, there must have been an element of the erotic in her weary lethargy which had sparked off an unparalleled passion in her partner. So much so that he had ripped the remainder of her clothing from her limbs, flinging himself forcefully between her brutally wrenched thighs and covering her neck with such livid lovebites that she had been forced into scarves for a week.

It had been an eye-opener.

Even so it had never occurred to her to reverse their sexual roles. Certainly not to the point where she would be paying him! And yet, why not! The more Blossom thought about it the more she applauded June for this revolutionary approach. Now it was the turn of Randolph to provide the sexual surprises, to wrack his brains for ways and means of titillating the sensual appetite of his wife. And knowing Randy as she did, Blossom didn't doubt for a moment that it was the sort of challenge that he would enjoy. He would be in a position to consult his considerable bibliography on the subject. His sexual section extended, as far as she could remember, across seven shelves of the library in his study. At one time this had been their favourite bedtime reading, with the advantages of practical application of newly discovered techniques immediately to hand. But of late, this pleasant practice had fallen by the way. Replaced by other seductions. Late night brandy. Bournvita. The undemanding bathos of end of the evening television. Or else, in his case, indigestible philosophical tomes. Or in her's, the latest well-reviewed novel.

It had arrived at the point, she could see now reviewing the situation from this distance, where their sex-life was really her responsibility. Like the cooking, and the shopping and the cleaning. And although it had never been anything short of idyllically successful (hadn't she, Blossom, devoted every waking moment to the pursuit!), perhaps a radical change of approach could bring nothing but a beneficial breath of fresh air. She only hoped that dear sweet Randolph felt this to be so.

Randolph did.

He had missed Blossom more than he had believed it possible to miss anyone. He pined for her as keenly as if she had died. She had been away from him for exactly two weeks, three days and five and three-quarter hours. Not counting the fifteen-minute delay in the arrival of her train. And yet, although his sense of loneliness had been so absolute that he had done what he vowed he wouldn't do – that is start pestering her with telephone calls – he had hidden his pain. The parting, after all, had been at his instigation. She needed a break, a change, and he had rather welcomed it himself. But the reality, by the end of the first day, had become unbearable. And worse at the end of the long, dream-logged night, threshing about in their vast four-poster bed. Feeling in vain for her smooth supple haunch, for the handful of breast to cling on to. In the morning, he had rung again in utter anguish, simply to hear her voice. And as unrecognisable though it was (the devilish misfortune to catch some miserable flu bug) it had been an enormous relief. So much so that this had become the pattern throughout the remainder of her visit.

He didn't find it strange that the girls had decided not to leave London after all. It had given Blossom a chance to wander around the shops, to visit exhibitions, the theatre, see films, eat at restaurants (even dance at one nightclub!). All things and places that in Puddlemouth she could only read about. He was well aware that Blossom had a butterfly side to her nature which responded to the less cerebral side of life. It was only right that she should be allowed – no, not allowed – allowed was altogether too much as if he were her keeper and she his possession, his little girl, his toy. She was his wife. She was his partner. She was his equal, his other half. And without her he ceased to exist as a whole.

After the first three nights on his own, his sexual frustration was making him shiver in bed. It was August and he felt deathly cold. At six in the morning he was driven to run a bath and for the first time in so many years that he couldn't remember the last time, he masturbated. It brought him no mental relief whatsoever. He watched the thin milky substance spurt from his cock, still grasping the shaft firmly in his fist. The all-black bathroom was lined with mirror tiles. Randolph was surrounded by images of himself. Cock-in-hand. He looked strained and unhappy like an adolescent boy caught in the act. He looked guilty and not a little mad. The next time he

111

wanked (the following evening) it was in bed, with the electric blanket for warmth and an absolutely appalling programme on the television. One which he and Blossom had even forbidden to the children – an American detective series of unparalleled puerility. But it was summer and there was nothing else better. He enjoyed it hugely, and what was more he lapped up a similar diet of pap for the rest of the evening. To his surprise he found that he had gone to bed at seven-thirty! At ten past ten, unable to stay awake any longer in this unendurable state of isolation, he tossed off at a frantic speed into a pair of Blossom's gossamer panties, then put out the light before falling asleep.

He slept an inordinate amount. Like a teenager, like a person unable to cope with the traumas of life, he sought refuge in sleep. By the first weekend with still ten more days to go before Blossom's return, Randolph was sure that he was suffering a minor breakdown. His behaviour had shaken him – not with alarm. After all he was a great thinker, one who had made a study of the human animal and the human reaction to enforced conditions, including stress. No, it wasn't alarm that he felt. But he was intrigued, he was surprised. His interest had been deeply aroused and was leading him towards an entirely new concept regarding the sexuality of man. His own behaviour, so out of character, would serve as the germination of necessary extensive research in the future. Blossom's absence had proved valuable to his work after all!

He began to take notes. He recorded the desperation of the dawn masturbation, the swift pleasure of the despoiling of Blossom's gossamer panties. And then he recorded the rest. The morning after the despoiling he had awoken with an erection whilst conscious of needing to pee. The erection subsided as he relieved himself, as he would expect it to. The hour was early, if he got up now there would be a further hour or so to wait before the light broke over the sea and the skies. But he found himself lacking his usual enthusiasm for the sight. His normal procedure of rising at dawn now appeared rather perverse without Blossom to return to at eight or thereabouts for their morning fuck – thence to proceed downstairs for breakfast (or the other way around, if she felt like it). He felt

112

disorientated, as badly as any person of firm habit whose normal programming has been turned upside down.

And so he returned to his bed.

The first sight that caught his eye was that of Blossom's spunky drawers. They lay pink and crumpled against the black sheet, a delicate reminder of their delicious owner. And of the purpose to which he had put them last night.

He fell on them with a groan and stuffed them to his mouth, kissing their sweet and faintly perfumed crotch. Sniffing them like a dog, rubbing them roughly all over his face, hugging them against his slack cock and balls. And then he bent down and pulled them on.

The effect was grotesque yet at the same time mesmerising. It was something to do with the contrast, the contrast of his muscled and rather hairy masculine flesh against the fine cobwebbed texture of the feminine garment. The sight seemed to contradict itself, it looked all wrong. But only, as Randolph later wrote in the appendix to his notes, because of a mental conditioning. It only looked odd and faintly obscene (also frankly perverse) because this was not the apparel one would normally expect to find on the body of a full-grown healthy man in this day and age. Apart from that, there was no viable reason why he, on studying his reflection in the mirrored ceiling of the four-poster (there must be an interesting explanation of Blossom's need to surround herself with mirrors – to do with being a twin and needing constantly to relate to her double?), should experience quite such a shock. Nor why, secondary to that shock and following hard on its heels, he should be aware of a growing excitement. Not even a specifically sexual excitement either, as yet. But an eerie and less familiar sensation, as if he were removed from the person reflected above him in the mirror. As if that person were being watched by an interested observer, a stranger, but one whose impartiality and distance was mutely denied by the expression of intense concentration contorting the twisted features.

His hand slid slowly down to the triangle of flimsy fabric barely covering his cock or his balls. Blossom's knickers, as he would have expected, were far too brief to begin to fit. His bollocks bulged out, one each side of the narrow crotch. Whilst his still inert penis, in no sense

113

extended (yet) lay pressed hard against his belly, the tip peeping out from beneath the line of the waist-elastic like the nose of an inquisitive puppy. And the constriction of his genitals was in no way unpleasant. Randolph even enjoyed it – it reminded him of Blossom and the way she had sometimes of squeezing him down there, cupping him tightly in both hands and whispering low threats.

At the memory his genitals jumped.

That evening he retired to his bedroom as early as the night before, around seven-thirty. Only this time he didn't retire to bed. Instead he stripped off, poured himself a large Scotch, adding a liberal supply of ice-cubes from the small bedside fridge (there solely for this purpose). Then he stood at the window watching the last of the summer visitors straggle off the beach below. He was wondering what to put on.

All day he had been like this, in a skin-tingling state of aroused excitement. As if he had stumbled upon a delicious secret, a forbidden activity, a subversive way of life. One open only to him. He could hardly wait for the evening to arrive.

The fact that what he was contemplating held no time limit, no rules or restrictions as to when and where this particular game could be played, was beside the point. The success of the performance lay in the ritual. His entire life until this point rested on order and a sense of logical calm. Only thus had he been able to explore imaginative avenues in his mind, creating mental chaos out of that which had first to be arranged with the utmost consistency. Had this not been so, had he instead chosen to live in utter turbulence and random theorizing, grasping at philosophical straws – then he should have felt obliged to devote his whole life in another sphere. To that of returning all back to square one. Restraining those impulses in himself toward revolutionary logic, all that he held most dear. His entire existence was aimed naturally towards reversal. Towards questioning the established order of things. But that meant *there had to be an established order to question*. The same applied to his sex life. He had never before in his (almost) forty years of life ever donned the intimate apparel of a female. Except once, when forced to borrow a cousin's warm vest when his own had blown off the washing line and lain all morning in the snow. Oh, and another time at school when he had played 'the vicar's sister' in a Christmas production of *The Black Sheep Of The Family*, by L. du Garde Peach. Then, it was perfectly true, he had warn a pair of passion-killer bloomers belonging to the late and lamented wife of the Latin teacher. The entire lady's wardrobe had been awarded to Drama Props on her death.

But these occasions could hardly be said to count beside what he had in mind now.

He took a deep draught from his drink, swallowing it in one gulp. It was not his custom to drink on his own, but then the need to do so rarely arose. Blossom was always here. But even tonight, various invitations had arrived since Blossom's departure, he had turned down the offer of dinner with friends, or the chance of a couple of beers in the Boozer's Gloom and an impromptu meal with Gascoigne Teate, the landlord. But this evening he felt he needed to drink alone. It was his intention to become rather delightfully tight – after all, this could be seen as a celebration. The celebration of a new departure.

The garment Randolph chose eventually to wear was less figure hugging than this morning's, and altogether more alluring – possibly because of this. But he had chosen it for another reason besides the fit. He wished to conduct an experiment with himself. The outfit was the slinky black satin nightdress, side-slit to the waist, with the matching negligée edged with the froth of maribou feathers. This was the seductive set of garments which Blossom had been wearing on their last evening together in this room. The night that she had been swilling champagne and scoffing soft-centres. He had good reason to remember the climax – he didn't think he would be able to face another chocolate for the rest of his life.

He shut his eyes tightly and began his experiment, conjuring up the image of Blossom as she had been that night. She had been lying, one thigh exposed, on the floor at his feet. On this very spot which he occupied now.

He crossed his legs, just as she had, and the action caused the satin to slither further apart at the slit. He explored the opening with tentative fingers remembering the softness of his wife's limb, immediately below the

115

profusion of pubic hair. He glanced down, then he frowned. Something was glaringly out of place – it was the lolling mound on his lap. His penis and testicles were giving offence, the sheer bulk of them brutalised the smooth surface of the satin nightdress. They should be tucked out of sight. Having crossed his legs, he now opened them, allowing his set to sink toward the floor. Then he pressed his thighs as closely together as comfort would allow. So far so good, now he had nothing – not even a crack! The folds of the nightdress flowed undisturbed from his hairy nipples, over his rib-cage, his abdomen, right down to the line of his thighs, and thence to his knees. Perfection. He closed his eyes again and this time with the memory of Blossom firmly in his mind he slowly began to caress himself.

And so it was and had been until the day of Blossom's return. The evening before had passed in the solemn ritual of parading slowly once (sometimes twice when the spirit moved him) around the bedroom, before the full-length mirrors. Each time he was adorned in an item of Blossom's vast collection of lingerie. And he wore a long ash-blonde wig, which he had discovered on her hat shelf, in addition to the discreet application of lipstick, rouge and eye-shadow. He had also discovered that wearing her perfume helped.

This interested him particularly, the sensory factor, and led directly to a regrouping of sub-sections in his notes. The last evening was the strangest of all, overhung with an aura of sadness, as he also recorded. It marked the conclusion of a fantasy. He very much doubted if such a period of time would occur again in his entire lifetime. The experience had been invaluable. The research had only just begun – for what he was starting to suspect would be his most important work. *The Spiritual Sperm* – A Proper Study of Spunk. The title had materialised during one climactic bout in a particularly pretty taffetta petticoat of Blossom's. No other title had ever come to him so easily.

Despite his secret idyll he could barely wait for Blossom's return. Although they had spoken each morning on the phone, he had been dreadfully conscious of the distance between them. Not just the physical distance –

116

there was something else. There was a sort of hesitancy, a shyness. Or had that been his imagination? Possibly so. And of course the poor girl had the most fearful cold, one that would have made anybody sound quite unlike themselves. Hard luck that, going all the way to London and having to spend so much of the time in bed. Poor Blossom.

Poor Blossom was being mobbed by a long bus-queue of schoolboys who had spotted her alighting from the Daimler of the Director General of Universal Television. The Director General had just proposed marriage in the back of the car in the full hearing of the chauffeur. Blossom considered this to be in rather dubious taste, especially since the Director General was already married.

'You're married already.' She had voiced her objections in a cold severe voice.

'I'm married to a bottle,' he had answered balefully. 'And have been for the last fifteen years, for what it's worth.'

Blossom, moved to pity, had taken his hand in hers and squeezed it sympathetically. There was something very cuddly about this large, lonely man. In the past four months, since the switch-around, she had to admit she had really grown to be rather fond of him. But this was true of all the rest of June's men. She couldn't think what could have allowed June to leave them all for Randolph. No – that wasn't true! She could of course, because Randolph was and always would be the most marvellous man in the whole bloody world! Putting it another way, only the lure of Randolph could have influenced June into relinquishing the fame, the financial benefits, the freedom and the love affairs of her fabulous London life. Each morning that Blossom awoke (wherever it was, regardless of whose bed) she had to pinch herself to see if it was all really still true. But what fears she had had at the start!

It was difficult now to remember exactly whose idea the life-swap had been. Though circumstances had dictated subsequent events. From the moment of her, Blossom's, arrival in town, she had been mistaken for June. But the real crunch, the first turning point, they agreed between them – was when Randolph had mistaken June for Blossom on the telephone. And thank Christ that he had!

As it happened Blossom had missed Randolph's morning

call by no more nor less than a mere fifteen minutes. A sixth sense had warned her that he might ring. Right in the middle of a passage of fine careless rapture with Professor Hamilton Hamilton, as he was moaning, 'June, dearest June – our very souls are in tune –,' and nibbling most effectively on the nub of her clitty, she just knew that at that precise moment back in Puddlemouth her husband was planning to speak to her. And she had rotated her pelvis at such alarming speed in her sudden agitation that she had almost torn the startled Professor's tongue from his throat.

'I'm coming!' she had cried out.

Then moments later, 'I'm going!'

And go she had, without so much as an explanation. Haunted all the way back to Flowers Hotel by the hurt bewilderment in the eyes of the Professor. 'But darling June – have I offended you? Tell me –' he had beseeched. But what could she have said! She could certainly not have told him the truth – that she was not June, but Blossom. Blossom behaving badly, Blossom being unfaithful, Blossom on the point of being found out . . . Jesus wept!

Her stomach had churned at the thought of poor Randolph's anguish, at the sweet baby's pain. What a blow! Shitballs – what a cunt she'd turned out to be! She sprawled back in the corner of the taxi mouthing a vehement stream of self-abuse.

The worst part of it was that she felt no genuine remorse. Her anxiety was simply the fear of being found out.

She leaned forward, and on impulse tapped the dividing glass to the taxi-driver's compartment. 'Could you stop at the next phone box, please?' She had hit on the answer. *She* would telephone Randolph now, she would beat him to it. She would say that her first thoughts had been of him as soon as she had woken, that she felt she just wanted to hear his voice. She would say all the things which she knew he was preparing in his mind to say to her. She rang. The line was engaged.

'You've just missed Randolph. He phoned about fifteen minutes ago. He was appalled by your terrible cold and said to stay in bed for the rest of the day.' June smiled

118

groggily. 'But he was most concerned, he'll be ringing tomorrow about the same time. You have two alternatives, either catch my cold and develop as croaky a voice as mine – or let me answer, as you, again tomorrow morning.' She gave Blossom a quizzical look. 'That might be best – now that you've had a taste of the alley-cat's life, there's no knowing what time you'll return . . .'

And so it was that each morning Randolph and June would conduct lengthy conversations of the most loving intimacy. It was a revelation to June, the warmth and the teasing wit, the closeness, the kindness, the erotic overtones, the small hints, the outright bawdiness, the sensual insinuations.

She had always, of course, been immensely attracted (as who wasn't?) to her brother-in-law. By the end of the first week she had fallen in love.

'I can't believe, Bloss, that Randolph won't know in bed.' June was getting cold feet.

'Fucking, you mean?' Blossom was trying to decide which of June's outfits she should wear on the television this evening. It was the continuation of a group discussion that had been started the previous night. An important event, that had been, marking as it did the very first *professional* reversal of the two girls. Blossom had emerged so far with creditable aplomb.

'Yes, fucking – he'll see the difference.'

'I very much doubt it, kid.' Blossom had turned to smile reassuringly. 'You see the whole success of our sex-life rests on the illusion that I am very many different people. It means that he is living out his fantasies, if you like. So that he wouldn't ever expect me to be the same from one fuck to the next. I do different things all the time – just to ring the changes. You'll soon get the hang of it. And if you don't, well Randolph will simply assume that your stupidity is just another pose.'

'Thanks.'

But that was, more or less, how it happened. Randolph was so ecstatic to have Blossom back again that he noticed no difference in her at all. She struck him as possibly somewhat subdued, but then she'd had a long journey. Also she had just recovered from the ill-effects of that

119

flu-bug. 'You could do with a holdiay.' He had hugged her close. 'Don't go away from me again,' he'd whispered in her neck. And they had drunk a bottle of champagne to celebrate her return – and then another. They missed the meal they had intended to have in the one decent restaurant Puddlemouth possessed, because by that time they were busy in bed. June simply presented herself as she was, overwhelmed by the trembling beginnings of love. For some reason Randolph was inexplicably moved by his wife's tenderness. So much so that at the point of the first orgasm he began to cry. They came to climax together, their faces wet with the saltiness of his tears.

Blossom managed finally to escape from the mobbing schoolboys. She was looking in on a discussion being held by The Coordination Committee in Defence of the 1967 Abortion Act, made up of sixteen organisations including the Family Planning Association, the National Council for Civil Liberties, The Abortion Law Reform Association and many members who planned to back up pro-abortion MPs and influence parliamentary opinion. Picket lines were under discussion. The meeting was being held in Mortimer Street. At the entrance to the building, a feminist group had posted various slogan posters on the wall, including the graffiti depicting the corner of a tiled public lavatory with the scrawled message: When God Created Man She Made A Mistake. It was one of Blossom's favourites.

It had been Hilda Vengeance's idea that Blossom should come along. Hilda was the official legal adviser to the group and had been since its inauguration. They were a set of admirable girls, but Blossom knew that already, she had met many of them whilst recording her recent Female Series. She whole-heartedly supported their work. Unfortunately she was not in the position to stay long today, she only hoped that her brief visit would not be construed as a sign of her lack of interest. She had no wish to antagonise anybody. But although she was as scrupulous with her time as it was humanly possible to be (after all there were only twenty-four hours in the day!) she found that she was becoming increasingly vulnerable to criticism from all sorts of unexpected quarters. Her daily

120

mail, delivered to Television Tower and opened by her two secretaries, contained open abuse from such diverse groups as the Milliners' Guild for never wearing a hat, to the Preservation of Rural Accents for the impersonality of her vowels. Her clothes and the styling of her hair were deplored. Speculative articles appeared discussing the fact that she had never chosen to marry. Several of them contained rather touching quotes from Tiny about their years together. 'I loved the girl dearly – I never did understand what exactly went wrong. Of course June was always very ambitious.'

June had rung up after reading the first of them. 'Sod that,' she shouted furiously. 'Trust that little turd to get in on the act! I'm surprised that he hasn't tried to creep back into your – my – bed.'

Blossom had laughed. 'I've got news for you –'

'You mean he has! Well, I tell you something – I shan't forgive you if you do. I had enough of that bastard!'

Blossom had laughed again. 'I shouldn't worry about that – I wouldn't begin to know where to fit him in even if I wanted to. By the way, that Czech film chap is back in the big city, he keeps leaving messages. What do you think I should do?'

June had snorted and then said cryptically. 'Well, it depends when you're next in front of the camera. I shouldn't see him the night before – it's too much of a risk. The girls in Make-up do wonders with black eyes, but it's not worth it. Everyone gets to know inside an hour and then they go round pulling your leg about it for weeks. And it could leak out further now that you're more of a celebrity – you don't want all that sort of thing in the papers do you? Oh, talking of the papers, isn't Zachary Ram going a bit overboard? Last week *and* this he's made mention of you in *Views*. It is becoming terribly obvious, even Randy was saying so –'

It was perfectly true that Zachary Ram was in danger of placing himself in a position of professional ridicule over June Day. Twice already his editor had had to have a word over the abuse of his powerful position as a critic. 'This, Ram, is not the place for the display of your personal obsessions. Up to several months ago your column was a hard core of positive and thoughtful criticism. Now it has deteriorated into the bashful scribbling of a lovesick schoolboy. Will you kindly conduct your wanking in the privacy of where the hell you care to. I positively refuse to carry it any longer on my pages!'

Zachary Ram had huffily offered his resignation, which his editor had grimly (and wisely) refused. Ram's column was widely read, his was a respected name amongst the readers of *Views*. Indeed, his name had already pulled a new and younger readership that the magazine had not enjoyed before Ram had started to write for them. This obsession with June Day was to be treated as a joke. It was a passing thing – for God's sake, everybody was obsessed with her at the minute. It was getting impossible to even pick up a newspaper or magazine without reading her name or seeing her photograph. Admittedly she had done a first rate job with those series of hers. She had lifted them out of the run of those rather pedestrian programmes by the very quality of her presence, the unaffected freshness of her forthright approach. She was that rare thing – an absolute television natural. There was an incandescence about her which glowed . . . The editor of *Views* abruptly checked his fey meanderings – he had begun to sound exactly like the more juvenile of Ram's views.

It was truly amazing how Blossom had taken to the medium of television. The very first time, of the group discussion, had not been the worst. She had sailed through that one, and the follow-up. But then she had not been on the screen by herself or with just one other person. She had been carried by the rest of the panel. She had also taken June's professional advice – two stiff gins drunk within fifteen minutes of appearing. Such that the spirit hits the stomach and begins to take effect just as you are needing the lift. It worked a treat. June had made her up a draught to drink from a flask. 'You down that in the lavvy so that no one can see. Otherwise you get the reputation of being a boozer. You get hospitality, but you can't rely on it. Some stations only give you a drink when it's all over – in case anyone goes over the top. And this is a live show – you're transmitting direct, so you may find it's like that. Best to take the flask just in case. You are sure now that uou want to go through with it? Because I don't mind missing this one – they know that I have been confined to bed these last few days . . .'

But Blossom had been adamant. 'This may be my only chance to try it and as you say it's not important, even if I don't say a single word. Though I should be able to do that –after all the subject is something that I know enough about. Woman's Changing Role in the Home. I probably have more than you to say on than.' And she had. In fact what Blossom had said on each of those evenings had in their way helped to establish June Day's reputation on television as being a fresh and original personality. One who, although being around for the last several years, was at last coming into her own.

'What is your opinion on that, Ms Day?' the chairman had addressed Blossom. The studio audience had waited expectantly for this attractive girl's reply.

'Sorry – how awful, I have just lost track of things. We were talking about wives and I was trying to remember the maxim. Would you like to hear it?' Blossom had smiled ingenuously.

The chairman and the rest of the panel made murmuring noises of assent. The discussion had reached a rather low point, it could do with a lift.

'Well,' Blossom had cleared her throat. 'I think this is it – I should know the saying well enough. My married sister has it pinned up –' June watching in, back at Flowers, rose from her pillow as if in silent protest, praying that Blossom wasn't going to say what she thought she would. Down in Puddlemouth, Randolph, attired in a pair of peaches-and-cream satin cami-knicks seated before the very slogan to which his sister-in-law would refer, raised his glass toward the television screen. It was as if he were toasting his wife. The resemblance was uncanny this evening.

'A wife . . .' Blossom cleared her throat.

A person coughed in the audience. Everyone was waiting for the precious gem. All those present in the studio, the director in the control room. the technicians on the floor, the vision-mixers, the sound controllers, the programme researchers, the publicity people, the receptionist in the foyer to Television Tower, plus the car-park attendant who had popped in from the cold. Along with the waiting taxi-drivers, ordered to drive the participants of the programme home later. Not to mention the four million viewers watching in their hojes (inclucing the emotional Randolph and apprehensive June).

Blossom began again, suddenly aware of being the undisputed centre of attention and squeezing the last ounce out of it. Her eyes twinkled roguishly. Here it came at last. 'A wife is an appliance you screw on the bed to get the housework done!'

And the following evening. 'A wife is a poorly paid prostitute with only one client!'

The telephone switchboard was jammed each time.

The effect on Cherie Pye's negotiating power, over the fees which she was now in a position to demand on June Day's behalf, was instantaneous.

'My angel – you 'ave pushed your earning up by almost a 'alf! Is true! I know, I can 'ardly believe it myself. The telephone it is ringing so much for your services. You are making yourself free I 'ope during these next few weeks, *non?* This is important, very – to strike while the h'iron is 'ot!'

Blossom hadn't said a word. She had just answered the telephone call from June's agent. Afterwards she said to June, 'Christ, that woman sounds absolutely *ghastly*! I'm not sure, if we do the switch, whether I'm going to be able to stand her. That high-pitched squeal – it's just like a stuck pig, surely it must put people off dreadfully.'

June had shaken her head. 'You would think so, but it doesn't. She's a bloody marvellous agent. I don't think you would find a better one, but of course it's up to you. That's if,' she had added hastily, 'we decide to do the swap.' Though really they had each made up their mind by then.

There had been one or two moments of heart-pounding panic the following week when Blossom had been asked to do an interview, lasting less than five minutes (and thus needing to be concise) with a much heralded novelist from North Cornwall. This was a woman who had once been on intimate terms with Emily Shawl. Someone whom Emily had actually brought round to visit Blossom and Randolph several years ago in Puddlemouth.

Coming face-to-face with each other for the first time in

the hospitality lounge, being briefed by the director as to the line of questions he would like to see pursued, the novelist refused to believe that she and Blossom had not met before. Despite Blossom's lengthy explanations that it would have been her twin sister and not her, the novelist remained unconvinced, as well she might. When the programme was suddenly on the air (a terrifying few seconds of countdown involving a beastly little light and someone waving their arms. And Blossom's throat as dry as the wings of a moth), Blossom completely forgot her briefed line of questioning. All she could think of was Emily Shawl's cruel comments regarding the famous novelist's inability to give a 'good-gobbing'. Those had been Emily's wicked words. 'A good gobbing.' And those were the only ones uppermost in Blossom's petrified mind, until the woman herself took the bull by the conversational horns (aware that precious viewing time was being wasted and that she was there with the express intent of plugging her latest book).

Afterwards June sympathised. 'You "dried" there for a second, didn't you – isn't it awful! I've done that –' And she had gone on to tell Blossom that people did it all the time. Even old hands like Nobs Plater. He had done it the other day in the middle of reading the Ten o'clock News. Afterwards he had explained that it had been one of his chest pains again. Though it had been pointed out to him – he *had* eaten that evening in the studio canteen. He should expect to suffer the ill effects of indigestion after that. And he had been forced to agree that a man in his position with the nation's news at the tip of his tongue ought to be more careful what he put in his mouth . . .

But from them on Blossom's self confidence slowly grew. Since she could never be certain which people her sister was familiar with, she went around with a permanent half-smile on her lips. Colleagues began remarking to each other what an absolute pleasure she had become to work with, eager to listen, eager to learn their opinions, never tiring of the old clichés everyone trotted out in the pub, in the bar, in the studio canteen, on location. It was almost as if she had never heard any of it before. Suddenly she was everyone's favourite, with producers and directors clamouring to work with her. Success breeding success.

125

And so it was with her love-life. Blossom was positively bombarded with invitations to dinners, to film openings, to previews, to first nights. Dimples (who was now manageress of Flowers – Mercedes having returned to the States to star off-Broadway) said she had never known anything like it. Nor had Blossom. But there was no room for any further lovers in her life than she managed to fit in already. And she had no interest in straying from the small but passionate posse that June had bequeathed her. They were a diverse enough group to satisfy her demands – she was able to play a different role with each of them (which gave her the warm feeling that she was still in a way with lovely Randolph). And besides that, she felt a sense of responsibility toward them, just as June was taking care of Randolph for her – so she, Blossom, must keep her sister's men under her wing.

She found that she had no favourites, though after, immediately after, being with each of them she would think that really *he* was the one.

Today she had lunched with the Director General after sucking him off in the grandiose seclusion of his office (an uneasy aperitif) with the distraction of secretarial sounds on the other side of the door – preferable to it being the other way around. The great man himself could have been caught by a member of staff tucking into what could have appeared to be a particularly scrumptious strawberry sandwich. For Blossom had her period, a fact which never failed to excite the Director General. He seemed to revel in the gore. And although it made no difference at all to her sex-life with Randolph (they fucked throughout that time as if all was normal), she had never experienced the positive appetite for it that the Director General displayed. She sometimes wondered whether that hadn't been the basic reason behind his professional success – the fact that he was out for everyone's blood!

Today for instance he had greeted her at his desk (after she had been shown through the door by an overtly discreet secretary) with a white linen napkin tied ostentatiously around his jutting chin!

'Are we eating here?' She had glanced around the large room for signs of a cold buffet and champagne on ice. That, after all, had been the manner of their second

126

luncheon together in this room. But no, there appeared to be nothing of that kind this morning.

And then she had got the message.

'Don't be a naughty boy!' she had scolded. 'No, I mean it. Take off that silly napkin – cunnilingus today is absolutely out of the question in my condition. No. Don't look like that. Really, whatever next! Your secretary would think you had a secret supply of raw steaks or were involved in some sacrificial rites on the sly – all that blood on your bib! Come on now, don't cry. I'll give you a nice cosy blow-job, really you're worse than a child!'

But they had a very relaxed lunch afterwards. He had taken her to The White Elephant in Curzon Street, which made sure that everyone in television knew. They would immediately jump to the conclusion that this was a business luncheon, instead of what it was – the open evidence that they were having an affair. Cynthia, the Director General's wife, was possessed of a highly unpredictable nature. He could never be quite certain how she might react to any given situation. 'Alcoholics are so damned unreliable,' he would confide to Blossom, shaking his large head. His conversation was peppered with these kind of dull truisms. Blossom couldn't for the life of her understand how in hell he had managed to get a Double First, but then, as she'd keep reminding herself, she was used to the wit and wisdom of Randolph. And Randolph, when he was on form, could make Bertrand Russell look like Mickey Mouse. More or less.

Even so the Director General aroused what she supposed must be her maternal instinct, she cared a great deal about making him feel wanted. She felt that he had suffered a short supply of love and sex during his life. Unlike Professor Hamilton Hamilton.

Professor Hamilton Hamilton had become obsessed with Blossom (believing her to be June) and June (believing her to be Blossom) as a twosome, with himself participating as the third in a sexual triangle. The idea had sprung to his mind during that very first dinner at The Gay Hussar when Blossom had masqueraded as June. It was because he knew that Blossom was in town (though as he had already been given to understand, she was confined to her bed with a beastly cold).

127

But he was impatient for her recovery, he could hardly wait to renew her acquaintance, as he kept telling his dinner companion.

'Tell me, June,' he had interrupted her in mid-sentence, 'had you and your twin-sister any desire for each other as small children. I mean did you explore each other's little bodies, that sort of thing?' Blossom had been surprised by the abruptness of the question. It was perfectly true that earlier they had been discussing the modern relevance of De Sade, over Victor's delicious Pike Quenelles. She gave proper consideration to the question. It was not the first time that it had been put to her, or to June for that matter. Many men appeared to find the possibility, that they would have discovered their sexuality together, immensely intriguing. Randolph had explored the subject often enough in the past. Though not for a long time – she wondered about that. Perhaps because June had not visited for some while.

She had answered with an honesty that had completely disarmed the Professor. 'I think we were more aware of each other's bodies when we reached the age of puberty. We would certainly compare our pubic hair, such as it was. And our breasts of course, there was never, ever any self-consciousness. As to whether we masturbated together, well yes, I remember that we did. It was rather like when we were small babies. They used to find us asleep, each with a thumb in the other one's mouth. In the same way I would play with – (she had nearly tripped up then and said June!) Blossom. You know, rub her clitoris. And she would rub mine. It only felt as if I was playing with myself in a way. I always felt it would have been more fun if there had been a second person present. Not a *third* person – do you see what I mean? For example, just a little thing, but at precisely the same moment without either of us saying anything, we would both reach to our mouths in the middle of this mutual masturbation to transfer some lubricating spittle to our slits. And what's more we always, always came together, rubbing like mad. That was very exciting now I remember it. We were as sensitive with each other, knowing exactly where and how to touch, as we were with ourselves. It was self-masturbation really. And another thing, we were always horny, in the mood for

128

that sort of thing at the same time. It was never a case of one of us not feeling like it, when the other did. But then when I (Christ! She had done it again – she *must, must* be more careful!), when Bloss and I went our separate ways – you know she got married to Randolph when she was only eighteen, then I suppose our sexual centres and horizons had altered. We have never caressed each other since then.'

'What a pity!' Those were the only words that the Professor had uttered. But he had seemed decidedly disturbed by what Blossom had confided. And there was a blazing light, which could be described as fanatical, shining behind his blue eyes.

Valentine, the fey and beautiful aristocrat, was quite a different kettle of fish. Describing her reaction to him, Blossom had admitted that half the attraction was that it made her feel as though she were actually fucking her own son. Fucking Pip – the erotic attractions of incest!

June had sniffed. 'Well, not having a son I wouldn't know about that!'

'No but June, his body – he's so delicately made – didn't you find that. Like holding a child – no?'

'Not where it matters.' June had been rather churlish altogether about Valentine. She didn't really know why on earth she should have felt like that either. It certainly wasn't that she minded about sharing him – neither she nor Blossom harboured any corrosive jealousy over any of June's lovers, or Blossom's husband. It certainly would have meant the end of the life-swap if either of them had.

'Perhaps it's the druggy thing that I've taken against, Bloss,' June had tried hard to rationalize her disquiet. They had to be completely honest with each other over any doubts. 'I always felt so guilty, we just used to lie around rolling joints all day. I confessed as much, I had to, to Cherie one evening after I had split up with Valentine. And she nearly went berserk as you can imagine. All those times when she'd been trying to get hold of me for jobs. It would be a terrible waste for us, or rather you, to have got this far in your career just to have it go up in smoke.'

Blossom was aghast. And then she laughed. 'When did you last see Valentine?' she demanded.

'It seems like years, but of course it isn't. It's just that he's never given up hope, I suppose. I dread to think what he's like now though. I heard that he was on to speed, coke and heroin too. What do you think – has he gone completely to the dogs?'

But all Blossom would do was laugh again into the telephone. This was one of their daily conversations (from Blossom's private line at Television Tower, so that poor Randolph shouldn't be landed with the gigantic telephone bill at the end of the quarter). 'Perhaps I shall refuse to answer that one. I'll just keep you in suspense – better than that I might pop down one weekend and bring Valentine with me – what about that! For that matter – what about bringing them *all*? Say for Christmas!'

At that point Blossom had really meant it as a joke. At that point she had not yet spent time with the Czech film director. Nor had she seduced the hysterical Zachary Ram.

By Christmas she had done.

Four

Blossom Tree (really Blossom) lay in her own four-poster bed with her husband's body in her arms. They had enjoyed the very first fuck of the New Year. In a matter of hours she would be gone, to be replaced by June her identical twin.

Randolph Tree was fast asleep, the entire night (and

the previous week) had been one of spent passion. With an exotic atmosphere of brooding lust hanging heavily in the air which he had been at a loss to explain. Though the easy explanation was there for all to see. His sister-in-law, June (really Blossom) had arrived for Christmas with the dazzling charisma of her current fame as the Television Celebrity of the Year. Or whatever she was now – perhaps it was Top Female Personality in the *TV Times* Readers' Poll. Blossom had explained it all, but he had been forced to admit to June herself that he had not taken as much account as had been expected of him. The reason being that these days his whole attention was on *Spunk* (his new book). She had laughed understandingly and listened with absolutely undivided concentration to the outline of the work, even questioning closely some of his tentative theories and offering a few suggestions of her own. What a good-natured creature this charming woman was! It never failed to please him whenever he was re-united with his wife's twin, to think that there were two such absolutely splendid girls in the world. Meaning (though God damn the ghastly thought) that if something ever happened to the one he was married to . . . Along with her incredibly potent presence, which seemed to ignite the atmosphere, had arrived the most amazing assortment of men. They had come out of nowhere! Pouring into the house, every shape and every size! Or so it had seemed to the bemused Randolph.

'Who the hell are these people?' He had cornered Blossom (really June) in the kitchen.

'All my sister's lovers, I presume . . .' She had answered with what he considered to be an astounding calm, almost as if she had intimate knowledge of every sodding one of them. Though, when he came to think about it, she must have met some of them when she had gone up for her holiday in London. He was on familiar terms with Professor Hamilton Hamilton, though it had to be said that the change in the poor fellow had been rather shattering. From having been a person of considerable charm and essential dignity, certainly with the clear evidence of a first class mind, he now struck Randolph as being simply a benign old fool. Almost gaga. Of course June was to blame. He clearly adored her, otherwise why in heaven's name should he make such a fool of himself careering all over the countryside in pursuit of his idol. Oh yes, he'd got the hots for her alright – it was rather pathetic to witness. Him in competition with so many men that much his junior.

Not that it was at all clear to an onlooker which of the assorted crew stood the best chance with June. For sheer physical beauty (though of too feminine an appeal for Randolph) he would have lain odds on the young Lord Valentine. The Czech film director certainly exuded a powerful brute force, there was no overlooking him. Him or his snarl! Nor was there any overlooking the chap who had the terrifyingly drunken wife in tow – the six-foot-four Director General. June had introduced him all around as her boss, but you didn't have to be a genius to see that there was more to it than that. The same with the clever little sod Zachary Ram. Randolph had enjoyed meeting him, he had been able to congratulate him on the bloody good job the chap was making of his Sunday television column. *The News* had made a shrewd move luring him away from *Views*. He was too bright to moulder away writing solely for a minority readership. That's what Randolph had been able to tell him.

But it had to be handed to June – she certainly kept her entourage under control! There was nobody flying at the others' throats. No scenes, no unpleasantness. Randolph could only wonder what sort of fools they were to be able to tolerate the situation. He certainly wouldn't have wished to share his wife in such a way!

Yes, it had been a strange week. Not as problematical as Blossom (still playing June) had expected. Christmas had passed in comparative calm. And there had been two of them to share the sexual load. She had doubts as to whether she would been able to cope on her own!

It was with this solution in mind that she had purchased several suitably festive outfits in duplicate before leaving London. It was years and years since she and June had dressed identically, it might be fun (and clever) to do so this Christmas. June had agreed. To be perfectly honest, both girls were rather excited at the prospect of Christmas – June was very much looking forward to seeing the 'team' again. It had been her suggestion – that

Blossom might care to sleep with Randolph for old times' sake. It was the least she could do in return for all the excitement that Blossom would be bringing with her.

Not that Blossom had expected the *whole bloody lot* to come!

It was amazing how many coincidences had suddenly materialised when each of them had learned that Blossom would be spending Christmas this year down with her twin sister in Cornwall.

'Puddlemouth,' Valentine had mused. 'Terrific surfing beach – yes, that's the place. Might be the very spot along that coast for the summer club I've been planning. A summer surfing club – a residential hotel on the beach, that would be the thing. "Valentine's by the Sea". What do you think? Christmas could be an ideal time to scout around for the right site . . .'

'Puddlemouth, not Puddlemouth in Cornwall? Good God!' Zachary Ram's vocal chords had careered off into the higher registers, as they did whenever he grew over-excited. 'My sister has just moved in that direction, near Lands End. She's gone to live with a potter. He's married. His wife continues to live on there as well, so I believe. It sounds a pretty cock-eyed set up, the sort of thing my sister would go for. She's trying to get me to go down there for Christmas. I had said no – but if you're going to be in the area . . .'

'Puddlemouth! Ha – what an extraordinary thing! A previous colleague and great friend of mine, now chairman of West Country Television, has a rather magnificent residence bang in the middle of Bodmin Moor. His wife went to school with mine, you know. And our children rather grew up with theirs – this was long before the old girl hit the bottle, of course. But I remember Puddlemouth quite well – don't they have that Arts Society there? Funny thing we were only discussing what to do about Christmas the other day. Basil was ringing from Bodmin, bemoaning the sad fact that now the children had flown the nest, Christmas wouldn't be what it once was. Matter of fact, he suggested then that the old girl and I should consider spending the festive season with them. Your being in the same neck of the woods puts a brighter complexion on things. I know the old girl would be

133

pleased as punch to go. Basil's cellars have rather a splendid reputation – she could be sozzled on the very best stuff . . .'

The Czech film director, riding on the crest of commercial success from *The Wing of the Rat*, had at last decided to begin shooting *Flying Fish* – a tense horror tale charting the first threat to the final extinction of an entire fishing community from a vast shoal of mutant fish which develop feathers and finally desert the ocean to flock the skies as predatory freaks, half-sprat, half-seagull. The location researchers had reported that Cornwall was the ideal setting for the saga. Hearing this the Czech director gave instructions that the tiny resort of Puddlemouth should be investigated since he himself had sound knowledge of a small fishing harbour there. A close friend of his would be spending Christmas in this place. It would be extremely pleasant if he could combine business with pleasure . . .

Professor Hamilton Hamilton had been the very first of the admirers to jump openly at the chance to be around at Christmas. He would really enjoy the opportunity to talk to Randolph once again. It was several years since they had been given the occasion for a lengthy discussion. He wanted to hear all about the extraordinary work that he had been given to understand Randolph was involved in at the minute. Was it really outright pornography? And he would be able to meet up with Blossom again. He had still not recovered from the disappointment of not getting together with her when she had been up in the summer. Now, at last, he would be in the company of the two girls together. He could barely conceal his impatience . . .

The girls had conducted many discussions over the phone regarding the arrangements.

'I think it has to be the rule, don't you, that no one can actually stay in the house – I mean we're not offering them a bed of their own.' June, who was in charge of the domestic arrangements (as mistress of the house) was anxious to know all these details.

Blossom agreed. 'Absolutely *not*. If you offered them a bed they wouldn't stay in it anyway. No, that's understood. Anyway, let's go through the list. The Director General will have what's her name – "four sheets to the wind" – in tow anyway. I should expect him over here about once, wouldn't you? And we three, you and Randy and me, will be invited over to Bodmin for dinner. We'll probably go, could be fun seeing how the other half lives.'

'What about Zachary Ram?' June still couldn't come to terms with the thought of Zachary Ram as one of the team. Well, that wasn't so strange because, as Blossom pointed out, he was the only one that June hadn't screwed yet. Though according to Blossom, he was quite an impressive performer, with great stamina and the biggest cock of the lot.

'Zachary? Oh well, he'll be staying with his sister, though of all of them I should think he'll be the one to try and wangle something. Because he's already explained to me that whatever he does he has to be near a television set over Christmas Day and Boxing Day – he has to file his copy for the following Sunday. Well, if he is over here, what will he do? Will we expect him to drive, pissed, back to Lands End? It seems a bit anti-social.'

They both thought about it. Blossom came up with the answer. 'If he expects to come over for both days, we should book him into Emily Shawl's for the night –'

June nodded, but dubiously. 'Perhaps we should stagger it a little. Perhaps coming over for both days is one day too many. Let's decide who'll come on each of those days. Nobody should come for both. I think Zachary Ram should have Christmas Day with his sister and come over here the day after. We know the Director General and Pissypops will be with their pals. We shall see either before, or after, the two crucial days.'

'Which leaves us with Professor Hamilton Hamilton, Valentine and –'

'And the European sadist! Will the Czech be arriving with members of his crew – surely not over Christmas?' June was surprised what a flickering anticipation she harboured at the thought of his arrival. *The Wing of the Rat* had been showing locally much to the fury of Pip and Willow who had not managed to con the desk that either of them was over eighteen. But she and Randolph had been to see the film and had enjoyed it immensely.

'He is one of June's, the director,' June had been able to say when the name had come up on the titles.

'Good chap, I'm sure,' had been Randolph's rather

abstracted reply. He had been pondering the application of a violent stimulation technique employed by the early Etruscans, as a means of maintaining an amazing extension of the male orgasm, without shrivelling the scrotum in the process. The shuddering foetus of an animal, ripped from the womb and used as a gripping background to the titles of this film, had reminded him somewhat of his own research. This Czech director must be a bit of a pervert, getting his rocks off on this sort of stuff.

'Is he a bit of a pervert? Does June say?' he asked June at the end.

'Why do you ask?' she asked innocently. The depravity of the film's violence had excited her. She even found that she was now squeezing Randolph's fingers rather more tightly than necessary as they strolled home through the darkened streets. Not because she was nervous, but because it gave her a small thrill to think that she might be hurting him.

'Ouch!' he exclaimed, suddenly conscious of the spiteful pressure, then adding rather irritably, 'Go easy on those fingers. I'll need them in the morning for typing, if you don't mind.'

June thought how much more pleasurable it would have been if he had landed her a blow round the chops.

'Ah – the European sadist!' Blossom had laughed softly, thinking with great affection of the violent bouts she had enjoyed with this tame brute. June had exaggerated the dangers. Why, these days Blossom had no fears at all of black eyes or similar trophies. Not on *her* body at any rate, though she felt proud of the liverish bruise *he* still bore to the left of his jaw. Not to mention the neat bite from the lobe of *his* ear. She still recalled the actual sensation as her front upper teeth met her lower – that, and his animal bellow of pain. Good fun. 'Well, the sadist is bringing his writer with him, and several others I believe. They don't celebrate the birth of our Lord, you know – it's against their political beliefs. They're no more believers than we are, so there isn't any reason why they shouldn't be working all through Christmas.' Blossom spoke with what June considered to be an unnecessarily condescending tone.

'Fuck all that,' she said loudly. 'I'm not some sodding

country bumpkin, I'm thinking of the Unions. He won't be coming with any of the crew members will he?'

Blossom chuckled down the phone. 'Keep your hair on – by the way I'm considering a change of hair colour again, are you?'

'Funny you should mention it – what about blonde?'

'Yes. I'd thought of blonde. Do you think my public would stand for it?'

June interrupted her, 'Never mind about that – do you think my husband will?

Each laughed contentedly, then Blossom said suddenly, 'It will be funny I must say. Seeing him.'

'And seeing the children again,' June added. 'And me.'

They went together to have their hair bleached and restyled, emerging from the hairdresser's like two sophisticated schoolboys. Planinum blonde, as blonde as Jean Harlow or Mae West. But crew-cut.

'You don't think this is going too far, do you Mrs Tree?' the hairdresser said anxiously to June. 'It's not you that I'm worried about, it's your sister. After all she is a celebrity. And the public is a funny thing, it likes to know where it is – you know what I mean. It gets used to seeing someone the way they are and then resents any drastic change.'

'Oh, bugger all that!' Blossom exclaimed gaily. 'Let's take the whole bloody lot off, that's what I say!'

'Well, if you're sure, Miss Day,' the poor girl had answered, concealing her private reservations. She had always thought that Mrs Tree was a little bit eccentric, her twin was obviously just as bad.

The end result was amazing. The entire salon had crowded round the two blondes. One on her own would have looked extraordinary enough, but the two of them together were truly uncanny.

'This is our most stylish – wouldn't you say, June?' Blossom (the real Blossom) had let the name June slip out without thinking.

The hairdresser looked from one to the other. Surely it had been Miss Day that had been sitting on the right, hadn't it? And yet Mrs Tree was addressing her remark to the twin on the left. Or had they switched around when

137

they had returned from the driers? That must have been it – for a moment there she had felt thoroughly confused. It didn't help matters that Mrs Tree was of a modern kind and so had never worn a wedding ring. That would have been one way of telling the two of them apart. Or if they were dressed differently. But no, identical from top to toe. Same jade green all-in-one sort of jumpsuits, latest London style (matching their eyes). Same honey-coloured cowboy boots (several shades deeper than their new hair). Only their coats were different, which was how the hairdresser had distinguished between the two as they had arrived for the appointment. Mrs Tree had been wearing her usual shaggy fur, racoon, that's what she called it. And there was no mistaking it. Once seen, never forgotten, like all of her clothes. Whereas Miss Day had come in wearing what looked like a very smart leather gentleman's overcoat, tightly belted with a huge stand-up collar. The same sort of honey colour as her boots. There was no doubt about it – they were an eye-catching pair. There were not many as eye-catching in Puddlemouth. Or anywhere come to that. There being two of them.

The twins looked at each other. Each knew what the other was thinking. The slip over the name had triggered off a new plan of action. Of course – why not revert back to being themselves! Just while Christmas lasted . . . They moved toward the door and took their coats from their hangers. June reached for the leather. Blossom wore the racoon, always her favourite winter coat. She had forgotten how very warm it was.

Professor Hamilton Hamilton maintained his erection throughout the Christmas dinner. He didn't want to, it was too damned uncomfortable for words. But there was simply nothing to be done that would ease the situation. Except the obvious of course.

And that for the time being was out of the question.

But he had plans.

The astounding (and immensely arousing) thing was that he simply could not tell the two girls apart. And though he had expected there to be this striking similarity, having never seen the two of them together like this, he had not imagined that it would have been this confusing.

Take this wonderful meal (wonderful though marred by the presence of a saturnine foreigner and a foppish English aristocrat) for instance. Each time either of the girls rose to bring various dishes to the table, and quite often they would be doing so together (each being as familiar with the kitchen as the other), he found that unless he actually kept his eyes on the one that he *knew* to be June then all was lost. He was completely at sea. There was absolutely no distinguishing between them. And what's more he couldn't even be sure that they were not playing a special sort of game between themselves. To deliberately confuse the guests still further.

More than once he had caught the dazzling clear green gaze of one of them settling on him with a special look of intimacy. This is June, he had been able to say to himself, reassured. Only to be the recipient of the same sort of meaningful half-smile from the other twin at the far side of the room. I was wrong, this must be June, he had been forced to correct himself. Which, he now wondered, had he made hurried love to this afternoon whilst helping with the washing-up? It had been a silent and short copulation, the most intense that he had experienced for some time. Schoolboy stuff, with the dreadful fear of imminent discovery – the rest of the household only up there around the bend of the stairs. All waiting to go for a wintry walk on the shore.

But he had to have her. There were no words spoken, not a single one.

She had been standing at the sink, preparing to tackle the saucepans. He had watched her tying a pinafore around her narrow waist, a striped red and white one. Curving over her flat belly and provocative hips, accentuating the tight fullness of the buttocks.

The atmosphere between them was tense with sexuality – he surely wasn't imagining that! If he was, she made no move to indicate that his attentions were in any way unwelcome. Though to suggest to him that time was of the essence, she had glanced warningly at the scarlet kitchen clock on the wall. He understood this. With an economy of movement he had brought her hips to his, skilfully unzipping his flies whilst slipping down the elasticised waist of her soft woollen slacks and the underlying tights. Then he plunged his prick in.

139

She was facing away from him, still at the sink, with a Brillo pad in one rubber-gloved hand and a soup-stained saucepan in the other. As he reared and bucked behind her, his fingers pressed around her front, amongst her pubic hair, to make sure that his excited penis should explode in the right hole. She bent forward from the waist to make this doubly certain. Once or twice, in his extreme rapture, he had withdrawn too far and in struggling to get back in had knocked on the wrong door. Buggery was all very well, but not best done in such desperate conditions. Not poised over a bowl full of Fairy Liquid.

Then he had come, panting and clutching onto the strings of her pinafore. Grappling to re-adjust his clothing and hers as he heard voices from the stairs. Hers first, since her hands were full – she had begun to scrub furiously with the Brillo around the inside of the saucepan leaving him to return her to respectability. He liked that. It showed trust. But the sacrifice caught him short, there was no time now to see to his own flies. People were here, they were pouring into the kitchen. Randolph was leading the way, followed closely by the young ones, Pip and Willow. Everyone seemed to be carrying a kite. The Professor felt faint, small specks of silver light suddenly appeared before his eyes. But he had the presence of mind to grab a dish-cloth from the draining-board and clutch it to his flagrant groin, fumbling beneath it to locate the lip of his zip. It had been a debilitating moment, quite ageing in a way, and it evidently showed on his face. Randolph had stepped back, staring. 'Professor – are you feeling yourself?'

Even that question had come as a shock since feeling himself was precisely what the Professor had been doing. His groping fingers beneath the dish-cloth had just come into contact with the slightly tacky surface of his still swollen cock. Nothing seemed to be in the right place.

He brought his hand guiltily to his face, leaving only one holding the fort. 'Feeling myself!' he echoed. His voice sounded hollow. The enchanting creature at the sink remained silent, though her shoulders shook slightly. No one could see her face. He dearly wanted to reassure himself that she was not in tears. The last thing in the world that he would have wished was to cause her distress. Now several of the others were staring at him too. The handsome effete young man, the cheerful son, and his sister. The sister was whispering, she was whispering to her father. At her words Randolph laughed out loud. 'Willow seems to think that you may need the lavatory and are much too polite to ask!'

'The Czech looks rather cheesed off – do you need any help?' Blossom was preparing to pour the brandy over the Christmas pudding, whilst June was busy with the white sauce.

June glanced over her shoulder towards the table. 'He shouldn't be. I gave him a bit in a gorse bush, his bum's scratched to smithereens. Didn't you notice? This afternoon we flew the kite to the top of the cliff. We were gone for about half an hour. I felt sure that you had noticed.' June looked at Blossom's face.

'Oh, I get it – you look like a cat who's been at the cream! Valentine?'

Blossom nodded. 'In your bedroom – we came back before the others. You remember, to put the kettle on for tea . . .'

It was necessary to keep checking with each other. As Blossom pointed out, they really ought to make a list as to who had had whom. Because if they were not careful, some greedy people would be getting more than their fair share. Doubling up, without them being any the wiser.

Randolph was the one who inadvertently found himself to be in that fortunate position. Like everyone else he had been bowled over by the new image that Blossom and June had presented. Though he had never said so he had always hankered after having a blonde in his bed. There was something so aesthetically pleasant about the sight of blonde hair on black satin sheets. And now that is what he had. And though loyalty to Blossom would have forbidden him from putting it into words, there was something decidedly erotic about having the two of them together in the house. Both blonde, both so exactly alike in their clothing. The whole set up delighted his senses. But he still prided himself on knowing which one was which – Christ he bloody well should after all these years!

On Christmas morning he arose at his usual time, it

141

was still dark, the first light had yet to break. He yawned and stretched. Blossom lay sleeping soundly in their bed. He looked at her lovingly then bent to kiss her mouth. She was ravishing, she was wearing a pearly white cotton nightgown, one with long sleeves and a ruffle of lace around the neck. The sort worn in times past. This summer she had used it as a summer dress on the beach, slipping it over her bikini. He had remarked then how well it suited her. But now with her short blonde hair she looked like a choirboy, or a cherub. She stirred beneath his kiss, arching her torso unconsciously as she slept. Randolph observed the shape of her breasts reform under the loose folds of the nightgown, twin pinnacles of cotton catching on her nipples. It was warm in the bedroom, they had reset the central heating to counteract this cold spell. The top coverings of the bed had been thrust low enough for Randolph to glimpse the cleft of his wife's buttocks, in which the nightgown had somehow got awkwardly trapped. She had rolled over and now lay as if in the womb, one leg higher than the other. Vulnerable. He sat on the edge of the bed feasting his eyes. Should he take her now, or should he do the usual thing – let her sleep and then have a session at a more reasonable hour.

His cock was fully erect, he looked down at it affectionately. 'That's all right, you greedy little sod – let's get upstairs and do some work. Plenty of time later for what you have in mind.' It didn't occur to him to masturbate. Since Blossom's return in the summer he had not done so once. With her handy, wanking seemed a terrible waste.

But his decision, he regretfully had to admit, was not very conducive to concentration. His research was not aiding matters. Studying Lo Duca's profusely illustrated *A History of Eroticism*, he found his thoughts wandering. Titillated initially by *The Turkish Bath*, a painting of voluptuous nudes by Ingres; he then found himself staring fixedly at the censor-cut shots of Brigitte Bardot's bare arse and suspenders from her film *Love is My Profession*. The shot is of her perched, skirts hitched and no knicks, on the edge of her lawyer's desk. She is offering him payment in the flesh. Lucky devil. Randolph leafed over without reading, until he came to three small frames from a French 'stag' film of 1925 (from *Sittengeschichte des*

142

Gehtemen und Verboten, Vienna). Then he gave up his attempt to work as a bad job. After all it was bloody Christmas Day – he could surely afford to take one day off. His brain wouldn't atrophy in that time and he felt he deserved to have the morning in bed with his wife. He sensed a special loving in her these last few days. He couldn't put his finger on it but it had been ever since the arrival of June. But then he might be wrong, it could be that he was approaching her differently. As if estranged yet, at the same time, sexually excited by her new blondeness. It was almost as if he were fucking a different girl! He gazed out at the calm sea, curiously calm today – yesterday it had been wild and too dangerous to swim. They had been forced to content themselves with simply skipping around in the surf, occasionally risking a daring dive beneath a particularly spectacular wave for the sheer fun of it. But being careful that at no time should any of them get out of their depth. Only last week a stranger had fallen to his almost instant death in this small bay, and swept out to sea before the rescue boats could do anything. The currents were absolutely treacherous with these tides.

Time for coffee. He would go and make one for himself and take one up to Blossom, but before that just a last lingering look at the cold apricot sky and the flat shining expanse of water disappearing to the horizon. As usual the sight filled him with elation.

It was in this mood, a mixture of spiritual serenity and sexual anticipation, that he descended the stairs on his way to the kitchen. He paused for a second at the closed door to his bedroom, thinking to enter. The inviting image of Blossom's rump had intruded on his mind's eye, it would be interesting just to investigate whether or not she was still asleep. But he decided against it, he really felt the need for a cup of coffee – to give him a quick boost for what he had in mind.

But she had beaten him to it! She was down in the kitchen already preparing coffee for him. He could smell the aroma drifting up the stairs even before he had passed the half-landing leading to June's bedroom. Oh, the darling! He hurried down. No one else was up, the rest of the house wouldn't be awake for ages even though it was

Christmas Day. He suspected that the kids would have opened their bedside presents last night, reasoning that by the time they had got to bed, well past midnight, it was already Christmas Day. There wouldn't be a sound from them for some time. Or June for that matter – not the way that she had rammed into the Remy Martin last night. She would have reason to regret that this morning! So, the way seemed to be clear. Blossom all to himself, a nice breakfast all on their own. But first . . .

'No Randy!'

'I insist.'

'But Randy –'

He had stripped her crimson kimono from her shoulders, finding to his pleasurable surprise that she had removed the demure and voluminous white cotton nightdress. This flimsy garment was altogether easier for the rape which he was perpetrating. Blossom enjoyed his rapes, they had discussed it in a detached fashion many times in recent months after he had violated her in this manner. But today her protesting struggles were really authentic. She knew how much her resistance excited him . . .

Rounding the stairs in her white cotton nightdress, yawning and rubbing her pleasurably prickly scalp (like a hedgehog, her short hair felt – or an unshaven cheek) Blossom paused on this Christmas morning. She thought she heard noises – were those kids up already!

She was coming down to check the turkey which had been in the oven all night on regulo 1, ensuring that it would be beautifully tender for this evening's dinner. It was also her intention to make coffee for herself and Randolph, he must surely be feeling like a cup by now. The question of whether June would appreciate being woken with the hangover she would be suffering this morning was something she hadn't yet decided.

She stood still, perfectly still. There was no doubt about it, there were people in the kitchen. There was a definite scuffling now and a suppressed snortling sound, accompanied by the unmistakeable heavy gasping of humans screwing . . .

'Fucking arseholes!!' Blossom caught her breath on her own involuntary expletive. It was just that the sight before her eyes was not what she had been expecting. Perfectly true she had anticipated a scene of vigorous fornication, with one of the participants being her sister. But she had not thought that her husband would be the other. It had crossed her mind that one of the team might have made it his business to arrive before the others – on the principle that the early worm catches the bird. But she was quite unprepared for it to have been Randolph.

She peered, fascinated, around the entrance into the kitchen. The sexual charade was being enacted beyond and through the open-plan dining area. Placed here at this hidden juncture, behind the giant dinner-gong, no one could witness her – observing.

It had often passed through her thoughts, the image of Randolph and June having it off. Many, many times since they had embarked on the life-swap she had tried to visualise it. Whereas at first she had preferred to blot it out of her mind, for fear of experiencing an oblique sensation of pain, she had later come mentally to fear it more and more. She wasn't jealous, she had never ever been jealous of June, of her twin. She couldn't be that. Such an emotion would be like being in competition with herself. It wasn't possible, not to be in competition – yet at the same time it was on the cards to wish to improve. To improve on past performances, to excel, to do better. In the case of making love and giving pleasure to Randolph it had always been Blossom's obsession to provide him with the greatest possible erotic enjoyment. These last couple of days and nights she had been going easy, letting him lead the way, encouraging but never taking the initiative as she used to before June had assumed the role of wife. Because with June, Randolph had seemed to have taken a different sexual role. More imaginative, more mannish, more perverted (if that was the right word) than he had been when she (Blossom) had been the instigator of their sexual games. His entire life was bound up with the subject these days, and for many years to come (so he had assured her joyfully) with the work he was writing. *Spiritual Spermatozoa – Significant Spontaneity* – The new title, now changed from *Spunk*. (*Spunk* being confusing to the British possessor of the lending library card, as also meaning 'pluck').

A rather fearful gagging noise now engaged Blossom's rapt attention. She peeped, recklessly taking a further step into the kitchen. Despite herself she found the experience of watching this tremendously arousing. She couldn't remember having had the pleasures of voyeurism before, but the circumstances – the fact that it was her own husband and her double (herself really) that she was privileged to watch, that made it even more arousing.

But what ferocity, what vigour, what brutishness he was displaying. This was rape! June was struggling, but to no end. Randolph's large hand was clamped over her mouth, from whence issued these strangulated guttural sounds. The poor girl appeared to be choking, but that made no difference to her fate. Her assailant was hell bent on getting his end away. Blossom's throat was dry with excitement. She thought of the time that she had ventured across the moors waiting to be picked up by Randolph in his big black limousine. That occasion had been one of pre-arranged rape. Since then she had not had the pleasure.

It only occurred to her now – Randolph must be under the impression that he was raping *her*! This was not a glimpse of clandestine infidelity at all! He had mistaken June for her – Blossom – the implications began to dawn on her. They had obviously not yet fully dawned on June (though she was to be forgiven for not thinking too clearly at this moment). She was struggling *too* much! June was playing it for real, anguished by the knowledge that Randolph was being unfaithful with her, the sister of his wife. Except that he wasn't – it couldn't be counted as that, not if he believed this person he was poking was his wife. *He must never, ever, be made aware that this was other than the truth!* Blossom felt this most strongly. If he knew of their life-swap, if he began to have any inkling that this was what the two of them had been up to, she knew the whole thing would crumble.

She couldn't have explained why, but in her mind it was extremely important to preserve the precious structure of her marriage. It seemed to her that the success of it rested on the foundation of absolute fidelity. She considered that she had continued to remain loyal and true to her husband. So far she had not once had intercourse with any other man throughout their entire marriage.

146

Not whilst she was being herself.

The affairs, the fucks, the sexual encounters, all the lovers since the life-swap had occurred whilst she was being June, not Blossom. The very first time with Professor Hamilton Hamilton, she had gone to bed with him as her sister – and he had never guessed that it had been otherwise.

She would have hated it to be common knowledge that Randolph Tree was a cuckold. He was too fine (he was too famous) a person to be tagged as that. And of course he could well, if he came to hear of any indiscretions on her part – he could very well start a little dallying of his own. What's sauce for the goose . . .

This way it was better, it was getting the best of both worlds.

She thought speedily about how to handle this current and potentially crucial situation.

June must be made aware that she, Blossom, was in the know. And that there was to be no spilling the beans to Randolph, above all. If she could catch June's demented attention over Randolph's heaving shoulder, she would give her the sign that everything was under control, that for the next hour or so she (Blossom) would pretend to be June. Would return to June's room and emerge at a time more convenient to all, giving June (and Randolph) a chance to collect themselves and present a proper public face. Then perhaps she (Blossom) would take over again . . .

Randolph was completely carried away on a dense wave of lust. He was having more than a little difficulty in breathing, his senses pounded. There was a dull ringing in each eardrum, accompanied by what sounded like a celestial choir. Christ Almighty, he had never heard music before! At one stage he had become dimly conscious that the struggling body beneath his own had suddenly slackened, passed through a brief period of limp inertia, and then had begun rocking in a thrilling rhythm tight with his own. He was aware that at the point of orgasm he shouted out. Afterwards he felt faintly bilious. And surprised to hear the strains of the heavenly choir still ringing in his ears.

The Salvation Army were singing carols in the street.

'That was a close shave – I didn't think that I would ever get your attention. To tell you the truth I was thinking of banging the gong. Randy wouldn't have noticed, he was really far gone.' Blossom giggled with June. They were comparing notes, keeping each other right up to date. Though that close shave had taken place almost a week ago, it gave both of them great amusement to relive certain highspots of this memorable time. Tomorrow was New Year's Eve, they were sitting in Blossom's bedroom putting the finishing touches to the costumes that they would be wearing at the Puddlemouth Society of Arts Fancy Dress Ball. They intended going as Tweedledum and Tweedledee. Of course.

The following morning Blossom would be leaving for London. It would be the first day of the New Year and in the evening she would be appearing on a new television quiz show as the mystery guest. From then on Cherie had booked her work through to the middle of the month. Personal appearances, radio programmes, magazine articles, photographic sessions. A gruelling few weeks, but it had reached the stage as Cherie had pointed out, where it was important to keep June Day's name in the public eye. Her career had to be carefully nurtured if it was to continue to be a success. They were already having difficulty in deciding whether or not to agree to a further Female Series. Cherie was tempted by the colossal fees that she had managed to negotiate. And yet she felt, as Blossom did, that there might be a definite sense of *déjà vu* in yet another series about women. Although this one would pursue the theme of women as entertainers, comic entertainers. Pure humour. And Blossom was very much drawn to the principle, especially since the plan would be to investigate countries other than Great Britain. She rather looked forward to a trip around the world. Even so she could not come to a decision. A sixth sense warned her to wait, she had the feeling that there was something bigger in the offing. So she and Cherie were holding fire, they had until the end of January to make up their minds. In the meantime, Cherie advised her to spread herself around the media as much as possible. She felt Blossom (believing her to be June) had been away long enough. It would be almost ten days since she had left London.

'Let's have a look at you then, you two!' Pip and Willow had barged into their mother's bedroom to inspect

Tweedledum and Tweedledee. They were about to be collected by their friends to spend tonight and New Year's Eve, and the following day on the friends' farm in the wilds where they bred lots of ponies. It meant that they wouldn't be seeing their mother again to say goodbye, but they were not aware of this. They were coming to say farewell to their celebrated aunt, so they thought.

Blossom kissed them, and hugged them very hard. It still surprised her how easily she could leave them. There was no pain at the parting. She wondered how they would have reacted to the knowledge that it was their true mother who was choosing to leave them. Would they have cried then? And would she? But this way, thank Christ, there were no emotional scenes. She had made a special point of studying the two of them very carefully over Christmas. It had been an inspired notion that she and June should revert back to being themselves. It had given Blossom a better chance of judging the reactions of Pip and Willow to herself, as their real mother. Had she noted any alarming symptoms of neurosis she would have reconsidered continuing with the life-switch. So far she had seen nothing to disturb her. She was certain that June was as warm and reassuring a mother figure as herself. There were certainly no worries in that direction. As Randolph so often declared, all that children really require is one positive touchstone. They had enough to cover a pebble-beach. She watched them now, kissing June.

'Bye Mum.'

'Bye Mum, mmm, you smell delicious.'

'Goodbye, my darlings. Have a lovely time – see you don't fall off any bloody ponies! We don't want to start the New Year with any broken bones –'

'No bloody fear, Mum –'

Blossom went to the top of the stairs to listen to the fragments of their disappearing conversation.

'She means *you* when she says falling off.' Pip's voice floated up accusingly.

'*Me*! You spiteful sod! She means you, if she means any bugger!' Willow's indignant answer sounded faint.

Blossom had the motherly instinct to shout down.

'And who the hell is *she* – the cat's mother?' But she didn't.

Five

Nice Nobs Plater collapsed whilst reading the Ten o'clock News on New Year's Eve. As a chilly cynic remarked, it was the final news flash of the dying year and turned out to be Nobs Plater's last.

But Blossom had no knowledge of the tragedy, not until she had managed to get the morning newspapers at Plymouth, running like a mad thing from the London train. The sad news was splashed over every front page.

He had suffered a fatal coronary before the entire nation. Being the professional that he was (a newscaster for fifteen years) he had reached the end of the news before keeling over, clutching violently at his heart. The reports suggested that he had died on the spot. Reading of the event Blossom felt a genuine tear spring to her eyes. Everyone liked nice Nobs Plater, a simple and uncomplicated man. Superbly suited to the job in hand. Grave and serious when the news required him to be so. Jaunty, even faintly flirtatious, when the occasion warranted a spot of jollity. A decent fellow, an all round popular chap, with not an ounce of ill-will in his entire body. It was, according to almost all of the editorials, as if a national monument was no more. The banner headline on the newspaper with the widest mass circulation read: *Nightie, night – Nobs!,* and beneath it in smaller print: *Alas – no more tomorrows!* 'Nightie, night – see you tomorrow.' That was how he had always ended his news readings.

'Snuffed it, poor sod!' the chap at the station newsstand had quipped, seeing Blossom stare. She had nodded. There would have been no point in disagreeing. She thought about it all the way to Paddington, about the implications and the repercussions of so sudden a death. What had he, poor old Nobs, been planning to do after the news. How would he have decided to see in the New Year. Certainly not in the way that he had!

She tried to think what she and June had been up to at the exact time of his departure from life. Had they not been leaving somewhere – the cocktail party at Basil's on Bodmin Moor? Or was that earlier – yes it must have been, because they could not have got back in time to see the New Year in at the Art Gallery otherwise. Although Randolph had driven like a demon. He was actually far from being sober. It would have been safer for them all to have accepted the offered lift in the Director General's chauffeur-driven Daimler. Randolph had pig-headedly refused to do that, he didn't care to abandon his own car on Bodmin Moor. Blossom secretly crossed her fingers all the way. But June had been prevailed upon to travel with the Director General. The Society of Arts Fancy Dress Ball was where he wished to see in the New Year. The real reason was that he was determined not to let June out of his sight. He had not yet had the chance of a Christmas poke.

It wasn't for want of trying. More than once he had manoeuvred it so that he and June should slip away from the cocktail party for a little spot of how's your father. 'How's your father' was the term that his friend Basil had used with a rather coarse wink, when the Director General had confided in him yesterday. It wasn't an expression that he was overkeen on himself and, as he had tried explaining to pal Basil, what he felt for this girl just wasn't like that. He had fallen deeply in love with her – further than that, he wanted her to be his wife.

Basil hadn't been able to see it. 'I know how it is, old man, you don't have to tell me. We all get as much as we can on the side, who doesn't in this game. But as for any marrying malarky – I should forget about that. For one thing you wouldn't ever be able to get rid of the old girl, old Cynthia, not without it costing you a bomb. And why bother? She turns a blind eye to whatever you get up to doesn't she?'

'A boozy eye,' the Director General said glumly. He was not too happy with the direction that this conversation had taken. Of course Basil had always been a crude bastard. It had been a mistake to confide his finer feelings to such a fellow, it had cheapened the whole thing. He didn't like discussing June as if she were anybody's whore. She was just not that sort of a girl.

He had missed her like hell this last week, and though they had spoken on the telephone as often as he had been able to escape from poor old Cynthia's drunkenly amorous clutches, it wasn't the same as seeing the wonderful child. And child was how he had come to regard her in the warmth of his growing love. As something golden and pure, as someone radiant and good who had come to him to bring life to his life. He wondered at these times of highly-charged emotional thoughts whether he might not be becoming a little senile. The first signs of an inner softening! For instance, in his daydreams, he and June were already married. More – she was carrying his child. She was pregnant with the son that he had never had. Her youthful body was bearing the fruit of their union. His entire existence seemed to have been geared to this fresh start. Cynthia was the only fly in the ointment.

It had been the hope of the Director General to have been able to slip off alone to the Fancy Dress Ball with June, he had already alerted his chauffeur that this would be his intention. But on returning from this mission to his despair he learned that Cynthia was aware of his plans. Not only was she coming too (she was upstairs at this very moment devising a fancy dress for herself and Basil's wife), but she had inveigled others of the party to come along too. There would be three car-loads in all.

But at least the Director General sat next to his love.

They had arrived in Puddlemouth by eleven-fifteen or so. All three cars stopping outside the Puddlemouth Society of Arts Gallery to disgorge the human content. The Director General noted to his annoyance that there had been enough room in the other two cars to have allowed him to travel on his own with June, had they managed to have given the extremely inebriated Cynthia the slip. His wife (how he winced at the term) had kept up a manic chattering the entire journey, high-pitched and completely incomprehensible to the other occupants of the Daimler. Every so often she would direct an especial leer in June's direction, wagging her finger and winking exaggeratedly. 'I sheen you beshore shumwhere . . .'

'You've seen June on the television, many times, Cynthia, my dear,' the Director General had eventually explained, sighing heavily. That was after the eleventh time that she had said it. The memory of Cynthia, slipping down the staircase in her sequined gown, returned to June each time. What a lot had happened since then. She wondered if Blossom wasn't beginning to long for a brief respite from the life of the career-woman, whether she might have liked to stay on down here for a while as herself. They hadn't really talked about that. As for herself, she was quite content whichever way it went. She loved either life – knowing that each was at her disposal. Tonight, on the walls of the Art Gallery, hung three of her large seascapes. Blossom hadn't seen those yet, it was to be a surprise. Tonight, apart from being the Fancy Dress Ball, was the official opening of the Society's New Year Exhibition. June looked forward to Blossom's reaction. She only hoped that the Director General's Daimler would not arrive much later than Blossom and Randolph, otherwise the tricky situation might occur of someone congratulating Blossom on paintings that she had no idea existed!

In fact, since Randolph insisted on parking his car in the garage, knowing full well that he would be incapable of doing so later, June made her Tweedledum entrance before Blossom and Randy. They were stumbling from the garage along the dimly lit cobbled street. The Gallery was situated in the very oldest part of Puddlemouth, there being barely room for the Daimler to even pass along the alleyway at some points. In view of this the chauffeurs parked a short distance from the Gallery and everyone at the end of the evening (whenever that occurred) would walk that short step to be driven back. June, of course would remain in Puddlemouth.

It had been difficult persuading the Director General (on Blossom's behalf) that she would really rather not travel back to London tomorrow with him in the Daimler. She very much preferred going on the train, and in any case with Cynthia in the car as well . . . He had regretfully accepted her decision. The real reason was that little Zachary Ram was meeting Blossom's train. Both she and June had felt rather guilty over Zachary. Neither of them felt that he had got much of a look in over Christmas. Though June had one sweaty session in the privacy of her bedroom with him after lunch on Boxing Day. Afterwards she and Blossom had compared notes on the impressive length (and width) of his cock. Blossom conceding to her sister, since she was the one who had last seen it, that when extended the whole thing reached up past the navel. Blossom harboured doubts about this, whilst granting that it would be easy to gain that impression. After all, Zachary Ram was quite a little person and it could be argued that the distance up to his navel was less than a larger person's anyway. It was a pretty hefty weapon either way. Both girls agreed that it was a wonder its owner didn't walk with a stoop, with all that weight hanging down in his drawers.

'If someone thought of tying a broom-head to his handle, he could double-up on his job as a street-sweeper on his way to work –' June began saying against Blossom's guffaws.

'Yeah –' they continued together, spluttering exactly the same thing. 'Without even having to bend over – ha ha ha!' Their gaiety was contagious.

By the time everyone had deposited their coats, and made small and quite unnecessary repairs to their make-up, it was almost twenty minutes to twelve. There would be a bar extension through to two o'clock in the morning, so there was no fear of not being able to get a drink. Even so, everyone wished to have a full glass in their hand by the time midnight was striking. 'Wozzont shat she pointa –' Cynthia kept saying, rather aggressively. 'Chew haff a lill chink for Snew Yere!'

No one could begin to guess what she had come as, but part of her fancy-dress consisted of her wearing a white bath-towel, wrapped around the bodice of her very expensive evening gown. That and an alarming amount of scarlet lipstick applied to the tip of her finely chiselled nose. June, feeling a pang of conscience, thought that someone ought to be doing something about Cynthia. She looked ridiculous, presenting herself thus – perhaps the lipstick on her nose had been intended for her mouth. 'You tell her,' June urged Blossom, whilst they were still in the cloakroom, 'and for Christ's sake take that towel off her as well. She wouldn't look too bad without those.'

But it was not to be. 'You have lipstick on your nose, I think, unless I am very much mistaken.' Blossom had ventured politely, attempting at the same time to loosen the towel.

Cynthia had spun round viciously, clutching the towel in talon-like claws. 'Shmine!' Then she had glared at Blossom through meanly narrowed eyes, thrusting her face forward like a ferocious rodent. 'I sheen you beshore shumwhere . . .'

The girls gave it up as a bad job.

'Come on Bloss – I've something to show you.' June led the way to the far end of the gallery where her three large seascapes occupied one of the most important walls of the exhibition. But others had already beaten her to it. Standing in an admiring group before the paintings were Randolph, Emily Shawl, Bodmin Basil, and, rubbing his hands together with great delight and appreciation – the Director General.

They all turned at the approach of the twins. Randolph had two full glasses in his hand, one for himself and one for Blossom.

The Director General had been similarly thoughtful. 'Your drink, my dear.' He had neglected to bring one along for his wife, secure in the knowledge that she would head straight for the bar. June stepped forward, smiling so warmly that his old heart somersaulted crazily against his ribs.

Randolph held a glass toward the twin standing behind. 'Blossom,' his eyes twinkled, 'a fabulous start for the New Year – you have just made your first professional sale!' And he lifted his own glass toward the nearest seascape. The Director General had purchased the painting for the foyer of Television Tower, it was exactly what was needed

155

in that concrete monstrosity. They had been looking for just this sort of breath of the elements, this glorious burst of vitality for a long time . . . Bodmin Basil endorsed his opinion and not to be outdone he bought the second of the three paintings. He had the ideal space in his house, he knew the wall. Between the windows in the dining room, with the westerly view of the moors . . . Emily Shawl sidled up with her box of tiny red stars in her hand and, biding her time, waiting for the most suitable pause in the conversation, she announced that the Selection Committee of the Puddlemouth Society of Arts had chosen to purchase a Blossom Tree seascape as one of their annual acquisitions for their Permanent Collection of Members' Works . . .

With four minutes to go to the striking of midnight June Day had sold one thousand, five hundred pounds' worth of paintings. A bewildered Blossom received all the congratulations.

Midnight chimed. Two telephone calls from London to Puddlemouth were being cancelled out, not only by each other, but by a third from Prague, and a fourth from the University of Oxford. All four calls had been firm arrangements made between June (or Blossom standing in for June) and Lord Valentine, Zachary Ram, the Czech director, and Professor Hamilton Hamilton. It was to be a secret, but each of the callers intended to make a proposal of marriage. Although at least two of them (Zachary Ram and the Czech) despised betrothal between human beings as the height of bourgeois mentality. Nevertheless this would be the intention of all – if there had been an answer to their call.

The thing was that June (and of course Blossom) had clean forgotten any such arrangement. And had they remembered, there was nothing that they could have done about it now.

As the chimes died away, after everybody had kissed everybody that it was possible to kiss, including kissing them twice if they happened to be handy – and then again if something special had accidentally been ignited – June stole out of the door. So did the Director General.

Cynthia was sozzled. She knew she was because, swaying here at the bar, she had begun to see double. However much she screwed up her eyes, however desperately she tried to focus – by closing first her left eye and then the other – she still kept seeing two instead of one. She was really searching for her husband, but there were so many people. Crowds that shouted around her, singing and linking arms in a ridiculous fashion. She thought she had seen him just a second ago. A person in baggy check trousers and what looked like a schoolboy's blazer had been beside him. The person had very short yellow hair with a little peaked cap sitting at the back of the head. And (this was where it began to be worrying) this person had their arms around another person who seemed to be the same person . . . Cynthia shut her eyes, blinked, then looked again. She was seeing double. There was no doubt about it. The thing to do was to steady herself with another little drink. She chose to drink brandy, although she had started the evening rather demurely on Champagne. Proceeding cautiously to Martinis, from them through to Bloody Marys. Then riproaring straight on to neat Scotch. She could probably do with a spot of fresh air, this was the trouble. There were too many people shoving and pushing. They were behaving like animals, it was absolutely monstrous . . . heaving all around her . . . she had to get out. Outside to some fresh air and to some sanity. A small sob broke in her throat as she wavered unsteadily through the boisterous revellers. Where was her husband? She needed him desperately, she needed him . . .

And then she saw him.

He was way ahead of her, as far as she could see – he was pushing his way through in the direction of the door. Now he had reached it. It was open already, the person ahead of him had opened it. That person was the one with the yellow hair and the little peaked cap. But now there was only one of her. Thank God she had stopped seeing double! And thank God –it looked as if they were going home.

The Director General was panting. It was extremely difficult to walk in this wind, even with their arms around each other he and June were finding it hard to stand upright. They had rounded the corner that led down to the beach – a romantic desire had swept over him – this was where he wished to make love to his love – on the beach and under the stars. But there were no stars, and there was barely a moon. The vast stretch of the sky was heavy with scudding clouds racing across the thin lemon light leaking through a shrouded crescent. The moon. These were heavy gale conditions, there would be no boats out tonight. The noise of the breaking surf was tumultuous in their ears. And the Director General found himself responding with an answering passing in his soul. This was the life! He lifted his face to the ferocious heavens, savouring the salt spray on his lips. Not looking, he stumbled. June held him tight.

'Be careful!' she warned. 'Best to look where you're going here – there's a drop down there straight into the sea. I'm taking us to a sheltered place I know.'

He followed her advice, humbly, consumed by his love.

Behind them unsteadily Cynthia followed too, consumed by her irritation. What a fucking long way to the shitty Daimler . . .

Six

'Guess what.'

'What?'

'Just guess.'

'What – guess anything?'

'Yes – anything. Go ahead and guess anything you like about me.'

'Ah – about you! That's a clue. About you. I guess –'

'Yes – go on, guessing.'

'I guess about you – I know it – I guess that you, June Day (though still posing in Puddlemouth as Blossom Tree), are –'

'Yes? What?'

'Are pregnant!'

'Oh Bloss –' June was disappointed, she had wanted to say it herself, not be told like this. 'How did you guess!?'

Blossom laughed into the telephone. 'Well, my darling, it was only a guess. But are you really? But that's wonderful, absolutely smashing! Christ, you must be thrilled! Have you told Randy yet? What does he say? When is it due? Ooh, I shall be able to be godmother!'

There was silence at the end of the line.

Blossom burbled on, heedlessly. 'Well, it is about time – let's face it. Every woman,' she assumed a purposely pompous voice, 'should experience the wonder of childbirth.' Eventually she realised that something was wrong and then she expressed her concern.

'I haven't told Randy yet because,' June responded slowly to Blossom's anxious promptings, 'because for one thing I wasn't certain till this morning. I got the results in the post from one of those Pregnancy Advisory addresses. I thought it wiser to do it that way than go to this new doctor down here.'

'Clever thinking,' Blossom spoke gently. She could tell that June was really upset. But why? With her sort of news she should be the happiest girl in the world.

'Yes. Although I sort of *knew* that I was pregnant –you do, don't you. Remember when you said you knew even before the poke was over that you had conceived Pip?'

'Yes, that's right, I did. Is that what happened with you? I mean can you actually trace it back to a particular screw?'

'Would that I could!' June wailed, raising her voice. 'You're not working it out are you . . .'

The facts of the matter were that ever since June had settled into the life-switch, really settled in, the idea of having a baby had appealed to her more and more. The set-up was so perfect, besides which she had waited long enough. It had never been her intention to travel through life childless, so why not start now? If she and Tiny had stayed together, a child had been one of the next items on the agenda. That had been the main regret when they had split up – that having a child would have to be postponed. If she didn't look out she would be leaving it too late.

But she hadn't told anybody that this was in her mind. Not even Blossom, particularly not Blossom. The reason being that she felt that it would be a form of blackmail, a way of preventing Blossom from returning to being herself (if she had wished to). June felt this very strongly. She didn't want it to look as though she was planning to stay for ever and ever. The whole thing needed to be open-ended at all times. It wasn't as if she had relinquished her career anyway, she still had it in mind to return to being the (now) very celebrated June Day. But it was just that of late she had been feeling exceptionally broody. She found herself unexpectedly peering into prams parked outside shops. For no reason at all she had purchased a tiny and exquisite Victorian christening robe – and had hidden it so that no one should see. It was ridiculous.

It was more than that, it was ridiculous and it was irresponsible. Two months running, in October *and* in December, she had inadvertently forgotten to take her Pill! This was something that she had never, ever done. Waiting for the first period to appear after the October carelessness had been a nail-biting time of wild delight and deep disappointment. She had been half a day late, by her hysterical calculations. And was already engrossing herself in the 'Naming the Baby' chapter of *The Guinness Book of Names*, secretly of course, when she had felt the all too familiar rush of moistness flooding into her knickers. At the sight of the scarlet stain she had collapsed on the lavatory seat and wept. She hadn't realised until that moment how much she had wanted a child.

Even so, in November, she had taken careful precautions. After all it wasn't up to her to decide, just like that, to become pregnant. Surely the father had some say in the matter. If she were anything of a woman she would discuss it all round. First talk to Blossom – it surprised her that her sister hadn't brought the subject up herself. They more often than not conducted their thoughts along the same lines. The fact that Blossom hadn't mentioned it

160

inhibited June from doing so. She supposed she would come round to it all in good time.

But in December exactly the same thing had happened all over again! This time June accepted that what she was doing was not even sub-conscious any more. What was worse was that it was not only once, but *three times*, on three successive mornings that she didn't take the Pill. And she had played a childish game with herself, pretending to be confused. Pretending that she had taken it, yet at the same time not checking up, not going to look even at the clear evidence on the sheet of pills. It was as if she were a gambler trapped in her own obsession. She was risking it, only risking it. This was her reasoning. Anyhow, whoever heard of anybody becoming pregnant after missing one pill (OK, three pills)? Hadn't statistics proved that it was virtually a million to one chance of this happening? So if she did happen to turn out to be that one, rather than the million, then the whole thing must be in the hands of fate. She was *meant* to conceive. This baby had been preordained – if it became a reality under such circumstance.

This was the way that June looked at it.

But something else had motivated this reckless behaviour – the knowledge that the team of lovers would be down. Knowing that instead of one man making love to her (Randy), there would now be five more – surely one of the sexy buggers would score a bulls-eye!

But now she was in a state of confusion. She desperately needed Blossom to tell her what to think.

'Fucking arseholes!' Had been Blossom's first wise comment on fully realizing the implications. Her second reaction had been to laugh. And laugh. It had been minutes before she had been able to speak again. By which time June had begun to see the funny side too.

'Very few people would believe this, you know, kid –' Blossom chuckled happily. 'A choice of six as to who is the father. Well, my darling, it's up to you. Every single one of them has proposed already. So it can't be said to be a shotgun wedding can it, whoever you choose – rather neat that. I must say that you have timed it a treat. Well, which one do you think? I'm afraid I can't be of any help at all. I wouldn't be able to choose, I haven't any favourites between them, have you? I think they're all absolutely gorgeous. Of course,' her voice became thoughtful, 'there are other alternatives. You could stay with Randy, I mean the baby could be his. It's a one in six chance – very low odds for anyone with a betting streak . . .'

June interrupted and spoke in a rush. 'That's the thing – I couldn't do that. I couldn't stay and have the baby. He's made an appointment this week for a vasectomy. He told me last night. He said he'd been thinking about it for a long time and now he's made up his mind. He says that we've enough children, no responsible person should foist more than two on the world. And that since we've got one of each anyway – both of them little sods, he said, but I'm sure he was only joking, you know how he does go on about them – anyway what he finished by saying was that the very last thing he wanted around the house was another stinking bundle of swaddling clothes, forever shitting out of one end and squalling out of the other. I had no idea that he felt so vicious about small babies – he was really vituperative!'

Blossom gave a long drawn-out sigh. 'I must admit that I'd forgotten. Yes. I'm afraid it's all coming back. He did rather loathe Pip and Willow when they were babies. Lots of men do. And of course they did disturb the nights, he was positively childish about that. I didn't ever tell anyone but did you know that one morning he put Pip in the dustbin. After a really terrible night when the poor little thing was teething and we hadn't had more than an hour of sleep all night. But can you imagine a grown man doing that! And the child's father too! Honestly it nearly split the marriage in two, I can tell you. I very nearly left him over that. There I was running around like a thing demented when I found the pram empty outside the front door. I mean I only looked in the dustbin because I wasn't myself and anywhere seemed possible – I even looked down the lavatory. That would have been a better place, that's what I screamed at him afterwards. Then, I said, the brute could have flushed the little thing straight into the sewers, no evidence. As it was, I was only just in time with the dustbin. The refuse cart was almost with us. It was just there at the top of the road – can you imagine!

And the bastard would have let me believe that the baby had been snatched by one of those baby-snatchers. There had been a lot about them in the news at the time, which is what had given him the idea. Of course, he was going through a bad time with his work around then. A small crying baby doesn't go with deep concentration, I must say.'

Both girls decided that staying on with Randolph would be a very bad idea. Hey-ho, time for another switch . . .

It was inconvenient that week. Momentous things were happening in June Day's career. She had been tipped as the likeliest successor to the nice and late lamented Nobs Plater. Yes – it was thought that the all-important position of prime newscaster for Universal Television should now be given to a woman. June Day was on a short list of seven. This week should be the decider. It was being put to the nation to choose their own newscaster. The situation was absolutely unprecedented.

A master-plan had been devised whereby all seven finalists should be given the Ten o'clock News to read. One a night. Thus providing viewers with the opportunity of seeing each of the candidates for the job in fair and unprejudiced conditions. A national poll would be conducted to discover the public's choice. The findings of which would be made known by the end of the day. It would be conducted exactly like a political event, just the same as the general election, with similar polling booths set up all over the country, hourly reports taking place on the television. Even at this point, before all the candidates had taken their turn, the betting shops were doing brisk business. June Day was already ahead of the rest – clear favourite with odds at two-to-one. Tomorrow, Wednesday night, would be her turn at ten o'clock. Although her detractors claimed that giving her a Wednesday night would be unfairly to her advantage since it was the one night that the masses watched the box – her supporters felt that she needed no such boost. Her popularity placed her automatically ahead.

She won.

Seven

Blossom Tree signed her name with a flourish at the bottom of her canvas, then she stood back to admire the painting. She had been worried that it wouldn't be dry in time for collection. Tomorrow all twenty of her works were being driven to The Sliced Eye Gallery in London. Her first one-woman exhibition would be opening on Monday. The whole family would be going up for the private view.

It was still difficult to regard herself as a professional (and financially successful) artist. June was the one who had started the ball rolling with her wonderful seascapes. Everything had taken off when the seascape bought by the Director General, had been so ceremoniously hung in the foyer of Television Tower. So many people had come to the party! Including – and this was what really had done it – the Art critic of *The News*. Zachary Ram had brought him along. Sweet thing. And the following Sunday the critic had made lengthy mention of the 'exuberant and absolutely splendid painting – the sea-spray flies from the canvas, of the Cornish artist, Ms Blossom Tree, wife of the famous philosopher Randolph Tree, and sister of television star Ms June Day'.

And then the London Galleries had descended.

It had been rather awkward really, all of them wanting to see her new seascapes. There weren't any new ones. Nor were there likely to be. Blossom was back, being Blossom, and try as she might she had been unable to find inspiration in the sea. Nudes were what she liked painting, nudes in the abstract with a touch of surrealism. The nearest that she could approach the sea in her work were her mermaids. She had plenty of those if anyone was interested.

The Sliced Eye Gallery in Soho was very interested indeed.

Blossom yawned. She was tired, it was almost ten o'clock. Good. June would be on in a minute.

It was lovely to be able to see June every day like this. To be able to watch her getting bigger every day. One more month, that was all till the baby's birth – the most publicised birth since Princess Anne had hers. And yet how the revelation of June Day's pregnancy had rent the nation in two only five months ago.

An unmarried mother reading the British news!

It had made headlines, and not just in this country. Many women everywhere sprang up in fierce defence of June Day. What courage, what honour, what pride and what bravery. June Day epitomised the position of her sex today. She was a champion. She was a cause. She was an example.

There was no way that she could have lost her job.

No one knew who the father was. In outrageous interviews of staggering candour June Day admitted as much. She had been, so she proudly announced, to bed with five (she and Blossom agreed to leave mention of a sixth out of this. Randolph was not too stupid to put two and two together) different men during the month that she had conceived. There was no way of knowing who the father might be. She had explained this to the gentlemen concerned. No she would prefer not to give their names, however if they themselves wished to reveal their identity then she had no objection. It was really up to them . . .

Her revelations, her flabbergasting revelations, made her the hottest property on television. The viewing ratings for the Ten o'clock News every night were the highest ever recorded for any single programme in the entire history of the medium. The rival station could do nothing, they were helpless. And the programmes either side of the news suffered too. The rivals made a colossal bid for her services. The figure mentioned was 'astronomical'. In panic her own employers made a similar offer simply to keep her with them. For the next six months at least June Day would be top news.

And when she had had the baby – well it wouldn't end there. She had already stated that not only did she have

165

every intention of resuming work as soon as she was able. But that she looked forward to having a large and happy family. She might even get married one day to one of her five gentlemen – they all seemed perfectly content to wait. Her child would be regarded as belonging, one fifth, to each and every one of them. Not every child was fortunate enough to be blessed with so many acknowledged fathers . . .

Eight

Randolph Tree kissed his wife's nipples slowly and with great love. She had been away from him for a week collecting June's children for a visit and he had missed her very much. In that time he had practised the habits of a monk. By the time of her return he had been ready to explode. For the very first time in their married life they had beaten their own record. He was forty-five and he had just fucked his wife ten times within twenty-four hours.

'You are my life,' he whispered to her tenderly.

'And you are mine,' she whispered back.

This was true. He was her life. Well, he was really, as much as any man. So June thought. But then that was how it should be – she and Blossom sharing everything as they always had. And as they would continue to do.

The door of the bedroom swung open. Two small boys

stood there, two absolutely identical children. June's twin sons. 'Blossom – your nephews.' Randolph smiled at the little bastards, knowing perfectly well that he was their father.

FAST AND LOOSE

For Sylvia, who taught me to make fun . . .

'Keeping this well-oiled, eh?' My medical practitioner eased his professional fingers up my uterus on his annual check, winking as he did so.

'Any warts on my womb?' I'd been going to ask. Instead I said, 'Well-oiled William, whatever do you mean?' And we looked at each other slyly, me naked from the waist down and he surreptitiously stirring the folded flesh of my innards. A bit pointless really, there was no chance of a poke, never would be. We both of us had much too much to lose, most precious of all being the long friendship between us. They were enjoyable though, these exploratory sessions. Titillating. I always slid off the couch wanting a whole lot more. It would have to be another nice bout with the old vibrator when I got back home. There'd just about be time for that and a quick bath before settling down to work again. Two more chapters to write before tomorrow.

'Plenty of sexual activity, that's what I mean as you very well know. A healthy body requires regular servicing in all departments.'

'Don't be dirty, doctor.' I quickly scrambled into my knickers, ones which I noticed, to my shame, had seen much better days, whilst William washed his hands at the sink. That was the trouble with not having a husband around any more, all sorts of personal things went to pot. My daughters were always telling me off about it, about the way that I'd let myself go. 'I leave the glamour to you lovely darlings!' I said to them. It was the wearing of Bertie's clothes that they minded most. 'Daddy's dead, Mummy,' they'd each of them take it in turns to say, 'and wearing his clothes is not going to bring him back again.'

171

No. The bugger.

'What I mean to say, Letty,' William had resumed his professional manner once more at his desk and was regarding me seriously behind the sober rims of his reading spectacles. He presumably would have removed those had we attempted consummation. Would he have washed his cock after the event, as carefully as he had just washed his hands? Or would it have been a more jocular occasion – a swift swill of the dick under the running tap, the friendly offer of a face flannel for my own fishy fanny, my pulsating parts . . .

They were pulsating now, purring away (presumably why parts were called pussies), so much so that as soon as I'd sat down opposite William I quickly crossed my legs, for fear his keen medical ears might pick up the whirring wavelength. The sound to me was like that of a trapped bird in a chimney. William was a kind friend and a fine physician, but he was inclined to hand out personal advice and medical prescriptions a little too freely. And whilst it was obvious that I was about to be treated to some home truths of a helpful nature, I hadn't the time or the inclination to queue up in the chemist's for a bottle of what William might consider a soothing cure-all for my clacking cunt.

But his next words showed that he was off on another tack altogether. He said, 'To tell you the truth, I'm becoming a little concerned about the proper balance of your life. All this work, all this writing, this new career you've carved out for yourself since Bertie's death – it's admirable Letty, dear. But I wonder if you're not neglecting other areas, to the detriment of the whole. Have you looked at yourself lately? It saddens me to have to say this, but the Lady Lettice Patch that I like to remember would no more have ventured forth –'

'Looking like I do?' I finished it for him and gave him the sort of smile I gave to Daisy and Tadpole when they started going on about it. Self-satisfied and utterly infuriating, according to them. 'You mean wearing Bertie's stuff still, is that what you mean, William? Well, I admit that when I first started doing it I did derive a strange comfort from the feeling that he was still there right next to my skin. But then as time went on there seemed no reason to change back into my own clothes. And as it is,' I gave what I meant to be a roguish twinkle, which failed to puncture his boring solemnity, 'the fashions appear to have caught up with me. Haven't you noticed – everyone's dressing up in gent's clothing these days. I must say I find Bertie's big old suits a bloody sight more comfortable now than my slinky dresses used to be.'

'A better fit, Letty.'

'What do you mean, William?'

'Just what I say. You've put on too much weight. Those slinky dresses wouldn't begin to go near you any longer.'

'My former figure must have gone the same way as your bedside manner.'

'I speak frankly. You are a fat person now and you must face it.'

'If I should ever develop a terminal disease, William, be a good chap and let the BBC tell me. They still know how to break news with a flicker of finesse. Get one of those telecasters to announce it to the nation. It wouldn't be any more wounding.'

He stared at me in appalled amazement as I threw back my head and began to howl.

I didn't very often cry, I had never been a crying sort. A sudden rush of tears caused by pre-menstrual tension was the most that I might shed in any one month. Even the month that Bertie had died. Instead of crying I'd started writing the first of my five novels. One novel a year. Five years of work. Five years of food. Five years without sex. Without the feel of human flesh crushed up against my own, sweat on sweat, pore on pore, two mouths mashing together, limbs lunging, lust equally lubricating the tongue and the twatty . . .

But there wasn't a waking moment when I didn't long for it though! Not a living second when some sensitive part of me didn't ache to be stroked, to be touched, to be coaxed, to be raped. Hadn't I strolled the streets, promenaded the parks, taken short cuts over the Common long after it was safe for a woman to be out on her own – in the desperate hope of a straightforward rape? And anything would have done, everything would have been acceptable to relieve my frustration. The newspapers were full of complaints from molested females (lucky things).

Young virgins, the victims of exuberant gang-bangs (how I would have welcomed such excessive attentions!). Shy spinsters soured by sexual overtures. Nice nursing mothers losing their milk from nasty, naughty suggestions. Sleeping wives seduced by absolute strangers. Geriatrics goaded to violence towards rude intruders. Trembling nurses into terror of persistent peeping-toms. Widows bewailing the attention of wankers. The list was never-ending, every bugger getting something. Every bugger, but me.

My nose was running, it ran down over my upper lip and spread into my mouth.

'Your nose is running. You look awful, here's a tissue.' William passed me the box. There was a calculating expression in his eyes.

'When you've blown a bit,' he said, 'stand up and come round this side. It's about time you were given some satisfaction, Letty, old girl.' I stopped crying and stared at him, licking my upper lip clean of the clear salty snot. I felt stupid and ugly, and sulky because of it. He was pandering to me, my doctor, as if to a plain, podgy child. Offering me a bribe in order to make me do something unpleasant.

'Satisfaction?' For one palpitating second when he stretched forward to take my hand, drawing me round to his side of the desk, I thought that I might be greeted with the sight of his open flies. No such luck!

'The weighing-scales,' he said, gesturing. 'My guess from just looking at you would be that you've hit the eleven stone mark. One stone up on what you were this time last year, which in turn was one and a half up on the weight you were at the time of Bertie's death. I would like to congratulate you, Letty, on this grotesque transformation. There –' He pushed me onto the scales; they registered eleven stone and three pounds. 'Now are you satisfied?'

Not really.

'Taxi!'

'Where to, sir?'

I looked at the driver, but he was perfectly serious. 'Oh – anywhere along Oxford Street,' I said, lowering my octaves. If he had genuinely mistaken me for a man, it was just as well not to disillusion him – it would only lead to embarrassment. I'd found that people took exception, as if you were trying to make a fool of them. Once a stockbroker type had become so enraged that he'd punched me on the nose. I punched him back, a low blow in the bollocks. And trod on his toes for good measure. A bit childish.

'Selfridges do, sir?'

'Fine,' I growled back, not too deeply, I didn't want to give myself a sore throat. I'd be in amongst people tomorrow at the health farm, my weight all too obviously my reason for going. I didn't want to have to start off by complaining of additional ailments. As it was, I would feel self-conscious enough, despite William's assurances to the contrary. 'They're all fatsos there, you won't feel out of place.' And he'd smacked my flabby botty through Bertie's fine serge. 'Believe me, Letty, it will do you the world of good. A dive in at the deep end. Drastic measures, that's what we need at this stage to break the eating syndrome. See if I'm not right. As soon as your body starts to regain its former shape, your natural interest in sex will return. It's a question of confidence, that's what it is. This preoccupation with food is a sublimation of your sex-drive . . .'

What did he mean by my *natural* interest in sex returning? Had he been aware, without even being told, of my present *unnatural* obsession with it?

The taxi dropped me awkwardly at the end of a straggling bus queue. Two smirking girls nudged each other and started giggling. I just smiled at them until each of their gazes faltered in turn. Their contempt failed to touch me. The real me, many layers inside, had nothing to do with the odd appearance I presented to the world. I got as much amusement out of the spectacle as everyone else. I laughed now at a tow-haired toddler tugging urgently at his mother's sleeve, but instead of returning my jollity, his saucer eyes filled with terror. I stuck my tongue out. Miserable little sod! I turned to join the teeming throngs of Oxford Street, God alone knew what I thought I was doing arriving just before rush-hour. Except that it was late-night closing, which gave me until seven to find something suitable to wear.

'Can't I go as I am, William?' I'd said to him mulishly

when he'd passed me a list of what I was to take to wear at this Slivers place, this health farm he'd booked me into. 'I'm certainly not in the mood for buying cocktail gowns and all that crap.'

He'd looked surprised. 'Cocktail gowns! Slivers isn't a social club, Letty, it's a serious establishment. The only cocktails you'll be served will be carrot cocktails. But I even doubt that. You will probably be put right away on lemon juice only. You'll be leading the life of a semi-invalid. This list doesn't contain any finery.'

Nor did it: *warm dressing-gown and shower cap for use in the treatment rooms; leotards, slacks, shorts, or track-suit for exercise sessions; swimming costume or trunks for use in the pool; sturdy outdoor shoes/wellingtons and warm clothing for cross-country walks; tennis and riding clothes for these outdoor activities; warm rug for sitting outside in spring and autumn. NOTE: Guests find that one of the most relaxing things about a stay at Slivers is that they have no need to dress up, and casual wear, such as track-suits or dressing-gowns, is acceptable throughout the day and evening. However, you may like to bring something a little more formal for the Saturday night dinner party.*

But I was feeling truculent, in the mood for an altercation. Christ, all I'd come to this fucking surgery for was a simple cervical smear. And now I was being talked into forking out in the region of four hundred quid for a fortnight of sucking on lemons. ('You can afford it,' William had cajoled. 'Look on it as a holiday, you haven't had one for over five years – when Bertie was still alive.' Bloody marvellous holiday!

'What,' I'd stabbed at the *Saturday night dinner party*, 'about this then? How am I supposed to turn up for this, eh? Wearing Bertie's tie and tails, I suppose!'

'Why not?' William had replied, perfectly pleasantly. 'Though after just a week's weight loss I think you'll find your ideas changing. Why not pack a nice frock in case? My mother-in-law found a perfectly charming outfit in Selfridges Outsize Department on her last visit.'

I'd glared at him savagely. It was the first time that I had been directed to the Outsize Department.

But it wasn't the last. 'Ladies Fashions?' I enquired of a passing assistant inside Selfridges. 'Outsize,' she said matter-of-factly, and gave me the floor. It didn't occur to her that Outsize was the last place I wanted. Inside I was tiny, tiny, tiny . . .

'If you'd care to jump onto the scales, Lady Patch?' Gunter Ragg, the resident consultant of Slivers smiled his suave smile.

I measured the height from the carpet up to the scales to be roughtly three inches, so I jumped. Just to show there was still life in the old girl and to introduce a welcome note of informality.

The din was stupendous. My show of athleticism appeared to have triggered off an electric charge. Bells began ringing all over the building; a radio blared forth; a television somewhere had been turned on full blast; the sounds of several powerful vehicles screeching to a standstill were now followed by the slamming of heavy car doors and an excited volume of words. New arrivals.

Gunter Ragg took no notice. 'Eleven stone, six pounds, shall we say – we don't record ounces.' I caught a whiff of an expensive after-shave. 'Why bother with ounces,' I said cheerfully. So I'd put on three pounds with last night's little

binge! A slap-up meal out with Daisy and this nice lesbian she's taken up with, and Tadpole with the rather terrible Toby still in tow. Though there was another little chap, with an unfortunate pimple on the side of his nose, who seemed fascinated by her. 'Darling Tadpole,' I'd whispered to her, 'I can't wait to know – have you had it off with Pimples yet?'

'Ssh, Mummy!' She'd hissed. 'It's all in the balance, I'm working my balls off – his name is Bart Deco. You've heard of him, he's brilliant. He manages Windsor Shag –'

'*The* Windsor Shag, the one who's been fucking Princess –'

'Yes, Mummy, *that* one.' Tadpole squeezed my arm sweetly. I know I do irritate my daughters by not being absolutely up on the latest things, but they try not to show how much it gets on their nerves. It pays off in the end if you bring up your children nicely.

'And,' she continued whispering, 'he has just taken over Kid Lips – you *must* remember from the sixties?'

I nodded. 'Dimly.' Then I looked over at the little chap

177

again, I could see the attraction. He was a short squirt of a thing, crew-cut, with one earring. But there was an undeniable power there. Butch. Bertie would have gone for him. 'You ought to buy him some Clearasil, darling,' I said, squinting at the livid pimple.

'Ssh!' By the sharpness of that 'ssh' I felt she must really like him. We were eating at Langan's Brasserie, one of the girls' favourite restaurants, around the corner from the Ritz and the Mayfair hotel. I was the fattest person in the place, and the oldest. Neither achievement was difficult. But I wasn't the oddest, not by any means. I'd watched the arresting figure of someone half-female, half-male making their way over to our table. It was as if a plumb-line had been hung down the centre of the body. The left-hand side was dressed as a man, in a man's formal dinner jacket, one leg wearing one trouser-leg, a black sock and a shiny patent shoe. Whilst the right-hand side was done up to the nines like a girl who had gone in for a 'Come Dancing' contest, in black and white sequins and yards of ruched tulle. The whole outfit had been skilfully sewn down the middle. But the head, handsomely leonine on the one side with a dark, heavy eyebrow and black, bushy beard, was the most disconcerting. The female half was so fragile, the carmine lips curling in a cat-like smile (reminding me of Vivien Leigh as Scarlett O'Hara in *Gone with the Wind*). The complexion was clear, flawless over the high cheek-bone, a subtle shading of rouge drawing attention to the dramatic slanting of the eye and the arching brow above it.

'Hello Mavis! How's things!' Bart Deco greeted the vision with obvious affection and I could see that Daisy and Tadpole were both pleased to make a welcome. 'Hi, Billy, you look great!' Daisy stood up for an embrace. But now I was confused as to what gender Billy Mavis actually was. Not that it worried me. I was used to the sexual ambivalence of those around me. But I had never before been presented with so definite a choice. The clue, I supposed, would lie in whether Billy Mavis was left- or right-handed. Whichever side I shook hands with on introduction would, I decided, determine the sex of this exquisite in my own mind. I didn't have long to wait.

'Mummy,' Daisy began, now wrapped in the contrasting arms of Billy Mavis, 'I don't think you two have met, have you? Unless it was before Billy went to the West Coast. He did look very different then, you might not have recognised him.' Everyone laughed.

'Oh really?' I was interested. It was after Bertie and I had been to Cornwall for a brief break that *he* had become noticeably more effeminate. Savage scenery can do that to human beings, bring out the basics. 'Where in the west did you visit, Billy? I have a weakness for Cornwall. I find Devon altogether a little too bland for my primitive tastes. The roar of the ocean, the howling embrace of the winds . . .' I looked around the table and smiled. Everyone was staring at me.

Tadpole spoke up. 'Should we order some Perrier water for Mummy, Daisy?' But Bart 'Pimples' Deco resented the inference. 'Your old Mum's fine, leave her alone. Are you sitting down, Mavis? – C'mon, grab up a chair. Budge along you others, let him get in there with Mum. Lady Patch,' he rose and bowed to me, 'this sight for sore eyes is the celebrated Billy. He's a cabaret artiste, you'll see him perform in a mo, he's just back from LA.'

'The West Coast of *America*, Mummy,' Daisy said kindly.

I took a quick gulp of my wine as a waiter poured a glassful for Billy, who was now seated at my side. 'To Mummy,' he said, lifting his drink. And the entire table joined him in his sweet little toast.

I found the whole thing, I must admit, quite moving. The young are so generous with their affection.

'I haven't broken the scales, Dr Ragg, not yet – though well on the way to doing so at this weight!' I spoke easily and without self-consciousness. On arrival in the foyer, I had passed two human elephants and a gross hippopotamus, whose hips made mine seem as slender as those of an earwig. I liked Slivers. What's more I was very impressed by the results that Dr Ragg and his team appeared to achieve. Several departing guests were being collected by friends and relatives while the receptionist, of diplomatically substantial build, had registered my particulars. And not one of these guests was capable of walking without aid, so frail and emaciated were they. Their

179

clothing hung around their bodies like carelessly furled flags, and one woman contrived to step clean out of her shoes, her feet had shrunk so. Whilst another kept blathering about how many earrings she had lost, she had not managed to retain even the flesh of her lobes. And yet these people appeared ecstatic, their eyes glowed with the saintly expression of martyrs, as ones who had undergone a cathartic experience. I regarded their staggering progress with envy but with the excited anticipation of feeling that the same success might soon be within my grasp. My admiring awe wasn't shared by all.

'Those people are *starving*! tragic!' the receptionist muttered to herself, whilst searching for the key to my room. Her impassioned outburst, not meant for my ears, had been caused by the sight of a swooning skeleton who had just collapsed against the boot of his relative's car. The relative, whom I had at first presumed to be his mother, was probably his wife. On closer scrutiny, and few could tear·their eyes from the riveting scene, the young man was obviously well into his forties. His face was familiar as an actor who appeared regulary in an excruciating television series, one which I always took great pleasure in switching off as soon as the titles and his fatuous features formed on the screen. In future, I reflected, it might be fun to sit it out just to check whether or not the poor sod was managing to hang onto his sylph-like figure. It hadn't occurred to me that one would catch these enlivening glimpses of famed persons, and their heartening humiliations, here at Slivers. My visit was becoming more interesting by the minute.

Gunter Ragg, whom I had addressed as 'Dr', corrected me smoothly, he was apparently not a medical practitioner. His many qualifications, which he rattled off incomprehensibly, taking the trouble to point them out in the Slivers' prospectus, turned out to be in other affiliated, though lesser fields.

'I don't give a jot, my dear Gunter,' I said to him gently, sensing a defensive chink in the sophisticated façade. 'It is not given to all of us to excel academically. I myself am a fine example of a child who failed dismally in school and yet now, in later life, I have manged to make a go of things. Have you read any of my books, by the way?

I always like to enquire of people as soon as I meet them. I find it clears the air and gets rid of any embarrassment that they may suffer in case they haven't.'

I beamed at him encouragingly, but my good humour failed to do the trick. Now the unfortunate creature was positively squirming, quite a usual reaction, I found, to my question. Few readers of literary pretension had ever read my novels. The sort of rubbish I wrote would have been considered much too much down-market. Pulp fiction with the special relish of crudely frank pornography, good-hearted filth. I had found writing it a fine way of hanging onto my sanity and lessening the painful ferocity of my sexual frustration in the beginning. But now I wrote this way because I enjoyed reading my own rude words so much, and it pleased me to pander to my public. Few of the stuff-shirted friends that Bertie and I had shared were able to countenance what they considered to be a degrading pursuit, but it exhilarated me to cock a snook in their direction. My reputation was my own, I could besmirch it in any way that I chose. And the girls, on consultation, agreed that it would be absolutely daft to write under a pseudonym. And so I write under Lettice Field, my maiden name. It only saddens me that Bertie hasn't survived to share my success. Though if he were still alive I should never have turned into a professional writer. I would still have been just doodling in my old diaries, and reading bits of them aloud in bed to titillate and delight us both, and by the end whoever was with us . . .

I bubbled with laughter at the pleasure the memory of those hectic bedtimes brought me, breaking the strained silence of poor Gunter Ragg's discomforture. 'Don't bother to reply, my dear,' I said to him magnanimously. 'Here,' I poked around in Bertie's briefcase, which I had taken for my own use as a handbag, 'I always carry some spare paperbacks. Peruse them at your leisure – they're full of fornication, but I expect that a man in your position, in the medically affiliated fields, won't be too thrown off balance by that, eh! Now if you'll be so good as to point me in the direction of lunch?'

But now Gunter Ragg had recovered his equilibrium, he was on home ground. 'Ah, well, now Lady Patch, don't let's raise our hopes too high at the prospect of lunch. Lemon and hot water, with a spoonful of honey, is all that you have to look forward to, I fear. Slivers operates on kill or cure principles.'

'I know,' I leaned over and punched his lean stomach, 'I saw some of the casualties on their way out. The poor buggers looked to me as if they were stretcher cases.'

He stiffened only slightly. 'Ah yes. Y Block. No, what you saw there were our cured anorexics. They were indeed stretcher cases when they were admitted. Slivers claims to aid the recovery of all those unfortunates who suffer problems with food.'

'You mean, Gunter dear, that they're not all in here for being greedy pigs like me.'

'Exactly, Lady Patch. I trust you will excuse me if I don't escort you into lunch. Would you kindly tell the next patient in the waiting room that I am free to see him?'

It wasn't a him, the next patient, it was a her. A her whom I hadn't seen in the flesh since my school days, Agatha Tatters, now Dame Agatha Tatters, honoured for her distinguished contribution to British politics. The unrelenting profile, the high-bridged nose, flaring nostrils, firm chin and challenging chest still put me in mind of the prow of a ship. Indeed, as countless political commentators had pointed out, it was this noble aspect of Dame Agatha's appearance (unchanged since as Head Girl she had captained the hockey team through to so many brilliant victories) that had so swiftly established her as one of Great Britain's political assets. She seemed so much to embody the spirit and strength of Boadicea that the public trusted her. Votes would have been cast in her favour, whichever party she chose to represent.

This had been well-proven already. Despite the waverings of Dame Agatha's political allegiance over the years between the three major parties, Conservative, Labour, and latterly Liberal (poor dears can do with my help, was the reason she gave in interviews), she had managed not only to claim a seat but to heartily increase the majority each time she stood. There seemed no way of imagining a House of Commons without Dame Agatha, no possible chance that she would ever cease to be part of British Parliament.

Except, except that now, standing back to encompass the entirety of my old school idol (I still harboured the heartache of my schoolgirl crush) I was disagreeably reminded of a recent cruel caricature of her that I had chanced upon in *The Times*. And having been reminded of that one, it occurred to me that I had seen others drawn in the same slightly malicious manner. Having been featured as Helen of Troy in the past, always treated by cartoonists in an affectionately respectful fashion, these latest line drawings seemed to be suggesting that Dame Agatha Tatters' proud prow was beginning to show signs of deterioration. That, like Britain herself, the brave Dame was in danger of sinking into torpor and flaccidity. And I was forced to admit that there were undeniable grounds for this view. Apart from the same unmistakeable facial structure and the angle of that imperious head, the rest of poor old Agatha was now submerged beneath a glutinous layer of soft, shifting flesh. Had it been headless, I'm afraid I would not have been able to identify the body. However, it seemed that she was having the same difficulty in placing me.

'Agatha Tatters! Christ-all-bloody-mighty!' I had hailed her with the same loud-mouthed exuberance for which I'd been exceptional at school. Just about the *only* thing about me which had been exceptional, not counting the doggedness of my devotion to this goddess before me. Only the iciness of her expression checked me from hurling myself to her feet and slavering over her ankles (now tragically swollen and frankly hideous).

'It's me,' I squeaked excitedly, lapsing into a schoolgirlish lisp, bobbing my recently-recorded eleven stone, six pounds before her proud and chiselled features, hopping like a child from one foot to the other. 'It's me.' I drew breath and plunged on, eyes shining, mouth loose in an asinine grin. 'It's Loopy – it's Loopy Lettice! It's Loopy Lettice Field . . .'

I waited for the penny to drop.

Someone farted into what seemed an eternity. At first I thought it was me, caused by my own excitement. But then the rude sound repeated itself. I realised that behind the closed door of his office Gunter Ragg was impatiently summoning his next client.

183

Neither Agatha nor I paid any attention. We were too engrossed with each other.

The penny had dropped.

'Little Loopy Lettice . . . it can't be . . . little Loopy . . .' The high fluting voice held a note of soft wonder as if recalling a loved one who was no longer of this life. As if by repeating the name she was able to summon from the past the shining memory of someone with whom she had been unforgettably intimate. It couldn't have been me. The furthest that I had ever got with the golden girl, and the nearest to intimacy, was cradling her hockey stick between my furtively parted legs. And pressing it hard against the sanitary napkin that Matron had issued for my newly menstruating body. But I had never confessed this to her (or to anyone else!). And I doubted that the hockey stick, though seemingly blessed with a magic capacity of its own on the field, was so exceptional as to be able to transmit my guilty secret to its glorious owner. It was, now I came to think of it, my very first sexual aid. Bertie would have enjoyed the tale.

'Well, well – little Loopy Lettice Field . . .' the muted fluting continued.

'Hm, hm,' I cleared my throat exaggeratedly. I couldn't stop myself from behaving like a first former. But my voice had returned to normal which was a relief. 'Not quite as little, I'm afraid!' I thumped my titties, one each side, like a gorilla beating its breast in the jungle. And then I thwacked my bulging backside. 'Not with bubs and a bum like mine, no sirree!'

Dame Agatha interrupted just as I had been about to get going on other obese portions of my anatomy. Now that I could sense that rescue and recovery from this imprisoning fatty encasement were being scheduled, I seemed not to mind about how ugly I had encouraged by body to become. She said, 'But surely it is no longer Lettice Field – didn't I read somewhere, though I'm going back a bit now, that you had married into the aristocracy, Loopy?'

Time had erased the memory of her snobbery, the snobbery of all the girls in that ghastly school. That world was so distant and ridiculous to me now. The phrase 'married into the aristocracy' I hadn't heard for years; it had a pathetically dated ring to it.

'Yes, I changed my name twenty-five years ago from Field to Patch, smaller package but a more impressive handle. But I don't pay much attention to being a Lady, it impresses other people more than it impresses me. I write under my maiden name. Yes, I'm a novelist now. I'm not like you Agnes, I didn't earn my title. I didn't do anything remarkable for it.' Dame Agnes drew a deep breath, her chest heaved and expanded as if someone had blown air into a barrage balloon.

'You sacrificed yourself in marriage to a man – I happen to consider that pretty remarkable.' She enunciated the words with great care and a touch of scornful pomposity. These were sentiments which she had given an airing to many times. They had a stale ring to them, but were delivered with such weightiness and wisdom that it was easy to understand her success in the world of politics. You poor bitch, I thought, you haven't listened to yourself for years. Not to what you've been saying. You've grown accustomed to regarding yourself as an authority, and now you simply perpetuate the image. No wonder you look as you do.

But that thought brought my train to a standstill. Jesus, there was only the difference of five years between us. Five years and a few stone. We'd both ended up here, in the same place searching for help. 'Bollocks!' I exploded. 'When I married Bertie I was all over the place. An overgrown schoolgirl – some people would say that I haven't changed – but it took Bertie and marriage to make a woman of me. I honestly do believe that.' Bloody liar.

The door opened behind me. Gunter Ragg cleared his throat politely. In the distance yet another bell pealed.

Dame Agatha's eyes widened. 'Whoops,' she said girlishly. 'We'd better get a move on Loopy, old girl. That's the lemon-juice bell – look, you run on ahead and bag us a nice seat near the window. I shan't be long weighing in here, then we can have a nice long chinwag. It will be just like being back at school!'

Doing as I was told, running on ahead to bag a nice seat near the window, it was exactly like being back at school. Not that I had ever been honoured there with a nice long chinwag with Agatha Tatters, but this running on ahead for other people was something I was very well used to.

All my forty-five years, so it seemed to me, had been spent preparing the path, oiling the wheels, softening the way for everyone else. Making it nice for them. Not that I minded, no – very much the reverse. I'd pounced on it as my role in life. A cheerful fetcher and carrier, an uncomplaining slave, a comforting companion. It was my devious method of making myself indispensable to those whom I admired; my way of being permitted to enjoy the company of persons whose special qualities placed them far outside my proper sphere. I had been at it since about the age of seven. It wasn't until later in my scholastic career that I realised how obviously obsequious my childish efforts must have appeared to the more discerning adult. It was a teacher who had said it, the words remain in my brain. 'It's that small girl I can't stand,' she had remarked to another, well within my hearing 'Uriah Heep, that's who she reminds me of.'

'Really?' The other had sounded surprised. 'I find her very sweet. She is the only one who stays behind to help clear up after class.'

'Yes – that's just what I mean.'

But now, running the short length of this opulent corridor, I found myself short of breath. It was no joke being bra-less like this, stripped down to Bertie's pyjamas and dressing-gown. No bloody wonder that old Agatha hadn't recognised me. At school I had been a shrimp of a thing, athletic and tautly strung, always springing up in her path. 'Like a little Jack-in-a-Box!' She had teased me one lyrical day, the first time she'd allowed me to carry her hockey-stick from the muddy field. And since these popping-up antics had seemed to find favour in my cherished darling's eyes, I had continued to use them. So much so that when I returned home for half-terms I brought the displeasure of my mother upon my head. She claimed my ducking and weaving, and bobbing and squirming had become an embarrassment. It looked as if I continually needed to spend a penny, though I had never shown evidence of a weak bladder before. Perhaps these were the early symptoms of St Vitus' Dance?

All I'd wished to prove was the agile flexibility of my body.

There wasn't much evidence of it now.

I had taken an honest look at myself in the bedroom at home after the dinner with the girls. It didn't stand up to inspection. 'Never mind, my darling,' I said to my mirror, 'this little sod's got no eyes. ' And I fetched my vibrator, the big black one with various attachments (all of them effective!), and stood there looking at myself with it stuck in between my crossed legs. Grinning like a sex maniac. It felt good.

It felt good but, it looked bloody obscene. There I was, poor old me, fat and over forty, feeling myself up with a plastic prick, purchased through the post. Preparing myself for a pretty savage orgasm, self-induced. Giving myself a naughty nightcap, a succulent sweetie, a nice sensation to send me to sleep. Pathetic! Pathetic, I thought, and I rammed my best friend up further, now spreading my legs as I collapsed onto the bed. Then throwing them up high in the air until my toes were in fear of touching the lowest tip of the tinkling chandelier.

'Woweeee! Yippeeyooo!' I screamed out at the top of my lungs, laughing and yodelling as loud as I could. The pain was exquisite, almost more than I could bear. But I rammed it in a bit more, rolling it round and round at the fastest speed.

That seemed to do the trick.

'Hooray! HOOray! HOORAY!!' I yelled like blue murder.

A pounding sounded on the door, which I had craftily locked first. 'Fuck off – I'm having fun!' I screamed from my bed, laughing hysterically. The pounding ceased, then came Tadpole's voice. 'C'mon Bart,' I heard her say. 'It's only Mummy doing her thing, best to leave her alone.'

So she'd managed to capture Pimples after all! Jolly good for her!

After I'd climaxed I lay and thought about things. Upstairs I supposed Daisy would by now be going down on her new friend, whatever her name was. They appeared so briefly on the scene, these pals of my daughters, that there was never much point in committing their names to memory. This girl, less boisterous than the usual run of Daisy's gay girlfriends, was called something like Sheila. From what I could gather at dinner, she was an Australian dentist, rather a useful contact. One never knew when one might require urgent attention in the molar regions, though, since Bertie, these hazards had receded from my life. The night that he'd brought back the Glaswegian docker, we could have done with someone like Sheila around. He'd knocked poor Bertie's upper dentures into a fine old mess, dislodging his jawbone whilst so doing – before dumping me with a dose of gonorrhoea. Very nice. Just what I wanted.

From somewhere came a burst of shrill music followed by the sudden slamming of a door. That would be Tadpole's powerful sound system. She lived day and night with the stereo full on. That the rest of us could barely hear it once her door was shut spoke highly for the solid structure of this old house. It was a very good reason for not moving, although in my heart I did feel that it was time the girls fled the nest and found homes of their own. After all, Daisy was twenty now, and Tadpole would be twenty in a month. I had remained with my own mother until I was twenty-four, but then she was an invalid. I had no other choice, though God knows I was longing, absolutely longing, to get away. Yet as soon as she had died I fell straight into marriage with Bertie. Silly bitch. Forfeiting one form of imprisonment for another, playing the same role again, accepting the responsibility for the other person's total welfare and happiness. As if I needed them just as much as they needed me, my dependants.

Perhaps that's what I was perpetuating with Daisy and Tadpole, making life at home so pleasant, so comfortable, so convenient, that it would seem pointless for either of them to consider leaving. Without consciously wanting to I had contrived to weave gossamer bonds as strong as the conventional sort. Was this my weakness or one which I had subtly encouraged in them? It was not only time that the girls struck out on their own, but also only fair that I should give myself the chance to see if I could go it alone.

Lying back on my bed at home, listening to the night traffic of Portland Place still streaming past, I had looked up at the magnificence of the chandelier above me. This room had once upon a time been our dining-room. What evenings, what gatherings, what gossip, what intrigues had taken place beneath that intricate assemblage of glittering glass! These days, thank Christ, I was no longer called upon to fulfil these social functions. We rarely entertained, or rather I rarely entertained down here on the ground floor in my suite of rooms. Upstairs, in their separate flats, God alone knew what Daisy and Tadpole got up to. It was with this in mind that I had the entire house converted after Bertie's accident. It wasn't as if the girls and I lived in each other's pockets. It's just that if I had been them I would have preferred not to be living on the same premises as my mother. Nor even in the same fucking city, if I'd had a choice with my own! Poor old thing.

Stretching high with one toe, managing (only just) to support my swollen body on my shoulders, I touched the chandelier and set it tinkling. Occasionally when Tadpole, immediately above, embarked on some marathon sexual bout with a young man, the chandelier would start all on its own. It was lovely.

I would lie there imagining exactly what they were doing to each other. Was he on top of her, or the other way round? Were her beautiful breasts (both my daughters were famed for the ripeness of their curves) in his mouth? Had he buggered her yet? Would she put her finger inside his arsehole? When he came would he cry? Would he withdraw his cock or remain in her cunt? Would she then choose to suck that same cock back to life, tasting herself in the process?

I used to find it arousing, thinking these thoughts. It was sad. A case of the elders feeding off the young. Age revitalised by youth. But better than nothing. It proved that there was still something left down there in my drawers. My own private parts hadn't atrophied yet, and with my substitute prick to see me through the nights and the technicolour images of what was going on upstairs aflame in my mind, I wasn't doing so badly.

In any case it all helped me with my work. My daughters willingly provided the source of invaluable research. And with one passing through a homosexual stage (though she currently insisted that it would go on forever), and the other eager to screw anything that moved, including the cat and the canary, it was no wonder that my writing was as torrid as it was. Why bother to indulge myself with this sort of sex-life, when my daughters did it so much better!

That's what I said to myself. But the true reason was fear

– fear of ridicule, fear of humiliation. Above all, fear of
rejection. I had been forty, almost forty, five years ago
when Bertie was killed. We had been planning an
enormous celebratory party. It would have taken place
five days after his death. Instead it was turned into his
funeral. He'd have laughed at that. 'Forty,' he kept on
saying. 'That's when life begins, Letty, my angel!' The
bugger. But I'd forgiven him now . . .

Coming to the end of the short corridor and rounding its
corner I came to a further one which seemed to lead
directly to the centre of Slivers. I had already reached this
junction once this morning from a different approach
when I was seen to my room. But I recognised the broad,
curving staircase leading up to the bedroom. Before, it
had been deserted, there'd been no one in sight. Now
human beings thronged down the steps, elbowing each
other out of the way, clinging to anything that would give
them support. The banister, each other, the picture
frames on the wall; several had dispensed with the use of
their legs and were simply descending like small children,
sliding all the way down on their bums.

The sight was astounding, I stared in astonishment.
The strangest part of it was that none of them were
speaking, there was no sound at all. It was as if I were
watching a silent film of the rush-hour in an Underground
station. Except that everyone here was clothed in night
attire, the variety of which was amazing. If I had
harboured any doubts as to the suitability of my choosing
to wear Bertie's old pyjamas and dressing gown, those
fears were now reassured. At Slivers, I was gratefully
coming to realise, nobody gave a fuck what you wore.

A blazing-eyed beauty of about Daisy's age fell forward
onto the shoulders of a pot-bellied dwarf, whose fiery
tresses curled down to her waist. The beauty was
completely enveloped in one of those snowy white Victorian nightdresses, so beloved of the young. Daisy and
Tadpole had gone in for them a few years ago, until the
ironing of all the frills had eventually got them down. The
dwarf had opted for a hideously unflattering quilted nylon
dressing gown, a harsh lemon yellow, which did devastating things to the ginger hair. The cascade of hair

completely obscured the face from my angle so that it was impossible to tell what age this rotund little creature was. Until, as bodily contact was made between her and the beauty, she spun around and I was able to see that this was a child, a girl of about twelve or thirteen at the most. She would have passed as pretty, had it not been for the babyish pout of her lips and the podginess of her face. There was something there that could have been salvaged, presumably somebody else thought so, too, or else she wouldn't have been here. But attention was also required elsewhere; her attitude to others left a lot to be desired. From my vantage point I could see her spitefully shift support from the beauty precariously balanced on her shoulders, knowing that the other would most certainly fall. Which she did, crumpling piteously in a decorative heap on the lower steps. Not a soul appeared affected by the sight. They continued to forge purposefully ahead, swerving to avoid the supine shape beneath their slippered feet. I was the only one to offer assistance.

'May I help you,' I said, in what I intended to be my gentlest voice. The beauty, and she was exquisite in close-up, raised her heart-shaped face to mine. The violet of the shadowed eye-lids intensified the brilliant violet of the eyes. I thought that I had never seen such aristocratic cheek-bones, nor such remarkably chiselled lips. This girl could be Russian, a descendant of the Czar; the tapering fingertips which she now held to her trembling mouth betrayed the royalty of her forbears.

I leaned forward to help her to her unsteady feet.

'Piss off!' she spat at me in a strong South London accent, 'I'm gonna puke up!' And she ejected a stream of vomit over the banisters. It drenched herself and an ornate velvet sofa, which being of an oyster hue, fortunately toned rather well.

'I'm afraid I left her to it. The sight and smell of sick has never been my idea of fun,' I said to Dame Agatha as we sat in the nice window seat that I'd managed to bag for her. 'I saw too much of it with my mother, poor darling. At the end she couldn't keep anything down. And it always put me off Channel crossings with Bertie. All those particles of regurgitated food flying around deck. It's more unpalatable when you happen to be an excellent sailor like me, you know.' I wrinkled my face up to show my distaste, though in truth it was the acidity of the lemon juice we were drinking. Was this really all that we could expect to be getting for the rest of the fortnight! My heart rose at the thought of the little edible items which I had had the foresight to stow away in secret places amongst my suitcases.

Dame Agatha's carrying voice cut through my greedy thoughts. 'Then you'll just have to get used to it, Loopy, old girl.'

'What?' I said, startled.

'Particles of regurgitated food flying around deck – plenty of it here. The only chance the troops get of having second helpings!' She gave a coarse laugh.

'You mean –' I couldn't think what she meant.

'I mean that there's bugger-all to eat here and so naturally, human nature being what it is, everyone has a go at cheating. They smuggle stuff in, they bribe the gardener – do you know what the going rate for a Mars bar is in this place? It's a fiver, but you can pay more if the stocks are running low. And of course, since the stomach has shrunk with all this drastic reduction of intake, it rebels. It throws up. That is what you've just witnessed, a dirty cheat. Her indisposition was only what she deserved.'

I looked at Dame Agatha with awe. Her lofty words must mean that she herself didn't cheat, that she would not sink so low as to deal in the black market for a Mars bar. It figured. Such honourable behaviour was only what one would have expected from Dame Agatha. Noble in countenance, word, thought and deed. It gave one an example to follow. I resolved to get rid of my illicit stock of goodies. What was the point of paying through the nose to lose weight and then sneaking sweets in like a child? Ridiculous!

'Damned ridiculous!' She leant closer so that no one should overhear. 'I wouldn't dream of advertising the fact of my own little indulgences. We all smuggle in whatever we can, but I've found that the act of eating is sufficient in itself. Once the morsel has passed the tongue one has no further need of it. Apart from registering on the scales –

and we are weighed every single morning, you know, Loopy – the body can humiliate one at the most inappropriate moments. Just like the young person you witnessed on the stairs. She'll be fined for that, it will be put onto her bill. And you can't blame them. The dry-cleaning bills must mount up alarmingly! No – I have my own way of coping. I induce my own vomit. Yes, it's much the best way. After I've secretly indulged, I retire to the lavabo and tickle the old tonsils with two fingers. It brings the lot up! It's a good wheeze, you should try it.' She chuckled wickedly.

'I must remember the tip. I'll make a mental note,' I said, greatly relieved. This was a new side of the old Agatha, one I had not guessed at before. This visit could be more fun than I had thought.

'How many days have you been here?' I asked, looking around. The room we were sitting in was like an ice-cream parlour in the style of Fortnum and Mason. Gold-lacquered, wicker-work chairs with cushioned seats in floral cretonne were tastefully arranged around low, glass-topped tables.

The tables were a necessity, since the hot lemon drinks were very hot indeed and there were those in the room without the strength to hold them for longer than a few seconds at a time. It was an affecting scene. I found myself having to avert my eyes from more than one distressing spectacle. Not far from where we were sitting, a corpulent gentleman with a fat cigar clenched between his dazzlingly white teeth, suddenly appeared to sag at the knees as he made his approach. The contents of his glass in its metal container, hideously hot to carry without the use of a hankie, slurped down the front of his expensive satin dressing-gown. Beneath the dressing-gown, a deep crimson with a monogrammed pocket, I could see a dashing pair of equally expensive pyjamas. They were identical, if my eyes didn't deceive me, to the ones of Bertie's that I was wearing. 'Snap!' I said to Dame Agatha, but she wasn't listening. She was surveying the room and the scattered unfortunates with open and undisguised mirth, eagerly devouring them with her eyes. At the sight of the satin knees buckling towards us she let out a roar of raucous delight which only succeeded in further flummoxing the approach. The knees appeared to give way altogether when only inches from our own, and had it not been for my own commendable presence of mind in grasping it from his clasp, the hot lemon would have also found its way to the floor. Dame Agatha sat convulsed in peals of loud and joyful laughter, whilst the rest of the room chose to ignore what they clearly considered to be a gross lapse of good taste. I couldn't decide what to think. Her behaviour was so unlike the Agatha that I had held in my memory for all these years, that I had difficulty in acclimatising myself to this merry and patently entertaining stranger. Perhaps the title of 'Dame' bestowed a sense of black humour; perhaps having spent so many years of her working life amongst politicians, she had developed a streak of private anarchism.

'Oh, oh!' she gasped now, wiping tears from her eyes. 'How amusing, first rate stuff, Pottle, old chap! Exactly how I felt!' And then as if only just remembering my presence (just like schooldays!), she turned to me. 'Loopy dear, this is Flab – Flab Pottle. Pottle contrives to keep us all sane, he's a real comedian. I can't think how we should manage without him. Pottle, I'd like you to meet a very good school chum of mine, Lady Patch. Known in school as Loopy, Lord only knows why. Why was it, Loopy?'

I laughed modestly. 'A bit bats-in-the-belfry in those days.'

'In that case, dear Madam, you and I will get on splendidly. By the way shouldn't I say "Snap!"?'

He had remained on his knees, but was now offering his hand.

I took it, the clasp was firm and hard, just as I liked them. The eyes twinkled and shone beneath heavy brows. The mouth, slightly lop-sided, stretched from one side of the face to the other in a wide, open grin. It was a boy's grin, cheeky and wild. He hung on so long to the hand he was holding that I began to feel silly. I could feel a blush rise.

'My pleasure, Mr Pottle.' I tried unsuccessfully to remove my numbed paw.

'No, mine, Lady Patch.' He leaned forward and brushed his smiling lips over my knuckles, remaining down there on his knees.

Dame Agatha lifted a hefty leg, kicked him hard on the shoulder, clouted him once around the head and shouted as if to the deaf. 'Come on now, we'll have less of that, Pottle! Stand on your feet, man, and draw up a chair.' And then to me in a more moderate key, 'You'll have to watch out for Pottle here – he fancies himself as a one with the ladies.'

'Does he indeed?' I allowed my gaze to stray to him as, removing his cigar, he settled himself into a chair as instructed. He appeared not to mind Dame Agatha's rough treatment.

'Eee, she's a one!' He laughed shaking his fist, employing an exaggerated northern accent. Was he from the north? He had the look of a successful self-made man, intent on displaying to the world how well he'd done for himself. I would have put his age at around fifty, a little older than Dame Agatha. He was heavy, certainly that, but with his height he could carry it. Though not conventionally handsome, there was a certain crude raffishness which would appeal to women. For the first time since Bertie, I blamed myself for allowing my body to get so out of hand. There was a time when a man such as this would have presented no challenge at all, I could have eaten him for breakfast. Now I clearly stood no chance, I was simply a female something on which to practise his charms. A sharpening device until the real thing came along. Shit!

He was twisting to survey the rest of the room. 'Where's Flower?'

I checked an irrational disappointment. Flower – the name alone conjured up a vision of youth and fragility. On neither count could I have reasonably hoped to compete, but moments later when Flower herself staggered into the room, I knew that I could forget Flab Pottle if this vision had already captured his interest. Flower turned out to be none other than the vomiting beauty.

She had changed from the frilly Victorian nightdress into a startlingly revealing satin negligée. Whereas before, the voluminous garment had successfully concealed every contour of her body so that it had been impossible to judge the shape beneath, this negligée did the opposite. On first sight I had been unable to believe the exquisite beauty of the face, but now I found my eyes drawn to the voluptuous abundance of breast.

Each one was as large as the heart-shaped face above it, easily that. And yet, despite the size and the imagined weight, they jutted unsupported from the narrow torso beneath. Each swelling in one sloping and unbroken line, provocatively dominating the upper half of the otherwise slim body; it was impossible not to stare. I had never in my life seen breasts like them. In my heydey, my own had been pretty sensational, though I say it myself. And both my nubile daughters were noted for their pneumatic charms. Even so, I can remember that it was around the age of thirteen that the girls', and doubtless my own, bosoms were at their most heart-achingly sublime. Able to pass the test, so beloved of magazine beauty editors, of whether or not a girl could qualify to go bra-less. That is to say that if a coin were to be placed beneath the breast and the overlap were to hold it in position, then she should not burn her brassiere. If the coin fell away, then she would be given the go-ahead. I had tried that same test myself a year previously and was still searching for my loose change! ˉ

But these breasts of the fair Flower gave no cause for that sweet regret that one suffers at the passing of physical perfection. It occurred to me as I gazed, that they might be man-made, that they were the sumptuous results of a silicone implant. I would know if I touched them, I could tell right away. But even I, who would dare to do more unorthodox things than most, lacked the presumption to lean forward and ask, 'Do you mind if I have a feel of your fabulous tits?' After all, we hadn't even been introduced yet.

I didn't have long to wait.

'Do you know Flower Fowler, Loopy? Lovely creature – something in films, mostly on the Continent. Pornography, according to Pottle.' Dame Agatha didn't bother to lower her voice as she said this, but simply smiled and beckoned at the staggering girl.

'She's the one I saw vomiting on the stairs,' I whispered back.

'Hear you've been make a public spectacle of yourself, Flower,' Dame Agatha chose to shout as the poor sweet

196

drew closer. 'My good friend, Lady Patch here has just been telling us that she caught you puking over the banisters, you undisciplined puppy.'

I turned scarlet and opened my mouth in protest, but the damage was done. Flower beamed her beautiful orbs in my direction, I felt my stomach somersaulting. Had I been a schoolboy I should probably have shot off in my trousers. 'Yeah, well, you can tell cunty to shut 'er fat gob!' Then brightening she turned to the now slavering Flab Pottle, 'What d'yer fink, Flab – I bleedin' lost a fuckin' pound! A whole pound!' She cupped the firm flesh of her breasts unselfconsciously in each hand, the nipples straining clearly against the stretched satin. At the sight of them I experienced a definite frisson, an actual sensation down in my clitoris. If it had affected me thus, what must have happened to the contents of Flab Pottle's pyjamas! I couldn't resist glancing in that direction, just in time to catch him crossing his substantial limbs. Clever move.

'Yeah – these buggers are shrinkin'. Won't be long now, not at this bleedin' rate!' Then she collapsed into the chair which Dame Agatha had drawn up for her. 'Fanks, luv,' she said warmly, 'did yer lose any today?'

'Nothing, I lost nothing. I appear to have reached some sort of *impasse*.'

'Shame, luv – still, never mind. Yer got yer enema today – that gits rid of a coupla stone, leastways that's 'ow it fuckin' feels! Ain't that right, eh, Flab? Flower turned her radiant gaze upon Flab Pottle, who had seemed to recover some sort of composure.

He nodded gravely and threw his eyes towards the ceiling, clasping his hands together over his big belly as if in protection of his private property. 'The sensation,' he began grimly!

'No, please –' interrupted Dame Agatha.

'The sensation,' he carried on, ignoring the interruption, taking no notice of her, 'is as if someone had taken a shovel –'

'I shan't remain, Pottle –'

'– to your arse, loaded with warm curried cement –'

We all laughed, even Dame Agatha, despite her anxious apprehension. But I understood how she was feeling. I had only suffered two previous enemas, each preceding

197

the delivery of my babies. These, and the skilled shaving of my pubic mound with a sharp hospital razor, remained amongst the more unpleasant experiences that I had undergone up to date. The humiliation of the enemas, the sensation of actually being about to explode as the hot soapy water was being pumped into the anus; the sickening lurch of the loosening excrement as it spun round the bowels; the agonised dive toward the nearest lavatory, fearful lest the sphincter shouldn't last the short distance – it seemed to me to be medical sadism at its worst. And yet here we were, the whole group of us voluntarily offering ourselves up for the experience. My ready laughter died on my lips.

Flower was still expressing her delight at Flab Pottle's description and was encouraging him to elaborate still further, when another inmate of Slivers appeared and joined our friendly group. It was the fat child in the lemon nylon dressing gown, little Miss potbelly, the one with the spectacular hair.

She was smiling now and looked altogether different. 'Two pounds,' she said triumphantly and help up two podgy fingers. Everyone clapped, including me since I saw that this was obviously the thing to do. The child's chubby cheeks dimpled with pleasure. She reminded me of an adorable little piglet, but more than anything I was waiting to hear her speak again. The voice had been so unexpectedly adult, husky and urgent. The sort of voice you would expect from a sophisticated chanteuse, full of tobacco smoke, recent sex and a special sort of desperation. Not at all in keeping with the cuddly creature before me. 'Hi!' she was hailing me now, offering her pig's trotters. 'Like your drag – hey, Flab, look – same pyjamas as yours!'

Flab Pottle leaned forward. 'That fact had not escaped my beady eyes,' he winked in my direction, but so that the whole assembly should see. 'The lady doesn't know it yet but I have plans to compare her inner seams with my own . . .' He looked satisfactorily surprised when everyone groaned.

'Do us a favour, Flab, eh? We all know you need a shoe 'orn!' Flower squeezed his arm affectionately to soften her words. But Dame Agatha guffawed. 'Shoe-horn!' she spluttered. 'Tea-spoon, more like!'

'Yes,' agreed the piglet. 'With the use of a matchstick as a splint!'

Flab Pottle raised his hands, chuckling happily, revelling in all this feminine attention. I was still trying to get over the change in Dame Agatha, but now I had been flung off my guard by the precociousness of the child. Had she really carnal knowledge of Flab Pottle's private parts? Perhaps she was not as youthful as she appeared.

As if to answer my unspoken thoughts, Dame Agatha introduced us. 'Fizzy, this is Lady Patch, best known as Loopy. We were schoolgirls together. Loopy, meet Fizzy Tornado. Young Fizzy has just recorded her very first disc, she has an extraordinary voice. Soon we shall be seeing her on "Top of the Pops". Isn't that right?'

Fizzy Tornado nodded and sighed. 'When this lot goes down.' She slapped her pot-belly and looked suddenly despondent, so much so that Flower jumped up and gave her a kiss. 'None o' all that cobblers, c'mon now, cheer up kid. You said yerself you lost two pound this mornin'. Christ, all-bleedin'-mighty! I only lost fuckin' one, and Dame Agatha 'ere she ain't lost nuffin! What about you, Flab?'

Flab shifted uneasily, this time he didn't welcome the spotlight being on him. 'Yes, well, ladies,' he began, clearing his throat. 'Actually –'

They all waited, it was like the Spanish Inquisition. Worse.

'Actually,' he mumbled.

Dame Agatha spoke first. 'You've put on, you've gained! You bastard!' She turned to the others. 'I told you he'd let us down – you silly sod!' She clipped his head sharply. 'They'll start watching us, you know that. We'll get thrown out if you're not more careful. Why not do as I do, throw up in privacy?'

Flab Pottle hung his head in genuine contrition. 'Sorry, girls. Sorry, Dame Agatha.' They regarded him sternly, all of them except me. Seeing my friendly face, he chose that moment to wink. I smiled back despite the disapproval surrounding me. Flower tapped my shoulder with unnecessary venom. I'd obviously stepped off on the wrong foot with her. 'Look cunty, don't you go fuckin' encouraging 'im. The old Dame is right, I nearly got us in

199

bovver this mornin' pukin' up all over the bleedin' banisters. This is only your fuckin' first day so you don't know what you've got in store – the diabolical nature of this bloody 'ole. Just you wait till you've done a few days! Ain't that right?' She appealed to the others.

Fizzy Tornado backed her up. 'Sure thing, Flower's right, missus.'

Dame Agatha rose from her chair and beckoned imperiously. 'Enough of all this inconsequential chatter. Come along with me, Loopy dear. Let me show you around Slivers. Pottle, I'm warning you – we shall have to exclude you if you let us down again. Is that understood?' She waited for an answer. I was suddenly confronted by the Head Girl at school again, only thankful that it was not me on the carpet. Poor Pottle!

'It is understood, Dame Agatha. From henceforward I shall be more careful. An extra hour in the sauna, that might do it each day. I could swim rather more than I do in the pool.'

'You could apply for the dreaded enema that you are so fond of describing, Pottle!'

His eyes lit up. 'That I could, sweet Madame. Pray at what hour are you expecting your enema today? Whatever it is, do not allow your mind to dwell upon it. We shall have to compare notes – you may find you liken yours to the casual insertion of a scalding hot drink, one liberally laced with freshly plucked stinging nettles, the retraction of which heralds the start of the snow-storm. Though on reflection –' Pottle paused, preparing to elaborate still further. Dame Agatha swept on, but behind her back I once again exchanged an encouraging smile.

Flab Pottle was my sort of person.

The guided tour which Dame Agatha promised me had to be postponed. As we emerged from the 'dining' room, we were both pounced upon by a person in uniform. 'Ah ha!' the person exclaimed with malevolent gaiety. 'Dame Agatha and – Lady Patch, I take it? I was told I might find the two of you together. This is for you, dear,' she said, handing me a sheaf of papers. 'It's your programme. Mr Ragg asked me to hand it over to you. Best to get started on your schedule right away. Dame Agatha, I

200

have you down for an enema at two-forty. If you don't mind too much I'd like to bring that forward to two o'clock.'

Dame Agatha looked disgruntled after consulting her watch. 'That's in fifteen minutes time.'

'Precisely.' The uniformed person pressed her fingertips together as if she could barely wait to get started on Dame Agatha's bowels. 'The sooner the better, that's what I say to patients. Get it over and done with –' She spun round on me. 'You'll notice, Lady Patch, that you are down for one later today, this is the reason that we are having to bring Dame Agatha forward. Mr Ragg felt strongly that we should try to accommodate you this afternoon. It is a departure from the norm, we don't usually give enemas as early as this in the patient's stay, but there have been exceptions. I'm sure Mr Ragg will have a perfectly sound reason – it's probably for the best. You'll find a drastic weight reduction will take place – and that, ladies, can never be a bad thing now can it!' She herself was as scrawny as a stray cat.

'That was Sister Severe, she's crackers. Pay no attention.' Dame Agatha tucked her hand comfortingly into the crook of my elbow as we moved towards the staircase. She didn't bother to lower her voice, it was obvious that the uniformed person could hear.

'I heard that, Dame Agatha! I don't know about paying no attention indeed! You are due on the enema couch in less than ten minutes and the longer you take to arrive the hotter will be the soapy water – I warn you!

Dame Agatha moved forward at a greatly increased speed. 'Need several things from my room, Sister. Shan't be half-a-mo.' I watched her sizeable buttocks swinging up the stairs ahead of me, not an unpleasant sight. She was still quite light on her feet, despite the added stones. And the proportions of the body hadn't changed, just expanded. so that the overall effect was not as aesthetically disagreeable as in someone such as myself who hadn't the height to carry it off. I puffed up the stairs behind her, giving out short explosions of breath with each step gained. I wasn't used to stairs anymore, living as I did on the ground floor.

She turned at the bend of the banister. I'd flopped out

down below. 'Loopy,' she said sternly, 'you're badly out of condition. I can remember the days when you ran everywhere like a little gazelle. Whatever has happened to get you into this sort of shape?'

'Thirty-five years have passed, that's all that's happened.' I glanced down to where the uniformed person stood studying her watch.

'Seven minutes, Dame Agatha!' she sang in a shrill soprano voice. It reminded me that I still had little Fizzy Tornado's singing to look forward to. If her speaking voice was anything to go by, then I had a treat in store. This place was the sort that Daisy and Tadpole would enjoy, meeting such people as Flower Fowler. Though what on earth that girl was doing at Slivers I couldn't imagine. It seemed to me that she had the perfect shape, especially if she performed in Continental erotica. But from what I could gather, it was her bosom that she was intent to be rid of – to become flat-chested! Why? It was useless to ask, I knew that very well. Nobody is satisfied with what they've got.

It was at that moment that they appeared, Fizzy, Flower and Flab Pottle. All three of them entwined around each other, laughing conspiratorially. The uniformed person, Sister, spun around at their approach.

'Sh, sh,' she placed her fingers on her lips. Ahead of me, Dame Agatha had disappeared from view. I puffed to catch up with her, I was interested to find out how far her bedroom was from my own.

The girls had encouraged me to lash out on the comfort of a room with toilet and shower, though I would have been perfectly content to reside in a much cheaper one without. The difference in price was about eighty pounds.

'After all,' I'd pointed out to them, 'I shan't be in much need of a shower, not if I'm to be spending all my time in the sauna and taking Epsom salt baths and seaweed baths and sitting in steam cabinets and such.

'You'll need a lavatory of your own, Mummy. That's hardly a luxury.'

'Well, Daisy darling, there won't be very much leaking out one way and another.'

I wondered if Dame Agatha had splashed out too.

It seemed she had.

'Come in, Loopy dear,' she shouted from her bathroom (no bath but everything else). 'Just getting my towel and things. The nice thing about places like these is how clean everything is; it's quite depressing when one returns home. Fresh towels every day, everything sparkling, everything so hygienic. And I'm such a slut, a hoarder, are you? I should really like to live here for the rest of my life. Perhaps I'll give up politics and start a health farm like Slivers. I have seriously considered it. But I suppose in the end one would be left without that sense of purpose, the gratifying glow which I personally get from being a politician. The knowledge that you are in there where it matters, shoulder to the wheel. with your weight behind the nation.' She laughed. We both did.

'Well, yes,' she said, 'speaking of which . . .'

I allowed her to hurry on whilst I made my leisurely way along the same corridor to my own room. It seemed endless, faced at the start and finish with lavishly framed mirrors, each banked by giant vases full of dried flowers and decorative foliage. If one had no idea of the culinary deprivation imposed on the paying guests, one might suffer the delusion that this was a very grand country house to which one had come for the weekend. Or an expensive and ostentatious hotel, the sort of place that Bertie always enjoyed (with the right rough trade).

My bedroom number was thirteen, but those superstitions had never bothered me. Rather the reverse. I .actually went out of my way to step underneath ladders, instead of walking around them. If a black cat happened to cross my path, the reason I would aim a well-placed kick up its bum would rise from my mild irritation with animals of any kind, rather than a fear of ill fortune.

Similarly I had no truck with the stars, all that codswallop about birth-signs and such. Daisy, at her hippiest, had become engrossed in it for a while, forever poring over the charts depicting the aspects of the planets and pestering people for the time, date and place of their birth. Until I'd had to have a word with her.

'I've worked it out, Mummy,' she'd woken me at something like one-thirty in the morning, draped in a crushed velvet sack which was scattered with badly sewn-on signs of the zodiac. Her long pre-Raphaelite hair

203

stank of stale pot. She was barely sixteen, her father not long dead. And although the hippie movement has such had long since passed its peak, there were still pockets of pseuds around who were keen to convert the young. Daisy, at that time was very drawn to the mystical. A classmate at school had recently drawn drastic attention to herself by pouring a can of petrol over her head and setting light to her drenched clothes in the centre of the netball court. This following the announcement that Daisy, and not she, would be playing the part of Shaw's St Joan in the school play at Christmas. The entire school had looked on in helpless horror as the girl burned swiftly to death. The Shaw production was cancelled, replaced by the rather odd choice of *Oklahoma*. I should have thought if the idea was for a little light relief, something by Noel Coward would have been more suitable, or Tennessee Williams. *Oklahoma* had meant that my Daisy no longer had the starring role, her singing voice was not up to it. She was relegated to the menial ranks of the humming chorus, merrily gesticulating with all the others in a hideously inept home-made dirndl. One of seventy-five hastily run up by the Dutch domestic science mistress, Ursula Ullrich. It was only when one saw the uncontrollable numbers whacking and banging about amongst the flimsy stage props, endangering themselves and the first five rows of the audience, that one realised the wisdom of choosing *Oklahoma*. Everybody in the whole school who had acting aspirations had a part. In future, the drama teacher had assured me after the show, this would become part of the policy. What had happened to that poor little sensitive child was just too gruesome to dwell upon. It was sad that dear Daisy had not been given her fully deserved opportunity to shine, but a girl such as Daisy, so mature for her years, wouldn't allow these minor disappointments to affect her adversely. 'Ah,' she had sighed, 'if only we had more here as balanced as your two!' that was before they had become unbalanced.

Waking your own mother up at one-thirty in the morning with a load of zodiacal gibberish was hardly balanced. I saw no point in learning that I was a subject born with Scorpio rising, the Sun and Mars in Aquarius, Moon in Sagittarius and under the Midheaven of Leo.

Not at that hour or any other would it have held any interest for me. Nor did I long to be told gravely by Daisy that there was a strong indication of intensity and sense of purpose, contrasted with considerable breadth of vision and optimism in my character. The fact that the planet Jupiter on my chart was in a very powerful position at the top of the sky, and that the sign Leo was on the area of the chart which had a direct say in the career, held no fascination for me. When she told me that I was an individualist, pretty extravagant and terrifically romantic at heart, I'm afraid I yawned in her touchingly serious young face. But as she went on to enlighten me on my powerful humanitarian feelings and my tremendously affectionate nature I cautioned her, I couldn't help it. 'My affectionate nature is showing signs of strain, darling,' I said as gently as my frayed nerves could manage. I was envisaging the tedious meeting ahead of me in the morning with Bertie's accountant, I would need all my wits for that one. But at the same time I had to be careful to be extra tender with both Daisy and Tadpole these days – they had been very close to their father. It took very little for tears to appear.

'Sorry, Mummy,' she'd said. 'We just thought that you'd like to know that we'd just finished your chart, rather than wait till the morning.'

'We? Who are we, Daisy?' I lay, struggling to remember who I had said goodnight to last night of Daisy's friends. Those were the days when I was still being consulted as to whether it was all right for her friends to stay the night. Not that there was every any reason for me to withhold my permission, they were all charming girls, every single one of them.

'Stewart.' She whispered the name as if it was holy, as if Stewart was one of the twelve sodding disciples instead of the drippy, Scottish drop-out that he was. My heart sank at her next words.

'That's the other reason for waking you, Mummy. I've told him it's all right to stay with us for a while until he gets himself sorted out. Please say it is. You see, that commune in Kent, it didn't work out and his family are being so horrible to him that he's sworn he'll never go home, never ever again.'

Lucky family. 'Well, Daisy, let's discuss it in the morning. In the meantime where were you thinking of putting Stewart to sleep?'

'Oh, he's sleeping with me, Mummy. I've put him in my bed, he's fast asleep already. He tried hitching from Coventry but no one would give him a lift, poor Stewart –'

But I'd sat up in bed. 'Now Daisy, be sensible. You're not on the pill. One thing we don't want is you getting pregnant, not with your "O" Levels coming up this year. How would you be able to concentrate on exams with morning sickness and all the discomfort? Answer me that!'

Her lower lip trembled, her expression was one of pain. 'Mummy,' she spoke with a dignity that I could not help but admire, 'Stewart's not like that. It's not how it is between us, sex doesn't come into it.'

I took hold of her cold hand and warmed it between my own. 'That's all right then, angel. As long as you know what you're doing. Daddy would have been just as concerned. I have to take care of you for him as well now.' It was a cheap trick but one which I knew would be effective.

'Don't worry,' she murmured and kissed me on the cheek. 'I won't let either of you down. As soon as I think I should go on the pill then I promise to tell you.'

She went on the pill the very next day. The occult was replaced by solid sex.

Bedroom thirteen was a pleasant enough room, about five along from Dame Agatha's and on the same side, so that we enjoyed identical views. It was still wintry, the trees were stripped bare of leaves and the impressive lawns appeared drab and balding in patches. But one could imagine how spectacular it must all be in the height of summer, or even in a few months time, in the glory of spring. We were getting the worst of it, coming at this time. On the other hand it made one appreciate the benefits of being indoors, the comfort of central heating, the general cosiness.

I consulted my watch and turned the television on, an image loomed on the coloured screen. I had caught a commercial break, a sudden flow of saliva flooded my mouth as the camera captured the succulent sight of a frying-pan full of sizzling pork sausages. It was the first time since my arrival at Slivers that I had experienced a genuine pang of hunger. In the normal way I would still be eating my lunch. Wolfing down whatever I had decide on for puddings in whichever of the eating places I had taken to frequenting around Oxford Circus.

It was a source of huge hilarity, the places I chose, sparked off by Tadpole and some of her friends who had spotted me sitting in the window of the tiny Bonbonnière Café opposite Liberty's. I had been eating an absolutely scrumptious treacle sponge with hot custard at the time, the enjoyment of which had been absolutely ruined by the senseless cavortings on the other side of the glass window. Since then I was careful never to accept a window seat again, not unless it couldn't be helped, and sometimes it couldn't because the time that I chose to eat was the same time as all the office workers and shop assistants took their lunch. The surrounding company was one of the really congenial elements of this sort of eating-out. The part, asided from the delicious food, that I really appreciated. It was fascinating to listen in on other people's conversations, it opened up worlds for me which I had never been given the chance to enter. Much more exciting than the exclusivity of the restaurants I had patronised with Bertie, waited upon by remote and excessively polite people with whom it would have been impossible to conduct any natural exchange, each of us in some sort of awe of the other, intent on preserving the traditions of the past. I had never liked the unbending formality of our dining-out from the very beginning. It was only when we were abroad that I had ever enjoyed it.

And yet I had been able to make use in my writing of even those stilted dinners. In my current pot-boiler, the heroine, a child of impoverished background (unlike mine which was never that), had found herself being fingered beneath the tablecloth by a wealthy would-be protector in a dauntingly plush restaurant. And I had found that a particularly satisfying passage to write, almost as if I had been able to identify with the poor girl's discomfiture.

The sausages remained on the television screen for an upsetting extended stretch of time. Did food commercials usually last this long? I had never really noticed them before. Now my taste-buds were on the rampage, I really needed to place a little edible item on my tongue. The urge to eat was desperate, try as I might to thrust the temptation away. Hadn't I vowed to be strong whilst sipping my hot lemon – hadn't I promised myself a clear run on the first day, without yielding once!

I had not yet unpacked, it would take me time to decide on the most discreet hiding place for my little goodies. But I had taken the precautionary measure of concealing each individual item within the contents of my large suitcase. It had crossed my mind before doing so that there might be in operation a sort of customs shed through which individuals were required to pass before entry into Slivers, scattered with blathering victims caught in the heinous crime of smuggling stuff inside. Accordingly I had skilfully substituted a slab of cheddar cheese for my bar of soap in its opaque plastic container. Two packets of Tampax contained a tin of sardines each, one with edible oil and the other with tomato sauce. Several sizeable screw-top pots ostensibly full of the super-emollient skin creams one would expect a woman of my age to use had been emptied and refilled with various temptations, the sort that I liked to dip my finger into at any time of the day or night. Long-lasting and mouth-watering Hellman's mayonnaise, with the piquant addition of crushed garlic and fresh lemon-juice. Nestlés wonderfully sweet and sticky condensed milk. Philadelphia cream cheese. Home-made lemon curd (half a dozen still sent each Christmas from an elderly maiden aunt in Suffolk), convincingly pale to pass as something one would apply to the face. Some thick, solid honey.

What seemed to be a packet of Lux soap flakes, essential for the daily swilling out of one's smalls, would have turned out to be on closer examination a seriously tampered-with container. Emptied and then re-sealed to hold wrapped packs of Smith's crisps, Whitworth's flaked almonds, dessicated coconut, mixed dried fruit, dried apricots. I was rather proud of this particular deception, despite the suspicious weightiness of the final product. It excited me to think of opening it up layer on layer, like dipping into a Christmas stocking. The big question now was what would I start with?

I ran my tongue around my lemony lips experiencing the tremulous thrill that always preceded the intake of favourite food, aware of the faint hammering of my heart. This hammering, according to William, was an unhealthy sign. Something one should not lightly disregard, not at this age and weight. It could be the onset of troublesome high blood-pressure. Another reason to cut back the feed. Starting tomorrow. For now I'd make do with a little sliver of cheddar sandwiched between two crackling Smith's crisps, with one dried apricot for afters. I had to ration myself, I was here for two weeks. It wouldn't do to hog the lot, and in any case it was nicer this way, sneaking up giving myself little treats with no one looking. Unless they were.

I turned to study the layout of the room. There were no obvious spy-holes in evidence, but then they wouldn't be obvious to the unskilled eye. It was because of my experiences with Bertie that I was suspicious. The first precaution he ever took on arrival in a fresh place was to check on whether or not it was safe from prying eyes. The fear of blackmail was never far from his mind, more especially as he grew older.

The mirrors were always the most suspect, and patterned wallpaper invariably induced paranoia. Bored holes through from the rooms next door were less detectable, more easily camouflaged if there was a pattern. From that point of view it was absolutely safe here, all four walls and ceiling were an anonymous and reassuring white. There were two mirrors, a full-length one positioned on the wall next to the door and backing onto the corridor; the other as part of the conventional dressing-table, that one would certainly not be two-way. Neither was it likely that passers-by could see in from the corridor, otherwise I would have been greeted with a glimpse of my own room before I had even opened the door. Nevertheless, just to make certain, I sidled over the carpet towards the door, popped my head out into the corridor to check that things were all right on that side, and then withdrew once again to safety. My hands shook as I opened the crisps and extracted two of the largest. The salty oiliness assailed my nostrils such that by the time I had scraped sufficient cheese together with my nail-file for a crisp-sandwich of any substance, the saliva was leaking from the corners of my eager mouth. Lifting the delicacy to my watery lips, I still had time to regret the lack of a little Branston Pickle. Just a touch to supply a tangy tingle. But Branston Pickle would have been too risky, too difficult to conceal, like many other favourites it had to go by the board. Never mind, they were all there at home to go back to.

But now the moment had come, the precise moment of entry, to use the sexual jargon. It was a toss-up whether to shut my eyes or relish the ecstacy in the mirror. I moved automatically towards my reflection and sank to face it at the small dressing-table.

Then I placed the crisps and cheese on my tongue and began munching very slowly in a strictly rhythmical manner to prevent myself going at it too fast and risk pleasurably choking to death in the process. It gave me time to observe myself, to study my face, to do what I hadn't done seriously for a very long time. That was to get an unbiased view of myself as others must see me. A frank focus of what I imposed on the world.

I wasn't a bad-looking woman, not an absolute wreck, not a positive affront to the human eye. On the other hand, I had to admit that the whole thing had rather gone to pot – and not the sort of pot that my daughters and their friends were so dependent on either.

I resembled a tousled yet amiable sort of animal. An unspecified species somewhere between a koala bear, a small seal and a shaggy English sheepdog. I would have made a loveable glove puppet, like one of the Muppets. Even as a girl, I was likened to cartoon characters out of Walt Disney films. It was to do with the odd arrangement of my features, the fact that my eyes and my mouth were proportionately too large for the rest of my face. Saucer-eyed and melon-mouthed was how Bertie described me, like an infant's happy drawing of an adult. And the hair, with a human life of its own waving this way and that in an effort to gain attention, that didn't help. And now that it had gone grey, the whole head had taken on the manic appearance of a used Brillo pad, a steel saucepan-scourer that had seen better days. Its dusty halo hugged my scalp, rebelling in bushy tendrils over my brow, curling in uncombed confusion around my ears.

Mercifully, the superfluous flesh which had so deformed the body below, had not wrecked as much havoc on my face. At some distance I doubtless looked my full forty-five years and more, nothing was more ageing than a stout silhouette, a good old middle-aged spread. And there was no denying that's what I had, with a vengeance! But the flesh of the face, though blurred along the jawbone and beneath the chin, bore no more than the usual signs of youth long since passed. I had small lines on either side of my mouth and many of them encircling my eyes. When I smiled, as I smiled now (not opening my mouth lest a precious crumb should fall out), these lines leapt into instant action, multiplying ten-fold into a cross-hatch of creases. Each intersection marking a fresh spin-off point until the whole area resembled a map of the British motorways. More than anything now I looked like a tipsy tortoise, wearing a merry wig upon its head.

It was time for my pudding, for my single dried apricot, although I had no longer any urgent desire for it. The yearning, the unspecified need had been satisfied by the minute snack I'd just finished. But I would go on now that the idea of the apricot remained in my mind. Indeed I could almost taste the thing already. And I looked forward to the change of flavour in my mouth, the sharp fruitiness of the apricot would dispel the slightly un-pleasant aftertaste one was left with cheese. Also get rid of an rancid odour on the breath, I must beware of these tell-tale giveaways!

The thought alerted me! Having taken my personal programme sheet from the uniformed Sister I still had not given myself a chance to study it. For all I knew at this very moment someone was expecting me, waiting to sweat, pummel, empty, or squeeze my bloated body into a recognisable human shape again. Meanwhile here was I nibbling away in the opposite direction, undermining my programme before it had even started.

I bit happily into my dried apricot, almost swooning with delight as I sucked the fruitiness through my teeth. My entire mouth was alive with exploding taste-buds, I was swallowing nectar. My stomach rose joyfully to my juicy throat . . .

Idly I studied the Slivers' brochure pinned to the

programme sheet. It was interesting to compare the brilliantly tinted photograph of the dining room with the place in which I had so lately supped my lemon juice. This dining room appeared to be afroth with roistering, revelling diners enjoying the delights of a full three-course meal, with wine on the side! A long central table groaned beneath a crammed cheese-board, banked by fresh celery sticks, a selection of crunchy bread-rolls and biscuits. Beyond this could be seen a vast fish-tank of a fruit-bowl harbouring a syrupy multi-coloured fruit-salad. Next to which was a clear cut-glass jug of what could only be double-cream, doubtless that really delicious stuff from Jersey (a full carton of which I could demolish in one sitting – and had done many times on my own).

To aid my concentration whilst deciding what to nibble, I had wisely switched off my television set. I didn't want any further food commercials to encourage me in my excesses. But at the sight of this photographed orgy I found myself reaching for another dried apricot – and a small fistful of crisps. The dining room snap was a falsification of the true facts, I thought to myself. It led would-be guests into believing that they could expect to be living the life of a gourmet Riley in this supposedly bloody health-farm. Unless what I was looking at was a different dining room, the one reserved exclusively for the anorexics, for these lucky people who needed to build up their physiques. Oh, to be encouraged to build up a bit of gut! I looked more closely, without my glasses it was difficult to make out the small print. My eyes were two of the many things which had deteriorated since Bertie, but they were being put to more strenuous uses than before. And I still only needed them for reading and writing. At least I found my way around the world without falling over furniture. Except on those occasions when I treated myself to a little drink . . .

The thought led me to check that my precious supply of alcohol was still safely intact in its perfume bottle. It was there, Glenfiddich whisky masquerading as 'Ma Femme'. Though it had taken many hours of soaking and scouring to rid the glass container of the clinging fragrance, I had eventually managed to do so.

Sniffing it now I felt there was something still lingering,

a certain sexy aroma. Taking a small sip to test the flavour of the contents I couldn't detect much wrong with the taste. Mm, mm – just what I needed at this point to pick me up. The last dried apricot had long since melted away, and the fistful of Smith's crisps with it. What was left in the packet was hardly worth hanging on to – was it my imagination, or were they filling them with fewer crisps than they once did? This packet appeared to have been barely more than half-full when I had started in on it, but now what remained I could finish off in two mouthfuls. Especially if I swilled each down with a good swig of 'Ma Femme'. I made a mischievous face in the mirror at the prospect; the next moment I'd put the idea into practice.

At the second cheek-bulging, tonsil-tearing, gobful of bliss, the first bang came on the door. Swallowing everything that was in my mouth (almost including the small upper denture that supported my back teeth), I staggered back in the belief that I was suffering my first coronary. The burning sensation was unbearable. Neat whisky, having seared the tender playing field of my tongue, tearing at trouble-spotted gums as it swirled sharp-edged, half-chewed crisps past my tonsils, was now scouring a fiery path toward my heart. Stark fear soured its progress, so much so that I was sure I was going to throw up. Was this possible whilst one went down with a stroke? Could there be medically speaking such a specta- cle as a vomiting corpse? If there could, then at least I would have one witness. Before I had sunk to the floor the door of my room was flung open. It was my first sight, in the flesh, of Kid Lips.

There was no mistaking him, I recognised him right away. The short, wiry body, the spindly bandy legs, the handsome leonine head, so at odds with the rest of him, had all now disappeared into a bloated parody of his famous former self. But the mouth still remained. He had managed to hang on to the marvellous mouth. That louche, insolent set of lips that had given him his professional name, had made him the sex idol of all those teeny boppers a decade ago. And not only the teeny boppers, the fans of Kid Lips and his group, The Lip-Lickers, had kept their idol at the top of the pop charts all over the world right into the mid-seventies. And then he seemed to have faded from the scene. Hadn't he become a tax-exile, wasn't he rumoured to be living in France, or San Francisco, or a faraway island in the Pacific? Weren't there terrible tales of drug abuse, sexual deviation, hard drinking and utter degradation? The usual stuff about pop-stars.

Gazing at him now in my shocked and weakened state I could see that he hadn't – what was the phrase? – taken care of himself. Though wearing the casually outrageous mixture of garments that one would expect, a set of formal coat-tails, tight emerald leather trousers, a canary yellow waistcoat, a black shirt and a white piqué bow-tie, with a rakish peaked cap on his head, he looked deeply uncomfortable in them. As though their exuberance had exhausted him. The leather trousers, whilst emphasising the formidable bulge of his genitals (the reputed size of which, along with his lips, had accelerated his fame), gaped open untidily at the top of the flies. The bright canary waistcoat refused to join forces over the low paunch, and a button was missing from the black shirt such that it gaped open immediately below the bow-tie to reveal a slice of bare chest.

The peaked cap, a crêpe paper one like those in Christmas crackers, was now in danger of falling right off. From the acute angle over the eye it slid wildly forward, resting momentarily on the tip of his nose before floating haphazardly to the floor. It lay there at my feet. Kid Lips looked, first at it and then at me with an expression of astonishment as if neither sight made any sort of sense in the world. The door slammed behind him adding to his expression of surprise. When he spoke it was with the slow deliberation of one who is being ultra-careful not to slur his words, in order to conceal his drunkenness. 'Hello love,' he lunged forward, then said politely. 'Tell me – d'you fuck?'

I should have said no, like anybody in their right mind, like any responsible person would have done. Except that responsible was the last thing I was feeling just at that moment. The full force of the whisky had just punched my stomach and was now racing along my wrists, towards my nipples, around my womb, pouring into my cunt . . .

The last answer on earth that I would have been

inclined to give at this moment would have been one in the negative. I may have been feeling not quite myself, but I hadn't taken all leave of my senses.

Ye gods, I was forty-five and hadn't fucked for all of five summers! And now here it was being offered on a plate by one of the world's sex-symbols!

Well, not exactly on a plate. We seemed to have taken up residence down on the floor midst the muted hues of a faded Persian rug. And whilst the bearer of the precious offer still bore the name of Kid Lips, there was little about his performance this minute to link him with any one of the legendary lovers in history. I couldn't be certain, but I thought he'd drifted into unconsciousness. Dreadful images of a girlfriend that Daisy had taken up with, a depressive who have overdosed herself in the bathroom above my own, suddenly flashed through my mind. What if this poor boy had slipped into a similar coma! With regret, not to say with a keen disappointment, I struggled to put sex out of my mind and began to think about getting some swift medical help.

My panic was pointless. There wasn't any need for help of any sort, unless it was for the services of a good old-fashioned lady's maid to assist me out of my clothing. After his brief respite, his two seconds of shut-eye, he was back on the job. Galvanised into action by the sight of my sprawled body (legs spread-eagled like some ancient, but gratefully abandoned houri) beside his own, Kid Lips was now scrabbling in the region of my pyjama cord. Bertie's beloved night attire was in danger of being ripped to smithereens. I had completely forgotten the aphrodisiac effect of such violent passion, it was years since I'd been granted the opportunity to enjoy a good rape. But now, with my pyjama buttons popping in all directions, my big soft breasts being munched by that beautiful mouth and my thighs as wide as a nut-cracker about to embark on a Brazil, all my innards melted to jelly. Christ, there was no substitute for the real thing! Whatever anyone said.

When it came my way, when I felt his cock press against my clitoris, I (or was it my clitty?) uttered a soft croak of delight. The sound reverberated, a high, long drawn-out cackle inside by throbbing head. I'd have to control these weird sound effects now that I had company.

All these years of single sex had led me into bad habits. I liked to do a lot of screaming, and singing and shouting as I approached the point of orgasm. It was a way of reminding myself of my existence, that outside the ecstatic ripples of intense pleasure the ordinary rest of me was still there. Just flesh and blood. I had a primitive fear of being transported entirely from my shell when I was all on my own, there was always the chance that I might never return.

I was being transported now all right! Orbiting off into sexual space on the end of Kid Lip's massive dick. It was the crudest cock I had ever accommodated, though I hadn't been given the chance to study its texture I wouldn't have been surprised to discover that it was covered in pores. Like the flesh on the rest of one's person, instead of the delicate membrane that I seemed to remember on other men. Not that this coarseness in any way detracted from the excitement of the insertion. Rather the contrary. When he whammed the thing in I feared I might faint, it felt as if someone had shoved up a leg of lamb, full width first. The last time I'd felt like this was when I'd given birth to Tadpole. And before that to Daisy.

It was a fitting return to fornication. I could feel myself falling in love a little, the way I always used to when the fucking was going well. 'Ooh – I love you,' I whispered to the human being in my arms, squeezing him tightly and kissing the nearest bit of him. The nearest bit at this point was his bow tie and his Adam's apple, both spearing my snout in an uncomfortable manner. For whilst the lower half of my partner's body was firing on all cylinders, going at it like a power-driven piston, the top half of him appeared to have lost consciousness again. He was slumped heavily across me, I couldn't see his face unless I managed to shift one of us. But I didn't want to disturb things when they were going so well. I was terrified that in the middle of all this the real Kid Lips might come to his senses, might look and see just what he was wasting his precious spunk on. Might withdraw in horror and spew up in the sink. Although my daughters and their friends displayed a fashionable compassion towards the infirm and the aged, lumping them along with the generally underprivileged, Kid Lips did not belong to that generation. He was older, he must be over thirty now and although the sexual barriers for his lot were sufficiently smudged to encompass screwing just about anything that moved, man, woman or beast, it didn't mean to say that fat old girls like me were yet entitled to a share. The machismo might not allow it. Not unless the man himself was so sure of himself that such petty considerations as a woman's age and the state of her body didn't come into it. But I didn't want to risk things by pushing my luck with Kid Lips, I was prepared to grab what I was getting and be pleased to do so. There's no gratitude like that of an old girl.

But something was happening – a rumbling commotion out in the corridor, a calling of names and a banging of doors! My mind spun with the thought of the sight we'd present sprawled like this on the floor. I held my breath and squeezed tighter, not just with my arms this time but with my legs as well. And I lifted my buttocks as best I could and began to rotate in an anti-clockwise direction to deliberately set up a separate rhythm to the one which was occupying my partner.

Within seconds we'd both shot off. He in surprise, as I knew he would – it was an old trick of mine that had never failed – and me because a spurious anxiety had heightened the excitement and imminence of orgasm. The commotion outside seemed now to be more distant. I guessed that whoever it was had now returned to the stairs and would be searching the corridors adjacent to mine.

It was time to expel Kid Lips from my room. The erotic idyll was over.

'People have been looking for you. Where've you been, dear?'

'Me?' I smiled radiantly at Sister who seemed taken aback by my changed appearance. 'I'm afraid, Sister, I was in my room. I lay down for a moment, I must have fallen asleep. I'm sorry if I've inconvenienced anyone.'

She seemed to warm to my charm, which came genuinely from the heart. Or more accurately from the cunt. I could feel it blasting from my refuelled sources melting all resistance on the way.

217

'Not really. I've given the sheikh's sister your sauna, but that doesn't matter. Your sleep seems to have been of some benefit, you look remarkably refreshed. And that is what Slivers is about – relaxation of the body and the mind. A loosening up of all life's little tensions. You'll find that in a few days' time you won't ever want to leave, you'll forget about food – there's so much else on offer to take its place.'

'Yes, Sister,' I said. 'I think you're right. I am finding that already.'

We were conversing in the stark white entrance of the Treatment Wing, where Sister supervised the scheduled programmes of the female patients. The male Treatment Wing was on the other side of the building, presumably to restrict the infiltration of male into female and vice-versa. From where I was standing, there was already a fair amount of bare female flesh on display. Draped ineptly beneath superbly laundered Slivers' towels, women and girls were wobbling all around me to and from the dry heat cabinets, the saunas, the Roman spa bath (hot, bubbling, communal, seaweed-charged, iodised) the massage rooms, the slim-and-trim gym, the solarium, the osteopath, colonic irrigations and enemas.

Branching off from this entrance was a long row of tiny cubicles, each supplied with a tiny bed upon which sufferers could collapse. Those who may have overdone things in the sauna, who felt that their premature end was upon them. Sudden heart failure was not unknown in the male and female Treatment Wings of Slivers, therefore a strict medical check was maintained over each cubicle and every one of the inmates. In the past there had been the fear of unpleasant publicity, resulting from the demise of the wife of a Danish diplomat. Excess fat due to the retention of fluid, it had said on her entry form. She had expired as dry as a Danish pastry, found abandoned in an unsupervised and distant heat cabinet. The body had been there twenty-four hours, but that was long before Sister's reign. Nothing like that would be allowed under her scrupulous supervision.

'You'll be required for your enema in half an hour, Lady Patch,' she said to me now.

'Yes, I'm looking forward to that.' I nodded happily

218

and smiled at her again. This time she glanced at me with an enquiring expression, tinged with the suspicion that I was being sarcastic, but then seeing that this clearly wasn't so she directed me towards one cubicle.

'You'll find your friend in their, just resting.'

'Dame Agatha?'

'That's the one.' Sister nodded grimly. 'But don't let her put you off your enema, she's been behaving like a child. I've never seen anything like it – and to think that we place our faith and confidence in politicians. My mother's dachshund has a greater sense of its own dignity. She was screaming the place down, it's a wonder she didn't wake you. Why not pop in and have a word to cheer her up. A nice smile from you should do the trick.'

Poor Agatha! When I withdrew the screening curtain I found her reclining in a state of shock on her stomach. Her face was turned to the wall away from me, so that she was unaware of my presence.

'Dame Agatha? How are you feeling now it's all over – better, I expect?' There was no reply.

'It's me, Loopy,' I said. 'Is there anything I can do for you?' I spoke humbly, casting myself back to the schoolgirl again. And yet I knew that the idiotic grin on my face was still there, the one Kid Lips had pasted on with his penis. 'I'm just off for my own enema in a minute,' I added casually, just to get some reaction. And I crept forward to take a closer peep at her averted cheek, suddenly afraid for what I might see. Tears, or the stunned eyes of a person betrayed by the bodily assault of another, I didn't know what to expect. Dame Agatha, after all, was still an unknown quantity to me. We had been out of contact with each other for all the important adult events of our lives so that I had no idea of her reactions under stress or in any given situation. Even so I was aware of a quickening concern. In my present euphoria I wanted everyone to be happy. And I was in the naughty mood to confide. I wanted to tell her, or somebody, about Kid Lips. It was too good to keep to myself.

'I've just been screwed silly,' I hissed at her sullen shape. May as well dive in at the deep end. 'Yes. Fucked on the floor up in my room by this fantastic pop-star. He

219

flung open the door and asked rather politely whether I fancied a fuck – or words to that effect –' I sighed contentedly. My words were doing the trick.

Dame Agatha rose slowly, large but graceful like a basking shark preparing to come in for the kill.

'I beg your pardon?'

'You heard,' I said blithely. 'I've just been shagged stupid by Kid Lips, the singer. Mind, I don't think the poor boy knew what the hell was going on but when I sent him away he seemed to be quite happy. As for me, I feel full of myself.' I gave a small skip in the air just to prove it, then looked properly at my stunned confidante. She looked ill, positively ancient, her entire face had caved in. 'Agatha, dear,' I said, horrified, 'I don't want to frighten you but you seem to have lost all your teeth!'

Her hand flew to her empty mouth, where her chin now met her nose, like a portrait of Punch. 'They went in the enema,' she mumbled miserably.

'But how ghastly, Agatha!' What on earth could she mean? Unsightly images clouded my mind.

'They're broken. I bit the nurse. Both dentures gone to be mended. Be back by tomorrow.' Dame Agatha shrank beneath my comforting gaze. 'I daren't look at myself in the mirror.'

'You look fine,' I said heartily. 'I tell you something – you look positively pounds lighter. Really thin in the face. I'm off for my enema in a moment, I hope it does that for me.'

Dame Agatha attempted a smile, keeping her lips pressed tightly together in case I got a glimpse of her gums. 'Don't bite the nurse,' she said out of the side of her mouth, 'not unless your teeth are all your own.'

'Some of them are, but not all. What do you think of my news – you haven't passed comment on that?' My imminent departure had made me bold.

Her eyes opened wide. The hand flew to her mouth again, this time to hide a laugh. 'He's jolly good at it, isn't he? Kid Lips! Yes I had him once, or was it twice in swift succession – I just can't remember, it was some years ago. He was only a lad then, long before he was famous, but I could tell he'd go far. Roy Baker, that was his name then. His father was a butcher in Barrow-on-Furness. Very reliable worker in the constituency, a political animal if ever I saw one. He always hoped young Roy would go in for politics and the lad was ambitious, but I suppose he just got seduced by the pop scene. Though I offered every encouragement.'

'Obviously!' I said succinctly, though without any malice.

'Oh dear, you say he's here. Well he musn't see me like this, nor must anyone else. I shall have arrangements made to have my lemon juice in my room until my teeth come. One's reputation and all that, Loopy. Will you make my apologies for me to the others. We usually congregate in the evenings over a game of chess, Marlene, little Marlene is our chess champion, if you can believe it! Or else we squabble over Scrabble, poor little Flower fails miserably at Scrabble. She can't spell, that's the trouble. Her education was sadly lacking, between you and me I don't even think that she can read. I think they got her to sign her film contract by simply placing an X in the appropriate place.'

Sister popped a wary head around the curtain. 'Time, please Lady Patch!'

Dame Agatha slunk down, her face hidden in her forearm. 'Come up and see me sometime, Loopy.' Her voice held a pleading note, it fell pleasantly on my ears.

'Difficult patient,' Sister muttered disagreeably.

'She was a model pupil at school,' I said ingenuously. 'But people do change as they grow older.' I was sucking up now, like mad, hoping that Sister might personally supervise my enema. Even my sexual euphoria couldn't hold at bay the dread I was experiencing now. I needed a sympathetic hand at the controls.

'We toast you, Lady Patch!' Flab Pottle's eyes twinkled as he held up his lemon juice. Flower Fowler and Fizzy Tornado clinked glasses with him and turned to welcome the newcomer who had joined our small group.

'Not Lady Patch, Flab – if I may call you Flab. My name's Lettice, or Letty. Or if you prefer, Loopy. Dame Agatha will never be able to think of me as anything other than Loopy.' I smiled at them all, encompassing the newcomer although no one had yet introduced us. 'What's the toast for anyway?'

I wondered if they'd had word of my abandoned

behaviour with Kid Lips, even Flower Fowler was regarding me with a friendlier curiosity than I might have expected from her. Perhaps Dame Agatha had spilt the beans, though I hadn't seen either of the girls in the Treatment Wing. And I believed Dame Agatha when she said that she had no intention of letting herself be seen without her tusks. Though my public persona wasn't anything like hers, I would have thought twice about flashing the gaps in my gums. The sight smacked a little too much of small country cemeteries whose gravestones have fallen away through general neglect and lack of proper attention. Besides which, while my top denture sported only five teeth, I felt it did a Trojan job in supporting my cheeks and the sub-structure of my face. Though I wouldn't look nearly as bad as poor old Agatha, the area around my mouth could suffer a minor collapse. As if I'd sucked overlong on a lemon.

'We toast you –' All three of them were saying it now, winking and nudging whilst they did so. The newcomer, boyishly-fleshed, beautifully groomed, aged about twenty-six, stood behind them smiling. He was obviously in on the act. A pal of Kid Lips, who'd been spreading the tale?

'On my enema?' I got it in first, feigning an expression of tortured agony and pointing crudely round to my backside.

'No. No,' Flab Pottle interrupted. 'Not on your enema – though welcome to the enema club, now we've all had one. The next thing is the colonic irrigation, old thing! No, we want to toast you on your bloody *joie de vivre,* on your sexual drive, on your animal appreciation of life, on the fucking great example you give to all these other lily-liv-ered mortals with your magnificent get-up and fuck-it, let's have a sodding go!'

They clearly knew about me. And Kid Lips. 'Well,' I said glowing.

'Yeah,' Flower Fowler clinked her lemon juice to suggest that she was under the influence. Not exactly inebriated, but high on something. 'Yeah, Flab's bin readin' us bits outa one of yer books. We never twigged that you was the Lettice Field that writes filthy books, me Mum's got every single one of 'em. She 'ides 'em away from me Dad. 'E's a bit of a prude, brought up Plymouth Brethren, if the old bugger ever got to see one of me films 'e'd go stark, ravin', bonkers! But your stuff – it's real good fun, just me cuppa tea.' And she leant forward and kissed me.

I was thrilled by her show of affection. I hated being on the wrong side of anyone, especially a creature as beguiling as this. Rare physical beauty such as Flower Fowler's casts a powerful spell, though she seemed unaware of being an enchantress in her down-to-earth manner and the warmth of her reactions. Now that I met with her approval, I could see that she was preparing to make a friend of me. Had I been the same age I might have had second thoughts, if I had been a normal girl and not used to bathing in the reflected glory of others. The competition would have been too overwhelming. But smouldering beauties rarely travel in pairs, they wisely choose drabber companions to enhance their own glitter. Or clowns to relax the electrifying tension which their perfection has created. I was perfectly prepared to play my part, any part she was preparing for me.

For the moment it seemed that I was to hog the limelight. It wasn't often that I enjoyed such literary acclaim, not so unequivocally as this.

I beamed at everybody. For the first time the newcomer stepped forward and spoke. 'I'm afraid it was my doing, Lady Patch,' he said hesitantly. 'I brought a couple of your paperbacks with me. Recommended reading by Tadpole, your daughter. I made her acquaintance over lunch today with Bart Deco.'

'My bleedin' agent,' Flower broke in with a scowl.

'Today, lunch today?' I said, surprised.

'Yes, I'm Windsor Shag,' and he held out a well manicured hand for me to shake – the nails would have graced an ad for nail polish. His teeth were as perfectly matched as a string of pearls. Yet there was no sexual charge to his presence. It was as if his development had been arrested at the stage of pre-puberty. He had the appeal of the small, scrubbed, shy schoolboy on his very best behaviour. The sort that mothers used to, or perhaps still did, want as a son-in-law. It was difficult to imagine him indulging in all the sort of things that the newspapers attributed to him. I didn't recognise him from his photographs, he looked so much younger and less worldly. Not at all the international stud, the plaything of the jet-set, the cause of the scandalous divorce in Royal circles.

But he did bring out the maternal. I wanted to mother him. To put my arm around him and bring him nearer the warmth. He was probably very much as I was, he'd find it easy to worm his way into people's affections. Many must have fallen in love with him that way, surprised into it from the unexpected intimacy.

'Yes, we were having lunch,' he continued pleasantly, 'and the question of my beer-belly arose.' He patted the subtle beginnings of a paunch which, together with the childish curve of his rosy cheeks, just stood between him and the contemporary idea of lean perfection. In another era he would have had no worries, but I could imagine him being dissatisfied with his shape. Wasn't that why we were all here! 'And Tadpole was telling us that you'd popped down to Slivers to shed a few pounds and before I knew what had happened Bart had organised me into coming too. It was arranged within the hour. He rounded up Kid Lips as well – he's really in bad shape. Needs to lose a hell of a lot before this new tour of his. The press are going to tear him to pieces otherwise, I can tell you.' Windsor Shag's cherubic features looked uncharacteristically solemn as he addressed us all.

I had been listening with the same silly grin on my face that I had been sporting all afternoon, but now I took my cue from the others and we nodded in united concern. There was not the remotest chance that I would ever be in the public eye long enough for the press to tear me to pieces and so I was not haunted by the spectre. But clearly every one else had entertained the fear, even jolly Flab Pottle.

' "A hideous barrel of lard, who nevertheless manages to keep his audience in hysterics!" That's what one critic wrote after my debut at the Hippodrome.' Flab gazed gloomily into his glass. 'I don't think I ever got a single review without my size being referred to. Mind you I was five stone heavier when I was in the business, it's only since I gave it up that I've had this svelte shape.' He sucked in his sizeable stomach and winked at me. If I'd have been any good at winking I'd have winked back at him.

But Flower was speaking now. All attention was on her. 'Yeah,' she spoke slowly with what seemed like a genuine sense of aggrievement. 'I never 'ad no fuckin' mention, 'cept for these flamin' fings!' And she punched her breasts so savagely that both little Fizzy and I winced. Only we, as females, could have any idea how painful the blow must have been. 'I bloody 'ate em! I've *always* 'ated 'em, if it weren't for the fact that I'm such a bleedin' coward, I'd 'ave 'ad both the bleedin' buggers off. 'Ad 'em seen to wiv surgery, you can y'know,' she addressed herself to me for some reason. I nodded in sympathy. 'They can do wonders wiv surgery, can't they these days? This German pal o' mine, the one I done them dyke scenes wiv, y'remember Flab, in that last film o' mine – she's 'ad er 'ole bum gone over, lifted up an' sliced away. Before that operation she 'ad shockin' duck's disease, she's shown me the snaps. Now she's got one o' the best bums in the business. But,' Flower sighed, 'when she said 'ow much it 'urt I thought to meself – blimey, girl, that aint for you!'

Now Fizzy took over. 'It's true, people can't take you for the talents you offer. Look at me. I was quite content winning that Radio One contest, I never meant it to go further than sending up the tape of me singing and hoping to hear my name over the air. I only did it as a dare with the girls at school. There were three of us who went in for it, Midge, Beryl and me. The same week as our "O" Levels I got the news that I had got through to the finals, we heard my name on Beryl's tranny while we were waiting at the bus-stop. There were lots of people listening, we couldn't believe it, any of us. And then one of the boys from the Grammar School shouted – it was really embarrassing – "if it was telly and not radio old Fatty wouldn't have got anywhere, she'd have broken the camera!" And then one of the others shouted, "they wouldn't have been able to fit her on to one screen!" And then everyone was laughing and making fun of me. It was so horrible that I started crying. I failed that history "O" level. I just couldn't concentrate, I felt so upset. And when I actually won, when Radio One did that interview and I

225

cut the first record for them, it was like a nightmare. Every time I see a photograph of myself I cringe. I try to get out of as many interviews as I can, just because I know they're going to want to take snaps of me. And now there's this television thing. They want me to go on Top of the Pops to tie in with the release of my first Melody record. I've signed up with Melody now, so they can really tell me what to do. It's Nick Zimmerman of Melody who's sent me here. He's said I'm to lose four stone before I'm to go anywhere near the television camera. He said that they put on about half a stone if they get you in the wrong angle.

He says that I'm to stay here at Slivers until I lose it all, they'll just postpone everything until I'm ready. So you see,' she looked imploringly around for sympathy, 'I really have got to do it, you can imagine the pressure I'm under.'

'But how old are you, Fizzy dear?' I spoke to her kindly. Until she'd mentioned her "O" levels, I would have placed her at fourteen, although my first impression had been even younger than that. But she must be seventeen or more since she was speaking of her school examinations as if they were well in the past. 'I mean to say,' I continued, 'that you shouldn't, at your age, have to be harassed into doing something you don't enjoy. What do your parents think about all this?'

' 'Er folks are dead. She's bin brought up by 'er Gran. Funny that, I should much to 'ave lived wiv my Gran, but she went an' died when I was a kid. Fizzy's Gran's bin put in an 'ome, aint she Fiz?'

'She's very old now, she was just hanging on till I finished in school. I always promised that I'd leave after "O" levels though I should have liked to have stayed on and done my "A" levels and gone on to University. No-one ever dreamed that all this would ever happen to me. I suppose it's what every girl dreams of, isn't it really – every girl except me.'

None of us spoke, we just sat there looking at her. Beneath the brilliant blanket of dyed hair, the first stab at the build-up of the Fizzy Tornado persona, was a perfectly ordinary, plump little schoolgirl. One of above average intelligence it would seem, capable of carving a good career for herself in the academic world. Apart from this

226

extraordinary voice. It was the effect of the voice that had reduced us to silence. Although she was speaking normally, with no effort to seduce, or impress in any way, we were all left wanting more. We wanted her to continue talking to us, stroking our spines with her thick, husky, honey tones. What, I couldn't help thinking, a combination it would make if Fizzy had Flower's face and body. Or the other way round. A publicist's dream, the chance to make millions. Fame without even lifting a finger! Though how the possessor of such bounty could cope with the pressures was another matter. Neither of these young women seemed to be satisfied with the reaction to what they had already.

'Wouldn't it be lovely now to be sitting at home in front of the television with a bag of fish and chips, knowing that when you finished them you could pop out for some more if you felt like it,' Fizzy was saying wistfully.

'Fish and chips and a pint of Guinness – no, make that two.' Flab Pottle wiped his mouth with the back of his hand, smacking his lips in imaginary relish.

'I could *murder* a fuckin' martini,' Flower Fowler murmured.

It was my turn. This was quite obviously a common turn of events, for the conversation to become dominated by the topic of food and drink. I thought quickly, being the generous soul that I am (always giving to gain a spot of friendly attention), I would have liked to confess to my little illicit hoard upstairs. And to share it around as far as it would go, though that wouldn't be very far, not with this number and their appetites. Best to say nothing – anyway this was my first day. Christ only knew what my needs would be like later in the week. The survival of self was the strongest priority in these circumstances.

'You mean what would I like most at this very minute?' I answered their expectant faces. 'Well, I wouldn't say no to a glass of champagne.' There were small mutters of approval. 'And then I might do justice to a nice big baked onion, with salt and freshly ground pepper, and masses of butter . . .'

'A bleedin' onion, blimey! Do us a favour!' Flower jeered.

'Very comforting, absolutely delicious, makes you sleep

227

like a top.' I assured her. I was enjoying this game. 'Well, would you like something else instead? What about a bread and butter pudding with currants and chopped candied peel and sliced bananas. And an egg custard made with cream and a good dash of rum.' Flab Pottle was slavering openly, I would have known that he'd be a pudding-person.

But Windsor Shag was pulling a face. 'All that cholesterol! I'd rather tuck into a decent steak and green salad and a bottle of claret. But then that's what I did tuck into at lunchtime, I hate to confess. So I'm not yet suffering like you poor bastards.' He spoke with a hesitant upper-class accent, the sort I was used to. But I could tell that it made him feel self-conscious in the present company, that he was striving to make it altogether slangier and more classless. I'd seen sweeping changes to accents in my lifetime.

'You wait a day or two, old boy. See how you feel then.' Flab Pottle leaned forward and patted his arm. Did I imagine it or was he mimicking the careful delivery of the other, even unconsciously?

'How long have you been in?' I looked around at them. 'And how long has Dame Agatha?'

'Dame Agatha Tatters?' Windsor Shag squeaked with surprised joy. 'Is Dame Agatha here too?' He looked around eagerly, hoping to catch a glimpse of her there and then.

'She's upstairs in her bedroom. She broke her false teeth biting the nurse as she was being given her enema,' I explained briefly. 'You'll see her tomorrow.' It was the first that the others had heard of the news. Everybody burst out laughing.

'She doesn't want to be seen without them. It's understandable,' I said.

'Oh, I don't know,' ventured Windsor Shag. 'When I first met Dame Agatha the assembled company was being invited to view her without her dentures. She looked a little like Punch, I seem to remember. Mind you we were all operating under relaxed conditions. Far from home on foreign shores. One of the gentlemen present unscrewed his false leg, it was all he had left.'

'Was you playin strip-poker, Windsor?' Flower asked coyly.

'Yes. We were as a matter of fact.'

'An wot was you left wiv?'

'I was left with my virginity. The very last forfeit.' Windsor spoke proudly.

'Ooh!' giggled both the girls.

Flab Pottle chortled. 'Don't tell me Dame Agatha Tatters was instrumental in the loss of your innocence, Shag, m'boy?'

'That would be telling, wouldn't it.' Windsor pressed his boyish lips prissily together, but still managed to hang onto his dignity.

I thought of Dame Agatha's revelation about Kid Lips. Had she relieved him of his innocence? He'd been very young too . . .

I cleared my throat. The memory of Kid Lips caused a sudden rush of saliva over my tonsils. 'You said you came down with Kid Lips, Windsor – where is he now?'

'Christ! Screw Kid Lips!' Flower spat with a kittenish venom. I wondered if she had screwed him at some time in her career. Snap!

'I wouldn't mind meeting him,' little Fizzy said softly. 'Kid Lips was always one of my idols. I used to have his poster pinned to my desk at school, we all did. He always looked so wonderfully dissolute.'

'Phew, dissolute eh! Wots up – you swallowed a fuckin' dictionary, Fizz?'

'It's a marvellous mouth,' I said casually, unable to resist joining in. Should I disclose my amorous encounter? Or not?

'Jesus – e's not got to you oldsters, that clapped out piece o' shit? Listen, Mum, I could tell you fings about that ratbag Kid Lips that would make you wanna, wanna . . .'

'Wanna wot, Flower darlin?' Kid Lips lifted her effortlessly into the air and then threw her carelessly back into her chair as if she were a rag doll. Then bowing to the rest of us, he doffed a very fine bowler hat. He had changed since the last time I'd seen him.

I had watched his approach, as had Fizzy Tornado and Windsor Shag. From where we were seated, facing the door, we had watched him being directed towards our group by Sister herself. She waved to me as she passed back into the corridor.

Perhaps Kid Lips had thought that my returning wave

was for him, although Windsor Shag had half-risen in welcome from his seat. In any event he felt friends were waiting, that his arrival was not going to pass unheralded. He looked – remarkable!

He was wearing a pair of ladies' lounging pyjamas, in pale peppermint green. The sort that screen sirens used to sport in the thirties, loose and floppy, made from slithery crêpe-de-chine for maximum cling and erotic appeal. Had these been all Kid Lips was wearing, it would have been positively indecent. As it was, with a fur-trimmed, velvet negligée (another feminine garment from some other age) draped over his shoulders, at least parts of his protuberances were concealed. Nevertheless there was enough on show to cause apoplexy amongst the other patients. In their weakened condition, in the exalted state that comes with extreme hunger, no-one had the energy to make a fuss. And there was no reason why they should. With his glamorous female garb, completed by the black bowler hat and the chic addition of an old school-tie around his neck, he looked the right addition for our group. I felt proud to be part of it, not odd at all, for although I too had changed from the clothes that I had been wearing for my enjoyable rape, I was still attired in Bertie's clothes. Nobody took exception, they were now accepted as part of me. I had on a crisp pair of striped black and white pyjamas, beneath a tailored black woollen dressing-gown. 'Rather natty,' Bertie used to remark of himself in this particular combination, 'Rather distingué, what!' And on him it was perfectly true, with his figure. On me it was quite a different story. My legs for a start were much shorter than Bertie's. One of the disadvantages when I began wearing his suits was that I'd had to pay to get the trousers professionally shortened. Similarly with the arms.

I had never got round to doctoring his night-wear to fit the length of me. Who would be seeing me in bed in any case? All the pyjamas had remained as they were with the exception of the red silk pair that I had been wearing earlier. Their legs and arms had been very much shortened to serve as the basis for the fancy-dress that Tadpole had worn some years ago at a school party. She was much shorter then, about the same height as me. She had gone as a Chinaman, smoothing turmeric from the kitchen into her skin to give herself the appropriate complexion.

And so I must have looked slight odder now, with my striped pyjama trouser-legs concertina-ing around each hidden foot, and my small hands concealed in the mandarin folds of my jacket arms. I must have looked a little unusual, to say the least. Not what you'd expect of a lady. That's what Kid Lips obviously must have thought, because after he'd greeted Windsor Shag and Flower Fowler he nodded cheerfully to me and uttered his well known phrase, 'Wotcha cock!'

He must have thought that I was a little fat man. His greeting to Flab Pottle was exactly the same, but nobody seemed to notice except me.

'It wasn't that I minded,' I explained to Dame Agatha in the sauna next morning, 'I had no reason to think for one moment that he would recognize me, that he'd come rushing across the room shouting "That was one helluva fuck we had back there! Come on, baby, let's give it another try right here!" '

Dame Agatha gave a small shudder of distaste that sent ripples all over her naked, steaming flesh (how huge, yet how firm she was still!).

'You mean to say that's how he speaks now – absolutely ghastly! All that "baby" stuff! Don't you agree? I do hope you don't encourage your daughters in this slovenly transatlantic slang. The young should be studying the languages of the Common Market, infiltrating the continental endearments into our vocabulary. I brought it up in the House recently.'

'You've gone off at a tangent again Agatha, dear. You keep doing it.' I tried to keep the irritability that I was feeling out of my voice. It took a considerable effort to do so. I had woken this morning with an absolutely appalling headache, which everyone had assured me was just what I should feel on the second day. Perhaps Dame Agatha, being several days of famine and fast ahead of me, was simply suffering from a normal loss of concentration rather than what seemed to me a quite unforgiveable preoccupation with *me, me, me,* and the inability to tolerate any conversation unless it was centred around herself. She was surprisingly urbane when it came to correction, however. I had to give her that.

'Oh, Loopy, my darling – you must forgive me! I'm just a selfish old woman, now what were you saying? I think it must be the relief of being amongst people again. It was absolutely awful last evening incarcerated in my room on my own. You didn't pop in to see me after all. I was hoping you would. I tried reading but you know, the concentration has gone. I kept re-reading the same sentence again and again, in the end I had to give it up. But watching television was completely impossible. Everyone was eating. They were eating all the time, and drinking! Do you know there was a play on and the heroine drank the whole way through. Just making her normal way around the world – she wasn't an alcoholic or anything remotely near it. And she was as thin as a blade of grass, I can assure you. And all the commercials! When I get out of here the first thing I must taste are all these new chocolate items they have out now for children. There is one called an Earthling, which consists of honey fudge and nut crunch which I simply have to sample. They show the tiny teeth of a creature from outer space sinking into this Earthling, and then a close-up of what happens when the tongue of the space creature comes into contact with the honey fudge and the nut crunch. Quite brilliant I thought, the way they do those special effects. Did you see *War Stars*, or *Several Encounters from another Close Planet*, Loopy? Frightfully good!'

'*Close Encounters of the Third Kind*, Agatha.'

'Oh, that's another good one is it? I must look out for it. Remind me to make a note of it when we get out of here. Phew – you don't think that we're overdoing it, do you dear? It seems to be dreadfully hot since that stupid woman threw water on those coals. Probably a Kraut, they always try to prove they can take things much tougher.'

The woman to whom Dame Agatha was so loudly referring to turned a pink, huffy shoulder in our direction and made an unpleasant remark about us to her nearest neighbour. She spoke in a strong Scottish accent. But it was cetainly true that the heat had now become unbearable. One boisterous and bonny teenager had collapsed and had to be helped out earlier this morning. We had seen her being dragged (there was no question of lifting her) along the corridor towards the shelter of the cubicles as we had arrived at the sauna. Everybody had been ordered out by Sister and several others of the staff.

It was rumoured that a body had been discovered in the swimming pool, though those premises were locked every night. A strange object resembling a human form had been discovered there this morning by the caretaker. I suspected that Kid Lips may have been behind it, but perhaps that was unfair. He was the obvious suspect when events requiring a degree of imagination and daring happened to have taken place. But in a place like Slivers these wild rumours were bound to circulate. It was like being back at school, except here no one was studying, there was not enough to occupy their minds. It would be easy for mass hysteria to take over, there was neurosis in the air.

'That's Madame Jean over there,' Dame Agatha pointed to a gross eighteen-stoner further along whose arms were festooned with bangles, bangles doomed to remain on her fat arms forever, unless someone sawed them off. She sat cross-legged on the wooden slats, with her eyes shut, like a Buddha.

'Good morning, Madame Jean.' Dame Agatha raised her loud voice. 'Taking a peep into the future, eh?'

The question clearly required no answer. Madame Jean merely inclined her head, without even bothering to open her eyes.

'She's a clairvoyant, Loopy.' Dame Agatha was shouting as if I was deaf.

'Don't shout at me, Agatha, you're making my head worse,' I said crossly.

'She's a clairvoyant, Madame Jean. Rather a good one, so I believe. Several of the chaps go to her. Idi Amin consults regularly.'

'From Uganda? Are you sure?'

'Absolutely, Loopy. Crossed wavelengths with the Chancellor of the Exchequer a short while ago, before the last budget. Could have been awkward for everyone concerned, you know what I mean.'

The conversation had drifted a long way from Kid Lips.

But I'd given up on it. Instead I brought things round to Windsor Shag.

'We spoke of you last night, Agatha. Windsor was explaining the circumstances of your first meeting – on foreign soil, he said.'

'Darling thing!' Dame Agatha chuckled. 'Yes, I remember little Windsor. I believe he was only about thirteen at the time. Lost his virginity to a rather feeble fellow with a peg-leg, Percy. Percy Partridge. Lost his leg in the Ministry of Environment, picked at a pimple on his left shin while sun-lounging out on the lawns. Damned thing turned out to be some sort of cancerous growth. They whipped him into the Charing Cross and had it off in a matter of weeks. Was touch and go whether or not to take the other one with it, one of those damned doctors diagnosed a tiny verucca on the big toe of his right foot as being cancerous too. Fortunately, a second opinion was sought on the matter, otherwise poor Percy would have been consigned to a wheelchair. He's no longer Environment. I'm not sure, but I think he's been shifted to Transport. Safe constituency, well, he's batting on a good wicket. The British would never ditch a chap with one leg, would they now!'

'Maybe so,' I said, not caring one way or another. The heat was getting to me too now. I felt dizzy, sweat was pouring over my forehead and into my eyes so that everything appeared in a blur.

There were about fifteen of us in this particular sauna, all women of around the same age. This tended to happen. In the sauna next door, where I had caught a glimpse of Flower Fowler and Fizzy Tornado stretched out beside each other, everyone appeared to be much younger. It was livelier, people were talking and laughing despite the debilitating effects of the steam heat. That was the place from which the teenager had been dragged – the young ones liked to push the temperature much higher that was safe. Despite what Dame Agatha had said about the heat in here, and despite what I was feeling now to be almost intolerable, I knew it would be far worse next door. They hadn't high blood-pressure and their hearts to worry about.

I lowered my chin down to my chest. Beneath my

breasts bulged the multiple folds of my spare tyres. Slumped, with no pretence at posture, I must have looked absolutely hideous. I knew that, but after the first few minutes of naked self-consciousness, I no longer cared. We were all in the same obese boat. Beside me Dame Agatha lolled in completely abandoned fashion, occupying the space of three normal-sized persons. She displayed little modesty in the pose she had adopted, thighs wide like a port prostitute preparing to greet the fleet. Her torso challengingly thrust towards anyone bold enough to take a glance, as she supported herself on her elbows. Head flung high in the air. 'Rubens would have done his nut in here,' I commented. My breath came in short, panting gasps as I said it.

Dame Agatha heaved herself forward. As she did so the sound of her heavy breasts falling against her ribcage made a moist slapping contact, like smacking a baby's botty.

'Phew,' she pursed her mouth in such a way that I was again reminded by her profile of the prow of a ship. 'Phew,' she repeated, 'I don't know about you, Loopy, but I'm just about done in here. I'm reluctant to give in – I do feel it doing me good. The pounds are literally falling away. And we're both due on the scales after this. I have been very good in the last twenty-four hours. Not a morsel has passed my lips, no secret tucking-in last night. I could have done, mind you – I have a little hoard secreted away up there like everyone else. But it's really not so much fun on your own. Did you lot get up to anything last night?'

'Up to anything?' I said innocently. 'We had a few games of Scrabble. Little Fizzy won. Kid Lips played chess with Windsor Shag – I was rather surprised by that. But I left them to it, I went to bed at ten-thirty.'

'You were hungry, Loopy, I expect. Did you eat anything?' Dame Agatha looked at me very directly so that it would have been impossible to tell anything other than the truth. That's why she'd made such a perfect Head Girl.

'A spoonful of Hellman's Mayonnaise. Oh, and a very tiny swig of Glenfiddich.'

'That won't have done much harm. Some people wolf down the equivalent of a seven-course meal, though how

235

they can imagine it won't show on the scales is beyond me. I think they think that because it's done in secret it somehow doesn't count. As if silent mastication makes everything all right. At the mention of the word mastication the Scottish woman scowled, she'd obviously misheard. There was little reaction from anyone else, though several lobster-pink buttocks wobbled past our eyes on their way out. People were beginning to give up.

'I think I'll have a cold shower now, Agatha,' I gasped. Sister's face had appeared at the small, misty pane of glass which was set into the door. 'Are you staying on a while?'

'Just a little, Loopy. You go on, it's only your first time in, best to be careful. You find you build up a resistance after a few days.'

There were few showers vacant but I managed to find one. Someone was singing in the one next to mine. It was a glorious voice, full and throaty. Its owner could have been black, but I guessed her to be Fizzy Tornado. I was correct. She was sharing her shower with Flower Fowler, I could hear their muffled laughter once the singing had stopped.

'Good morning girls,' I called over to them.

'Lady Patch?' Fizzy called back. Try as I could, I had not been able to persuade any of them to call me anything other than Lady Patch, not even Flab Pottle. Flower Fowler had explained it.

'Fing is see, Lady Patch, the rest of us aint used to 'avin titled people in our midst. So it sorta gives us a kick sayin' Lady this an' Lady that. If we was to call you Letty or Loopy, same as Dame Agatha do, you'd sound like the rest of us. Aint that true, folks?' They all seemed to be in agreement.

Kid Lips had not that he paid much attention to anything once he'd started on his game of chess with Windsor Shag. His fans wouldn't have recognised him. But I was waiting for the interesting confrontation between Kid Lips and Dame Agatha – and Windsor Shag.

'Yes, it's me,' I shouted back. 'How are you two this morning?'

There were scuffles from the next shower, followed by more giggles. 'What are you getting up to?' I shouted with a mock severity.

'Come an' fuckin' see for yerself,' I heard Flower gurgling.

But self-conscious modesty forbade me to move. It was all very well displaying myself amongst those of my own age group, whose sagging excesses were even more pronounced than my own. But to cavort amongst youngsters would be like stripping off before my own two beautiful daughters. I was old enought to be these young girls' mother. Even so, curiosity got the better of me, and I did have my towel to hide behind. And so clutching it to me, I edged around to where they were.

They stood before me beneath the streaming water unashamedly playing with each other. Flower had the soap in her slim fingers. She was using it between Fizzy's fat little thighs to work up a thick, creamy lather. There was already a sumptuous supply of it down there out of reach of the cascading shower. The white foam covered the entire area of pubic hair and yet Flower went on rubbing relentlessly to and fro, in and out. The effect on me was electrifying!

Fizzy, seeing the expression on my face, wriggled appreciatively against the pleasuring fingers. Her own were caressing Flower's voluptuous breasts, stroking them upwards with the palm of each hand, rolling the erect nipples softly between her knuckles. And then suddenly, still watching me, she bent over and pressing both breasts together she took the nipples into her mouth. Flower, squirming, threw back her head and burst out laughing.

'It is quite prevalent between the young I believe, Loopy.' Dame Agatha strode purposefully towards Gunter Ragg's weighing scales whilst I ran along beside her. 'They're all meant to be bi-sexual aren't they these days? If I'm to believe what I read.'

'Oh, yes. My eldest daughter is completely gay, though she started out a heterosexual. She may easily change back, though she says not.'

'How interesting, Loopy. And you, yourself, you don't mind one way or the other?' Dame Agatha steered me firmly around the corner. We ought to stop this conversation because ahead of us I could see Flower and Fizzy together. We were all on our way to be weighed.

'I don't mind anything, Agatha. It's all okay by me,' I said.

She squeezed my elbow affectionately.

'You haven't changed, Loopy dear. You always were a most accommodating child.'

By the time we had caught up with Flower and Fizzy, we were talking of other more innocuous matters. They had already teased Dame Agatha about her broken teeth and about biting the nurse. And now that they had allowed me to witness their sexual intimacies, which really had no more significance than a romp between two healthy animals (except that I couldn't get it out of my unhealthy mind) they treated me with a special teasing friendliness too. I could imagine them plotting together, 'C'mon, let's give the old girl a shock – let's give her something to write about in her dirty books!' I returned the special familiarity which had sprung up between us.

But now we all had something really serious to occupy our thoughts. We waited silently together in Gunter Ragg's outer office, behind the door we could hear the steady drone of a conversation.

'That will be someone who's gained weight. When you've lost you're in and out. It's all "well done!" and "top of the class!" But when you haven't he reads the riot act, in the politest possible way.' Dame Agatha spoke confidently, as one who had broken no rules. The rest of us fidgeted and looked apprehensive. Especially Fizzy. I was cross with myself too. I inspected my card, the one with yesterday's weight on. Eleven stone six. I must surely have lost something, my intake had been miniscule in the past twenty-four hours compared to what I used to guzzle.

'I shouldn't have had that sherry of Flab's,' whispered Fizzy accusingly to Flower. 'That was your fault, you encouraged me.' She began feverishly pummelling away at her hips, slapping and kneeding at the fistfuls of spare flesh.

'That aint gonna do much good, Fizz – won't come off, not like that, you silly bitch! Look at er!' Flower snorted derisively. She had tied her cloud of dark hair to the top of her head with a royal purple ribbon, which echoed the violet of her eyes. The long line of her neck was further emphasised by the unswept hair, and the stand-away shawl collar of the black robe she was wearing. She looked like Vivien Leigh in *Gone with the Wind*, except that her eyes were not green and her breasts were much bigger. I had to look away from her breasts, I kept seeing them in Fizzy's mouth. It gave me an ache between my legs.

This morning I'd woken with a similar ache, it wasn't only my head that was throbbing. All night long I'd been dreaming that someone was fucking me, roughly and brutally without any love. And although I'd been shocked by the lustful selfishness of my seducer and had cried all the way through, when I woke it was to find myself terribly aroused. I'd had to rub my clitoris to orgasm to relieve my frustration. And even then I felt that something was lacking. If I'd been at home I would have gone straight for a packet of corn-flakes and the creamy top of the milk. Instead I'd remained there in the warm, slowly stirring my moist folding inner flesh. I could have lain there fiddling with it all day.

I knew what it was. It was Kid Lips' doing. He'd given me a taste of what I'd been missing. The real thing. I wondered if old Agatha was getting it regularly, one wouldn't have dreamt of enquiring under normal circumstances. But at Slivers the normal rules of behaviour didn't seem to apply. I could see why people kept coming back again and again. It was a way of life that I could take to very easily myself. All I'd need would be my typewriter – and a spot of food to give me sustenance. I had brought my typewriter with me on this trip, but if how I felt this morning was anything to go by I wouldn't be able to concentrate on anything as exacting as writing a novel. Not even *my* novels, which though they read as though someone had scribbled them on the lavatory wall, still did require a measure of thought. Last night before retiring, with a scorching layer of whisky searing my tongue, I had tried to do a spot of reading. But it was no good, I was too tensed-up, too tired, too over-excited for the words to do anything other than dance wildly all over the page. In the end I had contented myself with slopping through the glossy pages of an Amercian magazine that Daisy had handed me for the train journey down. Mildly feminist, a sugar-coated mixture of glossy materialism and sexual independence. The fashion pages carried photographs of courting couples, all female, caressing in a sports car, in cinema seats, on a grassy slope, amongst deserted sand-dunes. None of the models were anywhere near as facially perfect as Flower Fowler and all were fashionably flat-chested unlike her.

'That's Marion there,' Daisy had pointed out to me one of those posing.

'Is it really, darling!' Marion – was she somebody that I'd met?

'You remember Marion, she broke the washing machine. The American one who stayed over last Whit-sun, she kept buying you all those bunches of daffodils and narcissi.'

'Ah, Marion! Very nice. Yes.' The washing machine had cost nearly fifty pounds to repair and I'd never cared for cut flowers hanging around the house. No one ever seemed to get around to changing the water or throwing the dead blooms away. So that they just sat there stinking the place out. Yes, of course I remembered Marion.

It was Fizzy's turn to go into Gunter Ragg's room. She turned pale and began trembling and would have run away into the corridor instead, and probably hitched a lift back to London in her nightie if we hadn't forcibly detained her.

'Dear Christ,' she muttered tearfully, 'please, please let me have lost.'

Her distress had communicated itself to the rest of us. The door closed behind her.

'I fink I got a bleedin' attack of diarrhoea,' Flower appealed, first to me and then to Dame Agatha. 'I fink I might be goin to 'ave a terrible accident!' The panic in her eyes was very real.

My own curdling innards churned savagely in sympathy but I tried to inject some calm. 'You'll be alright, Flower dear. You can't surely have very much to lose. You must weigh about as little as a sparrow.'

'Oh yeah, you'd be surprised – eight stone, two pounds. But that's not the fuckin' point. Wot I'm aimin' at is getting rid of these buggers, these tits o mine. It's for a reason, it's not just for fun.' She leaned forward. I had taken her mind off her attacking diarrhoea. 'There's this fuckin' part comin up, see, one that I got me eye on. I told

240

bloody Bart Deco that I want it but 'e just laughed 'is
socks off. See, the 'eroine gets mistaken in the plot for a
fella, so's this bloke gets off with 'er in this bar thinking
that's wot she is. Bit complicated, but the point is that the
actress playing that part must be convincin' as a bloke. I
mean she can't 'ave bloody tits this size, can she now – I
ask you!'

'I see the difficulty,' I started to say, but was interrupted by an unearthly high-pitched scream from the next
room, from Gunter Ragg's office. We all sat forward.
Flower, next to me, clutched my arm in apprehension.
The scream, though unlike any other that I had heard
from a human being, had the unmistakeable beauty of
Fizzy's tones.

'Wot's fuckin' 'appened now?' Flower whispered fear-
fully.

In immediate answer the door was flung open. Fizzy
Tornado stood there sobbing, her arms wrapped around
her body – as far as they could wrap around. We looked at
her aghast and then looked beyond her and the open door
into Gunter Ragg's office. There we could see him sitting
in bewilderment at his desk.

'I've lost three pounds since yesterday! Three pounds
I've lost since yesterday! Did you hear that – three
pounds!' Fizzy began babbling between sobs, then she fell
to her knees and placed her hands together in prayer.
'Jesus Christ, thank you ever so much – thank you ever so
much, Jesus Christ.'

'Jesus Christ!' Flower squeezed my arm. 'I never seen
'er this bad before. It's the strain, poor little bitch. She got
that cunt from Melody comin' to check up on 'er this
afternoon. Thank fuckin' God Batt Deco don't know I'm
in this place – though I wouldn't put it past that Kid Lips
or Windsor Shag to blow it for me. They wouldn't lift a
fuckin' finger to 'elp me, not either of them two.'

'Next please!' Gunter Ragg's impatient call came
through the door.

'Your turn, I believe, Loopy. Good luck to you.'

Dame Agatha was supporting the ecstatic but still
blabbering Fizzy in her arms. Flower Fowler looked grim
and gauntly beautiful. It was perversely ridiculous to
attempt what she was attempting, though obviously not

241

impossible. If she dieted long enough in the end she would be bound to lose her breasts.

'Well, and how's it been going for you at Slivers?' Gunter Ragg opened the conversation with the customary pleasantries, instead of getting on with the business in hand. The business of bouncing me on the scales like an overweight baby.

I stretched my gums at him bleakly in imitation of a smile, but he wasn't looking. He was studying my particulars instead. My headache felt as if it might shatter my skull, distributing itself all over his highly polished desk. Spoiling the effect with a surfeit of scarlet blood and splintered bone, and slivers of grey matter. Would he bother to heave a headless body onto the weighing scales, wishing to register the reduced poundage simply to keep an accurate record?

'I have a hell of a headache this morning,' I said, straining for sympathy before we got started. 'I feel that weighs a ton in itself.'

'Well now, we'll soon see whether that's true or not. It's perfectly normal to suffer migraine for the first day or so following the start of a diet of this sort. You'll find that it'll have disappeared by tomorrow. Now jump on. Lady Patch, let's see what the good news is.'

Yesterday I had taken him at his word – and almost broken the scales. This morning I was more circumspect and stepped up as daintily as it was possible for me to do. It must have looked like a parody of a ballerina. The scales clanged. I let my breath out trying to empty my lungs of all air. Air can weigh heavy. And I balanced as best I could on the very tip of my toes, I felt it all helped. I was too faint-hearted to look to see how I was doing. I shut my eyes tightly, like a child waiting to be told.

'Ah, ha!' Gunter Ragg announced. What sort of thing was that to say, insensitive twerp! 'Ah, ha – what have we here!' My heart did a somersault, I felt nauseous and ill. 'A four pound.' What? A four pound increase? Or a four pound loss? 'A four pounds loss – you've lost four pounds, Lady Patch.'

'I must have a hole in my pocket,' I laughed weakly with relief, allowing a lot of heavy air to flood back into my lungs – making certain to step quickly off the scales before it registered.

'That's very good, very good indeed, Lady Patch,' Gunter

Ragg was pleased with himself. 'Let's keep that up. Tomorrow you should be down into the ten stones. Within a week you won't know yourself.'

'How do you mean?' I looked at him blankly. I felt dazed and disorientated. If I'd had the energy I would have started screaming like little Fizzy Tornado. It struck me that I might have done myself a damage, hanging onto my emptied lungs in that foolish fashion. I'd once done that in the swimming-pool of friends in Cap Ferrat – swam an entire length underwater. Just showing off. It had been whilst Bertie and I were still heavy smokers. I hadn't the strength to heave myself out of the pool at the end of it. Midst all the cheering congratulations I was busy seeing stars. Bertie had been surprised that I hadn't suffered a black-out, so he'd said afterwards. At the time he'd been absent, scouring the beach. The bronzed giant he'd brought back spent the afternoon in our bed. It was the first time that I'd been buggered by a Bulgarian, I'd had to dine in the evening on an inflated air-cushion, much to everyone's amusement.

'I mean that by then you'll be down into the nine stones – what have we as your goal-weight? – yes, here it is. Eight stone, four pounds.'

'Eight stone, four pounds!' I wailed, suddenly coming to my senses. 'That's far too light for me – I'd have to be here all summer. I'd look like a scarecrow, all my loose skin flapping in the wind whenever I moved.'

'Isn't that what we agreed would be your goal-weight yesterday, Lady Patch?' Gunter Ragg was alarmed, not wanting a repeat of Fizzy's hysteria. He was frowning at me when moments ago he had been beaming. My behaviour must be the cause. I'd best calm down. I wasn't normally inclined to neurosis.

'We shouldn't have agreed on its being so low. If I did agree then it was before I'd had a taste of this appalling hunger, this headache, the strain of it all.' My voice had shrunk to a whisper, I could have howled I felt so sorry for myself. I seemed to be making a habit of losing control in consulting rooms.

Gunter Ragg drew closer to me and put an arm around my solid shoulders. Still solid despite the four pound loss – still a fat, plain whallop.

243

'Dear Lady Patch, don't distress yourself so. This is a normal reaction, I want you to see that. Until the system adjusts everything is going to be topsy-turvy.' The jargon of the medically affiliated fields.

I sniffed, a tennis ball stuck in my throat. My normal response to formal kindness from comparative strangers. The day before yesterday I had never even met Gunter Ragg, and now here I was in circumstances of intimacy – me in my nightwear, he with his arm around me. As if we were about to become lovers. But I knew these thoughts were not in his mind. To Gunter Ragg I merely represented two hundred quid a week. The suggestion of me getting down to eight stone four was simply a way of ensuring that my stay at Slivers would be longer.

'You want to be under nine stone though surely, Lady Patch?' His seductively smooth voice combined with the subtle squeeze softened my will.

'Mm.' I nodded my head.

'I should think so. You're not a tall person after all. At your height and given your age – what are you, five-foot two, and forty-five? You should be no more than eight stone ten at the most. I see that you were actually eight and a half stone some five years ago anyway. Probably a weight at which you felt very comfortable.' He was being suspiciously persuasive, or was I suddenly in the grip of menopausal paranoia? It was all so daunting, this goal that I was being harried towards. Why wasn't I being allowed to keep on eating contentedly, as I had been doing for the last five years? Why this compulsion, just from William my doctor, and now on the part of Gunter Ragg to strip me down to a bundle of skin and bones?

'My husband had just died. I didn't eat for a week, I was suffering from hay-fever, sneezing over all my food. Otherwise I would have been my normal weight.'

'What would you have said your normal weight was, Lady Patch?' His silly arm was still around me. I could smell his deodorant and see how expertly he had shaved around his sideburns. When he smiled, as he was smiling now, there was a glinting light from a gold tooth at the back. I felt myself growing curiously sleepy. It was soothing standing there slumped to his shoulder, nothing sexual as yet, but things could have developed.

244

Or was that my imagination again?

I lifted my mouth, meaning to say that it was so long since I'd been my normal weight that I could no longer remember. I had always been one of those people who, because they put on weight so very easily, veer violently from being on the brink of death from determined starvation to becomingly unrecognisably obese in a matter of weeks. So what was normal for me? It wasn't a topic that I was fond of discussing with any seriousness: my weight was something I could only joke about. I felt too much about it myself. Too defensive to accept any helpful criticism, because of the element of criticism. But who could I ever hope to confess all this to? Certainly not Gunter Ragg on one day's acquaintance. Besides, he was too busy kissing me.

How long we must have stood there kissing each other like that (oh yes – I was kissing him back all right!) it would have been difficult to say. My headache had vanished, though there was a buzzing between my ears that hadn't been there before. I was conscious, terribly conscious and ashamed that my left breast, swinging low and bra-less, had somehow got trapped under his elbow. So that we couldn't get any closer without wrenching the whole mammary away from its roots. Though that would scarcely have caused me more agony than it did already.

Also, and I couldn't quite believe this, he had such a stiff erection that I feared for the fragile flesh of my clitoris from the bared steel teeth of his thrusting flies. Bertie's pyjamas were no help whatsoever, sluttishly agape where they should have been shut. How, I asked my shuddering self, could the situation have arrived so swiftly at this pass! Granted I was ravenously hungry (Gunter Ragg had taken a chocolate digestive with his morning tea – I sucked like a vampire on his tongue and his teeth and gums) and was glad to get my lips against anything with blood in it, but what could possibly have brought on his bout of passion? I wasn't Brigitte Bardot, for goodness sake – I hadn't Flower Fowler's form and face. I wasn't wowing them on the Continent, unclothed or otherwise. It would have been as much as I could have managed in my present state to pull a parrot off his perch. If we'd been talking about the past . . .

I broke off to take breath, my blood pressure was soaring; my head was abuzz with a hive full of demented honey-bees. The regular beat of my heart had gone completly berserk. Lust was dangerous at my age, that's why the over-forties settled for love and electric blankets and Bournvita at nights. And if Bertie hadn't done the dirty and kicked the bucket before me then that's what I'd be enjoying too, allowing for the occasional sexual escapade. But always with him by my side, never alone. Not like this, not like yesterday. But I wasn't countin yesterday, nor was Kid Lips. He was out of his head on something or other, and I had been drinking on an empty stomach. So that encounter had been more in the nature of a dream. He obviously couldn't recall anything of it at all, while all I'd had to remind me was the radiant afterglow of satiated frustration. Was it this sensual afterglow that had set Gunter Ragg off? Was I giving off sexual wavelengths without even being aware of it? After all I had been tremendously aroused by the sight of Flower and Fizzy playing with each other's naked bodies. So that when I walked into this office I was already receptive, the idea of sex was most definitely on my mind. We are only animals, albeit human. Each individual is keenly attuned to the needs of another. What astonished me was that Gunter Ragg hadn't recoiled in revulsion before such as me, instead of going overboard in this ridiculous manner.

But someone had to call a halt, there were people waiting to be weighed. If Dame Agatha took it into her head to barge in, and I wouldn't put anything past her and her autocratic ways, we'd look pretty daft! I cleared my clogged throat.

'Mr Ragg,' I croaked.

'Gunter, Lady Patch . . .' His shaved cheek scraped my eyeball.

'Gunter – what about Mrs Ragg?' It was all I could think of to say. I was reluctant to end it all, that was the trouble. I was enjoying myself with all this kissing, it put me in mind of my mother's bank manager. He had fallen on me in this manner when I'd gone to him at eighteen to open my first account. His glasses had dropped off the end of his nose and one of us, I think it must have been me, had trodden on them. They lay in smithereens on the floor and when he'd bent down to retrieve them he'd gone temporarily insane and collapsed in a shaking heap at my feet. Staring up my dirndl skirt and plucking at his groin in a bestial frenzy – poor thing. After the initial fascination I decided to leave him at it, best get on with it by himself. Besides I had haddock to buy for Mother's lunch and her medicine to pick up at Boots, I had no wish to watch an old man scratching his rash. He should apply soothing camomile lotion or Vaseline. I had found Vaseline very good for Mother's bed sores.

But the kissing had stayed with me much longer than I'd thought it would, I could have done with a bit more of the kissing. I enjoyed being the object of desire, even without desiring the person to whom I was the object of desire. I thought it was a very nice knack to have, being able to bring men's blood temperature up to boiling point. But I remained a virgin until I was twenty-two. Daisy and Tadpole hadn't believed me when I'd told them this, but in my day girls were taught to hang onto it. Pointlessly. I regretted those wasted years.

"Mrs Ragg is no longer with me. May I visit you in your room, please Lady Patch?"

'Has she left you, poor man? Poor Gunter! Lettice is the name. I don't know about my room, do you think that's wise? You're a person with a position to maintain in this establishment.'

'I'm a widower.'

'Your wife kicked the bucket? In that case we're both in the same boat. The number of my room is thirteen, but it hasn't proved unlucky so far.'

'When is the charming Gunter Ragg, FLO, DRU, PhE paying you a call, Loopy dear? I must say you waste no time, you've hardly been in the place five minutes and you're fornicating like a ferret. I shall have to buck my ideas up. Trouble is I gave my oath to my posse of regular lovers, relationships which are very enduring and close to my heart. I promised not to take aboard any more passengers. I see little enough of each of the sweethearts as it is. One's parliamentary duties demand a heavy quota of one's free time. It simply cannot be sex, sex, sex, all

247

day long. The personality becomes too lopsided – there has to be balance somewhere. Don't you find?' Dame Agatha was bicycling behind me on a stationary tandem. It was heavy going up front, she certainly wasn't pulling her weight. Otherwise she wouldn't have had the energy to talk.

'I'm completely shagged, Agatha!' I stopped bicycling to gasp, sweat dripped all over the handlebars. But Doc Slack's attention was not on us at this moment. He was bellowing instead at a blowsy blonde badminton player who had managed to break her third shuttlecock in succession. She stood there poking her tongue out in sophisticated reaction to his bullying diatribe. I only wished that I had her courage.

'He's come already – quick work!' Dame Agatha chortled. 'Any good in the sack, eh? Gunter Ragg, FLO, DRU, PhE? I wonder what on earth they all stand for. It says in the prospectus, I shall have to check him out – see if he's up to scratch for you, Loopy.'

'No, he hasn't come already, Agatha.' I twisted around with difficulty in my seat to look at her. 'I said I'm completely shagged, how much longer have we got on this infernal machine? My muscles have caved in. He's coming after dinner.'

'Whose dinner!' Dame Agatha scoffed. 'Your dinner? Or his? It'll be pretty insensitive if he comes after his – all those wine fumes, et cetera.'

'I'll be able to eat of his gums. I got a good lick at them earlier today, he'd had a chocolate biscuit with his morning tea. It gave me a gorgeous after-taste.'

'Do you think he'll stay long, Loopy? We usually have a nice time in the evenings. I still haven't bumped into Windsor or Kid Lips yet. We missed them at lunchtime due to all your dallying with the good Gunter Ragg, they'd been and gone by the time we got there. Fizzy saw them though. That sweet little thing was beside herself with delight, having lost those few pounds. Three of the Melody team came to inspect her this afternoon. They took her off in a limousine the size of the swimming-pool. Apparently she had some work to do in the recording studios. As to Flower, I don't know where she has got to. Everyone is meant to be in this gym this afternoon. But I

heard her say she was going swimming with the lads –
Flower's a law unto herself.'

'Looking like that I suppose she can afford to be,' I said
on a wave of exhaustion. 'Ooh, Agatha, what I wouldn't
give to crawl into bed!'

'Can't wait, eh, Loopy old girl – you've given up sex for
far too long. What you confessed to me about your years of
enforced abstinence have obviously not done you any
good at all. You're behaving like a greedy child, do try
and control yourself.'

'God, no! That big bully – he's coming over again! Get
bicycling, Agatha.' But it was too late, Doc Slack has
caught us slacking. And even now was striding menacingly over to our corner.

'Lady bloody Patch, Dame Agatha sodding Tatters –
what the hell do you think we're running here? A sewing
circle? An afternoon tea-party? A bleeding debutante's
ball?!' His roar stilled the rest of the gymnasium. We
unfortunates had become the centre of their relieved
attention. Doc Slack, famed founder of the International
Egalitarian Gymnasium in Cardiff, one time Olympic
Trainer and now Permanent Consultant to Slivers Medically Qualified Osteopath, Confirmed Marxist and Mus-
cular Specimen of a Man was my class enemy. And Dame
Agatha's. He'd let that be known within minutes of our
arrival in his gymnasium. He despised us both, not only
for our rank and status in life, but also for what we had
allowed soft living to do to our bodies. We were barely
worthy of his exalted attention, we were a blot on the
clinical landscape of his exercise premises.

He shouted this, bending down so that we should
receive the full blast of it in our faces. He had been lucky
enough to be eating steak for lunch. Steak with a great
deal of garlic and other seasonings. It was worth being
shouted at as savagely as this in order to get the
mouthwatering whiff of what he had demolished in order
to sustain his strength and his shape. He was a man in his
sixties now. I could remember the fanfare opening of the
International Egalitarian Gymnasium some twenty years
ago when Doctor Evan Slack was at his physical peak,
though at forty still too old to be an active professional
athlete any longer. Yet looking up at him now, at the six

feet four of him, it was difficult to believe that any time had gone by. The Welsh Giant, they had called him. The Pride of the Valleys. Then black haired and flashing eyed, now completely bald, as bald as Kojak, but still with the fierce expression of the old days and his body unaltered. Only the baldness and the bitterness were new. And who wouldn't be bitter, faced with us lot – nothing but slack-muscled mounds of unspeakable corpulence. Not a single body-beautiful to lighten the scene. I should have been sick too if I'd been placed in his position. Oh, how the mighty have fallen! Even so I didn't enjoy being spoken to like this.

'Well,' I'd turned to Dame Agatha when he'd paused to take breath, 'we'd better give up and go to bed for a little nap if we're that much beyond redemption.'

He hadn't liked that. It was a mistake. I was heaping further coals of fire and fury upon my head for that spoilt and pettish reaction.

'Oh no you don't!' He'd caught my arm in a grip. I knew what horror it must feel like to be a rabbit in a trap. But I didn't struggle. I only hoped that when gentle Gunter Ragg visited me later in my room, that he wouldn't assume these savage bruises to be the outcome of another passionate encounter. I girlishly wanted him to believe that I was a respectable woman, not given to distributing my favours here, there and everywhere. I knew for a certainty that this vice-like grip on my arm would result in fierce bruising. Never mind, perhaps Gunter Ragg was not planning to strip me. He looked the sort who would simply and neatly unpeel his parts and methodically get on with the job.

I bent over my handlebars, head down, watching my knees wobbling up and down, up and down. My womb felt as if it had wandered away from my nether regions altogether, leaving a worrying void in its place. If someone had punched me in my solar plexus their fist would have shot straight through to the other side. I began praying that something like this would happen to escape from the fresh blast about to come my way. My gaze encompassed not only my pistoning knees, but also a close-up view of Doc Slack's plimsolls. He was drumming the side of his sculptured thigh with five furious fingers. His other hand rested firmly on my stationary handlebars. I chose to ignore both forbidding sights, but behind me I could feel Dame Agatha faltering on her pedals until finally she slackened off altogether. But I pedalled doggedly on.

The drumming fingers fell still, to join the others on my handlebar. Before me towered six feet four of menacing muscle in an unspoken battle of wills. Why I had taken it upon myself to become so bolshie I couldn't have explained to anybody. Perhaps the events of the last twenty-four hours and the comparative solitude of the five previous years had strengthened me in ways that I wouldn't have imagined possible. It had certainly never been in my character to invite trouble in this way. Whatever I had been it was never challenging – I had liked being liked too much for that. Daisy and Tadpole had been brought up in a relaxed atmosphere, ostensibly lacking all moral discipline (though not gentle guidance) because I couldn't bear to have bred children who ended up disliking me. A weak and cowardly attitude, but easily camouflaged by feigning an interest and belief in the Schneider Method of Child Development, which allowed for full freedom of expression in the formative years. I had even allowed the girls and myself to be interviewed by *The Psychiatric World* on the successful application of the Schneider Method, even though both girls had been in trouble that very week, Daisy for smoking cannabis in the school cloakrooms and Tadpole for stealing a tube of Trebor Extra Strong Mints from Woolworths. She'd never shown a liking for mints as a small child, although mints had always been my favourites. Especially Trebor Extra Strongs. *The Psychiatric World* had pounced on that fact as being of special significance.

Yet even in my relations with Dame Agatha I was no longer the soppy schoolgirl I had once been. She was my idol from the past. I had placed her on a pedestal and kept her there for so many years that yesterday when we had met again, I found myself adopting the sycophancy of my youth. Now I felt none of that, she was my equal, we were contemporaries. I regarded her as an ally and even a friend. We would continue to see each other, keep in touch when we left Slivers. When this present nightmare was over.

251

But I couldn't continue bicycling for much longer, the calves of my legs were about to cave in, and despite myself there were now desperate tears blurring the sight of those huge hands, now white-knuckled with fury, gripping my handlebars. And what was the point, where was the purpose? Why on earth was I doing it? I wasn't proving anything except my own stupidity and newly discovered pig-headedness! I'd stop when he spoke. But not before.

He spoke slowly and softly, with a terrible intensity. 'What the bloody hell is the point, where's the purpose in this? Why on earth are you doing it? – unless it's to prove your own stupidity and childish pig-headedness!' I remained where I was, still studying his plimsolls, refusing to even flinch beneath the lacerations of his quiet tongue. Though I had never in my life been spoken to with such barely controlled loathing, it stirred something familiar within me. The hatred was one that I had nurtured myself though never allowed to escape; it had remained buried beneath the innermost layers of my emotions. Against whom was it directed though? Did I even know? Was it my mother? Was it Bertie? Perhaps it had withered with their deaths. I harboured no hatred now.

But this poor creature was consumed with it. Like grief it was shaking him by the throat and would allow no escape. Shouldn't I give in and try to charm him with my usual suppliancy? Make this moment easier for both of us? Behind me Dame Agatha was making strange sounds of indignation, preparing to make some sort of stand in my defence. She had been oddly subdued by the bullying methods of Doc Slack, not exactly cowed, but as if preserving her dignity by pretending that she wasn't with us, as if her mind was on important matters elsewhere. It was a fairly effective method for herself, but I must devise means of my own. When a bull is incensed by the sight of a scarlet garment, the sensible wearer removes the offensive object. Not for the first time since my arrival at Slivers I rued the loss of my earlier seductive form. There was a time when if I'd done what I was doing now, peeling off my outer layer to cool myself down, the temperature of every male in the vicinity would have leapt sky-high. Not that a raise in temperature was what I was planning for the ferocious Doc Slack – if I'd had a convenient supply of valium I would have overloaded him with that. But the removal of my outer garment (Bertie's golfing windjammer) appeared to have the same effect. It was as if I had thrown a jug of cold water over him – the shock of seeing me strip!

It wasn't as if I was completely naked underneath, I was wearing a brassière and one of Bertie's string vests. Unfortunately the black brassière could be seen all too clearly through the open holes of the white vest. It was one of the old-fashioned sort dating back to the days when cleavages were all the rage, the only one that I could fit myself into at present. I had bought it when I'd been expecting Tadpole, to attend some charity do at the Dorchester. Ghastly thing! We'd quarrelled, Bertie and I, all the way home because I'd refused to perform – at eight-and-a-half months gone – with the Algerian wine waiter from Wapping! The spitting image of Omar Sharif. Apparently heavily pregnant women are considered highly desirable in Algeria, something I'd not been aware of – though Bertie had. His eye had been on this Adonis for some time. I blamed this black Berlei brassière for much of the trouble, the supporting shelf of the wired under-lift had a heap to answer for. Staunch-hearted mountaineers used to the Swiss Alps might have quailed at the sight of my slopes. And they looked much the same now.

'Good God Almighty!!' Doc Slack choked on his strangled vowels. Someone dropped a weighted dumbell. The blowsy blonde trod on another shuttlecock. A gamey geriatric got locked on the yoga mat in a lotus position. Dame Agatha appeared to have slipped off her saddle for she was now peering up at me in amazement from the floor. I couldn't think why – these were the very same tits that she'd sat next to in the sauna this morning. But they looked different now. Sexy. Suggestive. On offer, two hard-boiled eggs on a nest of caviare. I'd forgotten the sorcery of black lace – and a spot of skilled engineering. And thanks to Bertie's string vest the midriff, which I was trying to hold in like mad, was not so exposed that it spoilt the force of the effect. Though I could see that I must have looked fairly eccentric. Instead of shorts I was wearing a pair of Bertie's old swimming trunks, turquoise blue over some hectic plaid tights that Daisy had mistakenly purchased at the last Summer Sale at Scotch House and then passed on to me at an exorbitant price. Very nice and snug too, well worth the money.

I had noticed several silly smirks on the faces of my fellow slimmers when I had removed Bertie's dressing gown on arrival at the gym. Perhaps Doc Slack had taken exception to my jolly garb as well. He possibly took it to be a deliberate insult, not taking his exercise premises seriously enough to bother to turn up in the proper clothing. Wearing track suits and leotards and tailored shorts like everyone else, even Dame Agatha looked rather fetchingly trim in her Marks and Spencer track suit. The truth was that on my shopping spree I had seriously intended to purchase these items in Selfridges but had spent so long in the Outsize Fashions, having been directed there from Ground Floor, that I had lost all heart and had ended up in the Restaurant, much pleasanter altogether. Hot scones and strawberry jam, one eclair and a vanilla slice had helped me forget my feelings of inferiority. By which time it was cocktail hour at the Westbury Hotel where I was certain to bump into somebody from my publishing house. The Sales and Advertising regarded the Westbury as their pub, and if one chose to do so one could have been in there every day with them. But that would have meant becoming a creature of habit, an accusation which could hardly be levelled at me.

Thus I came to be turned out like an Italian beachball from Hamleys, each part of me a different colour, the only nod in the direction of feminity being this tart's brassière, worn now because I had feared that in Doc Slack's gymnasium I might be called upon to do some vigorous jumping on the spot. Or exercises which could result in serious injury, like a blow to the jaw (my own or anyone else's) from unchecked breast flying all over the gym. I had not worn a brassière for the past five years, finding that to do so somehow spoiled the line of Bertie's jackets, so I was careful never to run for a cab, never to move so abruptly as to knock someone's eye out, or to rise so swiftly from a seat that my unharnessed nipples might have found themselves still sitting there on the chair when I had already left the room. I'd trained my self to move as my daughters did, like all the bra-less women-libbers, with elbows pinned firmly into my sides. To my waistline – if I had still had a waist. With my shoulders thrown back like a startled stallion. On my daughters it looked absolutely terrific. On me it stopped this side of a physical deformity. Never mind, I felt oddly comforted without my bras. Back to being a child again, de-sexed and out of trouble.

I'd even managed to track down an extremely ancient liberty bodice in Gamage's Closing Down Clearance Sale. The elderly assistant had brought it out to show me for a laugh. She's had dyed red curls, frizzed up in a modern manner, a proper Afro. I applauded her spirit, she reminded me of a Toulouse Lautrec poster and I would have told her so, but I supposed that she wouldn't have taken it for a compliment. Instead I congratulated her on not having gone grey. 'Not a single grey hair in my head,' so she'd said, and had advised me to do something about my own dusty locks. 'They can do wonders with grey these days – so I'm given to believe.' I promised faithfully that I'd look into it. The liberty bodice had lasted me three years. But I still hadn't seen to my hair, perhaps now would be a good time to think about having it coloured, put a bit of life back into it. I was the only woman of my age that I knew who didn't. Everyone else had mingled their silver with subtle shades of honey and what they liked to refer to as mink. So that the tops of their heads looked like fashionable fur hats, light and youthful yet at the same time completely natural. As if they'd spent the past month playing tennis in the sun and were still tousled, their skins tanned, their locks lightened in strands. What silver was allowed to show through, just here and there, served only to enhance the effect. But it was not a look that would suit me. I had never aimed to be smart in the restrained English manner, or polished in the American style. And that sort of hair summed up a certain category of woman to me – one I had never had much in common with. Not simply provincial, but conservatively correct. If I were to start dyeing my hair I should prefer it to look obviously dyed, like the raven-haired women of Spain or Italy. Like the great Coco Chanel who was still dyeing her fringed bob a shiny boot-polish black until her

255

death, when she was into her eighties. Or Colette, whose frizzed ginger perm had been just as startling as the jolly old girl's who had served me in Gamages. On the other hand there was always a wig.

Passing through Selfridges on my abortive shopping trip I had paused on the ground floor to peer into the Wig Bar. There all manner of thatches greeted the eye, about two hundred scalps hung suspended in space. Some adorned plastic faces, featureless save for a painted mouth. Others graced pale, elongated shapes resembling the heads and necks of giraffes. Throughout the area had been placed a grotto of separate mini-shops, wig-bars within the Wig-Bar itself. Each intent on selling its own manufacturer's range. So that to stroll through, as I ventured to do, was to run the gauntlet of overtures from frighteningly glossy girls (all wearing wigs) inviting one to stop and try on any one of their gorgeous products. And they were absolutely gorgeous too. Headfuls of luxuriously glossy tresses, from inexpensive man-made to the costlier real thing. In every conceivable hair colour ever seen on a human head. And even those that one hadn't seen. In the Fantasy Range came the dream shades, sweet sherbert pink, pale turquoise, sharp lemon, deep purple. All guaranteed free of dandruff! No worries about split ends, lank greasiness, dry condition. No wondering what sort of shampoo to use or how often to use it. No fussing with hairdressers, rollers, clips, grips or heated curlers. These wigs were Wash'n Drip-Dry, ever so simple. Dame Agatha had shown me hers, a spruce auburn shingle, shaped close to the head at the back with an impressively deep wave falling over the forehead to be worn either swept back or swept forward. When she put it on she looked as she had on the hockey field at school, a girl again but for the extra flesh around her face and the inevitable lines that life had engraved upon the way. 'When I've lost the weight that I intend to lose in this place,' she'd confided, 'then I shall do what I've meant to do, Loopy, for some years. I shall invest in a face-lift. Just a little here and there.' She'd indicated the chin-line and the area around her eyes. 'Several Members in the house have gone in for it lately, and not only female ones either!' The change of hair would be enough for me to be going on with – and charm my class enemy, Doc Slack.

I looked at my wrist-watch, a full minute had passed since Doc Slack had started choking. Dame Agatha was still reclining on the floor.

'Phew!' I said, 'this bicycling is bloody hot work, Doc Slack.' And I lifted my bare forearm to wipe my damp brow. Half-a-stone of heaving breast came up with it. But I twinkled at him, turning my slice-of-melon mouth up at each corner, deliberately dimpling my cheeks and shining my eyes in a flirty way. I dare not begin to consider how utterly ridiculous I must have looked, trying this kid's trick on at my age. This was what I'd had to employ in the very early days for Bertie's benefit. To lure whatever it was he'd decided on for us both, even when my heart hadn't been in the game at all. No one saw through my simpering. None of the big strong men who'd been chosen, unknown to them. Some as huge and as superior in structure as Doc Slack himself.

Perhaps large men harbour a soft spot, a weakness, for little round women like me. Ones with big tits and sly come-hither smiles. And Doc Slack was of the generation to have appreciated what he would consider to be a feminine woman. I was wrong. Doc Slack turned and without uttering another word strode straight out of the gymnasium.

'I expect I sickened him, I suppose I must have turned his stomach – the sight of my bulging breasts.' We were tottering towards the swimming pool, arms intertwined, Dame Agatha and I. We had been instructed to swim for half an hour, minimum. I was hoping to get away with just floating.

'Oh, I don't suppose so for a moment, Loopy dear. Who's to say what his reaction could have been. He's a very odd character, I don't know what his personal set-up is. I believe he's been married but I don't think there's a wife around any longer.'

'A widower like Gunter Ragg?'

'Is Gunter Ragg a widower?'

'So he claims, Agatha. Why, do you think he's not telling the truth?'

Dame Agatha drew back. 'Not telling the truth! Since when has that mattered one way or the other, Loopy? You have no special interest in whether any of these men are married or not, have you? You aren't contemplating re-marriage yourself by any chance? People do come to Slivers for precisely that purpose – it has spawned many romantic attachments which have culminated in matrimony, and probably subsequent divorce. But that doesn't matter these days, does it? Just part of life's merry-go-round. I think I was always wise not to take a husband aboard, however. Politicians are still expected to be paragons of virtue. One couldn't have popped off with one husband after another. It never looks too good on paper, it's only really all right for socialites and film stars. And I could never have stuck with one husband for life. I can't imagine how your marriage lasted so long, Loopy – a lively little thing like you.'

'Do you think he's attractive, Doc Slack?' I asked, not really paying full attention to what she'd been saying. I'd found this was the way to be able to withstand Dame Agatha's domination of every conversation. The first few sentences were all that required absolute concentration. The rest was just her listening to the sound of her own voice.

'Do I think Doc Slack is attractive, an attractive man?' She weighed her words carefully. 'You mean would I care to go to bed with him?' She made an odd gesture, running her hands swiftly over her breasts and on down over her stomach, lingering briefly in between the stretch-nylon legs of her track-suit. She didn't seem at all aware of the surprised glances of those who passed by. One was the blowsy blonde who'd been banished to her swim some time before us. Doc Slack had not made a re-appearance for the rest of our time in the gym, one of his burly assistants had taken over our exercise programmes.

The blonde gave a wide smile to me as she passed.

'Is the water cold?' I called out.

But she shrugged her shoulders and made a helpless gesture towards her tongue.

'Fool doesn't speak English. Foreign,' Dame Agatha said loudly. 'Now to come back to your question – Doc Slack. Oh, yes, without a doubt I'd give that a whirl. There's something about those deeply disagreeable men, don't you think? They're a challenge. I've had one of them for years. Has a post in the Treasury, a chartered accountant by training. A deeply unpleasant person, accountants usually are. It's the result of regarding everything in monetary terms. He never fails to rile me, to put my back up. There are times when I vow never to see him again – but I do. It's very exciting sexually – a continual battle. If I require clitoral stimulation he'll unerringly decide to linger over my nipples. When I'm suffering from exhaustion and should appreciate a spot of wooing that's when he decides that it's my turn on top. Do you know that when I had a very nasty case of piles during the winter from those long parliamentary sessions relating to pay disputes and the unions, he actually chose to practise anal penetration! He'd chanced upon a school chum on his way home the evening before and it reminded him of what he'd been missing all these years with me. He's married. He's a grandfather. But he wouldn't dream of imposing his demands on his long-suffering wife. But we give each other as good as we get. That's why it's lasted so long. Fifteen years now – not bad going!'

'Extraordinary!' I murmured, fascinated. Perhaps I might disclose my life with Bertie to her if she was this much of a woman of the world! I had never told anyone about Bertie and me. Though whether *he* had, well that was another question altogether. He couldn't operate without an audience, that was part of him. So it would naturally follow that his exhibitionism would take the form of verbal boasting too. But he had never done so in my hearing. He professed to the end that his respect for me had remained unshakeable. I was his wife after all. I bore his name. I was Lady Patch. And there was never any doubt but that the children were his.

'Do you, to use the contemporary jargon "fancy" Doc Slack yourself, Loopy dear?' Dame Agatha's barely lowered tones interrupted my thoughts.

We had reached the mixed swimming pool now and were turning off towards the cubicles. I paused for a moment. High above us, poised on the top-most diving board of all, about to dive in a spectacular fashion into the pool, was the subject of our conversation. Doc Slack himself.

For a moment his figure was silhouetted against the arc

259

lamps of the ceiling. The long legs seemed to reach up to the normal length of an average man's body. The wide shoulders, stretched in the poised position, formed the base of an isosceles triangle from which his arms extended in one direction and his torso in another. There wasn't a surplus ounce of flesh on his entire body, it was a human machine in immaculate working order. He was a tough, virile sixty. At least that's what he looked. Whether he functioned sexually still was a matter of conjecture. A question which could only truthfully be answered by making love to him.

'Mm, perhaps I do fancy Doc Slack after all, despite the antagonism between us,' I murmured. But I was covertly studying his genitals as I said it, a bold bulge protruding between the Corinthian columns of his thighs.

'Interestingly enough, Agatha, in my experience it doesn't always follow that the very large men have the largest cocks.'

'Oh, you poor darling! Had Bertie a teeny dicky? There you are, you see – that was what you were stuck with all through your marriage. It's a wonder you weren't driven to look in a different direction. I know I would have been, I'm such a greedy girl.'

We parted at the cubicles, she went into the one next to mine. But we paused to watch Doc Slack's spectacular entry into the water. 'Well,' Dame Agatha announced above the small splash, seeing the tight buttocks disappear beneath the surface, 'I must say it does seem a bit of a waste. Either you'll have to have him, Loopy dear, or I shall!'

The Slivers swimming pool was of Olympic proportions, though there were at least fifty people swimming in it and one would not have thought so. But there was plenty of space. Dame Agatha emerged from her cubicle and after striding purposefully to the side, she executed quite a respectable dive into the deep end. I was rather more cautious. It was some time since I had visited a swimming pool. I had given up taking annual holidays or trips abroad after Bertie's death so I hadn't even been into the sea. I certainly could not have trusted myself to dive in, I needed time to familiarize myself with water again. But stepping gingerly down the tiled steps, lowering my apprehensive body into the shallow end, I was well aware of what a pathetic figure I must have made. I only hoped that Doc Slack wasn't watching.

No such luck. He swam upon me from behind with such unexpectedness that I would have sunk had it not been for his supporting hands – beneath my buttocks. He was holding them in an unnecessarily vulgar way, one that I was certain they didn't employ in life-saving techniques.

'You're a bloody little fool, Lady Patch,' we trod water together, our bodies touching, 'you shouldn't get out of your depth if you can't swim. This hour is strictly reserved for the experienced swimmers. It says so clearly in your booklet.'

I was speechless. Though my entry into the pool had been babyish to say the least, though in striking out towards the deeper end my first strokes may have appeared rusty and unformed, it still would have been obvious to anyone that I wasn't a beginner. I wasn't particularly proud of my swimming style, but it was competent enough. My breathing was not what it might have been, and I preferred not to submerge my head completely whilst doing the crawl. But I wasn't a liability as a swimmer, I had always won respectably in races with friends in the past. I certainly always beat Bertie.

'Doc Slack,' I began indignantly, spluttering water as the grip on my buttocks tightened. Rising hysteria threatened to overcome me, the combination of being held in such an intimate place and manner, coupled with the nearness of all the rest of him made me struggle to break free. 'I wish you wouldn't hold me like this,' I said. 'It's making me panic. And it's sort of –'

'Sort of what, Lady Patch?' His scowling eyebrows drew together. This close I could see that his eyes weren't dark at all, but a mixture of grey and green. Flecked and changeable in the reflected light from the turquoise depths. Was it my imagination or was he deliberately guiding one of his huge thighs between mine – adjusting our bodies so that now I could feel the full bulge of his private parts pressing against my own! His expression gave no indication of this intent. But now he had removed one of his hands from my buttocks and had placed it higher up my torso in the small of my back. My breasts bulged over the top of my swimsuit, uncomfortably so. I feared for the strength of the straps.

It was a halter-neck style swimsuit, one of the first on the market some seven years ago. Bertie had bought it for my birthday that year, from Simpsons, Piccadilly, one of his favourite stores. It had been on display in the Haymarket window, the one next door to the entrance. 'That's the one I want.' He'd taken the assistant out to the street to show her, the belligerent after-effect of having had an excessive number of brandies at his club. And he had actually meant that one, that very one. The window dresser had to dismantle the mannequin to remove it and had not been at all pleased. All rather a waste of effort, because it turned out to be at least two sizes too large. I could tell by the label as soon as I'd unwrapped it. Bertie had wanted to see me in it there and then but I'd promised him a special dressing-up display later that day. It had given me the opportunity to duplicate his present from Simpsons, but this time in the right size. I hadn't had the courage to ask for an exchange with the one that he'd insisted on having out of the window. I'd simply hidden it at the bottom of one of my drawers, never dreaming that one day I should have expanded enough to fill it. Now it was standing me in good stead. Black and slinky, skimming over my fulsome curves, it gave me a fleeting image of how I had once looked. Oh, the glories of the past! Poor Doc Slack and I had both seen better days physically, but that was inevitable. He could no longer perform the Herculean feats of his youth any more that I could – could what? What had I done that was of any distinction in my youth? Bugger all! The paltry achievements of Lady Lettice Patch! At least now I had taught myself to put pen to paper, and supported myself very comfortably on the proceeds. When I was young I hadn't even been given the opportunity to do that. Who knows what I might have done!

'Sort of what, Lady Patch?' He was repeating his question, but squeezing me so tight that each of my breasts had now eased themselves right up an over the top of my swimsuit. They fell free and unfettered over his broad chest, still held high by the halter neck. But the material was so strained that I knew it would give way at any second, it was fastened by a single button up at the back in the nape of my neck. Sure enough I could feel the whole thing sliding apart.

Doc Slack was staring down at it all whilst it happened, breathing so heavily that it sounded like a snorting animal. He had an enormous hard on.

'I've got to fuck you again, Lady Patch, are you listening? I'm going to screw you this time, you little cock-sucking whore, so hard that you'll never forget it! But this time you won't have your precious Bertie to protect you, do you understand? You're going to be fucked to within an inch of your worthless life!!' And having hissed those sweet promises against my surprised ears Doc Slack left me to struggle to the side of the pool, topless, whilst he swam effortlessly off in the opposite direction.

'Well, well Loopy dear – it looks very much as though you've beaten me to it with Mr Muscle Man. I somehow thought you would. It's the winning way you have – not just that you're so scrumptious. Edith Piaf, the froggy singer, she had it too. Right up until the end of her life she had chaps falling for her. All she had to do was lift her little finger. And she didn't have your magnificent frontage either. I saw the way he was staring at your bosoms in the pool.' Dame Agatha chortled. 'But then who wasn't? They don't allow topless at Slivers!'

I was in a funny state and not inclined to discuss Doc Slack further now. I had only blurted out the absolute basics of what he'd threatened to Dame Agatha. I didn't tell her the more shocking part, the fact that the proposed fucking would not be the first time between the two of us. That's what he was saying – that he'd already had the pleasure on a previous occasion. I couldn't remember the time or the place, or anything about him. It was as if it had all happened when I had been blindfolded. Or incapable through drink or exhausted sleep. I needed time on my own to think. I needed to go back in my mind to many years before. Surely something would come back to me.

'I'm not sure that I can face my lemon-juice this evening,' I said to Dame Agatha. 'I feel like flopping into a hot bath and falling asleep to be quite honest.'

She slapped me so heartily on the back as we climbed the staircase to our rooms that I missed my footing and nearly fell. It reminded me that my very first view of Flower Fowler and little Fizzy Tornado had been on this staircase. Was it only yesterday morning? It already seemed as if I'd been at Slivers for weeks, for half my lifetime in fact!

'To be quite *dis*honest you mean,' Dame Agatha hoisted me up the next few steps until we had safely reached the top. 'Phew – all this exercise is beginning to tell on the old thighs, isn't it?'

'Me too – what do you mean "dishonest"?' I looked at her wearily. I had gone past the painful pangs of hunger now. If she meant that I would be having an illicit little snack in my room then she was mistaken. The thought had certainly entered my head (when had thoughts of nibbles *never* entered it?), but somehow I couldn't summon up the usual enthusiasm. Too much had happened, there had been other stimulations. I was dreadfully excited by Doc Slack's revelation, sexually excited by the recent memory of his underwater erection pressing against me. I wanted to settle down in the dark and live it over again, trying to link it up with a previous experience of him in my memory. The trouble was that there had been so many of those brief encounters with me and Bertie! It would have been impossible to begin to imagine just how many there were. Hadn't he once joked that we should be making a record of them each time they happened? For future reference, he'd said. Then, rather more wistfully, to entertain us in our old age, 'when it won't be possible to play these games of ours any more'. That's what he'd said. 'What,' I'd joked back, 'complete with photographs like a police record?' We'd both laughed at that. Few of our 'friends' remained long enough to be photographed. But surely a man as principled as Doc Slack wouldn't have been one of those! And there had been others, other 'collaborators' eager to participate even without the exchange of filthy lucre. But these were not so much to Bertie's liking. He preferred buying his pleasures, it maintained the balance. The other way rendered him impotent, so he claimed. He felt excluded, out of it when there was no money involved. He needed to be in at the heart of things, and for that he felt it necessary to pull the purse strings.

'You plan to titivate yourself up for your other visitor,' Dame Agatha twinkled, distorting her face with a grotesquely exaggerated wink. 'Dishonest'? 'My other visitor'? – Of course! Gunter Ragg!

'Good God! Do you know, Agatha, I'd completely forgotten Gunter Ragg!' Perhaps Gunter Ragg was just what I needed to calm me down, to take my mind off the developments of the day.

We rounded the corner which led to our corridor, expecting to find it as deserted as everywhere else. We hadn't passed many on our way up. The time was around five forty-five. Most people were preparing for their dinner, whether they were on Light Diet in the Dining Room (the one illustrated in the prospectus that I had drooled over), or whether they were on straight lemon juice like us. Poor sods.

But as we approached we saw that there was a reception committee awaiting our arrival. Kid Lips and Windsor Shag were lolling against Dame Agatha's door, Flab Pottle sat cross-legged on the floor. All three had their eyes shut crooning a ballad – it sounded awfully like one which had been popular in my youth. That one called 'If you were the only girl in the world and I were the only boy', but it couldn't have been because both Kid Lips and Windsor Shag were far too young to ever have heard of it. Although it was true that dear old Barbara Cartland had recently issued (and she in her seventies!) a record album of reliable favourites from the glamorous days of her youth. Perhaps one of the punks had picked up the tune and put it out as a single, as a way of taking the piss. My girls would know the answer to that one. At the height of the punk thing, when Tadpole had snaffled all the safety pins from my sewing basket, I quite often came across her rifling through my possessions, especially old records.

'Just seeing if there's anything here that could be recycled. We're looking to put the mockers on some of the solid senders that people of your generation used to swoon to. Haven't you got any Frank Sinatra? – I thought all you lot had Frank Sinatra. Hey – this looks a goodie – who the hell was *she*? Doris Day, 'It's Magic'! Can I take this one?

265

– Nat King Cole – no, best not, he's black. It'll look like racism. Christ, Mum, you used to dance to some crap!' That was the week one of her boyfriends had been carted off to hospital with a severe case of septicaemia caused by plunging a pink nappy-pin straight through his cheek for facial decoration. I had seen it for myself, pus and all. Gallant lad. Though inarticulate with pain he had commanded the envious attention of his contemporaries. No one at that early stage of the punk game had gone so far as to do that, though in a matter of weeks millions would. Even Tadpole had toyed with the idea. 'What do you think – would it suit me through the cheek?' 'Look absolutely charming, darling,' I'd answered. 'When you get tired of the fashion you'll be left with a hole in your face, that's the only thing. But then,' I added cheerfully, 'you could always disguise it with a blob of Polyfilla.' I think it was the Polyfilla blob that put her off.

Dame Agatha's stride quickened. I shot her a glance and saw her expression of undisguised delight. She ran forward. Kid Lips chose that moment to open his eyes, lifting the bottle he was holding to his mouth. Tequila – Mexican fire-water – one of Bertie's weaknesses.

'Roy! Roy Baker – darling!' Dame Agatha shouted joyously.

The bottle hovered for a moment, then came slowly down. Kid Lips wasn't so inebriated that he was going to drop a bottle of valuable liquor. He placed it carefully on the floor against the door of Dame Agatha's room, far enough away from Flab Pottle's inert, cross-legged form, and began swaying towards us. He was crowing delightedly, stretching out his arms, waiting to be embraced.

And embrace him was exactly what Dame Agatha began to do, but not just him. Windsor Shag was quick off the mark. At the sound of Dame Agatha's echoing tones, her excited greeting, he too had opened his eyes. Clutched to his chest he had a litre of white wine, gutrot, I recognised it from the label as one that I used for cooking. The bottle was already three-quarters empty. But there was another poking out of the pocket of his dressing gown, weighing down the fine fabric, about to fall to the floor. But Windsor Shag seemed enough in possession of his faculties to take care of his treasures. Holding each bottle

266

by the neck he advanced upon Dame Agatha, arms in the air as if requesting the pleasure of a waltz. He was humming a tune, another unlikely one for a person of his age, 'Save The Last Dance For Me'. But it seemed to strike the right chord with Dame Agatha.

'Little Winnie! Oh, how absolutely lovely!'

Both reached her out-stretched arms at the same time, each covering her handsome, beaming face with kisses. All three murmuring excited endearments to each other, lost to everything else in the world at that moment except the warmth of the affection which surrounded them.

I looked on with curiosity, completely excluded – as was Flab Pottle.

He struggled with considerable difficulty to his feet. But he made it unaided.

'Well,' he said. 'Madame, Lady Patch, lovely creature – that seems to leave you and me! What do you say?'

For the fourth time within twenty-four hours I found myself enclosed in a male embrace.

Bliss. 'Bliss,' I murmured, my eyes closed, lying naked on my back. 'All the ladies they seem to enjoy it.' The voice of the Swedish masseuse seemed far away whilst her skilful finger-tips stroked my skin.

'Absolute heaven,' I smiled but I was day-dreaming of the night before. It was just that her fingers had reminded me.

An orgy at my age! Who would have thought it. A gang-bang of grannies! Well, we were old enough to be grandparents, Dame Agatha and me – and Flab Pottle.

Flab Pottle actually was a grandfather, so he'd confessed. A grandfather three times over by two of his daughters out in Australia.

'You must miss not seeing them,' I'd said out of the side of my mouth. His penis was short but quite thick, and his testicles were unusually tight and high for his years. So that chatting this casually took a bit of doing. I wasn't unfamiliar with the practice of passing the time of day while on the job.

Bertie had been very firmly in favour of it. But I could still recall the immense frustration of an explosive coitus interruptus caused by a climatic political clash with a

267

black bloke, who turned out to be a supporter of Ian Smith's Rhodesian administration. Since then I had learnt to stick to safer conversational topics. Politics were out, so was religion. Not that the young ones were all that interested in talking. Every now and again Kid would shout out, 'Fucking fantastic, man!' or 'Jeez, crazy!' Different phrases of that nature. And Windsor would raise his sweet face and look around at us all and remark from time to time, 'I say – isn't this really pleasant! Really nice!' And smile just as if we were having a summer picnic at Glyndbourne. Then he'd get down to fucking Dame Agatha again, or sucking my cunt, or easing Kid up his arse, or kissing Flab Pottle. We all had a share of each other, that was what was so nice about it. So Windsor was right when he said it was nice. It was gentle fun, no hurry. Everyone enjoying themselves and no-one getting hurt in any way.

Not one of us undressed. It was interesting that. It was to do with feeling that our bodies weren't up to it, not up to being the sort of bodies that one would normally associate with an orgy, I suppose.

Someone, I believe it was Flab, had started saying rather wistfully, 'You know what I shall do when I'm thin again? I shall –'

But he wasn't allowed to continue any further.

'Shut up – whoever's saying that! Make the most of this moment – do you think that you could better this? However thin you get, or don't get!' Dame Agatha had been the voice of sweet reason.

'You're absolutely right,' Flab had apologised all round. 'Sorry folks – let's get on with the party.' And we had.

The events had a curious ebb and flow to them. A dreamlike quality that reminded me of my erotic interlude with Kid Lips the day before. Would we all be embarrassed when we bumped into each other afterwards? Or would it be, as it had with Kid Lips, as if nothing had happened?

He still had no recall, no recognition of me – except that now he realised that I was a woman and not a man, as he'd thought yesterday.

'I thought you were a guy yesterday.' He'd giggled

268

sheepishly. 'It was your, y'know – your –'

'My clothes. Yes I know. I was wearing my husband's pyjamas.'

'What was he wearing, a nightie?' He'd giggled again. He was very attractive when he giggled. His eyes crinkled up and shone like silver paper and his mouth disappeared each side, almost to his ears.

I caressed his soft paunch beneath the short frock that he wore on top of the floppy Peruvian peasant pants. And then I moved down and took a hold on his springy erection. It reared wildly between the loose clasp of my fingers.

'My husband – was he wearing a nightie? Well, yes, in a way. The last time I saw him he was wearing a shroud, he was lying in a coffin. It was suitable to the occasion.' I squeezed more firmly than I should have done on his cock.

'Christ – go easy. That's better! You've done this before, girl, aintcha – I can tell!' And he'd pulled my mouth to him and kissed it good and hard. That 'girl' warmed me, right through to the marrow. I couldn't have pleasured him more thoroughly than I did from then on. But I didn't stint myself with any of them.

It was curious when, as the circle moved on from here to there, what occurred between Dame Agatha and myself. It happened after the particularly satisfactory and prolonged episode where I had been enquiring as to whether or not Flab was missing his grandchildren since they lived so far away in Australia.

'Not so much as that, to tell you the truth! He'd removed his hand from my right nipple to snap his fingers in the air. 'There comes a time in life when you can't be doing with small children.' He'd returned to his gentle twiddling. The sensitivity with which he did it told me a lot about his musicianship. I should have liked to have heard him tickling the keys, though the piano had never been my favourite instrument.

We were engaged in sixty-nine at that moment in the conversation so that I had to keep both ears open so's not to miss a word of what he was saying. I wouldn't have liked him to think that I wasn't interested in his nearest and dearest.

'What does Mrs Pottle think about it?' I shouted down at him.

269

'Which Mrs Pottle?' He shouted up. The removal of his tongue caused an unpleasant draught to whistle up my cunt. I must have shivered, ever aware of my needs he re-applied his tongue to me. That's what it felt like, but glancing down I could see that he'd actually corked me up with his thumb.

'How many Mrs Pottles are there?' This would have to be the end of the chat in a minute. Flab, whether he was aware of it or not was very close to coming.

'Apart from my mother, bless her heart, there are three Mrs Pottles floating around somewhere . . .'

He'd been married three times! I digested this fact along with his spunk, allowing both to sink gently. It was years since I'd had that taste on my tongue, though once when swallowing a sour strawberry yoghurt I had been very much reminded of what I was missing. I'd forgotten how crucial it was not to cough or clear one's throat as it slid past one's tonsils. The subsequent soreness was the same as spluttering on the segment of an orange. Much more of a hazard than gagging on the erection itself. But there hadn't been much fear of that with Flab's shorty. It was following this episode of mutual satisfaction, that I found myself fondled by Dame Agatha.

In the period of post-coital contentment Flab had been explaining his marital position to me. It seemed that he had been actually married just twice. His first wife had been killed in a car-crash on the way home from the pre-natal clinic which she attended in preparation for their first child. His next was a female ventriloquist whom he met when they shared the bill at the end of Skegness Pier. An Australian girl, the mother of his two daughters. But they hadn't ever got married. She was married already to a wrestler, though separated long before Flab had come on the scene. The third was the hotelier that he'd met in the Lake District, in an establishment like Slivers that he'd visited after giving up the entertainment game. He'd gone in with her as a partner. Sunk his savings in a hotel on the Norfolk Broads, sold the prosperous business at a tremendous profit, and ploughed those profits into building up a night-club on the northern circuit, just outside Bradford.

'And this Mrs Pottle – the current one?' I was curious to know.

270

'Cancer. Killed by Peter Stuyvestant Cork Tip.'

Poor chap, he'd been unlucky with his wives. But he didn't seem too put out by it now. It wasn't the moment for mourning those who'd passed on, even though I cast a thought towards Bertie.

Dame Agatha was tickling me, that was what it felt like at the very beginning, until it became obvious that there was a sexual intent. 'Well, Loopy dear, are you enjoying yourself?'

I was grinning widely, tippling on Kid Lips' diminishing supply of Tequila. Combined with the circumstances and the emptiness of my stomach I was well on the way to getting paralytically drunk, except that a safety device was operating somewhere in my subconscious. Though what exactly it was saying I couldn't work out.

'Hugely, Agatha.' I watched Kid Lips and Windsor Shag on each side of her, both sucking busily at a breast. Windsor had a feverish hand inside Dame Agatha's demure stretch-nylon knickers, the ones she was wearing beneath her nightie and dressing gown. It was clearly visible to everyone what he was up to. I thought how jolly convenient it was for these sort of practices that everyone went around at Slivers in a state of semi-dress. Although Dame Agatha had not (yet) removed a single garment her breasts were freely available to these two young amours by merely opening her buttons.

Similarly Kid Lips' cock, that I was to avail myself of in a minute, just hung out of the opening in his Peruvian peasant pants. And Windsor's parts, placed within easy reach of Flab Pottle's plumply obliging fist, peeped decorously out of his spotted drip-dry sleeping suit (American import, available from Aquascutum).

'But isn't it a shame that Flower and Fizzy aren't here with us?' The thought had only just occurred to me – up until then I couldn't think what it was that was missing.

'Oh, they wouldn't like this, Loopy dear – would they Flab?' Dame Agatha's arms, stretched high above her head entwined themselves around my neck, bringing my face alongside her own so that now I was in a fine position to view an incipient baldness on the scalp of Windsor Shag. And a fine dusting of dandruff on Kid Lips' shoulders.

Flab Pottle, tentatively fiddling with Windsor Shag's testicles, took a few seconds to answer. His attention was elsewhere, that was obvious. And who was to blame him! It was as fascinating as a slow motion film, watching Windsor's uncircumcised penis pushing through its sheath. The glans, a pale coral, looked naked and raw and even a little lost. It had the unhappy air of a bespectacled person without spectacles. Flab Pottle cupped it protectively within the palms of his hands and began tracing his index finger around the rim, bending now and then to brush his lips to the weeping eye and lick away any stray tear.

I found the sight very moving. What a loss to the medical profession Flab Pottle was, he would have made a first-rate nurse.

'I was just saying to Loopy that Flower and Fizzy wouldn't particularly enjoy what we're up to, wouldn't you say, Flab?' Dame Agatha wriggled appreciatively as Windsor Shag probed deeper inside her drawers. Her soft cheek threw off a faint scent of chlorine which reminded me of the swimming pool and Doc Slack.

This time Flab Pottle replied right away. 'Ho, ho, no! – not with us fellows around!'

'Fuckin' waste,' Kid Lips lifted an indirected leg in the air and left it to crash back to base. 'I remember that kid when she was straight, mad keen on fellas. A little groupie from Streatham. Number ten Sunnyhill Road, lived near my auntie.' Then he fell silent again.

Dame Agatha kissed me lightly on the lips. 'Little Loopy,' she said affectionately. 'I've waited a very long time to do that – if only you knew how much I wanted to at school. Do you know I used to dream about you. Yes, honestly I did! Don't look so astonished! There were several of us who felt the same. The awful Ursula Baglow, and the Welsh drip, Myfanwy Morgan – she was mad for you.'

'She was mad anyway!' I couldn't believe that what she was saying was true. It was probably the Tequila talking. But it interested me all right. I wanted to hear more. She had certainly aroused my vain interest.

'Oh, and Nicolette What's-her-name.'

'No, not her! Golly Moses!'

272

'Yes, Nicolette. Do you know what's more – I got a postcard from her at the time of your marriage. She'd stuck the newspaper cutting onto one side and written "Feared Missing – Presumed Lost!"'

'How extraordinary.'

'Wasn't it? The card was posted from Holland too, of all places. She had sent it to the House, it raised my secretary's eyebrows.'

'Must have done.' I couldn't believe that the story was true. The girl Nicolette that I remembered had never so much as flung a glance in my direction. Nor had any of the others for that matter. Surely if all this were true I would have noticed – being so keen on attention and the approval of others. Or had I been too obsessed with Agatha Tatters to take account of anything else? That was more like it. And all the time my adoration was being silently reciprocated, if only I had known!

I stroked her thinning hair from her forehead (the glossy wig reigned over her cosmetics on the dressing-table). The forehead itself was a network of finely etched lines, seeing it this close. But the strong brows were as commanding as ever, and the sockets in which the eyes lay were smooth and unwrinkled. She was still a remarkably handsome woman.

'From this angle, upside-down, you look like Ingrid Bergman, Agatha.' And it was true, the bow of her mouth, the high cheekbones did resemble the famous actress. Always one of my favourites.

'Sweet thing.' Then she smiled suddenly with such ferocious tenderness that I felt my stomach turn.

I saw that Windsor Shag had three whole fingers inside her.

'And how much you are losing. Lady Patch, since your arrival at Slivers? Already I am seeing that this is your third day.' The masseuse had a polite and hesitant voice and a delicate Swedish accent, out of keeping with the firmness of her fingers. But it was the sort of shy voice that demanded more care in the answering than that of a more self-assured speaker. So I made an effort to rouse myself from my euphoric memories.

'Um, let me see – I haven't been weighed yet this

morning, and I shall be having a sauna before I go for that, but yesterday I'd lost four pounds.'

'Ah is very good! Would you like for to turn over now onto the stomach, Lady Patch. That's perfect, thank you so much.'

I presented her with my buttocks, too preoccupied with anxiety over the confrontation with Gunter Ragg to feel any self-consciousness. As she began pummelling them (as if that would do anything to diminish their size!) so my thoughts juggled over the events that had caused me to completely miss Gunter Ragg's visit to my room.

I'd fallen asleep on the job! But I wasn't the only one. We all of us had. At least I was the first to awake but when I crept out of Dame Agatha's bedroom (leaving behind a heavenly smell of sex and spilt alcohol – it was Agatha's supply of brandy that had finally done us in) they were still dead to the world and each other.

The television set was still on, flickering bleakly. I turned it off, I had no recollection of it ever having been on. But there they were, all the rest of them seated, sprawled, slumped in a semi-circle around the television set. And at one time I had found myself, head in Dame Agatha's lap, holding Windsor Shag's hand, on the television viewing panel too. So we must have watched something after all. Perhaps it was after the brandy but before the smoking. Though I had declined the exotic pipe – my daughters would have been ashamed of me. But by then I was beginning to feel nauseous. It was just as well that I had practised Dame Agatha's finger trick. If I hadn't puked up I would most certainly have done so later, probably all over everyone else while unconscious.

But when I'd returned to my bedroom and looked at my watch I was horrified to see that the time was two in the morning!

Poor Gunter Ragg. I'd be seeing him in a few hours time, what on earth could be my excuse?

'You have the beautiful skin, Lady Patch – is a real pleasure to work on.' The masseuse was pummelling perilously near my anus. Last night my poor botty had received more in the way of dick than it had taken even during the earliest years of Bertie. It was still deliciously delicate.

274

'Have I really?' I said pleasantly. She hadn't surprised me, not this morning she hadn't. A week ago if anyone had complimented me on the condition of my skin I would have jumped out of it with amazement. But after last night I was in the mood to believe anything nice about myself. Perhaps the truth of the matter was that I hadn't deteriorated to the extent that I believed. Either way I didn't any longer feel the wreck that I had. I wasn't completely washed up, not yet.

'Ah, but yes, is true – you no believe some of the unsightly blemishes I am having to touch.' The Swedish accent shook with ill-concealed distaste. 'Only yesterday I have one poor lady come with me and she is blue and black, like the battering baby. I treat her with the soothing oils, but more I cannot do. Is her husband she says to me. More fool for to stay with an animal such as this!' I felt a furious dollop of cream land splat! onto the small of my back, and was aware of it being worked well into my pores. Just like polishing shoes, to get an extra shine.

'Oh dear,' I murmured sympathetically. 'How perfectly dreadful for the poor woman.' But I was reminded of the bruises that I had been expecting from Doc Slack's fierce clasp on my arm. They obviously can't have surfaced, otherwise they would have been remarked upon by this conscientious creature.

'Ah,' she said darkly, her voice dropping confidingly. 'Is much that I see in places like Slivers, Lady Patch. You, you are being the different kettle of fishes, but with some of the ladies – ugh! What they are abusing their poor bodies how!' She lifted my head so I could see the way she was throwing her eyes ceiling-ward.

'Really,' I murmured, again sympathetically. But whether the sympathy was intended for her or directed towards the suffering bodies made little difference to either of us. Her hesitant approach to our conversation had paid off, I was now a completely captive audience.

She chuckled contentedly and, laying my head down again, began to massage the back of my neck. 'Ha!' she said – triumphantly I thought. 'Is tense here, Lady Patch! Just here is tense, I am feeling. You will be having to go to Doc Slack for the deep massage and the pulling of all the rusty old joints.'

'Doc Slack?'

'Yes. Is the finest for the tension. Is very, very, gentle – some surprise for a giant, no!' She laughed happily. 'Appearances they work to the contrarywise, yes?'

'Very often,' I said. 'Very often they do.'

My session was over, the masseuse sighed as I stood up to shrug Bertie's navy-blue towelling wrap over my shoulders. 'Is silk,' she said, lightly touching the skin of my stomach.

I didn't agree with her there. Stretch nylon is how I would have described it rather than silk, thinking of all that this covering had been called upon to contain since food had become the focal point of my life. But I didn't say so. I smirked instead with a stupid show of false modesty and tugged the belt of the wrap much tighter than I usually did around my middle. For the first time since my arrival at Slivers I really felt thinner, as if I actually had a waistline again.

The masseuse was watching me. 'Good luck for the weighing – is fingers crossed for the kind scales, yes!' She nodded encouragingly, small, swift movements of her neat head.

'Yes. Yes,' I echoed, nodding my head too. But it wasn't the weight I was worried about, but who was weighing me. I didn't feel like being deflated this morning.

'Good morning, Lady Patch. Just you jump onto the scales whilst I consult your notes. Ah, yesterday I see you were eleven stone and two pounds. Well, you certainly look lighter than that to me, now then . . .'

Sister adjusted the scales as she spoke, but I was too shocked by not finding Gunter Ragg at his post to bother about breathing in or out as the crucial ounces were registering.

What had I done to him? Where was the poor creature? Was he hiding, couldn't he face me? My mind spun with these questions, I was already curiously light-headed since my sauna. I had definitely overdone things in there today, deliberately choosing the one in which the young-sters hung out in the hope of seeing Flower Fowler and Fizzy Tornado. And neither of them had appeared, I had seen neither of them since this time yesterday. Nor had

Dame Agatha surfaced as yet, surely the events of last night wouldn't have laid her this low, for so long? Afterwards, after my weigh-in, I'd planned to pop up to her room to see how she was. But first perhaps Sister would explain where Gunter Ragg was.

'Is Mr Ragg ill? Is he indisposed, Sister?' I showed a suitable mask of concern.

'Goodness me, indisposed! I doubt it. Mr Ragg takes his teachings very much to heart, he lives by his own book. I doubt if he has suffered any form of indisposition for the last twenty years!' Sister laughed at the idea. 'No, Lady Patch. This is Mr Ragg's week off. He'll be visiting his other establishment in the Lake District, it's always that way. We have to learn to operate without him until the weekend. Now, let's see. I don't know about you, Lady Patch, but it looks to me as if someone has been a very good girl. You're down in the tens! You have lost another four pounds! Keep this up and we'll have to start feeding you up – you'll be dining in the light-diet room before you know it!'

My relief at escaping the confrontation with Gunter Ragg was nevertheless tinged with a sense of anti-climax. It wasn't that I was disappointed as much as left in mid-air. I would have felt better if he'd sent me a message to show that I was forgiven for not being in my room when he called. But then why should he – this was simply me being me again, the childish need for approval. Gunter Ragg must believe that I had deliberately rejected him.

'You'll be all on your own now your fine friends have flown.' Sister's brisk voice startled me out of my maudlin thoughts. I felt too removed from life today to even take in my weight-loss. Down in the tens, ten stone and twelve pounds! But what did she mean about my fine friends?

I stared at her stupidly.

'Flower Fowler left yesterday with the short girl –'

'Fizzy,' I said. 'She was being collected by her recording manager, something to do with her –'

'Yes, well,' Sister interrupted impatiently. My conversation must have sounded as irrelevant to her as it did to me. The lack of sustenance had affected my intelligence, yet all thought of food was absent from my mind. The craving was gone, I couldn't understand it. It was as if I had risen above such venal considerations. I floated a few feet above the rest of the world in a saintly fashion – ten stone twelve pounds of pure soul. Even my headache had disappeared, in its place I was aware only of a delicate throbbing as my thin blood threaded its way through my body. Sister's voice was becoming increasingly distant although she hadn't lowered it at all.

'Anyway, they hadn't returned by last night and this morning we received word that their stay with us would be terminated and their belongings collected.'

'But why would that be?' I felt alone and bewildered, as if I had lost two of my closest friends, although I had known them for a mere day or so. But that's what happened in establishments of this sort. Under these conditions unexpected intimacies flourished. Flourished and then died as swiftly, but I had hoped to have gone on a little longer than this with those two.

'Why? I couldn't give you the answer to that one, Lady Patch. They'll be charged the full term, that's clearly understood. Not that money seems to worry that type of youngster these days. In the pop world they have the stuff pouring out of their ears, don't they? Mind you, I think that the short girl hadn't lost as much weight as they'd been hoping – and I can give you reason for that. Simple cheating. Simple cheating, Lady Patch. Yes, you wouldn't believe the food that was found amongst her belongings.'

I flinched inwardly, guiltily thinking of my little stock. But at least I'd had the guile to camouflage it all. Poor little Fizzy, that probably wouldn't have occurred to her and the last thing she'd dreamt of happening was that all her things were going to have to be packed for her. I wouldn't like to have anyone rustling through my cases, even though I'd taken my precautions, anyone on the lookout would sus out my edibles in a moment.

'They were nice girls, I shall miss them both,' I said lamely, moving towards the door.

'And Dame Agatha Tatters.' Sister sounded pleased with herself.

'I beg you pardon?'

'Dame Agatha left hurriedly this morning on urgent constituency business. But she will be back. We're quite

278

used to this with Dame Agatha. In her position one has to expect these small crises.'

'When will she be back?' I was appalled by the bleakness that had now assailed my spirits. Even my weight-loss couldn't make up for the loss of my intimates. And I'd been looking forward to mulling over the lovely orgy with Dame Agatha! Who would I have all that to confide in now?

But Sister had evidently had enough of our exchange. She gave a small, hard laugh and patted me on the shoulder.

'Don't look so woe-begone, Lady Patch! You will find many other extremely pleasant folk here at Slivers. Dame Agatha is a great personality – oh, I grant you that – but it would be a shame for you not to mix thoroughly with everybody else. Now is the time to make a start on it, in Dame Agatha's short absence. She's rarely gone for more than a few days at most. I'm sure she'll telephone you and inform you of her plans.'

'I expect she will,' I said tonelessly. I suddenly felt terribly tired. Perhaps lack of sleep was the cause of my light-headedness too. I yawned right into Sister's unwary face. 'Oh, I am sorry, Sister. I'm feeling dreadfully weary all of a sudden.'

She patted my shoulder again. 'Sleep, my dear Lady Patch. Go to bed and sleep. That's what you need now, plenty of rest. It's the body's way of compensating for the lack of food. You must remember that this is in the nature of a fast, Lady Patch.'

'I hadn't forgotten, Sister.' I smiled weakly. The question now was whether or not I'd make it up the stairs.

'I see on your programme sheet that you have a Slim and Trim Class with Madame Minerva at four.'

'Christ!' Madame Minerva's classes, based on her ballet training thirty years ago were a legendary crippling experience. I had completely forgotten that it was my turn today. Sister frowned.

'That's not the attitude I would have expected from you, Lady Patch. Exercise is very important when you're losing this much weight. We need to tighten and tone the muscles again otherwise you'll be flopping and drooping all over the place.'

'Like a crumpled carrier-bag.' I thought of my skeleton shrouded in withered and toneless tissue, about as sexy and delectable as dead leaves. 'Lovely,' I said. Now I'd gone into deep depression, even the thought of my lemon-tea didn't revive me. All I wanted was to drift into the land of dreams and relive the events of last night.

Sister shot me a sharp look, suspecting me of sarcasm. But she must have seen from my sloppish slump that there wasn't the spirit left for that. 'Come on now, Lady Patch,' she said briskly, 'up to bed for a rest. You have to work up some stamina for Madame Minerva, you know. You can do it!'

But I couldn't. 'I can't do it, Madame Minerva. It's no good . . .' I lay gasping, spread-eagled on the floor of Madame Minerva's Slim and Trim Studio with my feet placed up above me at an impossibly high angle against the wall. My instructions had been to touch my toes.

'Wubbish! Twy again – two, fwee, fouw – upsidaisy up, up!'

She was pulling my hair so hard that I screamed. The entire weight of my torso was being raised by my scalp, forced up from my follicles. The pain was excruciating, the only way to stop it was by making the superhuman effort to touch my wretched toes under my own steam. I lunged forward wildly, my fingertips stretched ahead of me like a sleep-walker but with the desperation of a long-disance runner within reach of the touch-line. 'Uuurgh!' My throat seized up in agony. I was not going to make it – again, and this was my tenth try. Madame Minerva, noting my failure, released my hair in disgust such that I fell back abruptly, banging my head on the floor. But I didn't care. It was sweet relief just to lie there doing nothing with my eyes closed.

Madame Minerva was the most odious woman that I'd ever met. She was older than me, well into her fifties, but one wouldn't have guessed this. She still looked like a ballerina in the Scandinavian style, tall and willowy. Blonde hair back in a bun, eyelids brushed with pale blue, the exact colour of her leotard and the unsmiling chill of her eyes.

The Führer would have approved – she'd have gone a

bomb with old Hitler. Shame Dame Agatha wasn't here with me, she'd have appreciated that little aside. But alas, my handful of companions showed no such streak of humour. Poor devils. They were suffering in silence, apart from my gasping confessions as to my own uselessness and the understandable scream as my hair was being yanked out by the roots. But my feelings were that Madame Minerva had had enough of me and my histrionics. A bucketful.

All that was left was to exchange grins of sympathy with the blowsy blonde, the one who had been attending Doc Slack's gymnasium yesterday. The same one that Dame Agatha and I had bumped into when we were on our way to the swimming pool. The one who appeared not to speak English. We communicated well enough in our way. I didn't have Dame Agatha's British reserve towards foreigners, especially not when we were both in the proverbial shit like this. Her blonde muscles seemed to have given up the ghost as well. Two spineless slobs together.

But I wasn't to be allowed even this short respite it seemed.

Madame Minerva's accent was a difficult one to pin down. There was a nasal North Finchley whine in it somewhere that was deeply unpleasant, overlaid with the perfect enunciation of a Harrods' shop assistant. But the inability to pronounce the letter *r* in the alphabet gave it a touchingly human quality. Or was it that I chose to see it as that? Was I warming to an apparent weakness – the only chink in an otherwise perfect façade?

I lay sprawled at her feet looking straight up those shapely legs into her snatch, wondering why there was no vaginal cleft there, no indentation at àll. Simply a stretch of sky-blue, flat and smooth as an ironing board. Whilst the rest of us – I glanced down to make sure that I was the same as everyone else – were displaying the dimpled signs of our sex, Madame Minerva had only this anonymous pre-pubescent cunt. I didn't know why but something about the thought cheered me.

'Weally, Lady Patch!'

'What?' Had the bitch read my thoughts!

'You are keeping the west of the class waiting for you.'

281

She stood running on the spot with her hands encircling her ludicrously narrow waist. On purpose, to emphasise to all of us fat pigs what could be achieved if we only tried. Not knowing that every single one of us would rather have died than turn ourselves into this undignified imitation of a kewpie doll at our age – let alone *her* age. The ancient old bag.

'The west of the class?' I repeated innocently, widening my eyes and looking up from my proper place at everyone's feet. Let the buggers trample all over me, run, jump, and roll. Suddenly I didn't care –

'Sod it!' I said. And rising slowly to my feet, from all fours at one stage, I limped painfully from Madame Minerva's Slim and Trim Studio. Leaving the west of the class to wescue themselves. I was joined by my ally, the blowsy blond.

In the corridor we both burst out laughing like two naughty schoolgirls, giggling together helplessly. In normal circumstances we would then have gone on somewhere to have a cup of tea together, or a drink. Something to cement the conspiratorial feeling between us. It passed through my mind that I could invite her up to my room for a spot of something illegal, but I was reluctant to do that. I wasn't keen on that degree of intimacy, not yet. And apart from that I had genuinely lost all desire to cheat, the thought of eating anything solid or drinking spirits made me feel slightly nauseous. It had been as much as I could do to force down my solitary lemon juice at lunchtime. I was thankful that none of the chaps had appeared, I wouldn't have known how to greet them without the moral support of Dame Agatha.

There had been a message from Dame Agatha waiting for me in my room. A brief note lamenting her departure and promising to ring me if and when she had the chance. The only reference that she had made to the sexual events we had shared was her PS: 'What glorious high jinks!!' It had made me smile, but I was childishly anxious for her return. Without her there in the building I felt curiously truncated and numbed, like at school when she hadn't come back after one half-term. For a week I'd felt as though I was sickening for influenza, to the point where I was even running a temperature. At her reappearance all these symptoms had vanished.

But now my new-found blowsy friend was studying her

282

watch and inviting me to do the same. I peered over her plump shoulder to stare at the small silvery object on her wrist. It looked just like every other watch I'd ever seen but perhaps she was wanting my admiration of a recently acquired present – a gift from a gentleman friend?

'Very nice indeed . . . verree . . . nice.' I mouthed the words slowly, stopping at various syllables to let it all sink in. And I nodded with furious pleasantry and showed my back teeth in gummy smiles.

She looked astonished. And then it dawned on her that I hadn't understood her intention at all. So this time she pointed to the darkening roots of her hair and then back to the tiny hands on the dial of her watch.

She was due to visit the hairdresser. Would I like to accompany her to the salon? The Beauty Bowl, of which the hairdressing salon was a sizeable part, branched away to the left of the intimately-lit Slivers Boutique. It was, both in architectural scale and atmosphere, the opposite of Doc Slack's vast Exercise Gymnasium or the Olympian swimming pool. As if the secret of feminine beauty as opposed to female fitness and health was one which could only be acquired through a certain amount of artificial mystique.

The patient prepared in the gymnasium, the sauna, the Swedish massage, the Roman Spa bath (which I had yet to try), the Slim and Trim class (which I never would again), and all the other Slivers' treatments, to be stripped free of vanity till a Spartan level had been reached. But here in the seductively perfumed confines of The Beauty Bowl, there was a completely separate set of ethics in operation. This was the frivolous end of the scale, the pampered part, the self-indulgent and narcissistic one. Where basics such as enemas and colonic irrigations were of another world. And although, as I had proved, I hardly belonged to the fitness brigade, I was too unfamiliar with the rarified plateau of professionally applied glamour to feel comfortable in its midst. And it wasn't even to do with being fat. Or in my forties. Even as a girl, as a slim young woman, I had been so indoctrinated by my mother (and by my school) to shun the cult of one's personal appearance that I viewed such places as beauty parlours with a mixture of derision and suspicion. The hairdresser's was somewhere to be visited only when one was forced to for the purposes of a hair-cut. But such frivolities as shampoos and sets were strictly for other people. As were new hair-styles. My hair, which in the last five years I had taken to trimming once a month myself with my dressmaking scissors, looked much the same now as it had done throughout my entire life. Mother had always insisted on its shortness – less risk of nits. And Bertie had approved too because from the back, he claimed, it made me look more like a boy. An extension of my appeal since the view from the front was so obviously female!

And so, it was with a conflicting set of emotions that I accompanied my blowsy companion to her destination, it was on my way in any case, so I reasoned. I wouldn't be forced to go inside, not against my will. And it would have to have been against my will, looking as I did. I couldn't help wondering now, catching sight of myself in the large, gleaming window to my left, whether Madame Minerva hadn't taken a dislike to me because of my clothing as much as my lack of physical co-ordination. Perhaps I had gone a little over the top this time.

I hadn't meant to, but my mid-day sleep had been so deep and dreamless (pity that, I'd been cheated) that I'd awoken only with the greatest difficulty. I'd set the alarm in good time for the class with Madame Minerva and yet was reluctant to leave my comfortable bed. And so I'd lain there, reflecting on my life, past and present. Of missed opportunities and wasted chances, and then of moments of surging happiness and fleeting glimpses of fulfilment.

'It's not been bad fun,' I'd said to myself cheerfully, and I'd turned up the transistor radio on my bedside table as it played a favourite tune of Tadpole's that reminded me of her and Daisy. Which made me even chirpier. And then I'd discovered this bone in my body, one that I hadn't felt for five years! It was my hip bone – there were two of them, one on each side of my stomach. I thought at first that I must be imagining things.

It was because I was lying flat on my back with my knees slightly bent, not my normal position. My usual was the routine return-to-the-womb, side-saddle, with my knees crushing my nipples. Lying in bed simply assessing my assets was not something that I'd spent much time doing since Bertie. My assets, physical and otherwise, had seemed too thin on the ground to make the pastime worthwhile.

When I'd very first had recourse to my vibrator, the muffled activity had been beneath blankets with me on my back, legs clumsily akimbo. But it hadn't been satisfactory. Bertie's pyjama bottoms had got in the way and then the vibrator itself had reared through my fingers and jerked convulsively off to some dark secret corner of the bed all on its own. Fornicating with the new flannelette sheets that I'd just switched over to for the winter. Besides which it felt lonely and shabby, doing it like that. Like wanking, rather than gleefully oiling the works. And so I had chosen to live out my love-life with the light on, not necessarily choosing bed in which to cherish myself. What I mostly did there was simply sleep, alone. And when I woke I immediately got up.

But now I was feeling my hip-bones protruding beneath the shrinking surface of my stomach. The sensation was so unfamiliar that I couldn't stop stroking them, taking pleasure from their jutting presence. They were like unexpected rocks on a stretch of soft, sandy shore. Would there be others elsewhere just like them?

Time, however, hadn't taken my preoccupation into account. When I'd next consulted the clock I found that it had left me a mere ten minutes in which to rise from my bed, change into suitable clothes, and get myself downstairs to Madame Minerva. I only had time to scramble into the nearest thing that I could grab hold of and run for my life. Madame Minerva was known to crucify late-comers.

And so it was that I'd found myself in my present garb, a pair of Bertie's winter long-johns. Ones that Daisy had unsuccessfully attempted to turn into a fashionable garment last winter by dyeing purple and sewing up the flies. With them I had tugged on a black long-sleeved lacy wool vest which had belonged to my mother and had seen better days as a meal for moths. There was a huge network of holes stretching over one shoulder, which though it could have been mistaken as part of the pattern, did reveal an unseemly acreage of upper breast. So for the sake of decency I'd had to slip a shirt over the top, the comfortably capacious short-sleeved Aertex (monogrammed) that Bertie had bought for himself in Bermuda. The time when he'd thought that we might take up tennis. I looked just about as wide as I was tall. But it struck me that for the first time my reflection in the corridor window appeared to be that of a woman!

It may have been because I had bound my head in a scarf. It was one of those scarlet and white cotton handkerchiefs that snuff-takers sneeze into and sailing wallahs tie around their necks. And the reason I'd donned it was not only that my unruly mop of hair was badly in need of attention and I couldn't find either a brush or a comb, but because I'd thought it might have charmed Madame Minerva to be reminded of her days as a fledgling ballerina. I looked like a serious dance student (from the neck up) give or take a decade or two.

Or was this new impression of myself as a female due to my recent sexual experiences? Perhaps they had even affected the way in which I strolled down a corridor!

I glanced at my blowsy friend. She was involved in fascinating preparations for her arrival at her hairdressing appointment. She was composing herself, applying a sumptuous strawberry gloss from a miniature compact to her upper lip with her little finger. Looking intently into the tiny mirror of the compact as we walked along, never for a second straying over the natural line of her mouth. And then she expertly pressed the top lip to the bottom, transferring a shiny sheen evenly over its surface. After which she pouted a few times at her mouth's reflection, before opening wide to examine her teeth for unsightly smudges of the strawberry gloss, running a pink, fleshy tongue over the whole to make absolutely sure. This completed, she sweetly offered me the little compact, pointing from it towards my own lips several times in case I was too thick to have connected the two together from watching her. But I declined. Cosmetics had never been my sort of thing.

But I was drawn to what she was doing. I watched her spit on another finger-tip now and run this first over one eye-brow and then over the other, before flicking up the eye-lashes with yet more saliva. She seemed to know the entire area of her face without having to look, because now she was busy pinching her cheeks at a precise spot on each. So that when she had finished a bright rush of blood like a maidenly blush glowed on either side of her nose.

Why on earth she was bothering I couldn't for the life of me work out. I had thought that the whole point of going to these beauty places was to let them do it all for you. That was what was so bloody off-putting about visiting the hairdressers, the fact that one was forced to sit in a line with a lot of tarted-up females, each of them staring at each other to see who looked the best and whether there wasn't another spare inch somewhere on their faces for plastering on something extra.

And yet I delighted in what Daisy and Tadpole did to themselves. I loved the excesses to which they went. As to whether their father would have approved, well that was another matter. When Bertie had died, the girls hadn't reached the stage of being obsessive about their appearance. They hadn't even begun to experiment with how to project themselves, their image was of little concern. I could imagine what tensions would have sprung up between Bertie and them if he'd lived to see the way in which they later chose to doll themselves up. Anything from a stormtrooper, a street-accident, or a Forties hooker auditioning for a Hollywood musical, was liable to emerge from either of their rooms at any time. I don't think that poor Bertie could have coped with the excitement. The whole success of our escapades, his and mine, rested on the fact that I was so overtly pure and unsullied. The model wife, not made of mistress material at all. Certainly not capable of being a whore.

It was because of this necessary element that Bertie disapproved of my use of cosmetics. Like my mother. My charm, so they claimed, lay in my fresh complexion and the completely natural look. To have tampered with that would have been a criminal act. If they'd either of them lived to see me now they would have been forced to acknowledge that time itself had tampered. I was corroded by nature, but even English roses eventually wither and fade away. And I had not even started life with the benefits of having been an English rose. More of a dandelion, or a communal-garden pansy, or a bright-centred daisy. All blooms with short stalks and a definite

287

presence to boast of, and little else besides the ability to pop up and flourish alongside the exotic. But never likely to win prizes for anything in the spectacular stakes, though perennially popular for all that.

Now that we had reached The Beauty Bowl it was time to part company. But my blowsy blonde had other ideas. She was clinging to my arm with a touch of desperation as we stood at the gold and white entrance, almost cringing. I could feel her fingers trembling through my shirt and wool vest. But what the hell was she expecting me to do – go into the beastly place with her! This was precisely what she was silently willing. It clicked into my mind that the poor creature hadn't an appointment, that she wanted me to arrange it for her. Me with my confidence and command of the English language. We stood there together, uncertainly on the brink while I gently disengaged her clutching hands and took the opportunity to peer inside the daunting façade. But this was difficult. The smoked glass of the windows made it impossible to gain a positive impression of anything other than a seductive blur of soft carpets, indoor plants and an immaculately groomed receptionist at the discreetly lit desk. I felt my heart plummetting down. This was not where I wished to enter, my friend would have to go in on her own.

I turned to let her know this, when I saw Sister approaching. She was smiling broadly and encouragingly at my companion before her welcome expanded to include me. Nodding and mouthing silent words in an exaggerated fashion, words that I understood as I lip-read what she was saying. And then to my amazement she began a series of rapid and efficient movements with her fingers, to which my new friend reacted in exactly the same way.

She was deaf and dumb! Of course! It had only been Dame Agatha's characteristic keenness to pigeon-hole people into separate nationalities that had led us into jumping to the conclusion that she was foreign. And only my gross insensitivity and crass preoccupation with myself had furthered this misconception.

I felt humbled and hot with shame. But Sister didn't notice, she was actually patting me on the back. 'Glad to see that you're making productive use of your time, Lady

Patch! Didn't I tell you that there were interesting friends to be found in Slivers?' And with that she went purposefully on her way.

I didn't look at the woman beside me, I couldn't bear her to realise that I had only just learnt of her handicap. When I'd thought of her simply as a foreigner I'd been treating her with a kind of amused sympathy. And she had responded in the same way. We'd chosen to appoint ourselves victims of the Slivers' harsh system and the fact that we were unable to exchange actual words made very little odds. We communicated quite happily in other ways. But now I felt differently. Now I felt protective towards her, though she would clearly have spurned my pity. I must watch myself for signs of indirect condenscension. I should have to stop myself from referring to her menatlly as my blowsy blonde. I was blessed with all my faculties, which she wasn't, therefore I was in a better position than she was to overcome fears of inadequacy. I took her elbow and stepping boldly through the door of The Beauty Bowl, I introduced myself to the receptionist and explained what was required. Five minutes later I found myself seated inside the hairdressing salon, along-side my friend, involved in a deep discussion with Tracy, the colour consultant, who was unhappy about the present condition of my friend's tresses. It would be far better for the general condition of the hair if she didn't apply the harsh peroxide but instead chose a different hair-bleach, one that though deepening the blonde shade several degrees, would nevertheless not harm it in the same way. It was my task to explain it all.

'What's your friend's name?' Tracy had asked at one point.

'Your name?' I mouthed energetically, raising my eyebrows to show it was a question. And then I hit upon the idea of writing it down.

She, in turn, wrote her name. It was Blanche. Blanche Regenbögen. Mrs Blanche Regenbögen. My eyes must have widened when she wrote the Mrs part, because she smiled and then struck it through several times. I took it to mean that Mr Regenbögen was no longer part of her life. She didn't seem unduly concerned.

But the decision as to the strength of bleach was

another matter. Tracy resorted to scribbling the facts as she saw them, but Blanche stubbornly chose not to agree with her. So that in the end Tracy accepted her defeat.

'Well,' she sighed, with a charming air of resignation. 'It is Madame's hair so on her head be it.'

'Quite,' I said.

'And what about your good self, Lady Patch? Shall we take a look at yours now?' She said it so matter-of-factly, removing my cotton scarf from my head as she did so that I was too taken aback even to answer. While waiting for Blanche to arrive at her decision I'd been idly leafing through Tracy's colour charts. They reminded me of all the shades that I'd seen in Selfridges Wig Bar. Each was represented by a looped strand of nylon hair secured at the edge of the printed information. One colour in particular, a brilliant russet red, had caught my eye. The colour that I would have chosen for myself as a child, I had always had a thing about redheads.

'Ah, now!' Tracy's eyes lit up. My wiry mane sprang into life beneath her finger, released from the confines of the cotton scarf. A hideous combination of dark brown and dusty grey, a salt and pepper mixture. Virgin territory to Tracy, I could tell by her expression and the way her tongue was running over her glossy lips.

When she met my eyes I shrank from their fire. 'There's only one question, Lady Patch. What colour will it be?'

I was on my way to becoming a redhead.

It proved how weak of will I was under circumstances as seductive as these. Blanche was there backing me up and egging me on, but I didn't really need her. I took to the world of the beautician's skills, to the pampering, the plucking, the perfuming, the pedicuring, as the manner born. It was nine o'clock at night when we eventually emerged! We had been in there almost five hours! Neither Bertie nor my mother would have recognised me. When I woke the following morning I found a stranger in my bed, scented and smooth of leg and under-arm. Plucked of brow, dyed of lash, clipped of nail, refined of pore and pierced of ear. But more startling than anything else was the hair. I stole stealthily out of my bed to take a look at it, as if scared that the colour might have bled out of it in the night. For although I had lain stroking the unfamiliar silkiness over my forehead and touched the tapered down behind my ears, it was the fiery colour that had made me first laugh out loud when they had shown me myself in the mirror.

A redhead at last – after all these years – me! I wanted to stand up and squeal with delight! What a bloody waste to have waited till now, but this wasn't a time for regrets.

It was Tracy who had started it (that girl should have been given shares in the business!). 'This is the boring part I'm afraid, Lady Patch,' she'd apologised when my red dye had been applied. 'What about a pedicure?'

'A pedicure?' I'd been astonished. Was a pedicure something that I was so obviously in need of?

But it was a clever suggestion, more cunning than starting off with the mention of a manicure. I would have hesitated at that as Tracy must have guessed, it conjured up sinful images of scarlet talons and long cigarette holders. All the things that Bertie and my mother so disapproved of. Whereas a pedicure smacked hygienically of Dr Scholl and chiropody. My mother was awfully hot on changing one's socks, and alternating one's shoes every other day.

'Yes. A pedicure sounds very refreshing. Thank you, Tracy.'

It was while having my pedicure that it was while having my pedicure that it was discovered how desperately I needed to have both legs waxed.

'Waxed? What?' I had heard them whispering over my limbs.

'Superfluous hair,' they had explained succinctly.

'No!' I was embarrassed. The way that they'd said it, so accusingly, it sounded as anti-social as syphilis.

And so they'd waxed me, spreading my legs from the knee downwards with a newly developed organic, honey-like substance. Warming it first and applying it to my skin in small areas at a time and covering each with a paper gauzed strip, which was later yanked off. With it came the distasteful superfluous hair. Afterwards a soothing cactus oil was massaged over each denuded leg. It wasn't as painful as I imagined it to be. I'd heard of women who'd been plunged into a catatonic trance from what they described as an experience of unmitigated agony. But the difference, so I was assured, between this method and the old (which lingered over from Egypt apparently!) was that this one gripped the hair and not the skin.

But while I was at it, wearing only my knickers by this time – stripped of Mother's vest, Bertie's long-johns and the Aertex monstrosity, I was persuaded into having my pubic area tidied up. The Bikini Treatment, it was known as. And another session under each arm.

Then, emboldened by this wholesale removal of the unsightly, I pointed out three stubborn hairs which had taken lately to sprouting straight out from my chin. They had always annoyed me, when reading or writing I often found my fingers straying to them. But I had to wait until they grew to a certain length before it was possible to get enough of a grip on them between my nails to wrench the wretched things out by the roots. The last time I'd resorted to snipping them off with nail scissors, it felt as if I were trimming a beard. And now they had come back with redoubled strength, harsh and prickly as thistles. It must be to do with the increase in the male hormones of my body. It happened, so I'd read, that at a certain time in the onset of the menopause these male hormones took over. They caused all sorts of alarming changes to take place, deepening the voice, thickening the waist, insinuating a sexual response towards fellow members of the female sex, and sprouting facial hair in the form of straggly moustaches and goatee beards – like the one I was growing.

And so electrolysis was employed to kill off these three hairs on my chin. I was warned that the results might not be absolutely permanent unless I kept up the treatment. This conducted an electrical current through each hair follicle to the hair base, thence destroying the papilla (whatever the papilla was). I couldn't pretend that this wasn't uncomfortable, but by then I'd become stoical and was prepared to suffer a little for perfection. I'd miss playing with those three hairs. But now I had my pierced ear-lobes to fiddle around with instead. Hadn't I been instructed to twist my little 'sleepers' each day to keep the pierced holes open and prevent them from closing up again?

They were sweet, my little 'sleepers', tiny gold rings like

the sort that Bertie and I used to see worn by the Spanish children when we stayed at the villa during the summers. I'd wanted to have Daisy and Tadpole's ears done, I'd heard that it was meant to strengthen the eyesight of small children. But Bertie had scoffed that away as being an old wives' tale – and a Spanish one at that. After his death they had it done themselves out of their own pocket-money. And had even tried to persuade me to do the same. But everything connected to the improvement of my appearance these last five years they had learned to give up as a bad job.

But what would they say now – what would their reaction be to a mother who looked as if she were trying to compete? Would they be proud – or horribly embarrassed? My mother's words hit me as I crept over to peep into the dressing-table mirror. 'Mutton done up as lamb.' She considered it the cruellest insult one could hurl at a woman. Would she say it of me now?

I was wearing Bertie's pyjamas as I usually did but now even they looked different on me. For one thing you couldn't guess at the shape of me beneath. They looked what they were, a pair of over-large gentleman's pyjamas. Whereas before they had rather clung around my belly and my bum, not to mention my breasts, now they simply sagged sadly over the whole. There was no doubt about it – I was definitely shrinking. I felt for my hip-bones. Now I didn't even have to lie flat on my back in order to feel them. Here they were below what was beginning to be an indication of a waist-line! But today it was me from the neck upward that looked most unfamiliar.

I bent forward and kissed the new me. Then, sitting down at the dressing-table I started to play with the two side-wings of the triple mirror. I needed to get a good all-round view of myself. I wanted to see what other people would be seeing from all sides. I had to practise at which angle to hold this new head, how to present this new self most favourably to the world.

Had my mother been able to see me now she would have sent me to my room to meditate and repent. My vanity would have had to have been scourged from my soul. I needed to be shown the error of my shallow ways.

I proved that I had been worshipping profane idols – but sod that. I looked bloody smashing, to me.

'Loopy, dear, everything is absolutely monstrous this end – my entire world seems to have turned upside down! I shan't bore you with the details but it's a case of mutiny in the ranks, a cuckoo in the nest – as odious a case of disloyalty as you could hope never to discover . . . Aren't some people vermin, haven't you found that? Probably not, Loopy,' Dame Agatha groaned over the telephone. 'Ah, would that I had led your sheltered life, then I too would share your sanguine view of humanity. You cheerful little soul, oh, but it's so comforting to hear your calm voice. Like an oasis of sanity, how I wish I were back with you at Slivers. I daren't ask how much weight you've lost – do you know how much I've put on in the last week? I shan't tell you! Now then give me all the gossip, do . . .'

But there wasn't any gossip. I had nothing to tell her, no juicy titbits. All I'd done since Dame Agatha, Flower Fowler and Fizzy Tornado had left Slivers was gently but relentlessly fading away.

I now weighed nine and half stone.

'I weigh nine and a half stone, Agatha.' I'd said it quietly.

Her scream must have raised the roof from the Houses of Parliament.

'But,' I said wistfully, 'I haven't had a single fuck since you left.'

'Serve you right, you – you – skinny little bitch! You probably haven't the bloody strength. What you need is a square meal. I haven't been off the nest since I left Slivers. Don't worry, little Loopy, we'll get you organised as soon as you're away from that ghastly place –'

'Oh, but aren't you returning? I'm sure that they're under the impression here that you are.'

Dame Agatha snorted. 'You mean I'm still paying! God almighty I shall crucify my secretary if I find that's the case. He's an absolute twerp, this chap. He had instructions to settle up the day after I left. That explains why my belongings haven't arrived yet. Bird-brain! I really shall have to find someone else. What sort of secretary do you think Windsor Shag would make, Loopy?'

'Windsor?' I could hardly remember what Windsor looked like even. That evening, those times seemed to belong to another life, another world. Kid Lips. Flab Pottle. Doc Slack . . .

It was as if I hadn't ever met them. I'd been existing in a void of my own making – again. I had deliberately cut myself off from their world.

But suddenly, just today, the light was filtering through the daze. Dame Agatha had telephoned and snapped me out of myself.

Her call had woken me up, I peered at my watch. It was only eight-thirty in the morning, but the post had been already, I could see three letters on the carpet. They'd been pushed in beneath the door together with my usual *Guardian*.

'Yes, Windsor.' Dame Agatha sounded excited. 'He's been staying with me here, but I really do think that he should do some sort of work. I could put him on a crash course of shorthand and typing. The poor lamb is sadly lacking in qualifications and as I tell him he can't hope to live on his looks forever.'

I was bewildered by this sudden turn of events. As far as I knew Windsor Shag was still here at Slivers. 'But what about Bart Deco and all those plans – wasn't he going to launch Windsor as something or other?'

'Ah, but what, Loopy dear! I'm afraid poor Windsor hasn't the drive or the ambition to make anything much of himself. Sweet thing hadn't the will-power to even stick it out as Slivers, as soon as he discovered that I'd left he came running after me. You should see his paunch now, he's gained a further five pounds!'

'Oh dear.'

'Yes, I think your Mr Deco has washed his hands of him. There was talk of a small film part but of course he's too fat for it, and I'm afraid that I'm not much help to the angel there – not where food is concerned. But there's more to life, I tell him, than just the body beautiful. Though now you probably would disagree with me, Loopy – you and your five and a half stone!'

'*Nine* and a half, Agatha –'

'You probably look like someone with anorexia.'

'Not really, no. I look quite nice I think. I've had my hair dyed.'

'Dyed! What colour, Loopy?'

'Bright red.'

'God Almighty – like a carrot on a chopstick!' Dame Agatha chortled. 'No wonder you haven't been getting your fair share – you've been frightening the fellows away!'

'I've been keeping myself to myself.' My voice sounded prissy.

'Whatever for, Loopy? Are you suffering a religious conversion, my dear? Haven't you been spending time with that nice Flab Pottle? I heard that Kid Lips was thrown out, Windsor told me all about that.'

'Really? I didn't know Kid had gone, I haven't seen Flab Pottle, Gunter Ragg's been away, and I decided not to visit the gymnasium any more. I've been avoiding Doc Slack – I just couldn't face him without your moral support, Agatha.'

'Nonsense, darling thing! I can tell you that you've gone into positive decline. You're starving, you've lost your energy – where has all that *joie de vivre* gone to? You must leave that place. I shall organise to have you collected this morning, I'll get my twerp onto it. Or shall I send Windsor along for you? Trouble is that he doesn't drive yet, though I have booked him up with B.S.M. He's starting lessons next week –'

'Don't be silly, Agatha –'

'Silly? I think everyone should hold a driving licence, one never knows when it'll come in handy. Especially useful for Windsor to be able to drive if he hopes to be of any use to me.'

'I didn't mean that. I agree that Windsor should have driving lessons, it'll help him to be more independent.'

'Oh dear. I'm not sure that's such a good idea. I rather like babying him along Loopy, d'you suppose that it's because I never gave birth?'

'Possibly Agatha. But what I was saying was that I'll stay on here a little longer. I thought that I'd try to get into the eights.'

'How ghastly! You make it sound like a rowing team. Well, Loopy dear, do promise me that you'll emerge from this ridiculous shell you appear to have retired into. Get hold of old Flab Pottle and stroll down to the pub, that's what we used to do. It won't show on the scales if you puke it up as I showed you. Oh – and next time we talk I hope to hear some real gossip, sexual stuff – you know the kind of thing I enjoy!'

I should have rung her right back there and then. All three of my letters were from men, I discovered this when I got out of bed.

Gunter Ragg's was the only one with a postmark and so I had opened it first out of curiosity. The other two, from Flab Pottle and Doc Slack, had been written on the premises and must have been pigeon-holed for me down at Reception. It was interesting to compare the writing styles – in each case they were a true reflection of the man behind them. It came as no surprise that all three missives had arrived on the same day. Coincidences had quite often happened to me in my life – an abundance of wealth following a period of poverty, the flocking of friends after a long patch of loneliness. Even the sexual saturation of the shared orgy was sent, I was sure, to make up for all I'd been missing. And I'd had to give myself a chance to think about all that too. I'd needed this time of withdrawal to get the whole question of my future into some sort of perspective.

But there hadn't been any doubt in my mind that I should hear from these three. About now was how long I'd thought it would take.

Poor Blanche's departure might have had something to do with it. Since yesterday I'd been free enough to cast my thoughts in other directions, maybe I'd subconsciously summoned the three chaps onto my wavelength. Placed myself firmly into their thoughts. Sometimes it is plausible to believe that one can will things into existence. The letters could be proof of that.

Gunter Ragg's was the most formal, as I should have expected it to be. It was typewritten on an electric machine, the letters were thin and spidery, as was his handwritten signature below. He had been hoping to return in his usual manner by the weekend but bad news had cropped up, his son had been involved in a minor

297

accident. He hoped to catch me before I left Slivers, he'd heard that I'd made exemplary progress and looked forward to greeting the new sylph-like Lady Patch. P.S. He had very much enjoyed reading my books!

I grew a little hot at that. The fact was that I'd forgotten how I'd forced my filth on the poor fellow! Those were early days then before I'd become my current circumspect self. I wondered whether the books had been what started him off in the first place, perhaps they had precipitated the passionate lunge in the office. Who could tell?

Doc Slack's short note was terse and to the point. He felt he owed me an apology and an explanation. Would it be possible to meet at the gymnasium this evening at around eight o'clock? If I didn't turn up or leave a message he would understand and he wouldn't try to get in touch with me again. The writing was large and practically filled the entire page although it was barely more than a few lines. Written with a ferociously black felt-tip pen, each full-stop and comma looked as if it had been spat onto the paper. The signature had gone through to the other side.

Flab Pottle's started off, 'Dear Little Lady Lettice Patch – are you by any chance avoiding me?'

I was sad that he should have thought this to be the case, though it wasn't so far from the truth. Blanche had monopolised my attention more than I had intended, but it was a situation which I had allowed to develop. One which I was very familiar with, hadn't I had it with both my mother and then with Bertie? Me devoting my life and time to making them feel happy and important and loved. And I was proud of the change that I'd helped bring about in Blanche, even Sister had congratulated me. That was pleasant, to be in her good books without having to do my usual arse-licking act. I found it gave me an unfamiliar feeling of genuine self-respect. Florence Nightingale must have had a fabulous ego.

But in any case it had been a two-way thing, Blanche had introduced me to a world that I hadn't entered before. Each day we had found a reason for popping into The Beauty Bowl. If we weren't having ourselves tanned with ultra-violet rays (I looked now as if I'd spent a fortnight in the Seychelles) we would be enduring one of our Slender-tone spot-reducing treatments, or allowing the therapist to eradicate the tension lines from our faces, or coaxing the cellulite from our upper thighs with the aid of special creams. I had never been so familiar with my own body in my whole life, I knew every nook and cranny, pustule, pore, failing and follicle. It was fascinating that I'd managed to get this far without knowing it all before. Narcissism. Narcissism gone bloody berserk!

We did other things as well. We neither of us, for different reasons, wanted to patronise Doc Slack's gymnasium so took our exercise in other ways. We each hired a bicycle and wobbled around the extensive grounds of Slivers, even venturing out onto the highway on several occasions. But then Blanche had spotted a Stop Me And Buy One ice-cream vendor whose habit it was to park outside the local prep school. The first time I'd weakened and had bought us both a vanilla wafer, but after the first lick (which tasted so wonderful I almost swooned) we'd both begun to feel dreadfully sick. Neither of us were able to finish – I could hardly believe it – not able to wolf down a babyish ice-cream wafer! When only a month ago I had purchased a two pound tub of American Coffee Fudge'n'Nut from the deep freeze counter at Harrods, thinking how nice it would be to have a supply of ice-cream in the house in case the urge for the taste should overtake me. But, alas, by the time the Ten O'clock News had come on the television I had polished off the entire tub. All by myself, not a spoonful for the girls. Without so much as a twinge of nausea.

The next time we cycled on past the Stop Me And Buy One, but Blanche's will gave out when we got to the village store. She would insist on sausage rolls, paying the shopkeeper double to heat them up for her. He gladly agreed, he did enormous under-the-counter trade with patients from Slivers. I recognised two customers skulking amongst the biscuit and cake section, but pretended never to have crossed their paths before, though less than a few hours ago I had seen them both stark naked in the sauna.

As we were leaving, my heart pirouetted against my pullover, such that the shop swung around before my eyes. I steadied myself against a clustered group of early potted hyacinths, breaking several of the fragile blue blooms by so doing. More money changed hands with the urbane owner of the place and flustered apologies on my part.

'Not to worry,' he said beaming. 'There's lots keel right over – laid flat on the floor – of you folk from Slivers. I've been afeared that I'm coming round from my side of the counter to pick up a corpse.' He chortled at the thought. 'You sure you're going to be alright now, Miss? You look as if a puff of wind would blow you over – nothing that a good meal wouldn't put right.'

His words were sweet to my ears, I could have swayed there all day hearing such honeyed stuff. But I was more interested in the cause of my sudden dizziness. I hadn't been the terrible ecstasy of the hot sausage roll flaking over my tongue, squelching through my tight teeth, slithering past my taut tonsils. But rather what the warm sausage meat had reminded me of, that and the fact that a person entering the shop had looked uncannily like Flab Pottle.

It wasn't him, it was someone else, but even so it had unnerved me. Had my companion been anyone other than Blanche I would have had to make an effort to conceal the sudden moodiness I felt. I recognised it for what it was, a fierce bout of self-pitying sexual frustration. What was the point of all this beautifying of the body if there was no-one around getting the benefit. My vibrator couldn't have cared less if I was twelve stone or two, as long as I fed it a diet of fresh batteries.

'Christ, Blanche baby – I could do with a bit of a poke!' I shouted into the wind as we cycled along.

Poor Blanche, she couldn't hear but she knew I'd said something. She offered me another hot sausage roll by way of an answer, her own cheeks bulging with the same. But it wasn't what I wanted. I wanted crude cock, preferably uncooked and joined on to a male person at the appropriate point. And the ridiculous part of it was that I knew perfectly well I could get it, but still something held me back, causing me to make myself unavailable.

It was as if I was paying a penance by keeping constant company with Blanche. As if I first had to deny myself, live the chaste life for a little longer in order to justify the reward. The reward that I knew would eventually come my way. That's how I looked at it. I could have, Dame Agatha would have pointed out, opened life up even more for Blanche by introducing her to Flab Pottle. Making up a tasty threesome, if not with Flab, then certainly with Doc Slack. Or Gunter Ragg, when he returned?

But sexuality had no place in our friendship. I had no way of enquiring but something told me instinctively that Blanche had had enough bruising experience of men to last her for some time. There were times when a battered and defeated droop betrayed an inner hopelessness, despite the jaunty façade it was enough for now that I was there just for fun and companionship. We demanded no more of each other than that.

When she had departed yesterday, considerably thinner (three stone, according to Sister), glossily polished and preened and altogether in the pink, we had both shed an affectionate tear of regret. It was doubtful as to whether we would ever meet again, although we'd exchanged addresses and had promised to do so. But I didn't very often find myself in Southampton and she rarely undertook the journey to London. I really missed her after she'd gone and tossed up in my mind whether or not to go in search of Flab Pottle then – but I didn't.

His letter might have been written at that very moment, just as I was thinking of him! The question now was when and where should we meet.

The wedding caterers were coming to measure up the premises. It was not my idea to hold the reception at home. I would have chosen somewhere jolly like Langan's Brasserie or one of the new clubs like Curdles. Or even Flab's latest place, The Singed Fringe. But I'd been over-ruled by everyone, as they all pointed out – it wasn't my wedding. Tadpole should be allowed to have the last word. And I agreed with that, after all she was to be the bride. Though I couldn't quote my mother's words, 'A girl only has one wedding day in her life', since I no longer believed this to be true, the first wedding is tremendously exciting. Tinged with a trembling trepidation that the subsequent ones just don't have. I suppose one has more

301

of an idea what to expect of marriage the oftener one samples it. While it loses the appeal of the unknown on the one hand, and I have certainly found this to be the case, experience helps to overcome the emotional mayhem of living together as man and wife.

But I have confided few of these reflections to Tadpole. She has reached that stage in pregnancy, mere weeks before giving birth, where the entire universe revolves in ecstatic whorls of creative contentment. Her world is radiant, golden, and as warm as her swollen womb. She is hoping, and we all cross fingers with her in her wish, to celebrate the birth of her child on the exact day of her wedding. The betrothal between her and Bart Deco was announced when they had a firm date for the baby's delivery. I only hope that she won't be too disappointed if her timing comes unstuck. As I pointed out to Dame Agatha, delivery dates are not what they once were. There was no sure way of relying upon them at all. I was still awaiting the delivery of a guinea-pig from Harrods, one which I had taken pity on more than two years ago in the Pet Department. I could only conclude that the poor mite had passed out in transit, delivery having been promised for the following day. The man at Harrods probably hadn't the heart to break the news. It was a dear little guinea-pig, with rather a nervous disposition and more than a hint of a cast in one eye.

But on the other hand, as Dame Agatha had replied, few deliveries arrive *before* the arranged date.

'Babies do!' I'd said darkly. 'Babies make their own arrangements.'

'Not an area with which I'm altogether *au fait*, Loopy dear. But darling Tadpole appears a fairly ordered child, the sort who'll deliver the goods right on the dot. And since three of the guests are qualified obstetricians, everything's bound to be alright. If she looks like being late, can't they start the thing in motion – break the waters – isn't that right? Stick a knitting needle up, or a candle from the wedding-cake? All sounds slightly nauseating to me, I must say. I'd rather stand back and be fairy godmother, more dignified at my age, don't you think?'

It had already been decided that Dame Agatha should be godmother to Tadpole's child. It helped to make up for the disappointment over the cessation of her menstrual cycle. Whatever she may be saying now about motherhood I knew how desperately hard she and Windsor Shag were striving for a child. And how ecstatic they had both been when Dame Agatha had missed that first period. William, her gynaecologist as well as mine, was the unfortunate one to break the sad news.

She was not with child.

The diagnosis was corroborated by three highly respected obstetricians (the three who would be present at Tadpole's nuptials). Old Sir Chilly Gilly was at school with Bertie and had been in attendance at most of the royal births, nevertheless Dame Agatha, distrusting his cold hands, had called for a further opinion. An inscrutable Ghanaian from Guy's Hospital pronounced that the well of Saint Agatha was now dry.

'Saint? Didn't he mean Dame?' I'd said, perplexed, to William. William against all rules of medical ethics had confided the case to me. It made one wonder how much he used to reveal to his wife, how many confidential titbits about patients she'd taken to her grave. Like the gonorrhoea that Bertie brought back for me from the Grampians, a fortnight after our return from Guatemala. Unfortunate soul was invariably unlucky on home soil.

'In Ghana, so I gather, Saint Agatha represents female fecundity.'

I'd nodded sorrowfully at William's reply. 'Arid pastures for poor Agatha – nil de water dans le well. No possible chance of a child then?'

I didn't wait for his reply. I was thinking about myself. I wouldn't have minded a blow-torch on my bloody innards, high at the source to stem the flow for good and all. One arrives at a point in life when menstruation becomes meaningless, a mockery. Although I could sympathise with Dame Agatha in the urge towards procreation, now that she was no longer as politically active as she had once been. But something would turn up – it didn't have to be a baby. And she'd always have Windsor, he was a big enough baby himself, more than full-time. I should have a word with her about Windsor, he really was getting too fat. As if he were dosed on an exclusive diet of Farley's Rusks. And to think what an Adonis that boy had been. Tragic really.

303

Whilst Dame Agatha herself now has the sylph-like figure of a seventeen-year-old. Like me.

Only the other night when we were strolling towards Fenchurch Street for a cocktail at Curdles, before meeting Flab for Dinner at The Singed Fringe, we were mistaken for mere girls. Well almost.

It happened that we'd paused for a second at *Pussy*'s to study the delectable underwear display. When suddenly we were conscious of a commotion behind us, the raucous sounds of high-spirited youths on the rampage. Neither of us looked around, we were wiser than that, though it was an ignominious position to be in, gazing at crotchless panties with such slavering interest. At that time of day!

They approached from the rear, uttering rather fearful guttural sounds, whistling and shouting. The things they were shouting were, to say the least, of an aggressively personal nature. I'm familiar with the noun Cunt, and a wide selection of euphemisms for the same, but there were ones here that I had never heard before in my life. What flattery!

I tried to concentrate on what sort of view we were presenting from the back. Pretty tasty, to borrow a phrase of my daughters'. My red hair was still red, if anything a fiercer red than it had been dyed at Slivers. But now I'd had it permed and it had grown so much in the nine months since Slivers that I was able to wear it piled high in a mad frizz on top. My clothing had undergone sweeping changes in that time too. Bertie's wardrobe no longer existed, it had been ceremonially burnt by my second husband on the eve of our wedding.

Little did we guess as we watched the ashes swirl upon the light April air that within the week his ashes also would be scattered against the wind. Flung from the topmost peak of the Welsh mountains between which he'd been born. The Pride of the Valleys, the Welsh Giant was dead. A Russian tragedy for a Welsh hero. Poor Evan, drowned on the second day of our honeymoon, diving into the treacherous rocky seapools of Petropavlosk. His first and last visit to the U.S.S.R.

Flying his broken body back, magnificent even in death, I reflected what a mercy his death had been. A man as physical as Evan Slack could never have survived in a wheelchair. And I had been assured that this is what would have resulted from his injuries. Permanent paralysis.

As his widow it was my task to reply to the thousands of condolences I received. They had arrived from all over the world, but I was especially touched by the vast numbers that had been sent by ex-patients of Slivers. Doc Slack, for all his ferocity, had found a place in their hearts.

My photograph had appeared in the press. There had been much publicity surrounding his death, just as there had been over our marriage. Although the ceremony itself had been a very quiet affair, this was Evan's first stab at marriage and despite his deeply held Marxist convictions he seemed to regard our union with an almost holy reverence. He loathed all my friends. He openly disapproved of both Daisy and Tadpole, though they were as sweet to him as they knew how. At his insistence I had placed the Portland Place house on the market, not daring to tell him of all the other properties. The villa. The Irish mansion. The farm in Shropshire. The clutch of mews cottages off Marble Arch. And all the others that I had so neglected since Bertie's death.

He so despised property, and all that the owning of it conjured up in his mind, that I naturally had assumed that he himself possessed nothing. It was beneath his political principles to discuss matters of that nature. And since I had no interest in doing so the subject never was raised.

So it came as a complete shock to discover that there was to be an unpleasant investigation into the suspicious circumstances of the death of my late husband. At the instigation of his insurance company!

Doctor Evan Slack, the Welsh Giant, The Pride Of The Valleys, had invested his professional earnings very shrewdly indeed. He was a wealthy man.

But I was a widow who had no need of Evan's fortune. Quite clearly I wouldn't have knocked him off for my own profit, though the insurance enquiry agents were so obtuse that it took them an insultingly long time to reach that conclusion. It was Dame Agatha who'd had the brainwave. 'Why not give Evan's money away, Loopy dear –

then you'll have these bastards off your back for good and all. I mean you don't want the bloody stuff anyway. Donate it all to a charitable trust, sign it all over to the Athletics Association, dump it on the Junior Olympics Training Scheme. I'll organise it all if you like. Big publicity for Evan – a memorial playing field, sporting scholarships, the Evan Slack Award for Endurance – all that crap!'

And so that's what I'd done, it made me wonder why Evan hadn't thought of doing it himself instead of accumulating his profits like a capitalist.

The following months I was deluged with mail of a different nature. Fan mail, proposals of marriage, invitations to meet.

'After your money, Loopy! Burn them all, don't bother to answer. These rats have figured out that if a woman is in a position to give away a fortune, then she has plenty more where that came from.' Dame Agatha was adamant. At my insistence we sifted through them in case anything genuine came up, anyone really searching for a partner in life but too shy to make the first approach other than by letter.

I never intended remarrying. My marriage to Evan had been a whirlwind affair, he had swept me off my feet in spite of keen competition from darling Flab and dear Gunter. He courted me like a person truly possessed, but even whilst I was marrying him, whilst I was whispering 'Yes', I knew in my water that it was a mistake.

Reflecting on it now from the safe harbour of my present happiness, from this nuptial bliss, I think my marriage to Evan was founded on guilt. Even to the horrifying hour of his death I still couldn't recall having shared sex with him and Bertie. Try as I might no image came to mind, and as I pointed out to him it wasn't as if his penis was one I'd ever forget. Me or anyone!

Couldn't it possibly have been someone passing themselves off as Bertie's wife. Though the thought was painful to me, it was not outside the realms of probability. Bertie had travelled extensively without me when Daisy and Tadpole had been tiny babies. One couldn't imagine him denying himself sex simply because I was not there.

But it had become an obsession with Evan to prove it was me, though he admitted that the incident had taken place at a time when he'd been dropped from the Olympic team and had taken to hitting the bottle. Yet he still insisted that his drunkenness had in no way impaired his performance then or his total recall now. He was deeply wounded that I failed to remember him, and nothing that I said could reassure him or cancel the hurt. So I married him to make up for the blow to his ego. Though I couldn't pretend that the chemistry between us wasn't superb, because it was. Lying alongside his body was like owning a public monument. All mine to explore whenever I wished, every crack, every crevice; over smooth surfaces, into dark passages. Losing myself for whole hours within its confines. He was very keen on back-ways, had been like Bertie actively homosexual in his youth. I think, having had a more conventional outlook than my own, he was afraid the disclosure would shock or disappoint me in some way. We had a lot to learn about each other.

And yet his death had come as a release, though I wouldn't have admitted it to anyone. Naturally I suffered from the shock, who wouldn't. And it was a sobering thought that if I had allowed him to persuade me into the churning waters I would have followed him to my death. But there had been small, significant signs that our life together might eventually have proved to be intolerable. His maniacal jealousy would have been unlivable with, and the terrifying violence that resulted from that jealousy. At London Airport, suspecting that a fellow passenger, a particularly mild neuro-physicist from Prague, was trying to chum up to me, Evan had seized the poor fellow's hand baggage and flung it across the departure lounge. Cursing in Welsh as he did so. And this was only the first in a succession of similar *fracas*; by the time we had arrived at Petropavlosk my flattered amusement had begun to wear thin. This was pure caveman stuff and had no place in civilised social life. Me no Jane! Tarzan's breast-beatings were an undignified bore. I was too old to be regarded as a chattel.

The Fenchurch Street lads were almost upon us, I swayed on my shiny black boots. French patent leather from my recent trip to Paris with Tadpole for the fitting at

Yves St Laurent. He had begged Bart for the honour of designing her pregnancy/wedding gown, and of making a present of an outfit to me. I accepted of course: it would have been churlish not to, but it has placed me in an awkward position nevertheless. I shan't be wearing the Yves St Laurent at the wedding, I only hope that the sweet boy won't take offence. It's just that my loyalty to our wonderful British designers wouldn't allow it, though which of these I shall patronise I haven't decided. The only part planned yet is my David Shilling chapeau, a real *pièce de resistance*, a memory of the famous concoction which Salvador Dali and Schiaparelli created between them in the thirties. The Shoe Hat, the hat in the shape of a shoe. I'd had to reliquish a favourite pair of stiletto-heeled sandals in order that the adorable David might use them as a working model. I'm promised that the hat will be ready for me this week, but I've been given a detailed drawing of it to be shown to whichever designer I decide upon. And one can only hope that they will agree to run up a little something to tie in with it. If not, I've told Tadpole, I shall have to appear clad in just the basics. Bra and pants. She said, 'As long as it's Janet Reger . . .'

I was wearing Janet Reger now, sexy scarlet cami-knickers. The slippery satin of them sliding between my buttocks so that they looked, according to my fond spouse this morning as he watched me get dressed, like two hard-boiled eggs dipped in blood.

It was an exaggeration in my favour, which was why I loved him. His compliments are cunning. I knew what my buttocks looked like, more the peeled plum tomatoes that come in tins. Slightly fibrous and tending to droop.

The gang had passed on with a fresh outburst of admiring comments. Dame Agatha in her new blonde wig (Selfridge) was looking like a million dollars. Her cream trouser suit had come from Manhattan, cut in the way that only Americans know how. Drip-dry down to the last wrinkle-free crease. Her image had changed, but not everyone agreed that it was an improvement. The autocratic profile had gone, all character ironed out under the scalpel of the plastic surgeon. She was still undeniably handsome, a beautiful woman now in the more stereotyped style of Grace Kelly, since Grace settled into the role of Princess Grace of Monaco.

The loss of face, the original face, had contributed to

Dame Agatha's disastrous drop in the polls. Contrary to her convictions, the loyalty of her constituents had not been affected by her recent critical press over the last few years. Rather the opposite, her obvious ageing had endeared her to them more than ever. It was this unfamiliar image that had lost her votes. She now represented a wider world outside, she no longer epitomised the crumbling edifice of Great Britain. But more the sharp modern architecture of a newer nation. An international symbol. The dreaded Common Market. The United States of America (which was where she'd had her face-lift). Before anyone knew where they were it would be the U.S.S.R. on our very doorstep!

Dame Agatha's political opponent gained her seat with an overwhelming majority. But Dame Agatha was a survivor. Something would turn up.

We neither of us spoke, there was now complete silence in Fenchurch Street. Our young fans had fled in search of further glamour. The whole thing had been so delightfully swift that it was all over before it had begun. But there was an odd animal odour in the street, one that hadn't been there before. Apart from that it was as if nothing at all had happened, as if there had always just been the two of us looking into Pussy's window. The acrid smell was strong in my nostrils.

'Have you farted, Agatha, by any chance?' I turned disdainfully to my companion.

'I may have passed wind, Loopy dear. But that's my prerogative. I'm entitled to air my opinion, am I not?'

'You certainly are. And so am I, darling. What say we proceed in a leisurely fashion toward a drink? Rather divine being taken for teenagers.'

'A celebration is called for, Loopy. I shall have a Buck's Fizz. Several in fact.'

We linked arms with each other, laughing.

'Though one learns as one gets older, doesn't one, to accept sexual rejection too,' I said companionably.

'Certainly not!' She stopped short in her tracks. 'Speak for yourself.'

I turned to see if she was being serious, but from the expression on her face it seemed she was. 'I suppose it must be more difficult if you've always been beautiful and used to spectacular success with the opposite sex.'

'Well, you have very little cause for complaint in that department, Loopy. Three husbands and God only knows what on the side!'

'Not any more, on the side I mean. Perhaps it's because I fear possible rejection, just as I did all those years after Bertie.' For some reason the street encounter had drawn out a philosophical streak in me.

'Don't mention that ghastly turd to me! It's a wonder that you didn't turn lesbian, Loopy, really it is. When I think what that depraved animal put you through, precious pet.'

Dame Agatha bent down to peck me on the cheek, engulfing me in a heady drift of her new perfume. *Norelle*. She'd brought buckets of it back with her from the States, buying it from Bendel, the nearest store that New Yorkers have to our own Libertys.

It was a perfume that the old Dame Agatha would never have dreamed of wearing being far too actressy and up to the minute. It had about it the special scent of success, completely in keeping with her glossy appearance. Whereas before she had exuded an aroma of dusty lace and Yardley's Lavender overlaid with camphorous moth-ball. Such as one would expect of an aged aunt. *Norelle* had a far more cheering effect, it would make butterflies drunk.

'Though I suppose,' she continued, warming to one of her favourite themes, 'you were really asking for trouble. Marrying a chap of that age, a person older than your own mother. Especially one who'd never been married before.'

'Oh,' I interrupted, 'he had been married before. He ran away with one of the maids and got married when he was eighteen. The family managed to get it annulled, but the girl had left him before they even found out. Poor Bertie. I don't really think that he ever got over it. I thought it a brave thing to do in those days, run away with a maid. Rather romantic.'

'Rubbish, Loopy. You know you do have a ridiculously slushy streak for someone so sensible.'

'Am I sensible?' I said, surprised. Surprised and pleased at the same time. To be sensible in Dame Agatha's book was something that one took as praise. She still had that effect on me, the wanting to please her even

310

though we had become such intimate friends. She would always hold the trump card.

'Perhaps capable is more the word.'

She steered me across the street though there was very little traffic. But that wouldn't affect the business at The Singed Fringe. Members drove miles every day of the week to get together at Flab's newest club. And tonight there was the added attraction of Fizzy Tornado, whose hit record SHOVE had been top of the charts for the past seven weeks. And this new one of hers that she had recorded with Kid Lips, a week before he had so tragically O.D.ed, had only entered the charts the day before yesterday and already looked like overtaking SHOVE. One couldn't help wondering how much of the record's pre-determined success was due to the ghoulish curiosity of the public. It was clear to all of us, all of his friends, that Kid Lips' drug problem had got out of hand, but there seemed to be nothing we could do to help. Since the flop of his concert tour he'd been heading along a course of vicious self-destruction, even cutting the disc with Fizzy – it was Tadpole who had given the brilliant idea to Bart – had only distracted him momentarily. William, who had recently monitored the confinement of a young mother-to-be who was a heroin addict, maintained all along that Kid wouldn't be satisfied until he had killed himself. The end was inevitable so William said, he had little faith in the rehabilitation of addicts.

It had been an awful year for deaths. First Marion, William's wife, had passed away in the spring; not completely unexpected, cancer had been diagnosed. It had always been a matter of time.

Then Gunter Ragg's suicide on the eve of my marriage to Evan. The two events were not linked despite Dame Agatha's continuing naughty insistence that they were. No, I hadn't broken poor Gunter's heart. It wasn't that at all, though I conceded that had I agreed to marry him the financial muddles that had driven him to end his life would have been solved without any fuss.

If only I'd known. If only he'd told me. But the last person one would expect to be a gambler was Gunter. His debts were astronomical and the amounts that he had embezzled from both the Slivers establishments had run well over fifty thousand pounds. According to my accountant's clerk, who was keen to discuss the scandal with me because I had known Gunter, he must have been little short of a financial wizard to have got away with it for so long. All of seven years. 'That's the sort of chap we need in the Treasury!' he'd proclaimed. 'Put this country back on its feet.'

'They don't embrace gamblers in the government, Sydney,' I'd said.

He had chortled so vigorously that his spit showered my face. 'That's a good 'un, I must say – the entire system of government is based on a gamble! Bloody gambling on how long those fly bastards can go on pullin' the wool over the eyes of us poor sods, Joe Public!'

'Mm. Maybe so.' Sydney's diatribes weren't conversation as most of us know it. What he really wanted to do was pin whoever he was addressing up against the wall and bang their head repeatedly until they lost consciousness. But I was wearing a hat today and didn't much care to risk having its sleek contours crushed. I had moved swiftly through to the inner office.

I seemed to have been spending far too much of my time these days at the accountant's. Me of all people, who loathed talking about money!

It was because of the film that Flower Fowler and Daisy were doing together, based on my latest novel, *Up and Coming*. They were shooting it in California at this very moment, so far completely on schedule, making it more or less sure that they would be back in time for Tadpole's wedding.

'We ought to combine it with a ceremony of our own, oughtn't we –' Daisy had written. 'Masses of gay girls get married to each other over here, they wear wedding dresses and everything. It's really nice. Though as to which of us opt for the wearing of white – well, that's another ball game. One which we don't play. Our status within the relationship is intersexual, we neither of us are acting out male or female roles. But I don't need to tell you that, you can see how we are . . . The film is going great, really great! Maria Schneider and her girl-friend came over to the set on Sunday – you remember she was the girl in Last Tango (get Tadpole to explain!). And we went to a party at Ken Tynan's, I talked with Woody Allen. He's that little comedian with the glasses that you like a lot (ask Tadpole!). Next Tuesday Flower and I are celebrating our anniversary – eight whole months together! And we love each other more than ever! And to work together too – she's a dream to direct! It was hard at first coming to terms with seeing her fuck other people (we don't simulate anything in our movie – all of it is for real!), but now I approach it professionally. As she does. I think it probably has made us even closer. There is an avid amount of interest in everything we do, as you can imagine. If *She* does as well at the box-office as everyone predicts you can expect the cinemas to be flooded with gay girlie films, imitations of ours. But ours will have been the first. And they're never going to find a director/star team like Flower and me, partnerships such as ours are made in heaven!'

She was always a prolific letter-writer, Daisy, even as a child. If she couldn't find her note-pad she would scribble on lavatory paper. We had always taken it as a sure sign that she would become a writer when she grew up. But later we came to realise that it wasn't the writing that engrossed her. But simply the need to communicate, to pass on messages, to keep in touch. She was intrigued at the thought that out there in the wide world there were others who were eager to learn what she had to say. By the time she was twelve she was in communication with as many as thirty-seven penpals! Every postal delivery was flush with missives from afar, each stamped with the strange insignia of the exotic country of origin. Finland, France, Switzerland, Sweden, Germany, Austria, China, Japan, Australia, New Zealand. It was an endless stream, all for Daisy, the trade she did in the schoolyard with foreign stamps was spectacular. She didn't collect stamps herself. Only the strangers with whom she communicated. It was no surprise when she announced that she wished to make films. Of course, we all said. And she was packed off to the British Film School to study her craft for three years, this year would have been her final one. But she had been making her own cine-films from the age of fourteen, when Bertie had bought her first cine-camera. There are cupboards full of family antics, recorded on carefully itemised reels, stacked wall-to-wall up in the attic of Portland Place. Home-movieland gone berserk – every one shot by Daisy. Some awful, out of focus, with only a person's shoe occupying the foreground. Or the close-up of a left nostril. But run consecutively it can be seen that there is a gradual and then an even remarkable improvement. By the time Daisy was eighteen her films, though clearly amateur, showed considerable ability. They were bold and imaginative. They unfolded small stories with humour and unexpected twists in the plot. And the colour was really adventurous, always using unusual contrasts in lighting. She would rise before dawn to capture the greys preceding the daylight. And stand for hours awaiting the fall of dusk.

This year she was making her first professional full-length feature with the backing of the California Film Company, Inc. A commercial enterprise. Straight-forward erotica, but all gay. With Flower Fowler, a huge name not only on the Contintent, but in China and Japan.

All I'd had to do was change the hero into another heroine. It hadn't been all that difficult adapting *Up and Coming*. Though since Daisy wanted to do a specifically lesbian tale of love and lust, obviously the title couldn't stand(!) as it was. That's how it came to be called *She* instead, nobody seemed to think that there'd be any complications over the *She* of Rider Haggard. The American producer, a young person in jeans with the moustache of a Mexican bandit, had never heard of Rider Haggard. Or his *She*. So that was alright. I must say I'd been surprised on meeting this young man, my idea of Hollywood moguls was restricted to what I'd heard of monsters like Harry Cohn or Louis B. Mayer, or chaps with the stature of God, like Sam Goldwyn. But this casual lad, the transatlantic equivalent to Bart Deco, was big business.

He had made his first million with a low-budget, soft-porn version of *Peter Pan*. Then had gone on to consolidate his reputation by employing the young German director, Wolf Wankein, for *Titty Anna, A Shakespearian Dream*. 'Shakespearian *Wet* Dream!!' The reviewers had hurled critical abuse from all sides, but it hadn't affected the box-office. Now everyone was trying to jump on his bandwagon, hustling to work for him, sending him scripts. Which made it even more prestigious than he had approached us, made us an offer. We'd come as a package deal, with Bart dealing as our joint agent. Now there were fresh plans afoot involving me selling off all my properties (Evan would have approved!). As Bart pointed out, if we could get it together to raise our own capital, pool all our resources, why not finance our own film projects! He was managing little Fizzy Tornado too now, so the next thing to think about would be a musical, starring Fizzy and Flower together. But though we'd considered various other books of mine as a basic plot to work from (why buy in another property, as Bart said, when we've got a ready-made writer sitting at home twiddling her thumbs!), not one of them seemed quite right to me.

What I was trying to do now was come up with something. Something new. And then the idea of Dame Agatha hit me!

'Have you ever thought,' I started tentatively, 'of writing your memoirs, Agatha?' She had been going through several days of deep depression, even Windsor had been worried. So worried that he had telephoned William at the surgery, feeling that she may be in need of menopausal medications but was too proud to admit to this herself.

'Me, Loopy?' She'd been drinking all through lunchtime instead of having anything to eat. Depression put on weight, so she claimed. Ignoring the fact that she'd just drunk more than her full day's calorie allowance in the space of two hours. But she wasn't drunk yet, she hadn't reached any plateau of high spirits. One knew that she wouldn't either, not in her present mood. She'd just continue drinking to the borders of consciousness, then simply spiral off into oblivion. I felt that I'd just caught her in time.

'You, Agatha.'

She stared at me in a maudlin way, suddenly bleary-eyed. But there was a spark of the old Dame Agatha aggression for a moment when she spoke.

'What a bloody asinine idea! You talk absolute balls,

Loopy, from time to time. Married bliss is softening your brain!'

'No, seriously, Have you thought of it? After all your life would make a fascinating tale, lots of scandal. Plenty of power. Sex with the famous . . .'

'And infamous, darling . . .'

'That's what I mean, Agatha – you could reveal all . . .'

'All! Could I really, Loopy? Without fear of repercussion?'

I had captured her interest now, that was clear. She adored the thought of stirring up a spot of bother. 'Mm, I could really put the political cat amongst the pigeons!' Her eyes began to sparkle. 'We'd have to get a pretty good libel lawyer – I know just the chap, Gummidge – he's first class on this sort of stuff. I believe he put a lot of spade-work into the Crossman Diaries. The only thing –' She looked suddenly dejected again. 'The bugger of it is that I can't write.'

'I can.'

She stared at me, the whole idea gradually dawning. 'You mean . . .?'

'Why not?' I spoke briskly. It was the best way to be, get the thing moving before she had second thoughts. I was ready to start work on it as soon as possible. Why not tomorrow, with a tape-recorder? Just start at the beginning and bring everything up to now, to the present with Windsor Shag, to the ignominious defeat at the polls, the subsequent end of her political career. To the prospect of an uncertain future, not knowing which way to go professionally . . .

My mind was racing ahead, I was thinking what a great number that closing song could make for Fizzy. I was wondering what Flower would say to having her hair bleached back to the honey of Agatha's as I'd first seen her at school. Though Flower resembled the young Agatha in no way at all, other than their both being extraordinarily handsome, I didn't think that mattered. And we could overcome the problem of speech. The entire soundtrack could be recorded separately, in song. Fizzy would sing the Agatha part throughout. Flower would simply perform as if in a silent movie.

But I didn't reveal any of these thoughts to Dame

316

Agatha. Her mind was only running along the lines of a scandalous political autobiography, with me as the ghost-writer, incognito behind the scenes. And there was no reason why this should not be the case. Any publisher would jump at the chance to publish this bombshell, I was only surprised that none had already approached her with the suggestion. Dame Agatha Tatter's affairs well concealed from the British public, due to the cautious discretion of the media (and the Members concerned!) were legendary within certain circles. I had had no inkling of this when we had renewed our acquaintance at Slivers. It seemed that since that time I was hearing a fresh rumour from her past everywhere I moved. I supposed that her enemies were gloating over her downfall and were squeezing the final piece of gossip from her poor corpse before it finally sank from the scene.

Well, this would show them!

'I'll put the wind up a few of those old farts! Eh, Loopy!' Dame Agatha caught hold of my hand and squeezed it hard. She was excited. It was the first time in months that I'd seen her like this.

'It would make a wonderful film – the film of the book, Agatha,' I said casually.

'A film!' Her eyes widened, she sucked in her breath. 'Do you think so? The life of a female politician? Would the public find that interesting?'

'They're flocking to *Evita*.'

'Yes, but she was a tart, Loopy.'

I didn't say anything. I couldn't really see that it made any difference, charging for it. The worst thing about Eva Peron was her politics, not how she put about her private parts. 'What shall we call it, the book?'

'Now you've got me.'

I thought. 'What about "*Up Agatha*"?'

And so that's what we were involved with, *Up Agatha* (simply our working title for the project!) after the excitement of Tadpoles nuptuals. Several leading publishers were already in the auction to secure the rights of what now promised to be merely Volume One in the saga of Dame Agatha Tatters. We were having to limit her number of television appearances. If we weren't careful the pre-publication publicity would cancel out the chance of any after the event.

Dame Agatha, herself, had been besieged by anguished ex-lovers begging not to be included between the covers. 'Just as you'd expect,' she'd expostulated, 'the very ones who pleaded hardest to slide between my sheets!'

We would have an hourly conference on who to mention and who to leave out. And it was amusing how many past amours wished to be included. It was obvious that reputations would be made as well as shattered by being in the book, or not!

I laid down a clear plan from the start, after that first memorable meeting with Oliver Gummidge, the Q.C. (another of Agatha's!) I thought it best, and so did he, to commence the gigantic task of recording the events, romantic and otherwise, by censoring nothing. Putting the whole lot down.

'Spilling the beans left, right and centre, you mean?' Aunt Agatha had the light of battle in her eyes. She became demoniacal over every explicit detail, ringing me up at all hours of the day or night in the very beginning. Until I hit upon the notion that she should record it herself into a tape-recorder. This she did with a vengeance, carrying the infernal machine with her everywhere. Until we were getting irate reports of Dame Agatha from hosts and hostesses whose dinner-parties had been ruined by her eccentric behaviour.

'She left the table in the middle of the first course, leaving her soufflé untouched – much to the rage of our chef – and didn't appear again until we had assembled back in the lounge for coffee and brandy. Well, really, it was too bad – I had concocted the entire guest list around her! She is enjoying such a spectacular *succès de scandale* at the moment that the whole of London is thronging to meet her. Though what on earth the book will read like is another thing altogether. I gather she can't write for toffee – but I suppose that with pornography it doesn't really make much odds. One doesn't need literary skills to write such stuff.'

'Oh, I don't know,' I'd replied to this particular caller with a certain cool irritation. She was somebody that I hadn't heard from for many, many years. Her father had been a great friend of Bertie's, she and I roughly were about the same age. But since my name had been so often in the news she had taken to inviting me continually to her dreary gatherings in Belgravia. Especially now that I was married again and so could be relied upon to come with a ready-made escort, instead of buggering up the numbers by being a middle-aged widow on my own. I chose not to forget which of the so-called friends of Bertie's and mine had dropped me after his death. Without exception they had surfaced from the painful past and tried to get in on the act.

Especially now, realising how close a friend I was of Dame Agatha. Though not having any notion at all of how closely involved I was in *the* book of the year. Just as well too! Even I was flabbergasted just how many men Dame Agatha had been through in her time. Many of them the husbands of the very hostesses who were pressing for her presence at their tables now. It gave us hours of amusement.

Meanwhile Bart Deco, my son-in-law, was setting up the film. It was his idea, an ambitious one, but one I was sure he (if anyone) could pull off. It was his idea to stage *Up Agatha* (still only the working title) as a musical, too. Whether or not to use Fizzy and Flower for this venture, on completion of the film of course, or to try other stars – was the big debate. I didn't think for a moment that Flower would agree to playing live on stage. For one thing it would mean working with a director other than Daisy. Those two were a team now, they refused to split up. If anybody wanted one of them they had to take the other. With the success of *She* the world was their oyster. But in any case, if I was reading correctly between the lines of Daisy's latest letter, they had plans of their own. They were still on the world promotional tour for *She*, last heard from in Hamburg where police re-inforcements had to be summoned to protect them from the enthusiasm of the Gay Liberation Front.

On their return they would start filming *Up Agatha*. We have referred for so long to the project as that, not seeming to be able to agree over a new title, that now it seems likely to stay as the final one. Daisy is very keen on it, and it is an appropriate title for a musical comedy. And the book has ended up as a farce, in every way. Three resignations, and the possible downfall of the present government!

At least it's put Britain back in the headlines. And all this before publication day.

Dame Agatha was really pleased with herself!

But Daisy and Flower have both become broody, it's the result of Garth, Tadpole's baby. They each of them would like to have one of their own.

'There's no problem about impregnation,' Daisy had explained to me in her earnest way, her arm around Flower's finely boned shoulders as she spoke . . .

It was the evening before their departure on the publicity tour and they were trying to fit in an early night for a change.

Looking at Flower I thought how much she had changed since she and Daisy had been together. If it was possible she was even more beautiful than before but she was a woman now. Her marvellous face had matured, the mouth was more relaxed. The eyes were more serene. That she was a film-star there could be no doubt. This glamour was classic Garbo.

Only the inimitable voice had remained unaffected by time and the stupendous burgeoning of her career. Which was nice. It made her somehow accessible still.

She spoke now, squeezing Daisy's free hand between her own.

'Yeah, I mean there's no bleedin' way either of us are goner agree to 'avin it off wiv a guy. I'm never fuckin' for a kid an' neither is Daisy, right mate?'

Daisy shook her head of tangled curls violently. Both my daughters were much better looking than me, they had inherited a sculptured cast to their features that contrasted interestingly with the way that they turned themselves out. It gave them a casual elegance that I had never possessed. Though I had often been described as *belle-laide*, especially by the French in France who have a high regard for those with beautiful/ugly features like mine, I couldn't look as Daisy was looking this moment. Like a cross between Lauren Bacall, Julia Christie and Bianca Jagger, dressed in a trilby hat, a pair of khaki combat trousers and a cream cashmere polo-neck so vast that it could have doubled as a mini dress.

'That's right – no way! None of that number!' Her words made me wince.

'Is it that one is getting more intolerant with age?' I'd appealed to Agatha, 'or did youth always speak in meaningless clichés? If I hear "she's a lovely lady", or "no way", or "doing a number", or "pulling a moody", any more from the young people cruising through my home I shall, I shall . . .' But Dame Agatha had only laughed. 'The slang of the day.' She was right, I was growing crusty. I listened with sympathy to what Daisy was saying, despite the limitation of the vocabulary. It seemed that there were especial medical provisions being made now for females who were in the position of Flower and herself. Women who longed to be mothers but who had an aversion to men, or rather an aversion towards having a sexual relationship with them.

In short they could now apply to the Sperm Bank. They could become impregnated without having anything at all to do with the male, without ever even knowing who the father of their child might possibly be.

It seemed the perfect solution.

'But I had thought,' I was showing my ignorance now, 'that the governing body of the Sperm Bank operated under the most rigid strictures. I understood that they were as tightly controlled as Adoption Societies. That you had to prove, if you were a prospective parent, that you had the full happy family set-up to offer an adopted child, proving your religious affiliations even. I'm probably hopelessly out of date – am I?'

It seemed that I was. As with everything, events happened too swiftly for me to keep up with the changes around me.

Daisy had laughed out loud. 'Darling!' Then she'd become serious again . . . It was the Gay Liberation Summit Conference, held in Stockholm two years ago, who had forced the law to make these overdue changes. And earlier this year the whole position had been clarified at the Swiss Summit Conference in Geneva. It was now an International Charter, fully agreed by the United Nations. Homosexual persons of either sex could now adopt unwanted children with no difficulty whatsoever. Whether or not they were single. All that was required was that the person was financially secure enough to continue to support the child until it came of adult age, here placed at eighteen. And that the aforesaid person should prove him, or herself to be of sound character (ex-convicts were frowned upon).

But the Sperm Bank was altogether different. Previously it had existed solely for married couples, to solve the problem of infertility amongst husbands. Anyone could donate spunk to the Bank, indeed there had been a major drive planned several years ago. An international appeal was to be mounted, until this was invalidated by doubts over the long-term safety of women taking the Pill. When this alarmist report was published, thousands of married women immediately stopped taking the Pill as a contraceptive device and prevailed instead upon their husbands to assume the responsibility.

An unprecedented rush towards vascectomy had been the result. But to preserve their sperm for posterity, and in order to have a supply of it on hand should their wives wish to increase the family later, most husbands banked the results of their final wanks. The Sperm Bank was now full to overflowing.

It was interesting that Daisy and Flower wished to be pregnant at the same time. In essence it would mean that each would be mother and father to their own child, whilst supplying the structured warmth of a family unit by simply being together.

It made very good sense to me, and sounded like fun. It would give both babies an instant brother or sister, as long as Daisy and Flower managed to conceive simultaneously. And William, when I questioned him about it, didn't anticipate any difficulty there. They were both young and healthy and at least one of them, Flower, had conceived before (she'd had her first abortion when she was fifteen). As far as I knew, Daisy had never had an abortion – but she may have had one without telling me, though I shouldn't have thought so. Whatever Daisy did she liked to share it with everyone.

The interviews which she and Flower had given about their love for each must have been a Journalist's dream. There were no holds barred, Daisy had divulged every single detail of their life together, the difficulties, the drama, the pressures, the tensions, the jealousies, the occasional fights, the ebb and flow of their sexual need for each other. Being naturally more articulate than Flower, though Flower was hotter on unusual expletives, Daisy had become the spokesman of the two. Rather she had become the *spokesperson*.

It was impossible to pass a news-stand without seeing at least one magazine with them entwined on the cover. If this fervour continued they would soon find it impossible to lead any sort of normal private life. Already one could spot scattered look-alikes on the streets, gay girls and otherwise, arm-in-arm with each other, or openly holding hands, striding along. Tall and leggy and slender. Free and easy – and exuberantly liberated. They made Dame Agatha and myself seem hopelessly outdated, orientated as we were exclusively towards a sexual life with men. I envied them a little, knowing that it was all too late now for me to embark on that particular band-waggon. It had passed me by.

'Don't you feel, Agatha,' I'd said to her, 'that you and I were born just a little too soon?' We were buying a minute punk romper-suit for Garth, her godson and my very first grandchild.

'No.' She examined what looked like a miniature space-suit, shiny silver with soft zips. 'Does this look right to you, Loopy?' There was doubt in her voice. 'Perfect,' I answered. 'He'll love that, little Garth. He likes anything shiny, you should see him with Flower's diamonds. His eyes follow her everywhere.'

'Well, he is male, Loopy!' Dame Agatha gave a crude laugh. And then picked up an imitation leopard-skin boiler suit, buttoned up the front with an attached hood. 'This has a certain animal appeal! Would Tadpole put Garth in it do you think?'

'I'm sure she would, but you mustn't spend any more on that child – she's got masses of stuff for him already. David Bowie gave him a snake yesterday, can you imagine – a boa constrictor.' I laughed at the memory of Tadpole's face. She had just been given confirmation of her pregnancy by William and was trying to decide whether she was glad or sorry when the snake had arrived. 'Just what you need, darling,' I'd tried to soothe her, there were definite signs of hysteria.

'What a bloody stupid present!' Dame Agatha exploded. A midget ran forward from the back of *Cute Kids*, he was dressed up as little Lord Fauntleroy, though he would never see thirty again.

'Trouble?' he lisped. Now he was closer I could see that he wasn't a proper midget – or rather, little person. I had learned, through Daisy, to be scrupulously careful over collective names and the least offensive terms for minority groups. No, this wasn't a little person, but simply one with a truncated length of leg. He suffered from what used to be known as duck's disease, his buttocks were barely clearing the ground.

It was strange that I should have noticed this. I hadn't caught myself gazing at the bodies of young men for what seemed like centuries. *Cute Kids*, specialising in the sort of clothes the wealthy *avante garde* delighted in buying for their children was next to The Bonbonniere, my old guzzling ground opposite Liberty's. I could recall how I'd sit just inside the window slavering over the virile aspects of the passers-by. Crotch watching, the favourite spectator sport of women with my particular itch.

I didn't do that any more. I didn't guzzle, nor did I slaver. Was that what marriage and grandmotherhood had done to me? And a year of fulfilling work? Had my sexual avariciousness departed forever? Would I embark again on bouts of marathon munching – or could I look forward to a future in this present calm harbour? Trim enough to trip up flights of stairs. Sexually controlled enough to make do with a screw morn and night, seven days a week (including the seven rather messier ones during menstruation).

I would have thought so – and yet it didn't do to take any of these things for granted. After all look at Dame Agatha! One couldn't have envisaged the dramatic changes that had swept through her life in the last year.

Her appearance was altogether different to what it had been just three months ago. She must have gained at least three stones in weight and looked larger each time I saw her. I couldn't believe it.

'What's happened, Agatha darling?' I'd met her at the airport to welcome her home from a trip that had taken her from Aberdare, in South Wales, to Ayutthaya, in Siam. *Up Agatha* in its various translations was heading the best-seller lists in twenty-two countries.

Dame Agatha had been fêted all over the world, wined and dined on every imaginable national delicacy. And didn't she look it!

It was as if the glossy, slim, up-lifted Dame Agatha had never been. I stared at her, hypnotised by the spread of her hips as she squeezed through the crowds of Heathrow. I was unable to believe that this smiling, sun-tanned, larger-than-life goddess was the svelte creature that I'd waved away at this airport, the month before last.

Then she'd been wearing a simple Jaeger suit, a shade too conventional for my own tastes. Slate grey with a gunmetal silk shirt and court shoes, hand-made for her at Lobbs of St James's. I'd recently ordered several of them myself, though in rather jollier colours, and found them so comfortable that I was wearing them as bedroom slippers. Much to my darling's excitement, I kept them on throughout a bout of cunnilingus the other evening in front of the television. Not deliberately, though he refused to believe so, but simply because I hadn't realised that they were still on my feet.

They were an emerald green, that pair, with a heel that was rather higher than the rest – to save me shortening the green velvet trousers that I usually wore with them, ones which turned out to be a trifle long in the leg.

I wasn't wearing the trousers of course, not for cunnilingus! I think I may have been reclining in a night-shirt of his. Though this wearing of his garments is not something that he encourages. He, rightly, claims it to be reminiscent of how I'd worn my first husband's clothes everywhere around the place. And it's surely time that his ghost had been exorcised. Bertie. It's extraordinary how difficult it is for me now to summon up the memory of his face with any clarity. The man who had so influenced my smallest movement that I'd called to tell him when my bowels had signalled to be relieved! My every motion at his command!

Yes, that's what she'd been wearing, Dame Agatha at take-off. Jaeger. But I doubt that any designer of note had much to do with what she had on for her return. It looked

to me to be a reckless gesture of Mother Nature, as if it
had been woven from actual leaves and small plaited
grasses, and fibrous tendrils. And she was festooned with
exotic blooms of blazing hues, they hung as a surrealist
row of beads around her neck, dropping petals at every
turn. I couldn't imagine how she had travelled looking
like this – gay and ethnic though it may have been. My
heart bled for her fellow-passengers, especially the poor
sod sitting next to her. Like flying through the skies with a
shrubbery at one's side hardly conducive to conversation!
Unless tucked in amongst her foliage was concealed such
a thing as a cockatoo, an amusing travelling companion.
One wouldn't have known what on earth she was
carrying, it was difficult to tell where she left off and her
clothing began. But her spirit was stupendous.

'Loopy – my angel! Oh, you are such a pet to meet me
. . .' And she'd enveloped me within the branch-like
confusion of her arms, showering the small family to the
left of her with what looked like acorns.

'Fertility,' she announced, spinning around. Flab,
who'd driven me to the airport and had been parking the
car, chose this moment to make his appearance.

'Holy cow!' He fell back at her approach. I wondered
how liberally Dame Agatha had applied herself to the
hospitality of the airline. In first class they allow one as
much champagne as can be drunk.

'In a manner of speaking – yes, darling Flab!' She
extended her mossy hand towards him, he was luckier
than me not to get the full embrace. I felt a weal rising
along my cheek already, the flesh broken by what had felt
like a thistle. 'Holy Cow is exactly what I'm meant to
represent. Holy Cow, the symbol fertility. My new
religion, whether you heathens approve or fucking not.
Loopy,' she'd turned to me, 'I want you to be the first to
know that I am leaving these shores. I've had Great
Britain up to here!' She gave a generous gesture to
indicate her genital zone. 'I'm returning to my followers in
Kahoolawe . . .'

'Kahoolawe – Christ, where's Kahoolawe, Agatha?'
Flab and I said together.

'Kahoolawe happens to be the Hawaiian Island that I
bought yesterday, my subjects await my return . . .'

And she'd gone.

'You were her doctor, William. Do you think that she went a little crackers at the end?' We talked of her often in this way. But he didn't enjoy the discussions, he said to talk of Dame Agatha in her absence like that was to assume that she wouldn't pop up again when any of us least expected it.

She'd been gone a year now and nobody had heard from her. I didn't give up hope of having a letter. My own, which I wrote regularly despite doubts as to whether or not she received them, were always full of the sort of news that she'd enjoy.

Garth, her godson was walking now. His sister Tilly was teething. And Tadpole was expecting twins in the spring.

Both Daisy and Flower were also in pod, due to produce at any time. They were willing it that the babies share their birthdays. Nerve-racking stuff, just like Tadpole's wedding. But as Daisy pointed out, Tadpole managed to deliver on the right day – just, five minutes this side of midnight! I hoped we didn't have to go through all that again. But this time there would be a greater onus on timing. Daisy had arranged for a camera crew, with her assistant director, to stand by and film both births. Because of this she had made preparations for the two of them, herself and Flower, to be in the same delivery room. They planned to grip each other's hands throughout. A triumphant end to the most highly publicised pregnancies since Eve was with child.

And as for me – my child-bearing years were completely over. I contemplate this with nothing but relief, still awaiting the anguish that I'm told to expect from the menopause. Perhaps I shall be fortunate and escape them.

Today I am due at William's surgery. The time has come around again for my annual cervical smear. This will be the first, I now realise, since I ceased menstruation. I wonder do I look any different as I approach William's receptionist? Apparently not.

She looks up and smiles. 'Good afternoon Lady Marylebone, you are expected. Do walk in.'

Moments later I am lying, naked from the waist down,

upon William's examination couch. And he is easing his professional something up my uterus. It feels like a cock and of course it is.

'Highly unethical, Doctor – what you're doing is frightfully rude!'

'Is it frightfully rude to fuck one's own wife?'

A BITE OF THE APPLE

For Patrick
my first and my last

One

'Whose bloody idea was it anyway? This . . .' I stagger against the open door of the bathroom, addressing the three heaving bodies on the bed. They are all naked now except for me, I'm still wearing my evening clothes. My spun-gossamer gown of gold lamé thread, frothing into its shower of seductive maribou over each shoulder, still encases my body. My shining Cinderella slippers, delicate crafts of smooth satin, continue to arch my insteps at their usual elegant angle. The couture confection of feathers to the side of my sleek head, is still – somehow – miraculously in its place, moored to the scalp by millinery magic. Only my mouth appears at odds with the rest of me, I must have left that behind in the back of the cab. One set of Sophisticated Siren painted lips lost between Broadway and Lexington Avenue. We were passing through Central Park when the communal kissing started.

'Your idea, Eve – get your clothes off and come to bed!' Impossible to tell whose muffled voice has answered me. Surely I'd recognise my own husband's tones. You'd think that.

'Adam?'

But there's no response to me this time, only an increasingly alarming crescendo of sucking noises. And the definitely disturbing view of this free-for-all fornication, buttock upon belly, belly upon breast. With a space in it for me, where I am expected to fit.

'Like rutting pigs,' I mutter to my reflection in the bathroom mirror.

But pigs always have been my most favourite of animals. Ecstatic memories survive from childhood in which pigs feature as my playmates. Calico skirts crammed as full as shopping bags with squealing piglets still wet from the womb, burrowing like maggots for the dark place between my legs. And me silent and excited, squirming along with them.

Last summer on an English country walk, before we'd definitely settled on living in the States, I unexpectedly found myself in spiritual communion with a geriatric sow. Snout-to-snout we were, she and I, her slit eyes engaging my own in rueful sympathy. The disappointed jowls of her heavy features belied by the humorous curve of the mouth.

An optimistic face, I said to myself. A soul-sister. And we continued staring, each spellbound by the other, until I could hear the rest of them shouting for me. Urging me to join them.

Like now. When all I want to do is go home.

'Prudery. That's what it is, my angel. You'll get over it with practice.' Adam squeezes my fingers affectionately, pressing his long thigh against my own in the home-going cab. My eyes fill up at this show of togetherness. I would have appreciated it more if it had come four or five hours ago, before – before – all of everything happened.

'Not prudery is it to happen to be in love with your husband and want him all to yourself?' I'm dismayed by the wail in my voice, the way now that it's rising. 'It's not my idea of fun to wake up in the morning and see my husband being sucked off by a stranger.'

Adam leans forward to close the glass partition between us and the avidly interested cab-driver. A fine example of English reserve.

'Hardly a stranger, Eve. We've known Cherry for ten years, almost all our married life.'

'Not intimately though, we've never known her intimately.'

'Few would have guessed that from the way you were kissing her last Christmas, darling.'

'Me!' I swing around in the seat to stare at him. 'Me? Kissing Cherry? Last Christmas?'

He gazes back at me without blinking. 'Wasn't the only one.'

I nod several times, mean triumph twisting my mouth. 'Ah, now we come to it – you were kissing her too!'

'Not at all. I have always been the model of propriety in public.'

'And in private?' I spin round again, my scowl stiff with suspicion. I daren't dwell on how ugly I look.

He puts his arm around my shoulder now, trying to hug me close. My wide silver wedding ring winks up at me from my white knuckles, which are clenched in uncharacteristic tension. There's something wrong with me this morning, that's what I want to say to him, all to do with last night.

'You know better than that, Eve. When would I ever do anything behind your back? When, come to that, have I ever done anything to upset you with anyone else? You are the one who goes around kissing people – that's what I was just saying. Cherry wasn't by any means the only one in your passionate embrace last Christmas. Everyone got their share, they were queueing up by the end.'

'I was drunk.'

'You were drunk last night.'

'I wouldn't have behaved like that if you hadn't have been there.'

'To take care of you. To see to it that things didn't get out of hand. Well, last night things did get out of hand. I warned you they would one day. It's you who's been calling the tune all these years, but now it's happened, you suddenly don't like it.'

I draw away from him coarsely, endangering my maribou, crushing my feather hat against the upholstery of the cab. What on earth would they think at the desk of the Eden, of me waltzing in at this hour of the morning still dressed in last night's finery! A stray cat on the tiles. After only one month of Manhattan life, dabbling in the depths of depravity.

'It'll be nice walking into the Eden like this.' I manage to make it sound like an accusation. 'Very nice.'

'They won't turn a hair, it's what they're used to at the Eden. Artists. Eccentrics. *La vie bohème.*' He is wearing a relaxed expression, in contrast to my own.

'Moral reprobates,' I mutter moodily, staring out of my side.

'Well, I must say that for someone who displays such self-loathing this morning, you seemed to be enjoying yourself well enough last night. What did you think of Roger's cock?'

'Roger's cock?'

'That object at the end of his torso that you attacked with such relish – once we'd winkled you out of the bathroom.'

'Oh, that. I remember. Sweet.' I speak dully. 'Not as nice as yours.' My eyes fill with tears. 'Didn't get much of a chance at yours though – too busy bunging it to Cherry.'

Adam laughs, the deep dimple in his right cheek darker from having missed his late-night shave. The red-haired girl driving a gleaming Cadillac alongside idly glances at us as our vehicles stall in a traffic jam. Her eyes flicker over me and return to rest on Adam, with interest. I am glad he is looking my way.

'You did a fair bit of bunging it to Cherry too.' He leans to kiss me. I hope that the red-head is still watching. 'It excited me, that, to see you kissing her cunt. And to see you being brought to orgasm by her. Was she better on the clitty than me?'

But it's too late to make a reply, too late to dwell on an honest answer. For the question demands a certain deliberation. And we have now arrived at the Eden, it's time to brave the foyer.

Mercifully it's deserted. The desk clerk, however, catches sight of me as I attempt to slink into the lift – or the elevator, as I must get used to calling it.

'Mrs Smith!' I ignore him, as I ignore anyone who addresses me by my married name. This morning it serves my purpose. If there is a message, then he can just as well give it to Adam, when he comes in after paying off the cab. Adam would have stopped at the desk in any case to collect our letters – our mail. Both having careers which are basically based in London, we each receive regular daily amounts of correspondence.

'Ms Lynn!' I turn at my professional name, conditioned by the bark of too many impatient editors, too many irascible bosses, to ignore the command nonchalantly. Besides, this is a different voice now. Sexy Lewis, the black telephonist. An out-of-work actor who has taken the job in-between roles. What woman, or man (Adam says), could fail to be stopped short by this candied growl.

334

'Urgent call, Ms Lynn, from London. Here's the number to ring back.' He flashes his big teeth, as bright as bleached tombstones, and passes me the piece of paper with the scribbled message on it. As he turns back to his switchboard I find myself unexpectedly studying the shape of his bum. Altogether higher and rounder than on a white man, than Adam's for instance, whose lean frame hardly sports any sort of an arse at all. And the thought sparks off another, that I haven't yet had the pleasure of a black lover in my life. Not unless you'd count that time in Tunisia (between marriages), when it had been a case of spontaneous combustion on the dance floor during a conga. And a dawn awakening in the desert, with no remembrance of anything in-between. Then a quickie, imminent to departure, in one of the hotel chalets with the airport charabanc hooting impatiently and half the passengers cheering me aboard. Whilst my Prince of Darkness, a post office employee from Djerba, waved me off with his white cotton shorts at half-mast. I can't even recall if he was circumcised (now why would I consider that important?).

The elevator doors are drawing to and I attempt to dart in, but too late. Adam has caught up with me.

'None of that! Cheating!' He looks stern and steers me towards the stairs.

We have a pact whereby we always walk up to our flat – our apartment – even though it is on the seventh floor. Good for the legs. Excellent exercise. The last thing I need this morning.

'You, or someone, will have to carry this then,' I grumble in misery, waving my minute evening bag in the air.

'Too heavy? Here, give it to me – Jesus, what have you got in it?'

'Your girlfriend gave it to me when you were taking your shower. It's a talisman, a silver pig with her key through the nose. I expect she gives them to everyone who spends the night.'

'*Our* girlfriend, not just mine. Let's get that straight, Eve. You notice that I'm not taking this aggressive attitude over Roger. And I could . . .'

'Where was Roger this morning then?' I say this to

divert him. Disturbing images are forming behind my eyes of precisely what the four of us had got up to, for it was true, once they had managed to coax me out of the bathroom, I had *hurled* myself into the orgy.

'He had a breakfast meeting, big business. He left after the main event.'

'The main event?' I stop halfway up a flight of stairs, grasping the ornate brass banister. We were approaching the third floor landing, already my breath is running short and the backs of my thighs are pulling. I look longingly at the elevator doors as they close upon two fellow guests, passing trade. Not residents like us.

They gaze back with amused interest, inspecting my garb. Outlandish for this time of day, even in the Eden, whatever Adam may say.

'Good morning,' he nods at them before they disappear from view, receiving an equally pleasant greeting in return. He does that all the time in New York now, he has adopted the urbanity of Americans. Their sanguine side, the sunniness in the smiles of strangers. He's not terrified of the city and its sidewalks as I am. He doesn't palpitate when vagrants veer crazily across our path, when bag-ladies babble past, or when menacingly servile destitutes demand a couple of dimes for a drink.

'I'm suffering from paranoia about this place and the people in it!' I sometimes gasp, shuddering from the shortest foray into the shopping jungle. I have inadvertently brushed against a Hispanic hysteric as he's reaching for his Budweiser beer. He has threatened to crack my skull in two with it, hissing and spitting straight into my open mouth. My beseeching glances receive little support from my fellow shoppers, for they too are frightened. Frightened that he will turn on them, that bedlam will break out and widespread mayhem will erupt. I don't wait to buy what I want, but rush tearfully back to Adam at the Eden. I am so disturbed that I fear I may sustain my first coronary.

But Adam pooh-poohs it all. 'Paranoia,' he says, 'is not what you're suffering from. Paranoia,' he continues, 'is an irrational fear that one is being persecuted, sometimes known as persecution mania.'

'That's me,' I wail. 'That's what I've got.' And I refuse

336

to go out on my own again, I wait for him to accompany me until my confidence returns. Until I can walk down Twenty-third Street without dreading that my bowels might void themselves at any moment, that my heart will leap straight from my throat to the pavement – or should I say sidewalk – each time a lurching stranger catches my eye.

'Avoid eye-contact, whatever you do, Evelyn!' It was Cherry who'd advised me on that (before last night's seduction scene). 'New York's not London, you know. I've been here two years and it took me two days to learn this street-smartness thing. You have to keep your wits about you when you're walking about in order to survive. By the way, first thing to do is buy yourself a shoulder bag, instead of that silly clutch purse you always carry around. Right away it'll make you less vulnerable.'

'Vulnerable?' Vulnerable to her? And her sexual advances?

'To muggers, Evelyn, vulnerable to muggers.'

Neither Adam or I have been mugged yet – touch wood and whistle. And yesterday afternoon (before we became orgiasts) I did inadvertently stumble upon a method of self-protection on Twenty-third Street.

'I'm off to the repair shop to collect your typewriter,' I shouted into the studio. The Eden is an exceptional residential hotel in this sense. It harbours and has harboured many creative people. Artists such as Adam, and writers like myself find the odd structure of the various apartments congenial to our work. The residential roster of the place reads like a *Who's Who* of artistic achievement, which is one of the reasons that we have chosen to settle here for the year. Already Adam has completed at least a dozen small paintings, gouache on paper images. Gouache being a cross between tubes of designers' colours and thick poster paint, in contrast to the quick-drying, glossy, oil-based paintings on huge pieces of hardboard that had built up his reputation in Britain.

'Airmail envelopes, large olives, carbon paper, salt and pepper,' he shouted back, 'and don't forget that I love you.'

'Love you too,' I murmured to myself, writing down his

list of requests. At one time I would have gone in to kiss him goodbye, would never have dreamed of leaving to go anywhere, even to the postbox, without doing so. But our eleventh wedding anniversary is just about to come up. Small-scale kissing got left behind a long time ago, even with as passionate a pair as us. In any case Adam is preoccupied these days with painting for his end-of-the-year exhibition in London. With both of us, when we're faced with the devastation of creative frustration, when hours pass and all one has to show is a page of meaningless doodles, irritability can erupt at any interruption. This is why our working alongside each other is so successful, the understanding is there. More than if I were simply his wife, attending to his every needs as if he were a child. Cossetting him along, like the wives of some of his contemporaries. But then those are marriages which began when both partners were starting out in life, where the girls sacrificed their careers in favour of their husband's chosen calling. Like Adam's first wife. Staying at home and seeing to the children. More or less as I was in my first marriage, bogged down with babies (beautiful though they were). My years spent as a student reduced to the proportions of a lucrative hobby, whilst the occasions for celebrations were reserved for my husband's promotional successes in his law practice. Enough of all that . . .

'Love you too,' I repeated, runing out of ball-point pens as I'm about to scribble down SALT'n PEP. So, 'Salt'n pep and ball-point pens,' I mutter as I drag on my street disguise, letting myself out of the apartment as I do so. Practising Zen and the Art of Harnessing Rising Hysteria as I approach the ominously empty, echoing stairwell of the Eden.

My blood jolts in my veins passing the fourth floor. A shadow still dressed in pyjamas flits from a door on one side of the passage to another on the other side. The door opens miraculously without his even having to knock. In the subdued gloom of the light I catch his white face for an instant. He is harmless, one of the several young junkies who inhabit the hotel. The lost son of some wealthy family who still mourn his wrecked life. A youthful musician no longer even fighting the addiction, a creature of the small hours. For some reason they foregather on the Fourth. We, up on the Seventh, are a sunnier lot altogether. Nearer to heaven.

The junkie disappears, I continue my downward journey. He was probably as disturbed by my appearance as I am by his. My street disguise makes me look disgusting, Adam turns away whenever I wear it. But until I get acclimatised to the city I feel I must merge into it, look like everyone else on Twenty-third, between Seventh and Eighth. And so now what I wear is this dingy, over-large overcoat, covering the gaudy excesses of my clothes beneath. I am known back in my own country for my eye-catching outfits. When we are interviewed by magazines, as a celebrated artistic couple, many column inches are devoted to detailed descriptions as to what I'm wearing. 'Elegant kitsch,' has been one of the more accurate descriptions, the one most to my liking. But I am too timid to venture forth in this city dressed as I normally would, the object here is to deliberately not seek to draw attention to oneself in the street. For the first time in my life I am attempting to assume the grey mantle of a mouse.

Adam says I go too far, that this camouflage is extreme – as is everything I attempt, every effect I strive after. A normal person, he claimed, would have bought their street clothes from an ordinary shop like everyone else. That would be the way to achieve anonymity (*quelle horreur!*). Instead of which my garment, my unspeakable purchase, was something I found in a mound of second-hand throwouts at the Salvation Army Thrift Shop, down on Eighth Avenue. The equivalent of a jumble sale, or an Oxfam shop in Britain. Two dollars, I paid for it. A dollar more than the asking price. The assistant was absolutely astonished, but even I considered that two dollars, the equivalent of a pound in our sterling, to be a positive bargain. Adam claims never to have seen me looking this plain. 'In almost eleven years of marriage I'm allowed to lower my standards now and again, aren't I!' My defence is that it's a matter of safety.

'Salt'n pep and ball-point pens,' I mouth my way through the lobby. Lobby is the American word for foyer, one that has slipped easily into my new vocabulary. 'In no time at all you start sounding like Yanks, talking with a twang,' friends had said accusingly before we left. 'Hope so,' I'd answered back.

But it hasn't turned out like that, quite the contrary. They adore the British accent over here. Everywhere we go people plead with us to go on talking (not that I ever need much encouragement in that department), just to slaver over our accents. So it would be stupid to start aping the way in which they speak, throwing away one of our greatest assets. The thing to do, as Adam pointed out very early on, is absorb the idiom of the American language so that those around understand what you're saying. The other day, for instance, I was trying to explain to the desk clerk that a friend of ours would be visiting in a fortnight for two nights and wished to return for a whole week later in the autumn. It was clear from his bewildered expression that he had no idea what I was talking about. A fellow guest tactfully interceded on my behalf. Fortnight, the word 'fortnight' was one of the stumbling blocks. There is no such word meaning two weeks over here. And instead of autumn I should have said 'fall'. Very confusing.

'Salt'n pep and ball-point pens,' I step out onto the sidewalk, nodding to the emaciated cleric entering as I leave. He looks startled, but I assume that this is because no one has acknowledged him so pleasantly of late. I've been told that he is behind in his rent, hasn't managed to pay it for as much as six months or more, But the management is tolerant in such cases, they won't throw him out yet. The foyer of the Eden is – the *lobby* of the Eden is lavishly hung with the paintings of former residents who have presented their work in exchange for their rent. One supposes that the elderly cleric has bartered with devout prayer – all that he has on offer.

I clutch my shopping list in my hand whilst keeping the extra requirements to the front of my brain, at the tip of my tongue. The palms of my hands are already beginning to sweat with the familiar nervous trepidation. Not for the first time I wonder whether living here in New York isn't the ultimate in masochism, if this is the effect that it is having on me. But I've discussed it with Cherry and other British people we've met at parties, indeed I talk of little else but this irrational fear of mine. And they assure me

340

that it will take up to three months for the panic to subside, for me to feel as at home as I would in London. Something to look forward to, at least!

'Salt and pepper, salt and pepper . . .' What the hell was the other thing? Already it has flown from my mind. That is because a battered colossus is approaching me, the entire right side of his face caked with dried blood. He is white, but the congealed gore is black. His eye is completely obliterated on that side. I can't tear my own eyes away from the sight.

'Salt and pepper, salt and pepper.' We are almost face to face. I engage the one working eye in frantic communion with my own, my lips moving continuously now, memorising my condiments.

'Salt and pepper, salt and pepper, salt and pepper . . .'

He has passed. He has lumbered straight past me, backing slightly away as my gaze searches the horror of his face. I am so amazed at his reaction, by the shiftiness of that darting eye of his, struggling to avoid mine that I am momentarily rendered speechless. Why did he recoil like that? From me!

Shaking my head I continue on my way. The grocery shop – the delicatessen – is only half a block away. Between me and there the sidewalk throngs surge my way, I detect menace in each looming shape.

'Salt and pepper, salt and pepper, salt and pepper,' my lips curl soundlessly around the syllables, I stride purposefully forward staring straight ahead.

But now something strange is happening to people as they approach me. I notice that they are stepping aside to avoid me, deliberately turning their heads away, doing anything rather than have me engage them in dreaded eye-contact.

They are frightened of me.

'Because you were muttering in that asinine manner – by the way, where are the ball-points? There's not a pen in the place that works.'

'You think that was it? They all thought I was crazy?' I ignore Adam's bit about the ball-point pens, my forgotten item. But I don't mind if I have to make a second journey down to buy them, not now that I've stumbled onto this unique method of self-preservation. The pandemonium of

341

the passing traffic pounds through the closed wondows.
Though the central heating in the Eden is way over the
top, so stiflingly hot that at times one can't breathe, I love
it that way. Someone used to this luxurious American
heating would probably open a window to let in some
fresh air. But not me. I was brought up in houses where
the only warmth came from the coal fire, kept in day and
night, summertime included. Where every member of the
family suffered blistering chilblains on their hands and
their feet from the cold. Where all of the women, all of my
aunties, bore the unsightly evidence of chronic circulatory
problems all down the front of their legs and at the end of
their noses. Technicolour discolourations from sitting too
closely huddled around the fire.

And yet that glowing image, from childhood – the fire –
has remained with me through the rest of my life. No room
seems complete without that crucial focus, even when the
personalities in it would diminish any flame with the
brilliance of their conversation and wit. It's a visual thing
too, my theory being that the secret of television's
universal success is that human beings need this flickering
light in the corner of their home. The modern equivalent
of the primitive hearth (best gazed at with the sound
turned off in the States!).

'The main event, what do you mean by the main event?
Adam!' But Adam has disappeared from view now,
probably reached our apartment with the kettle on
already to greet me with a comforting cup of decaffeinated
coffee. A health precaution we had adopted, the decaffeinated, before we even came to New York. Here everyone we
know seems to drink it that way, whereas back in Britain
we were ridiculed as being health-freaks. For that and our
daily half-mile swim in the pool. I study my tiny gold
cocktail watch, a present from Adam on my last birthday,
given to me at midnight like an extra anniversary
celebration. Neat that, getting married the day before my
birthday (the day his divorce came through). It gives the
excuse for a prolonged celebration, two days instead of
one running into each other. Soon I shall have to decide
what to do, how to celebrate the two events over here this
year. Without our usual friends and all the family. I feel a
stab of homesickness at the thought of them, but breathe

deeply and blink hard to dispel the rising emotion. Jesus Christ, I feel *frightful* this morning! When did I ever before have such a hellish head as this, a scalp bristling with lethal shafts of pain as sudden and swift as shooting stars. What did Adam mean, that Roger had left after the main event – had there been more fucks than one? And if so who was screwing who?

A paralysing thought hit me, as I looked at my little watch with the date winking up at my dazed eyes. *Did Roger come in me, did he shoot off inside!* I am slap-bang in the middle week between periods, with no protection any more. No contraceptive device at all, not for the past five years, not since Adam had his vasectomy and I went to the clinic for my IUD, my coil, to be removed.

'This will keep you in order now,' Adam had teased at the time. 'There'll be trouble if you get pregnant from now on!' And we'd both laughed, as if either of us would ever even dream of having anyone except each other.

Oh, why wasn't Adam taking care of things better last night! How did it get so out of hand!

Our marriage is over. *We have committed adultery.*

I'm crying by the time I reach our apartment. A reluctant divorcee, pregnant with Roger's child.

'Welcome home, infidel!' Adam opens the door with an exuberant flourish, grinning wickedly at my wilting body, lifting me up and whisking me across the threshold. Like a bride, instead of an almost ex-wife.

I cling onto his shoulders, hugging him tightly, snivelling all down his neck.

'I'm upset,' I sob into him. 'Terribly, terribly upset . . . we've committed adultery . . . we've been unfaithful to each other . . .' I hear myself actually *howling*. 'We've spoilt everything now . . . it'll never be the same again . . .'

'Cup of coffee,' he says softly, in his very gentlest voice. 'Cup of coffee, that's what my darling can do with.' And he cradles me in his arms, sitting down now. Rocking me slowly to-and-fro like a small child.

'My head hurts, Adam. Dreadfully.' I whimper as my sobbing subsides.

'It will hurt.' He sounds so sensible. 'The way you were whacking into the amyl nitrate, there was no holding you

343

once you got sniffing that stuff. There's no checking your appetite, Eve angel, once you get the taste for something new. It's always been one of your troubles.'

But I don't know what he's talking about. I honestly have no memory of it at all.

'Amyl nitrate?' I whisper. It even hurts now to open my eyes.

'Amyl nitrate. The main event. It was after the amyl nitrate that Roger left.'

'You married, Eve?'

'Sort of.' I answer carefully.

'Yeah? In a meaningful relationship anyway, they're the best. I haven't had one since last fall. Right now though I'm too busy with Sister Solidarity to worry 'bout love. It has a way of hitting you when you least expect it, anyway. Plenty of time, I'm not worried.'

'How old are you, Jody?' Twenty, I thought when I met her in the Sister Solidarity offices. But now in the open air, with the wintry sunshine soft on her smooth complexion I guess that she's probably even younger.

'Me, I'm twenty-six.' She tosses her long brown hair back from her face, ignoring the admiring glances from a group of young thugs lounging against the corner of Forty-second Street. One of them calls out something, but it's unintelligible to me.

'Creeps!' she mutters witheringly. 'Stick close by me now, this is the pits along here. First we go into *Show World*.'

I am being taken on one of the twice-weekly tours of the Times Square organised by Sister Solidarity, to raise the consciousness of American women.

'Part of your new-found puritanism?' Adam has been pleasantly ironic about this desire of mine to go on the advertised tour. I'd brought back the leaflet from one of the SoHo galleries downtown.

'It's an important issue,' I'd answered primly. 'Especially if you have daughters. How would you like it if one of my girls were manipulated into performing in those hell-holes along Forty-second Street? Or forced to appear, needing the money, in some hard-core movie, committing unnatural acts with animals? Or any of your boys, for that matter – they make use of kids of both sexes, you know.'

'Unnatural acts with animals must be one of your fantasies – probably because you weren't allowed a puppy when you were a child. You're always on about it, you really are.'

'A neat side-stepping of the main issue.' I'd turned back to my desk and creased my forehead in a frown of concentration. It was the second time that morning I had started this magazine article. And I had yet to work out my angle for the piece on Sister Solidarity. The work was not going too well these days.

The night with Cherry and Roger kept preying on my mind, and the reason why I'd hung back so reluctantly in the bathroom.

Vanity. I was ashamed of my body.

I haven't been self-conscious about nudity, about myself with nothing on, for eleven years. Not for the whole of my married life with Adam.

In the communal changing rooms favoured by stores and boutiques now (except the more exclusive ones with subtly intolerable sales pressure), I strip down to the bare essentials along with the best of them. Rather proud, in fact, of my athletic frame. My firm breasts, my small waist, the smooth silkiness of my skin – or have I been deluding myself these past years? For I must face it now, if there is to be a confrontation, a comparison with such as Cherry (a girl of twenty-nine, almost twenty years younger), mine is plainly the body of a mature woman.

Starting from the top of me, compiling an abrasively honest list (for my eyes alone!) of my assets and defects, I still have all my own hair, and plenty of it. I feel that I should say this after being told (in strictest confidence) recently by a hairdresser at a party, just how many famous film-stars have had to resort to wearing wigs now they are approaching their late forties. That shook me. I shall peer more closely, in future, at snapshots of the acknowledged beauties of our times. But, alas, like me, none of them are getting any younger.

This morning I read a spiteful item in a tabloid newspaper. Adam reprimanded me for even buying such a rubbishy rag. He, himself, was purchasing our regular reading material. *The New Yorker. The Village Voice. SoHo News.* The first for erudite enlightenment, and the last two for local events and items of interest. But my tabloid headlined the miserable, reclusive existence of Doris Day (with a *rare* photograph!). And in addition an inside report on the recent marriage of an international sex symbol to a Frenchman, *five whole years younger*!

'It is unallowable for one person to impose their own intellectual snobbery on another,' I had retorted to Adam's expression of disapproval at my avid interest in these 'degrading' journalistic scoops.

But reading them, in *Pretty Polly's Coffee Shop*, salivating over my English muffin and marmalade (neither of which I would ever dream of eating in England for lunch) I was left with feelings of depression – while Adam was busy ordering himself a second muffin, a bran muffin this time with grapejello. 'I'll have the same, please,' I said quickly, avoiding his eye. Whilst I'm on a perpetual diet (this muffin phase has *got* to stop!), Adam can eat anything he likes and not put on a pound in weight. At least that is how it has always been in the past, but the advancing years are catching up with him now, so he claims. Not so long ago he stood in front of the bathroom mirror, 'Well, the big race is on!' he announced.

'Which big race is that?' I'd said. It was the day after the Marathon, which we'd gone to watch in Central Park (our very first foray into the midst of an organised crowded event). I'd thought that he was referring to another such sporting fixture.

'The *big* race,' he'd repeated, 'as to which will win first – the baldness or the grey!' And he'd proffered the top of his head for my inspection. Later that day he had written saying this to my youngest daughter, who hugely enjoys any joke at another's expense (I can't think who she gets her sadistic sense of humour from!). And he'd got the reply in return, written tersely on the back of a postcard of the Queen. A BALD MAN DOES NOT FEAR GREY HAIR!

Soon Adam will be forty, he is seven years my junior. He was twenty-nine when we met, and I was thirty-six. I couldn't wait for that first birthday of his to get him into the thirties, alongside me.

Similarly I secretly can't wait for this his fortieth birthday, the one that he is dreading so much. I don't know what it is about forty that so distresses men. Women feel worse when they hit their thirtieth year, all my friends claimed suicidal thoughts as theirs loomed up. I remember ringing a sophisticated female friend of mine on the final evening of my twenty-ninth year. 'It's my *thirtieth* birthday tomorrow,' I'd wailed. 'Hard cheese!' That had been her crisp reply! Then she'd softened it with, 'From here on in, kid, you'll find it can only get better.'

And she's been right about that. It has got better. Until now, the time for agonising reappraisal.

But, yes, my hair is no problem. No *new* trouble with greying, my follicles started falling dead somewhere around my seventeenth year. Prematurely silver by the time I was twenty-four, like my grandfather before me. It is said to be hereditary. 'How stylish!' New friends who didn't know me in those early years exclaim to me now, thinking that I walked around with a shock of silver hair looking like a Christmas sparkler each time I made an entry into a subtly-lit room. As if I would have had the panache to have carried off that sort of thing then. Now I could do it, now I wear my hair any colour – green, purple, electric blue. Not recently, of course, because that punk thing has past. And when I wore the violently-coloured hair I went the whole sophisticated way, putting on only clothes and accessories of the same or toning shades. The impact was stunning, though I say it myself!

Those years I must have appeared in more glossy magazines and newspaper supplements than I could care to count. These days, when reporters call, it is usually for an in-depth interview. Serious stuff about the work and the direction in which I consider myself to be going artistically. The photographs that accompany these pieces are run large, sometimes from the top of the column to the bottom. But they work just as well in black and white. The colour photograph is no longer essential, since my impact is now more to do with the line, the shape and usually the extraordinary chapeaux that I choose to wear. Black is my favourite colour currently. It is the colour which I now have my hair dyed.

I stayed away from black for my hair for something like ten years, the last ten, now I come to think of it. Though I was black when I met Adam. Only just however. Three

347

weeks previously I was still red, bright red each time the re-growth had been done. And then fading through the month to what one of my many lovers of the time termed, 'a mangy tabby on the tiles'. When he'd said that I went into the hairdresser the next morning and returned to black (my childhood colour before turning naturally silver).

It had done funny things to me, the red. I'd envisaged myself as looking like Rita Hayworth. Flaming, exotic, hot-tempered, a temptress. But instead of that, what happened was that people started treating me more like that other demure red-head, delightfully English Deborah Kerr. I could hardly believe it, but it started happening right away.

The very evening that I'd had it done my ex-husband called around as usual to kiss goodnight to the children. His expression had altered as soon as I greeted him (self-consciously) at the door. 'Hey, you look good tonight – what have you done that's different?' 'Nothing different,' I'd said sourly. 'It's something,' he stood, staring. 'I've never seen you looking as, as, feminine and pretty as this before.' Obviously red hair is the answer to flagging marriages, I'd thought. It really seemed for a moment there as if he was considering re-proposing. And to my horror I'd gone along with it, simpering and blushing.

Worse than that, as the same reaction started coming from strangers at parties, and from old acquaintances and the usual posse of lovers (though all of the posse admitted afterwards that they had felt uneasy about the new image), I even went out and bought a new wardrobe to go with the new me. Sedate and subtle garments started infiltrating themselves into the house. Camelhair over-coats, casual and sporty tweeds in soft russet colours, chiffon blouses in shimmering bronzes, chrysanthemum silk shirts, cashmeres in yellows and natural fawns. All the sort of clothes that I had always so despised. And with this new wardrobe came unsuitable suitors. Stockbrokers, physicians, financiers, select members of the English aristocracy. All the sort of men with whom I had so little in common during my first marriage. If only I had looked like this then, it might have solved all of our mutual problems, Henry's and mine.

Since I have been with Adam I have never suffered such an identity crisis. The only time was for that one summer when I decided, with his encouragement, to return to my natural (now) silver. The style was flattering, I had it all permed into a tight rippling shoulder-length mop and then pinned on top of my head in a Lucille Ball sort of frizz. People would stop me in the street to ask where I had it done – the colour. Few would believe it was my own. Except in Italy, on the beach one of the young lifeguards, who was pursuing my eldest daughter, mistook me as the mother of Adam, along with being the mother of his three sons and my two girls. That *didn't* please me. On my return to London I got rid of the silver and all the grey clothes I had bought to tone along with it. The colour of hair has a huge bearing on personality. However chic it is considered to be to wear one's hair grey now, however unwise the radical feminists consider it to interfere with nature, grey hair is undeniably ageing. One looks older, more solemn, more responsible, wiser, less fun, lots of things like that – with steel-wool tresses. I pin my faith on artificial aids. Artifice has always engaged my aesthetic enthusiasm.

If only artifice could come to my aid now!

The light in Cherry's bathroom was mercilessly cruel, the bathroom of someone youthful enough to be able to afford it, someone with few things to hide. Standing, stripped, beneath the central bulb I saw myself more clearly than I had done for years. Unflattering shadows were cast from overhead, emphasising the 'laughter lines' around my eyes, turning them into something uncommonly like *wrinkles*!

Smiling sympathetically at myself (to soften that blow), my entire countenance congealed into a relief map of Europe. Main arterial highways met at crucial intersections around the nose, around the mouth, branching alarmingly into deep ravines which ran from the centre of each cheek, disappearing down under the chin. Didn't those used to be dimples? And not that long ago either!

Peering more closely towards the mirror, ferociously full-length, I tilted my head at what I imagined to be a more flattering angle. This was a tip given me recently by a veteran photographer when I had posed for him in his studio.

'Your left is your best side,' he'd said to me kindly.

'Yes, I've been told that before.' I'd cocked my head in the coquettish manner that I'd always employed (since the age of six, or thereabouts, I imagine). It was an integral part of my bag of tricks, could generally be counted upon to elicit compliments on the sensuality of my lips, or the unusual lustre of my uncannily clear eyes. Though I had never been described as a pretty girl, camps appear to be evenly divided over my looks. I have been variously categorised as having the pert features of a pedigree filly, 'an irresistible equestrian', to being that elusive of all beauties – the classic contemporary, or the contemporary classic. If my life were ever to be filmed (a possible project, not beyond reasonable speculation one day), I should probably be played by an actress such as Jill Bennett. Or, in the French version, by Jeanne Moreau. Or in the American, perhaps Ann Bancroft.

Though, doubtless, there are younger actresses coming up . . . now why should that thought occur to me, why *should* I be portrayed by someone younger than myself! Is that more acceptable to my vanity? If so, then I find it vaguely disturbing, for I've never been concerned about my age – or anyone else's – before. But perhaps this is how it is with everyone, it hits them unexpectedly. Death has inched imperceptibly closer whilst they were looking the other way.

But it isn't death that concerns me now. It's this sexual thing. Suddenly I have found myself in the competitive sexual arena again. And it is of my own making too, Adam is right on that. I have behaved in too licentious a fashion in the past, getting drunk and embracing all manner of people – but without meaning any of it, truly. Oh, but what is the use of saying that now! I have pushed Adam to the limit, and placed our relationship in jeopardy. Stupid bitch!

We haven't spoken of it yet, not in connection with us and Cherry, but there was an incident almost two years ago, when my irresponsible lewdness got us into the same sort of trouble. I thought I had managed to blot it out, but every time I think of being in bed with Cherry (kissing the amazing hairiness between her legs – burrowing in there to ease my tongue into the wetness of the flesh), I remember the girl, Stella.

She'd been sent to see us both by her magazine, a Paris publication. Coinciding with a surrealist exhibition in which Adam was represented over there. We had carried on a lengthy correspondence with her prior to her arrival, so that by the time she arrived it seemed only natural that she should stay overnight with us in our house before catching her flight back to Paris.

She was a practised interviewer, rather older in the flesh than she had sounded on the telephone. 'A dyke, do you suppose?' Adam had whispered to me whilst she unpacked her few belongings in the bedroom we had given her.

'Never!' I'd been certain. Her clothes were too stylish. Scarlet leather jeans and matching jacket, crimson tee-shirt beneath clearly revealing a pair of arousingly pointed nipples. And her short hair was not 'butch' enough, it curled in enticing tendrils around her small head in altogether a feminine way. The sort of girl, one would have thought, who had strings of beaux to her banjo. Nevertheless, Adam's observation had awakened me to the possibility. He was usually right in these matters, I inevitably am proved way off the mark when it comes to people's sexual proclivities. Halfway through dinner that evening I admitted that he had guessed correctly. By that time, with the libation of alcohol and the generally pleasant mood into which we'd fallen, I was getting very strong sexual messages from Stella.

Sexual messages, for me, are not in any way unusual. I have been pursued by members of the oppostite sex all my life. I enjoy it enormously, the flirtatious part of it. The holding of a gaze, the unspoken agreement between consenting participants. And the messages have not simply been from men. But I have always been too timid to dabble as deeply as I would have liked with members of my own sex. I have never indulged in an intense lesbian relationship. Certainly Stella was the first female that I had kissed with any serious passionate intent – since I have been with Adam.

It came about in the bathroom (bathrooms obviously have started figuring pretty large lately in my sexual life). That's where we fell upon each other first. I am still not too clear who made the initial move. At one moment I was

351

extracting an extra pillowcase from the pile in the airing cupboard, bending across Stella as she was wiping her hands dry on a towel – and the next thing is that we have our arms around each other. We are kissing like fury.

And laughing, laughing so hysterically that Adam comes to see if anything is the matter. By that time we are both in a partial state of undress. Stella has wriggled out of her scarlet leather jeans, removing her high-heeled shoes in order to be able to do so. Now she stands, a little shorter than me, more on a level with my breasts. When Adam enters, the sight he is greeted with is Stella sucking enthusiastically on my left nipple, twiddling the right one between her fingers.

My expensive angora sweater, white no longer, lies at our feet. The sole of my shoe is pawing the front fastening as I thrust an impatient knee between Stella's willing thighs.

'Many husbands would have been absolutely horrified to witness a scene of debauchery such as that!' Adam said the next day. Just when I couldn't bear even to contemplate the memory of it. The guilt had been absolutely horrendous. For we had gone on from the mere kissing. That was only for starters!

It had ended up with the three of us in bed together, but some of that time I had chosen to get up out of the bed and just sit in a chair and watch. Watching Adam and Stella together screwing the arses off each other – or just me with Stella, poised in the position of sixty-nine – I don't know which disturbed me most.

Just as I don't know now about Cherry and the two of us. I feel jealousy somewhere. I am insecure about myself suddenly. But is that because I am not certain of my own sexual identity any more?

'Let me pay your money for you – we'll sort it all out afterwards if you like. Doesn't do to hang around the entrance of *Show World*. These slobs assume that you're touting for trade. They can only think of life in terms of sex and money, Eve.'

Jody is steering me capably forward. We are engulfed in the throbbing beat of full volume disco music. Men surround us on every side (we are the only females in the place), some openly leering, licking their lips in an exaggerated way. Others brush roughly past us as if angry at our intrusion into this their male domain. Still more pretend that they haven't seen us, some of them actually blush and appear sheepish. It's as if they had been caught out by their mothers or sisters. Just one or two give crudely knowing glances at the two of us, this girl and myself, obviously sure that we are a pair of lesbian lovers. For some reason I find this reaction the most offensive. I must remember to tell that to Adam.

'I'm only interested in showing you one of the "attractions" here, Eve.' Jody steers me up the stairs towards a large flashing sign advertising a display of live sex for an extra of five dollars.

'Only simulated sex.' Jody sees me reading the sign. 'Not worth the extra cash, like everything in this dump.'

We pass several transparent telephone booths in which are seated girls wearing brief, chiffon, baby-doll negligées. Beside each of the booths there stood an empty one for a caller to ring through an obscene telephone call to the girl on the other side of the clear partition. 'It costs one dollar to mouth five minutes of filth, the object being to see how the recipient recoils!' Jody quipped from the corner of her mouth. 'Some of these girls are pretty good actresses, they pretend to gasp and faint. But they've heard it before. We've all had our share of dirty phone calls, huh?'

I nod. I'm self-conscious, uneasily so. I am finding this experience oppressive, more than I had expected it to be. But before I can articulate these feelings to Jody, knowing that she would understand absolutely (many women who take this tour are suburban wives, for Christ sake, not sophisticated sexually, like me), we seem to arrive at where we've been heading.

'The Carousel!' Jody announces. And I'm gently pushed through a curtain and find myself in a dark enclosure with barely room even to spread my elbows. In front of me is a small light above a slot in which I'm meant to drop my coin. As soon as I do so a partition falls immediately, or is it raised (?). The action takes me completely by surprise. More than that, the sight before me – luridly bright, and alarmingly close – causes me to forget my previous discomfort. I am crotch-level with a

353

dozen completely naked girls, their bodies congregate on the other side of my open partition, but they are higher than me by about six inches. It is as if I am in the front row of an intimate theatre, with them onstage and me in the audience. Except that they are close enough to touch, to smell, to lick. And I am not the only spectator – though I am the only woman. Surrounding this enclosed arena are at least a dozen small cells, like the one that I'm in (cowering in!) now.

Males of all ages, from youngsters who look as if they have barely had their first shave, to whiskery senior citizens, stand sweating at each of the open partitions. Now and again, one of these shut abruptly – more money is obviously needed to keep the shutters open. I shall *not* be placing another coin in the slot, however. I am already dissolving in my own embarrassment.

For, in seconds of sighting me, I am surrounded by this excitable throng of giggling girls. They are jostling with each other to get as close to me as they possibly can. The more they press their bellies and buttocks into my scarlet face, the further back I am trying to shrink.

And this amuses them even more, they are taking an absolute delight in taunting me. Jody explains afterwards that the Sister Solidarity tours of joints such as this do afford the girls working in them a great deal of fun. And that since they are our 'sisters' (exploited sisters) we should try not to give them any hassle. As if I bloody am!

Now the ringleader is pushing herself to the forefront of the bunch. I had noticed her from the very start, as being slightly older than the rest. Which would put her in her early twenties! But she was noticeable for her confidence above all, the way she carries her body, the thrust of her hips. And the electricity leaping from every pore.

In addition she is the girl with the most dollar bills in her garter, the same garter as the rest of them are wearing around their upper thighs. The object of the garter, according to Jody when we discussed it later (why hadn't she told me all this *before*?), is to persuade the clients to touch. A dollar a touch. And the ringleader is determined now that I should not get away without contributing my dollar a touch. Though I get the impression that the challenge for her is more that our flesh should meet in

some form of contact, than the mere money involved. It is
my demure reluctance that she is all out to sweep aside.

By God, she is formidable too! I have never been
subjected to such sexual enticement as this in my entire
life!

'C'mon, honey, you wanna kiss me?' She raises one
haunch, high in the air, resting her knee on the wall above
my head. It enables her to show (and me to see) the entire
stretch of her genital area. Right from her arsehole around
to the tip of her clitoris. Her *rouged* clitoris, I swear that
this is so! I have yet to see such a rosy apparition – and
one as juicily plump and swollen.

My throat is dry, I long to lick my lips but dare not do
so, even if this were possible. There is a violent churning
down at the bottom of my stomach (mostly to the front –
the part described as the pit?).

The other girls buzz around their Queen Bee, also
beseeching me to let myself go and TOUCH.

'Go ahead and lick her, lick Delphine,' one of them is
coaxing me. This child cannot be more than fifteen at the
most. I thought of my daughters, and what they would say
about me sitting here passing the afternoon in such a
raffish manner. 'A piece of sociological research, darlings,'
I would have to explain it away like that. I could hear
their scornful replies as if they were here next to me.

But they are not here next to me, Delphine is here next
to me instead. And Delphine is losing patience with me,
with my spoil-sport ways, with what she would call my
British reserve (if she knew for a moment that I am
British).

And it is absolutely ridiculous, too, the adolescent way
that I am behaving. Jesus, these jolly girls are only doing
their job as pleasantly and efficiently as they know how. I
mean the brief is to titillate the customer, after all. And
perhaps that is the trouble. Delphine has succeeded only
too well with me. My cheeks are aflame with distress, I am
almost close to tears.

And more sexually aroused than I dare to admit, even
to myself.

The money is due to run out. My partition is about to
slam down and obliterate the scene of debauchery and
delight – unless I am prepared to save the day and do

something about it. Which I am not. Like a real trooper, determined to save something from the lost battle, salvage something if only her prideful pride, Delphine leans down to me so close I taste her breath.

'I got your number, hun, you get your rocks off just lookin'.' The partition crashes down, slicing the silky smile into smithereens. It cancels out her cunt, the mockery of her mischevious thighs, and only leaves the purring words winding into my brain. And the muskiness floating into my nostrils.

I stumble out towards the steadying arms of Jody. A small gang of passing boys snigger at the sight of me. They are on their way in to sample the Carousel themselves. Delphine will fare much better with them.

'Strong stuff, huh!' Jody smiles sympathetically. But I am too preoccupied, too shocked somewhere inside to respond. To my surprise I am actually trembling, I feel weak at the knees. I am sticky down there, down there in the cotton gusset of these American pantie-briefs. Like a young girl in the back row of a cinema with her very first date. Oh, the discomfort of the walk home afterwards! I remember it still! And here I am now with the same problem.

'Where we're headed into now is nothing more or less than a masturbatory parlour.' Jody's upper lip curls disparagingly as she says this. I think back guiltily on all those past times of pleasuring my own person. Perhaps it is more excusable when performed in private, or don't the young bother with masturbation any more? There was a long review yesterday in *The Village Voice* headed 'Lust Bust', which put forward the claims of a newly-published book, *The New Celibacy*. 'A glut on the sexual market,' according to the ground-breaking research of Gabrielle Brown Ph.d, 'has led to a deterioration of the product. Emotion and sex have rolled over to the opposite edges of the kingsize water-bed, leaving in their wake boredom, frustration and an increasing desperation to find the Real Thing. Some post-sexual revolutionary die-hards haven't given up yet on the quest for unalienated sex: they persist in looking for trusted lovers, on working things out with the lovers they've got, or, if things feel awry, on going into therapy. But other more pragmatic folk have apparently eliminated the problem altogether: they've simply stopped having sex.'

I'd read bits out to Adam, despite his saying he'd read it himself earlier. Marriage does that to you, it leads you to want to share things with your loved one – regardless of whether they have already experienced something and may not necessarily wish to re-live it. But it's a kindly compulsion, not meant to irritate. I can be very irritating though, I know.

'The New Celibates', I'd continued reading out, 'are an attractive crowd. Like most trendsetters, they are "successful, positive, strong people with a goal of personal fulfilment in life . . . quite happy and remarkably healthy-looking . . . into good food, exercise, no drugs and so on." These people aren't running *from* anything, they are seeking either "achievement in work," or "more complex human pleasures, such as emotions and ideas" . . . "something more eternal, more permanent . . . a further self-expression" than is possible when you're having trouble breathing because of "blocked air passages caused by swollen blood vessels." Sex for these people is, as one man put it, "a leak in the energy pipe".'

I put down the newspaper and had sat looking at Adam. For the first five years of our marriage we had made love on average three to four times a day (including the night). Four times, or three, every twenty-four hours. Between twenty-one and twenty-eight times a week . . . if I was any good at arithmetic I would be able to work out how many times a year we had done it. Oh, I am forgetting to include our wedding anniversaries when we have made a concentrated effort to exceed our own record.

'Adam?'

'Mm?'

'What does our record stand at now?'

'Eleven, I believe.' He knows exactly what I'm talking about.

'Not eleven and a-half? I thought that we were trying to make it a round dozen.'

'Possibly so.'

'Won't be doing that again.' I don't even feel inclined to ask quite which year we last attempted it.

'Not without help, Eve, my angel.' And he'd winked at me lasciviously.

'Christ!' But I laugh anyway. What has this marriage come to that we can say things like this to each other. Hasn't our intimacy overbounded into indecency. But I don't say this for not wanting really to talk about it at this point. The whole thing needs much more thinking about.

'See this guy with the mop and pail?' Jody precedes me into what looks like an amusement arcade, opening onto the sidewalk. Again we are immediately swallowed up in a milling group of men. They are more sinister this time, they look much of a muchness in age. Around forty seems to be the average. Most have their hands deep in their pockets and are hunched over with worried or preoccupied expressions on their faces. Around the four walls and along a central partition their are tiny curtained booths. The contents of these booths are advertised outside each of them. They all represent mini-viewing theatres. Each is showing a short film. Or perhaps it is a video. The titles of each are clear to see.

'Take your pick,' Jody directs me. 'This is a real honey!' And she shows me the tiny picture of a young female being tortured in chains by a heavy man in nazi uniform. 'Or this.' I study the title. FUN DOWN ON THE FARM. There is no accompanying illustration.

'Oh, boy – look at him go mop up!'

I look towards where she is staring, still standing outside the FUN DOWN ON THE FARM kiosk. The gorilla-like man with the mop is entering a recently vacated booth. There is an overwhelmingly nauseous drift of strong disinfectant as he swishes the contents of his pail over the walls and floor.

When I return my watering eyes to where I am, I see that a small queue is already forming behind me. Jody has retired to the far side of the arcade. I am left on my own to wait for FUN DOWN ON THE FARM.

'Hey you dumb broad,' someone is addressing me! 'Hey you, can't you see that this booth is occupied. 'The guy points angrily up at the red light on the booth.

'Sure buddy, the dame knows. What you think we doin' here. We in line. You wanna see de film you get in behind us.'

A Sir Galahad has come to my rescue! Normally I would have turned around gratefully to thank him. But the circumstances have numbed my usually impeccable manner. All I can do is stand staring straight ahead. But the murmuring noises behind me now lead me to believe that the numbers waiting for FUN DOWN ON THE FARM are increasing every second. It must be the magic of a line-up. This obviously has to be the hottest show in the place otherwise why would I be waiting like this? I see that the management would be well advised to hire a token woman in the place to draw customers in – just place her in front of any of the film-clips which appear to be doing flagging business.

My eyes wander along the rows of stalls, the next one is showing something called FUCKING AT THE HEALTH SPA. On the other side is LIKE MOTHER, LIKE DAUGHTER, about someone pleasuring both at the same time.

But now the curtain before me is being whisked to one side. The red light has gone off and the queue behind me is pressing me forward. Before I have time to shrink back and allow the mop-and-pail man to do his job, I find myself forced into the small kiosk – fighting for breath. There is an overpowering stench of rotting mushrooms. The air is fetid, the walls are suspiciously shiny to the eye. I make certain that there shall be no contact between them and me by drawing my clothing as tightly around me as possible.

The previous occupant, frantic at finding himself the centre of attention as he attempted to slink out unseen from his furtive viewing, had been a surprisingly ordinary-looking man.

'How did you expect him to look?' Adam asked afterwards.

'What I mean is that he could have been any number of our friends,' I had floundered. 'He looked rather studious. He was wearing spectacles.'

'Very sensible too. He didn't want to miss anything, not when he'd paid out good cash. Sounds just like any one of our friends.'

After the first involuntary intake of breath I take the sensible course and begin breathing through my mouth. It

359

is what I used to do when I changed my babies' nappies. Same trick, no smell. Otherwise I would have gagged – unlike the young (*really* young) heroine of FUN DOWN ON THE FARM. Gagging looks like something that she has never even heard of, she must have been taking lessons from Linda Lovelace in deep-throating. Her mouth (and I could imagine all the tubes down to her navel!) is fully occupied by donkey-dick. *This cherubic child is sucking off a donkey*!

It is a stomach-churning scene, topped only by the grotesque shots of her friend on the far side of the field doing the same thing with an alsation dog. At one point the shaggy hair around the dog's dick gets entangled in the girl's mouth and disappears up her nostrils. Was this what made the spectacled professor shoot off?

'Could have been a hair-fetishist, you never know,' Adam took an altogether more sanguine view of it than me. But then he hadn't seen FUN DOWN ON THE FARM himself. Nor sat through the convulsive coming of donkey and dog, arrived at together (those girls must have worked before as a team!).

'I feel queasy. Quite ill.'

Jody nods grimly. 'You wanna know how much those poor kids get for doing that? They don't receive more than two hundred dollars a film. Can you imagine!'

'Degradation deserves a higher wage scale,' I said.

She looked at me approvingly. 'Those girls in the Carousel only get fifty-six dollars for an eight-hour stretch, that's why they go for the tip-a-touch so hard. And this is a four *billion* dollar-a-year industry where all the profits are being creamed off by men. Who dares to say that these women are not being exploited!'

We are out again on Forty-second Street amongst all the pimps and pushers, the drunks and degenerates. I have never (who has) flowered in hostile environments and feel like discontinuing the tour right now. I want to go home, to have a comforting cup of tea with Adam. I like knowing that I have a husband and I am nothing to do with any of this. I am just a tourist in this street of cheap thrills.

'I wonder what the NSPCA would have to say about the film I've just seen. They'd probably stage a protest

360

march to Parliament claiming that the natural dignity of the dog and donkey had been violated.' I am trying to lighten my plight. But Jody is looking at her watch and frowning.

'Have to cut this a little bit short, I'm afraid, Eve. Do you mind too much. We usually take people on to one of the topless bars around here, but I'm running short of time. We'll get you some "literature" in here though. You should get a couple of these gems.'

We swerve off into a tiny bookstore, no larger than a tobacconist's kiosk. A swarthy, villainous-looking creature scowls from behind his money-till. I grab a paperback quickly from the many on the rack, he scowls even more but grudgingly accepts my money.

'He obviously doesn't welcome our custom.' Jody walks with me to the corner as I settle up the money with her. 'But there is nothing that any of these bastards can do about Sister Solidarity. We are going to win. One day this whole strip will be unrecognisable. Decent people will be able to walk along here without worrying again.'

'She said "decent people", Adam. That's not you and me. What would she think if she'd seen us with Roger and Cherry? It's hardly a happily married scene is it?'

But Adam is refusing to answer me. We are on our way to the swimming pool over at the YMCA. He says that this is not the time or place for a serious discussion on sexual ethics. Or on morality. There are certain issues which have to be cleared up between us, him and me. Tonight he is taking me out to dinner for this serious discussion. That is to be the purpose of the outing.

We take the elevator in the Y up to the third floor, for me and the Ladies' locker room where I change. Adam goes on up to the fourth. I glance down to see that my bag is all right. One of the fears is that this bag will be grabbed even in the safe confines of this Christian building. I see that the 'literature' I bought with Jody is still protruding from the top of my bag. Its lurid cover, AUSCHWITZ TERROR, shows a girl writhing in ecstacy. Her nipples are nailed down on to a wooden bench, a vicious instrument is jammed cruelly between her legs. I still have to show it to Adam. He'll say, 'Great! Something juicy to read together in bed!' I can just hear it.

361

'See you in a minute,' he calls after me as I leave the elevator. A girl gets out with me, 'Hi,' she smiles at me. Strolling the short length of corridor to the Ladies' locker room, we pass the karate class. It is mixed, men and women in equal numbers. But in the next large room which is devoted to body-building and weight-lifting there are no girls present at all. Though there is one girl who uses these facilities, a magnificent young negress. When I saw her from the back, sauntering naked from the sauna the other day, I had a shock. I'd thought she was a boy, the body was rippling with so many muscles. And the shape, the strong shoulders tapering down to such high and tight, tiny buttocks. Only the certain knowledge that no male would dare enter, or be permitted to infiltrate that far inside the female domain, made me think again. And when she turned, it was perfectly obvious which sex she was. Her breasts were as high and tight as her buttocks, and probably just as firm to the touch.

There are many beautiful bodies over at the Y. A great number of dancers come here to work out every day. And since it's normal (though not for me) to stroll around with nothing on within the confines of the ladies' quarters, there are ample opportunities to covertly study them. No one stares directly at anyone else's torso, wouldn't dream of it. As in a nudist colony, nudity is the last thing on anyone's mind. Except mine.

I greet the black woman seated at the desk in the entrance to the locker room. To the far left of her lie the showers and the sauna, further beyond is the television lounge. If you were on your own in New York this club would be a nice place to come to, a good way of meeting people and making friends. Adam and I don't make anywhere near as much of the facilities as we could. But then we are only interested in the swimming. Without our half-mile a day swim we'd feel dreadfully deprived. It has become one of the pivots of our life together.

The black woman bursts out laughing at my, 'Hello.' Her eyes shine with delight. 'Hi there, how're you doin'?'

We have this exchange every time I arrive. I can't make out whether it's my Englishness that pleases her so much, or the fact that I acknowledge her presence. I notice that few others ever greet her. But I have to because she's coloured, whilst aware of the condescension in my desire to make her feel important. Since every one else treats her as they treat each other, with a mixture of friendly indifference, they are paying her the greater compliment. They regard her as their equal, whether or not she is an employee of the establishment, regardless of her being black. To them she is a fellow woman and as such a sister. I am years behind in terms of this liberation.

I glance up at the big clock as I enter the locker room and approach a free locker. Security is ultra-strict in this place – even so there are warnings pinned up on the walls to keep an eye on one's belongings. Last week I stupidly left my watch in the bottom of my locker and realising this I rang as soon as I reached our apartment back at the Eden. But it was too late, the watch had disappeared.

'That's two watches you've lost in the last ten months,' Adam had said. An hour later I came back to him.

'Let's look at it another way. That's two watches I've lost in ten years.' Irritating when you can't think of the snappy answer right away.

I keep meaning to buy myself a new watch. A cheap one which I'd be cheerful to lose.

I start to undress, looking out of the corner of my eye at a girl, thin enough surely to be anorexic, weighing herself on the scales. As far as I can see from here she is ninety pounds, but this doesn't have the same meaning to me as when I translate it into stones and pounds in the English way. Six stone, six.

She remains rooted on the scales, staring with disbelief at the outcome. As she turns away I see that her lower lip is trembling, there are not many such troubled souls in the Y.

'Hi!' I look across the room, halfway into my swimsuit. A friendly wave accompanies the voice.

'Ah, hello.' I wave back. One day I must try to get over my blockage about using 'Hi' as a greeting. Hello sounds so stuffy and blimpish somehow. This informality thing takes some getting into.

The person I'm waving to is someone who had advertised a fur coat, forties style, when we first started coming to the Y. And I had answered the ad feeling the coat might be just the thing with the weather getting as cold as it is. But the colour had been wrong, too brown for me. Still the owner and I had 'gotten along fine'. The only thing is that I still have no idea what she's called. It would be embarrassing if I were expected ever to introduce her to someone else. We are on too good terms now for me to ask her name.

She is an attractive woman, in her mid to late thirtes. Her hair is grey, cut into a long bob, which makes her look older than her years. But that may only be because of my own feelings regarding grey hair.

Her face looks pleasantly 'lived in', a crooked mouth and small, lively eyes that laugh a lot. I look immediately at the left hand, at the married finger, from force of habit still. To see if it carries a gold ring on it. Old-fashioned. It means nothing now, the matrimonial band of gold. The sophisticated young don't bother with marriage, the sophisticated middle-aged have dispensed their spouses. Only Adam and I remain married, but even I am considering removing my wedding ring. It is no longer the thing to flash around as it used to be, 'look at me – I am lucky enough to have caught a husband.' I could survive on my own.

Now why am I thinking these thoughts? Why have they started to creep into mind? And when did they even begin to formulate?

There is a permanently funky (my new American word) odour in the female quarters of the Y. Fresh sweat, old sweat, stinky feet, stale armpits, menstruation, farts. All these are never quite eliminated by the camouflaging sweetness of talcum powder, spray deodorant, and the concoctions of coconut oil and cream which so many of us use. There is a continuous assault of agreeable sounds. Lockers being slammed and kicked, voices calling back and forth, showers spattering followed by a shriek about the icy water, a whoosh as the steam room door is opened, hair dryers roaring into action.

Once out of street clothes, members don their own idiosyncratic gym costumes. Leotards with stirrup tights; jogging shorts and tee-shirts, leg-warmers, flannel sweat pants, Spandex, Danskin, knee-socks. And just about everyone has a theory about the best unform, so she swears by a magic formula of club activities: swim, sauna, steam; run, swim, sauna; martial arts, sauna, shower.

But I'm still too shy to join in with all the banter. Heads turn even now at the sound of my British voice. I don't yet fully believe that I belong. So I wrap myself in my towel, modestly, to make my way up the staircase to the sixth floor. BUSINESS MEN'S SAUNA and SWIMMING POOL, it says above the door. And I slink in, past the guy at the door. His name is Curly, I know that at least. We greet each other with silent smiles, but one day soon I shall pluck up courage and say, 'Hi Curly!', just like everyone else. That way he will make an effort to find out what my name is. He is friendly and polite enough to do that, I know. By these small means I shall start to feel more at home in this city. It's all got to come from me in the end.

Adam is already in the pool, he is usually faster than me at getting undressed. I linger in the locker room listening to everything. He claims there is considerably less action in the mens' locker room, that nobody speaks to each other at all. Which I find hard to believe. I am convinced that this place must be a hot-bed of homosexual cruising between the male members. Perhaps Adam needs his eyesight retesting.

I have this impression, that all the men (even Curly?) are gay, because of their physiques. They are all so fit, so well-developed where they should be developed. I don't just mean down there – though I have to admit that these days I am looking at very little else when I am up in the pool. Being one of the minority – far fewer women swim that men – I have plenty of opportunity to reflect on male bodies.

All of them work out, it seems. I have never been so surrounded by pectorals as pronounced as these in my life. Or by such bulging biceps. The men in my life would all have run like lunatics from any body-improvement programme. The mind is what occupied their time and effort. Anything else would have been dismissed as vanity. It is only since our arrival in the States that it has occurred to Adam and me that all this (aside from vanity) is related to health. Health and the ascetic pleasure given to others. That and the difference that a good body must make to one's love life. If one were single, of course (or depraved perverts such as us).

I look down at Adam swimming sleekly through the water. They have a very civilised swimming procedure here in the Y pool. One must wait in line, seated at the edge of the pool, until a lane becomes free, before one is allowed into the water. That is if you wish to have a swimming lane (like the Olympic champions) all to yourself. Otherwise you just take your chance and swim in the circuit-lane, following on the tail of the swimmer in front of you. Round and around, up and down, up and down. This is what I prefer to do, the pressure is less. No one is staring at you waiting for your place – perhaps a more competent swimmer who considers it a waste that you are in one of the single lanes which would be better employed by himself.

But Adam likes to use the more professional lane, he always chooses to wait his turn until one becomes vacant. Sometimes it means that I have swum my half hour, my half-a-mile before he has even stepped a toe in the pool. In which case I dawdle in the ladies' locker room. I wash my hair and dry it more carefully than usual. Or I put on a more special face of make-up, whilst looking discreetly around me at all the girls in their various stages of undress. And listen in on their conversations. I love it. Waiting for him to finish is no hardship at all. It would be different if it were the other way round, I'm sure. Adam doesn't care to wait for anyone. Not even me.

He cleaves through the water from one end of the pool to the other, turning adroitly when he reaches the end and continuing as though there had been no interruption at all. When we met he couldn't swim at all. Had never swum, had been timid of the sea. One holiday, the first that we shared abroad, he had stood anxiously at the edge of the ocean wildly waving me in from where I was swimming when I wasn't even out of my depth!

Then he took lessons, goaded on by me. Now he has easily overtaken me, in style, speed and confidence. I may have more dogged endurance, that's all. Otherwise, the competetiveness is typical of his approach to everything. 'Simply a question of learning how.'

He is wearing his contact lenses beneath the goggles that all the serious swimmers wear in the pool. Or are these his new goggles, the ones with his prescription lenses actually in them? I must remember to ask him. I don't wear goggles, but then I keep my head above water when I swim. It looks amateurish, as if I don't have the correct breathing technique. But it's to do with wearing my eye make-up really. There are just three of us who swim with make-up on. One is a person of my age group, who wears light, bright-pink lipstick and rouge. The other is a young model with lashings of mascara and shaped cheeks but no lipstick. The three of us acknowledge each other with small smiles, as if we are sharing a secret that the bare-faced girls amongst us with their natural appearances are missing out on. And these others probably regard us with the same tolerant contempt. Fat is a feminist issue, so it is proclaimed. And the use of cosmetics is open to query from that same faction.

Adam catches sight of me and waves up. His smile transforms the irregular features of his face, reveals his good teeth, dimples the one cheek, and makes him irresistibly attractive. To me.

I wave back, watching his long body turn. His legs are the legs that I would really have liked for myself, the sort that go on forever. Marrying him was the next best thing to owning them, and better really because they are always there for me to admire on him. I am not the only one staring in appreciation. Two guys in the line-up for those swimming lanes are gazing speculatively at Adam too. There is not too much conversation in the hushed atmosphere of the pool area, the air is heavier with the concentration of the swim. The only real contact is eye contact, nothing much spoken. Certainly not between members of the opposite sex. Adam and I are the only couple, married or otherwise, who swim together. And as such are the subjects of a certain curiosity. The British accents intrigue as well.

'Have you ever had a homosexual encounter, Adam? Any of that sort of stuff?' I had asked him very early on when we were still at that stage of finding everything out about each other.

'You really want to know?'

'I wouldn't have asked otherwise.'

'Once.'

'Only once? Once what? I'm avid for details.'

'Was with a student of mine, many years ago. I was pissed, we both were. The evening ended with me shagging him, but anything would have done. He just happened to be there that's all. Hardly edifying.'

'You mean you stuck your dick up his bum?'

'I think I did. If I didn't I certainly meant to, but I might have aimed way off the mark. I remember sucking his cock though, that I do remember.'

'Why do you remember that?'

'So bloody nice, I suppose.'

Cherry is due round for a drink in about half an hour. Not just for a drink, obviously, this is a pre-arranged date. The three of us are going to bed together (though it's only five-thirty in the afternoon).

'When it's all over maybe we'll go to the cinema, or something,' I say in a brave voice to Adam.

'It's not an operation, Eve, my darling. "When it's all over", indeed!'

'Don't laugh at me.' I am nervous, unhappy about it all. I was feeling like this when it was being planned for the four of us. Roger was meant to be in on it at first, but has had to fly off to London on business. It was Cherry who suggested that we could get on with things without him.

'But that leaves us short of a man, doesn't it, Cherry?'

'So?' She'd laughed at the other end of the phone. Adam, on our own telephone extension, had echoed her laugh. 'More for me to enjoy,' he'd said it with such obvious relish that a sudden rage had swept through my body. But I'd remained silent, saying nothing. What I was feeling was a terrible jealousy. Why was I not enough for him? Why were we even considering sharing ourselves with anyone else? It was on the tip of my tongue to say why not cancel. Why not wait until Roger gets back to have our affectionate orgy – as Cherry called it. It was all right for Cherry, she did this sort of thing all the time. She spent her life in bed with married couples. 'Cementing their marriages.' But ours doesn't need cementing, it's idyllically happy. I didn't voice any of this though. I didn't want to be thought a spoil-sport. And that's why Cherry is due in half-an-hour's time.

368

'Did you put the champagne in the fridge, Adam?' I call from the bathroom. I am having a second shower, though I am perfectly clean already. And I know that Adam has put the champagne in because I saw him do it only an hour ago. But I have to keep on talking, I can't bear to think about things. I am actually dreading what is about to take place. It's all so, so *premeditated*, so *unspontaneous*. Falling into bed drunk and irresponsible is one thing, that's excusable – but doing it in the full light of day is another thing altogether.

Adam pokes his head through the shower curtain. 'It's in the fridge. Would you like a glass, my angel?' He looks so loving, so familiar, so reassuringly as he's always looked with his close-cropped hair, and his twinkling eyes, and his curling-up mouth, that I have to kiss him. Just that. Scraping my teeth on his teeth and dripping water all down his front.

'Oh, Adam,' I choke, holding his head between my hands and staring, stricken, straight into his eyes. 'Is all this all right? Do we know what we're doing?' The telephone is there on the table, Cherry won't have left yet. There's still time to call it all off. I am praying that the suggestion to do so will come from him, that I will be spared from making it. No such luck.

'Glass of champagne coming up.' He disentangles himself, gently, as if not to hurt my feelings. Nevertheless he disappears.

I continue to stand, disconsolately, under the streaming water, going over and over in my mind – as I have done so often lately – all the times in the past when we've been together with Cherry. Had Adam expressed any particular interest in Cherry then? Were there undercurrents between them that I had been insensitive to? Was he falling in love with her now?

By the time he returns, two glasses in hand, I am feeling as sorry for little me as it's possible to feel. Christ, I'm beginning to bore myself!

'Are you in love with her? Would you rather that I dress and go out before she arrives? You don't want me hanging around gawping at the two of you on the job, do you? It would be better, don't you think, if you were both to go off and have an affair on your own? I honestly wouldn't mind as much as I mind this now . . .' There, I've said it! I can't look at him, I'm too appalled by my outburst. I can't bear to look at his upset face.

There is no answer, no reply. My eyes are tightly shut now so that I can't tell whether he has quietly left without saying a word, or whether he is still there. Still there with a pitying expression on his humorous face. That I couldn't bear.

I open one eye, and then I open the other in startled surprise as I feel his nakedness against my own. He has stripped off his clothes and stepped into the shower with me.

'What are you doing – what!' I gasp, then start laughing. Hysterically laughing within seconds as he seizes the soap and starts lathering it over my breasts and then under each arm. And then he plunges it down in between my legs. 'Adam . . . Adam, no, no . . .' I'm convulsed. It must be ages since we were in the shower together. As much as a year? Even longer! The realisation of that gives me a jolt. At one time back in England we used to spend hours in the bathroom, we used to treat it as an extension of the bedroom. Our special playground for doing dirty deeds together, dreaming up dirtier and dirtier ones all the time. Pissing on each other, that sort of thing (though we've never told anyone *that*!).

'She'll be here in a minute – she'll catch us in the shower – Adam, stop it!'

'Who will catch us in the shower?' He is down on his knees now, pressing his wet face into my soapy pubic hairs and holding me firmly to him with a hand on each of my buttocks.

'Cherry will, you fool.' I still can't stop laughing. Oh, but I wish she wasn't coming. Especially when I hear Adam's next sentence.

'Ah, Cherry – our lover! Best place to greet her, here in the shower. Get the proceedings off to the right start.'

That does it. I stop laughing, it's not very funny. 'Champagne? Where did you put it, I could do with my glass now.' I'm trying to keep my voice as light as possible. I'd like to crash the glass in splinters through his scalp.

The telephone, the internal one, rings as he reaches

through for the drinks. It will be Cherry downstairs in the hotel lobby to say that she has arrived. No one comes straight up without ringing first. New Yorkers refuse to answer their doors unless they are expecting a specific caller. Security measures.

I listen to Adam telling Cherry to come right up, his greeting sets off a downward spiral of depression in me. I turn off the shower and step quickly out of the bathroom, dragging my white terry towelling robe around me. In the mirror ahead of me all I can see is the unrecognisable face of a stranger. Wild-eyed and grim-faced.

'Christ, I look awful!' I say. And I grab the glass of champagne from Adam's hand, drinking it all down in one gulp. 'Quick, another,' I gasp. My heart is racing, I feel sick. Like the very first time all over again.

'Are you always going to need a drink before we try to make love, Evelyn?' That's what the boy had said, plaintively complaining. The operative word had been 'try' in his case, or rather in those days. It had eventually taken a fifty-year-old *roué* with a French mistress and three ex-wives to crack me open without the aid of alcohol. All fifteen stone of him. A case of brute force. He's dead now, that darling of a man.

'You're acting like a virgin being led to the slaughter, Eve.'

'That's what I feel like, Adam.' I look at him coldly. I feel it's all his fault and I want him to know and not enjoy himself because of the friction that I'm deliberately setting up between us. But I think now that I've left it too late. Either that or he is so over-excited by what is about to take place, that he is not receiving any of my desperate wavelengths. Shit. The doorbell rings.

'Answer the door. Here comes your date, Adam.' There can be no mistaking my sneer, each syllable is spliced with venom. But Adam, eyes shining, leans forward to squeeze me. '*Our* date, my darling.' He sounds like a small boy at Christmas, about to open his presents. It was this quality of boyishness, combined with what I perceived to be a sophisticated wit, that had drawn me to Adam in the first place. Now I can only see how inappropriate his enthusiasm is in a man of his years. Almost forty and behaving like a fourteen-year-old. I must have a serious word with him about it later.

'Cherry, darling!' I stand rooted to my same spot, listening

371

to his silly voice, smarming with false charm, lathering all over our unwelcome guest. For the life of me I cannot bring myself to go forth and greet her. Let the bitch make her own way in – on the arm of my husband. She has never been a particularly close friend of mine anyway. If it hadn't been for Scot, our old friend (now, alas, dead), we would never even have got to know her. Not someone with this much of an age-gap between us. A girl too old to be a friend to any of our kids, and too young to be part of our circle. Except as a piece of stuff for one of our friends, a lady-killer such as Scot. Someone who we'd already seen through several failed marriages. It was only from loyalty and affection for his memory that we had ever shown any warmth to this girl after his death. And now she turns out to be the viper in the woodpile. The instrument of wreckage in our marriage – just as she had been between Scot and his last wife. It is with great difficulty that I form my stiff lips into a smile, waiting for her to come in from the hall. I am trying to capture a lasting impression of her, one to mull over in my mind after she's gone.

The first thing that strikes me is how, how *sunny* she looks. Is she wearing yellow – a colour associated with the quality of sunshine? She looks as if she has been running, as if she couldn't wait to get here (to grab hold of my husband in her strong, young arms). There is a sense of fresh air and breathlessness about her. As her eyes fall upon my (resentful) face, they light. Really light up, start to sparkle and laugh.

'Eve, darling!' she says it in a kind of breathy whisper. As if we share secrets that no one could possibly guess at. Despite myself I am responding and meaning it too.

'Cherry, little Cherry.' I hold out my arms, aware that the towelling robe is falling open to reveal my full nudity. She rushes forward to be held by me, hugging my neck and smothering my face with small butterfly kisses.

'Oh, I've *missed* you so much,' she is breathing in my ear. 'I really have, I really have.'

My grasp on her tightens to show that I understand completely, as if to let her know that I have missed her too. As if I have thought of very little else but her since we parted (which is perfectly true. The cow).

'I've been thinking about you,' I whisper back. Looking

over his shoulder I can see Adam's delighted face. His torso is still dripping with water from the shower, down onto the emerald green towel which he's secured around himself for modesty's sake. He is still brown from last summer, there is a thin strip of white circling his left wrist where he wears his watch. And a matching pale shade beneath the towel – which we will doubtless see in a moment. That thought clouds my present engulfing euphoria. I can't stand here embracing Cherry like this forever – at some point the action will commence.

'Champagne, Cherry?' Adam breaks the spell.

'Mm, mm, lovely.' I release our guest as she stirs in my arms. She spins around to look at him, running her eyes appreciatively over his body as she does so, whilst encircling one of my breasts with a cupped hand.

'Have you two sexpots already started without me? I'm feeling decidedly overdressed.' And she unwinds her wintry scarf and peels off her chunky sweater, and the woolly vest beneath it. No bra, I note. No need for a bra. I envy that. All my life I have had to wear a brassiere, starting at twelve years of age when my breasts were as big as my buttocks. Each one of them fuller than my face, perched up high on my frame, come-hither birds on my rib cage. And though, since then, they have shrunk to less spectacular proportions in relation to the rest of me, I still have not enjoyed the rare occasions of being without 'support'. For a brassiere does more than control, divide, restrict, and uplift – as the advertisements boast. It protects, it shields, it provides a defence against the lustful attentions of the male species. Once, crossing a busy thoroughfare on a sweltering summer day, clad merely in my working jeans and a cotton tee-shirt, I all but caused a full-scale collision of vehicles. The traffic lights were about to change and in order to reach the centre of the road in time I was forced to run for my life. My mammary glands were my undoing. They bounced about me like beach-balls, uncontrollable in their excitement at having been taken for a trot. Like toddlers let loose, like puppies off the leash, they hurled themselves this way and that in their happiness. Oh, how I longed for the despised brassiere then! What could have persuaded me into relinquishing it I can't imagine, probably the pressures of fashion when every fashion photograph showed parades of models with nipples flaring on flat chests. Not a cleavage in sight, considered old-fashioned. And all the young girls, my own daughters, jiggling joyfully around town. I returned to the protective comfort of my 34C cups (36C at certain times of the month).

'Lovely titties, lovely little ones, Cherry,' I say generously. The envious bile is alive in my throat.

'Don't be cruel,' she laughs cheerfully. 'Nothing here worth writing home about.' And she looks down at herself and pulls a face. 'What I'd really like are your magnificent pair, Eve.'

Adam steps forward towards us both. 'Quality, not quantity. That's what you've got, Cherry darling.'

I look at him. It's as if he has smacked me across the face. But it's left to Cherry to retrieve the moment. 'Eve has both.' I shall save up asking Adam what he meant by his remark until later.

'Cheers, Girls! He raises his glass, unaware of what hell is in store for him when we will be alone again.

'Cheers!' Cherry echoes, unaware too of the corrosion she is causing to my stomach-lining. Medical expenses are astronomically high in the States. They don't have the financial harbour of the British National Health scheme. I wonder if sexual jealousy would be accepted as a justifiable cause of an incapacitating malaise on an insurance claim. And are we still insured since our arrival in America, or was that policy simply to cover loss, illness and accident whilst travelling? I must remember to ask Adam, if I ever speak to him again. 'Empty glass, angel?' The swine is addressing me now, but all I can do in place of answering him is thrust my glass forward and nod like a mute. He is going to have to get used to this form of exchange.

Cherry is now down to her tights, her panty-hose as they call them here. Pale turquoise, to tone in with the stylish boots she has on over the navy-blue corduroy dungarees. She dresses well, but conventionally, I have always noted with my consummately skilled eye. The sort of girl who adds charm to a table setting, brings a feminine grace to a party gathering without necessarily elevating it to a higher sartorial plane. Yet when fellow guests know that I will be present they strive to greater efforts to compete, unsuccessfully as it turns out. But it all makes for more fun, the dressing-up part, it introduces frivolity. An element I admire.

I must be frivolous now, if only to relieve my own suffering.

'Isn't it time for a little frivolity, boys and girls?' I gesture towards the bed.

'You're our leader – thought you'd never ask!' Excruciating boyishness from Adam as he bounds forwards. 'Oh, whoops – there goes my modesty. Naked as nature intended.' His towel has fallen from his loins (wouldn't you guess). I see with satisfaction that his bum seems especially spotty. They call them 'zits' over here, the American for boils and pimples. A much more descriptive word. I look forward to informing Romeo what a zitsy arse he has, I shall say it the very second that Cherry shuts the door on her departure. Just to wipe the smarmy post-coital smile off his simpering chops . . .

'Great idea,' grins our guest and bounds bedwards to join my husband. (*By the time I join them his erection is in, right up to her epiglottis, wavering an exuberant greeting to her womb on the way. When she opens her mouth to smile at me I swear I can see the tip of his dick down there with her tonsils. Easing up to trickle its spunk out all over her tongue. If I kiss her, as she is inviting me to do now, I'll be able to suck him off with Cherry's body strung out on the length of his prick between us. The loathsome, lecherous toad . . .*)

I am imagining this as I sit on the lavatory seat staring catatonically into space. I have left the bathroom door open onto the bedroom. To torment myself further with the filthy sounds of their fornication. I have no intention of joining in – ever. Sod the both of them, they can get on with it together, get on with their sordid game.

'What on earth are you doing now, Eve?' Adam appears suddenly before me. He is wearing a bewildered expression on his face. He has no sign of an erection.

'Piddling,' I mutter, amazed. Why on earth is his dick so limp?

'What's she doing?' I hear Cherry shout from the bed. 'Come on darling.' Who does 'darling' refer to? My absent husband? Or does he mean me?

I remember how it felt, accompanying my older sister on her early dates. 'Mind you take care of little Evelyn, don't lose her now,' my mother would warn my blossoming sister. But I wasn't a spoil-sport, even at that tender age. And I didn't intend to be one now. Let them have their fun and games. Perhaps I could slip off to the cinema . . .

'Piddling, so she says,' Adam calls back to Cherry. They are talking about me.

'Come on, Eve! Get her out here, Adam, so that we can start the proceedings. No fun till the three of us are on it.'

'Come on, silly.' Adam is on his knees, kissing me all over my face, stroking my neck and hugging my shoulders. 'We've been waiting for you. *You.*' He lifts my chin to look straight into my dull eyes, I can see their drabness reflected in his own bright pupils. I probably have never loved anyone in my whole life as much as I love this man at this moment.

'Just coming!' I shout back at my best friend in the bed. 'Just making myself fragrant for my two favourite people!' And I join in their joint laughter, spraying myself extra-vagantly with *Bal A Versailles* (the French perfume I share with Elizabeth Taylor and Her Majesty The Queen). But before leaving the bathroom I slip into a black satin nightgown, one that encloses my breasts in sheaths of intricate lace (whilst still allowing for nipple-sucking).

'Mm, sexy.' This gown is a favourite of Adam's. Why, knowing that, have I worn it so seldom, choosing instead the unflattering comfort of my old-fashioned flannelette? When we were first together I wore nothing in bed at all, wouldn't have dreamed of doing so. I delighted in the all-night contact of our skins, relishing rubbing myself against him, taking every opportunity to arouse him. And then one bitterly cold Cornish winter, staying with friends in their unheated country retreat I took to wearing my monstrosity. I'd found it in an antique shop, frilled and furry to the touch, totally enveloping in its Victorian modesty. Like returning to the warmth of the womb. The following summer, it must have been in that same year, we had a heatwave. Instead of spending sweltering nights trying to separate our sticky bodies in bed I wore a gauzy silk slip. Adam said it excited him, the feel of me beneath the slipperiness, the way that the material clung to my nipples. And how it fell between my buttocks. One night we tried it on him. I wanted to take a photograph of his erection, with him lying down it looked like a ludicrous tent. He refuses to pose, saying that if the photograph were to fall into the wrong hands it wouldn't do his reputation as a serious artist any good at all. I thought it would make him even more interesting to his public. He said that he was thinking of posterity. And of the people who actually purchase his paintings. I remember how pretty he looked in female attire (for the silk shift wasn't the only thing we tried on him).

I look down at myself, then twirl into the bedroom. 'Fashion show for you, Cherry!' My exuberance is evaporating, I must do everything to hang onto it.

'Oh, I *love* that, really sexy! Is there one for me to put on?' She is lying naked across the bed, legs wide open. Masturbating. I tear my eyes away from her face and let them rest upon her busy fingers, just for a moment. Embarrassment forces my voice up two tones higher, she is continuing to play with herself freely.

'You don't want to wear anything, darling – not at your age. Does she, Adam?' And I laugh, a thin constrained sound. 'Nightgowns and negligees are for old girls like me whose bodies have seen better days.'

'But I *love* dressing up, let me wear something. You must have masses of marvellous things – make her, Adam, bring me something.' Her radiant face turns from me to him but the rest of her remains unchanged. Her hand continues to rub rhythmically around and around, in and out, up and down . . . I won't allow myself to look at Adam's face, I couldn't bear to see the expression, for if he is anything of a man he is finding this terribly arousing. This abandoned hussy on our bed.

'Well,' I drawl the words, finding it difficult to speak naturally. 'Let me think now, what would suit you. You and your colouring.' Surely Adam must have an erection by now! Despite myself, though everything in me warns against doing so, I move towards him and (as if without meaning to) I brush my hand across the top of his thighs. His cock jerks immediately to attention, springing eagerly up against my knuckles as if all it had been waiting for was my blessing. My permission to appear interested.

Now I am excited too, suppurating where I should be. Wanting to feel something hard and firm between my own flanks. Ready for action, or else.

'Phew,' I say, pretending to sway, leaning my full weight against my tall husband. 'Is it my imagination or does it seem tremendously hot in here?'

'Pretty steamy my way!' Cherry parts her legs even wider. She's a jogger, she jogs something like an hour every morning. She's trying to show off how double-jointed she's become. Either that or she's trying to tell us something.

'Are you trying to tell us something? I think the child is trying to tell us something, Daddy.'

'Less of the "Daddy", Mummy.' Adam pinches my arse. 'Perhaps we should attend to the child.'

Cherry wriggles around, removing her fingers from the vital spot, and throws her legs up in the air like a little baby. This way, I am pleased to see, her upper limbs look even more substantial than usual. Thick on the thigh. She has the sort of shape that one sees on ancient statues, Venus de Milo. High, small, tight tits. Solid arms and legs And a well sculptured torso in between. Her hands are square and capable, but the fingertips are tapering. She has a sensitive touch, as befits an artist (she constructs intriguing objects from flmsy fabrics around centres of crudely cast metal). As befits a person as keen on playing with her own pussy as she obviously is.

I am pleased as well, ridiculously so, with my 'child' and 'Mummy and Daddy' line. It seems only right to treat Cherry as something outside our marriage, too young to be anything of a serious threat. Our baby, for us to share between us, a person from another generation.

It's all bollocks, this reasoning. Cherry is twenty-nine now, the age-gap between her and dear old Scot was even wider than it is between us and her. Especially wider than the age-gap between her and Adam. Whilst I could (causing a scandal in my own family) just about be old enough to be her mother, Adam would have had to sire her at something like ten years of age. Possible, I suppose, considering how early he flared into puberty (losing his virginity at the age of thirteen, father of his own three by the age of twenty). But not probable.

But she likes being treated as the baby, Cherry. She enjoys it. I can remember that Scot used to treat her like that, indulging her, dressing her up like a little doll one day and like an ingénue whore the next. Girls do like it. I used to myself, when my lovers were all of them veterans of the world. Worldly and wealthy – and unbelievably ancient. 'Why on earth would you bother with old men like these, Evelyn?' my girlfriends, my flatmates, my colleagues, would say to me. Bewildered that I failed to share their enthusiasm for dashing young blades in bright scarlet sports cars. Or for pimply – zitzy – intellectuals in turtle-neck sweaters (worn high to the ears to hide a crop of fresh boils). Existing on diets of cornflakes and Kafka. And they wouldn't have understood, even if I'd bothered to try to explain, that special *cossetting* that old men can give to a young girl. That daring expression of the desire for one's father (grandfather yet!) that had up till now been stifled and denied.

But something tells me that Adam does *not* represent a father-figure to Cherry. Whether she regards me as a mother-replacement is quite a different question.

I am shutting my mind to the possibilities that all this mental conjecture is presenting to me. Time to get on with things.

We land on the bed together, Adam and I, one each side of our guest. And she enfolds us both equally with her strong arms, so that suddenly we are snout to snout with a nipple in each of our mouths. It feels surprisingly nice in this position, meeting each other this way. I smile at Adam with my eyes and he winks. Cherry's hands are busy below.

She has managed to manipulate herself into such a position that she has hold of my clitoris in one hand and Adam's cock in the other. My own fingers trace a path down to her private (no longer) parts – and encounter Adam's fingers there already. We join forces, tapping and stroking together. Cherry is moving in a different rhythm to ours, but we quickly adapt so that now the whole bed is rocking to-and-fro, creaking exultantly. It has never been called upon to take more than the two of us before.

379

I glance down at myself, delighting in the sexual pleasure that I'm feeling, but still preoccupied with self-doubt. There is an uneasiness that prevents me from letting myself go with the same abandonment that I usually bring to my fucking with Adam. A part of me is outside this triangle, looking on. And worrying. Wondering whether or not he finds her soft cunt springier than mine. Mine that has stretched to afford access to the bodies of my two living babies (hardly babies now!). Mine which has folded limply back into itself with the grief at the loss of the last eagerly cherished foetus. And before that the discreet and expensive abortion.

Oh yes, it's been through some battles this genial uterus, and if the scars aren't exactly in evidence, the elasticity can't possibly be as taut as at the start of my sexual indulgences. That's the forfeit that any woman pays for the pleasurable pain, the pain and the pleasure (correction) of bearing children. But at this moment I am experiencing regret. I would like to be young again. Very much.

While I've been thinking all this, things have been happening beside me. Turning my head I see that my husband is kissing my friend, Cherry, on the mouth. And she is kissing him back.

They are kissing each other. *No one is kissing me. This has never happened before.*

My first reaction is to get up and go – in a huff. Back to the bathroom to contemplate my (wrinkled) navel. My wrinkled navel, compared to the navel of Cherry's is one of the causes of my self-disgust. Where did my other one go? The one, like hers, that resembled a child's, no more than the indentation made by a drop of rain falling in snow. Instead of this poorly planted raisin, set in a haphazard field of fine furrows. Where has my *smmoooth* stomach gone? No wonder my husband seeks sexual solace elsewhere, in the firmer flesh of youth, in the poreless surface of perfection (near perfection – no not even that – the arse leaves a *lot* to be desired).

But I don't get up and go. I've been reared in England where boys and girls at school are taught to be gallant losers. Instead I lie there and contemplate just how drab my future will be without the solace of a husband by my side.

Well, I think to myself, at least I'm in the right country, at the right time. Women, betrayed wives, divorced or bereft from death, widows, women who have never married – all are flourishing here and are in the pink. Every magazine I flick through gives bracing reports on how expendable men have become. Just this month there have been startling statistics published on the strides that women have made in the professional fields over here. In banking, medicine, journalism (not just on the fashion pages), law, even in the previously male dominated movie industry. Is it Universal or United Artists, one of those movie companies anyway, which is being run by a thirty-five-year old girl? Ousting all the males who were in line for the promotion . . .

And it will be nice for Cherry to settle down and rear a family. Only last time we met (before we all fell into bed) she was saying what yearning emotions the sight of small children aroused in her these days.

Except that Adam has had a vasectomy. An irreversible vasectomy. One in the eye for old Cherry. She and Adam will have to adopt. As for me I shall take up the single life again.

Two

'Yeah – well, like we'd been up all night and it was nearly noon and I was all for getting rid of this guy. But you know, well, we'd been pals for a long time and I hadn't run into him since college – so I figured it was somehow easier to throw him a fuck than politely ask the poor sod to leave . . .' The speaker adjusts her outsize glasses, smoky-brown at the top fading out to absolute transparency on the cheek. Flattering glasses, chosen with skilled self-knowledge and care like everything this girl has on. Transforming a short-sighted, stooping spindle into a supremely self-assured, sexually attractive feminine package. Complacent, and coldly frigid to the core. Or is this a tritely superficial snap-judgement on my part? Am I falling prey to the New York habit of writing off people one meets at parties within mere moments of introduction?

I smile warmly and clink my empty glass against her empty one. 'We should drink,' I say jauntily, 'to these sort of fucks. It shows that you harbour a compassionate streak beneath your veneer of sophistication. Or should we consider it a screw of simple convenience? Either way it illustrates just how independent we women have become – able to decide which course of action to take. Proving that your body is yours, that you can do what you like with it.'

'Do you write too?' Her eyes sparkle behind the elegant specs. I nod, and a passing waitress takes the inclination of my head to mean that we need our glasses freshened with yet more liquor.

'When you say "too", does that mean that you wield the pen also? That you earn your livelihood this tortuous way?' I conjure a roguish grin to soften the heavy pedantry of my words. Too often in these past few months, I have been treated as some sort of serious academic – the combination, I assume, of my English accent and what I'm saying. So few seem to understand that I speak with tongue in cheek. Perhaps I am moving in the wrong circles.

This gathering that I am attending is a literary one, a party given to celebrate Mitzy Guttenberger's new volume of poetry. I am gate-crashing it, I have entered without having received an invitation. I am a 'literary ligger'.

I have already been introduced to Mitzy Guttenberger, been photographed with her by a bevy of pressmen. 'Who

382

are you? Why are we being photographed together?'
There was ever such a tiny edge in Ms Guttenberger's
fluting tones, a lemon-juice flavour to her wide smile. 'I'm
a writer from England.' I'd repeated my name. But it
wasn't for that reason I'd been picked out for photographs. I was wearing one of my extraordinary hats, a
Carmen Miranda concoction filled with fruit such as
cherries. That hat has been photographed more times
than I can remember. It's what I wear when I desperately
want to be noticed, the fitting accessory for a ligger who
hasn't been invited. Looking as I do at this moment, no
one could possibly believe that I hadn't been on the
official list. I look as much as if I belong as anyone
present. Even as much as Ms Guttenberger herself. It
makes one think that to get ahead (as the ad says) all one
needs is a hat. What hours of writing time authors could
save themselves, what years of creative agony!

But we parted on good terms, Mitzy and myself. I was
forgiven for my presumption at posing beside her. And it
hadn't even been my idea in the first place. On arrival, my
heart pounding in anticipation of a humiliating scene
where I imagine being asked to leave as I sidle in, heads
had turned at the sight of my startling chapeau. 'Mon
dieu!' 'Who the hell is *that*!' 'Jeez, a walking fruit salad!'
But all passing comments were couched in admiring awe
as if I had to be a somebody to brave the moderate
confines of Madison Avenue with such extravagant
splendour.

That was when the photographers descended, first one
and then a streak of them searching for anything to make
an interesting snap for the picture editor's desk. 'Say, do
you know Mitzy? No? C'mon along here, I'll introduce
you two. Just wanna get a shot of that hat – make some
picture – hey, where you from anyway? London, great!'
And with that I had found myself hustled through the
waiting crowds, throngs of literary groupies surging to
shake Ms Guttenberger by the hand, or at least get a
closer peek at her.

So now I'm basking in my momentary success, long
since edged to the outer fringes of the frenetic sycophants
(who for a few fraught seconds back there pressed me for
my autograph too, not even knowing who on earth I may

be). No one knows who I am in New York, I am becoming used to that now. My reputation hasn't spread this far. And even if it had, no one would be overly impressed. To become a celebrity here one has to achieve it in their terms. In American terms, by their standard of acclaim and best-sellerdom, and big money. And all these so far have eluded me. But there is plenty of time for it, the dream, to come true. Everyone in this city harbours the same aspirations, they are all waiting to be discovered. I have been discovered already – in my own country. This is a separate continent.

It is a double blow to my ego, this non-recognition. Suddenly, unexpectedly both my identities are under review and found to be wanting. That is how it appears to me. My sexual identity and my professional identity. I am no one all over again. My balance is shaky with the shock of it all.

But at the same time I am exhilarated, astonished that my nerves can still be so raw. That strong shafts of pain can still surface when I least expect them. That, instead of the dull ache of despair, the sort of despondency that could cause me to give up and retreat from the battle of life, I am alternately flooded by a fierce optimism and fearful vitality.

I am not resentful. This surprises me. 'I am not resentful, Adam,' I'd said to him.

'Resentful?' He'd answered, seeming to be astonished (astonishing in itself!). 'What's there to be resentful about? We're having a *gorgeous* time – aren't we? Your're not feeling homesick for England any more?'

It is touching, Adam's solicitude. Without his sympathetic support I would have returned to England. Back to the warmth of family and friends, back to the security of professional respect, back to being a someone. Back to safely being his wife again, with nobody else in the bed.

It has seen some activity, our bed, this month. Busier than the back room in a brothel! But first I had to sort out my insecurities about Cherry, and the turning point came about when I decided to dress her up. When we played out our charade for the benefit of Roger and Adam, preparatory to the four of us fucking.

It took place on a Saturday, a Saturday evening, a

prearranged mini-orgy. I say mini-orgy because since then we have had others with more people. Six participants seems about the accepted number to qualify for a proper orgy with a generous interchange between partners. Fewer than that and it becomes more intense, more emotional, more like a proper (as compared to an improper) relationship.

The occasion was planned as a return surprise for Roger, who had spent ten days over in London on business. During that ten days, unbeknownst to him, Cherry had been to bed with us three times. Before he'd left New York on his trip he had taken her to dinner several times. 'Cherry is not overly interested in sex, you know. Nice lady, lovely lady, but not much of a one for the old beddikins – probably performs best with all of us in it like that first night. Wouldn't you say?'

Saturday night. Sex and then something to eat at a sumptuous restaurant. And us, Adam and me, staying the whole night. The venue was to the luxury loft in SoHo, belonging to a pal of Roger's in advertising. He was pretending to his wife that he was out of town for a weekend conference in Connecticut.

'Do you suppose Roger's wife is getting anything herself,' I'd said to Adam, 'in the way of dick, I mean?' But all he'd done was laugh, laugh and shake his head.

'You'll be thinking of starting up a Wives' Union next.'

'What do you mean by that remark, Adam?'

'For deprived wives. Why are you looking at me like that? You're hardly a deprived wife, are you? Eve, now Eve, come here to me – oh, don't start crying. What have I said now to upset my darling?'

I keep getting upset. For no reason at all I dissolve into the most ridiculous tears lately. 'Perhaps I'm pregnant,' that's what I said to Adam last week.

'Maybe you are, Eve. I admit I am becoming increasingly worried on your behalf in this respect. It's obvious that you are going to have to get some form of contraceptive device, I doubt if any of our fleeting lovers have had vasectomies like me. Even Roger, he hasn't, let alone any of these kids. And why should they, they will all want to start having children one day.'

'None of those came in me though. Neither did Roger.

I'm not pregnant.' I spoke emphatically. 'I'm too old, you don't get pregnant at my age. Over the age of forty there is only something like a one-in-a-thousand chance of becoming pregnant.'

'Rubbish!'

'Not rubbish. I was reading it the other day.' I was onto a losing wicket here, I knew. No one can beat Adam on hard factual statistics. 'In any case,' I added hurriedly, 'no one has actually shot off inside me . . .'

'Penetration is more important than the proof of ejaculation, Eve.'

'Yes, well, I must see about getting protection.'

'Would be the wisest course if we are to go on having fun like this. You must accept the responsibility for your own body, nobody else can. I am just here to advise you.'

'Is that all?' I'm near to tears again, can hardly get the pathetic words out. Jesus wept, what a drip!

But I'd looked forward to the foursome with Roger and Cherry. 'I'm going to dress you up, my darling. It will be an erotic charade – don't ask me what I'll dress you up as, that is to be the surprise.' She'd squealed on the telephone, she likes a surprise. 'She's like a small child,' I'd said to Adam when I put the phone down.

'Yes, she's a charming girl.' He'd said it absently, concentrating on his work. The structure of a particular skycraper was giving him trouble.

'The breasts of a female giraffe are the largest of any in the animal world, barring those of a human. We are both mammals you know.' It was a test just to see how hard he was concentrating.

'Mm, delicious nipples,' he murmured.

'Who's, Cherry's nipples or the giraffe's?' My voice had a streak of steel running through it. But he didn't answer, I'd lost his attention altogether. But did he subconsciously think of Cherry's nipples even when he was working?

I took my American Express card with me when I went shopping for Cherry's outfit. 'Would you like to come with me, darling?' I'd invited Adam on the jaunt, but he had refused.

'You're better on your own at that sort of thing. What are you getting her anyway?'

'Just something to wear in bed.'

'Does that mean she won't have to borrow stuff of yours any more? I find it disorientating fucking her when she's wearing your flimsies. Get her something that's not black, for God's sake.'

'I'm getting her dressed up as an innocent, young and dewy,' I replied, 'to pinpoint the difference between us. I'm playing the experienced, older woman.'

'The sort I like best.' He said it as if he really meant it, only I knew that he didn't. Who in their right mind would?

The place I chose for Cherry's outfit was *Lovely Legends* on Ninth Avenue. A tiny shop selling retro clothes – or antique ones as we call them in Britain – everything in immaculate condition, exquisite, and expensive.

'I'm buying for my daughter,' I explained to the assistant (who turned out to be the owner). 'She's getting married and I thought to buy her something pretty for her honeymoon.' I didn't flinch as I lied to her so glibly. But why, I reflected on the way back to the Eden, hadn't I had the wit and courage to tell her the truth . . . 'My husband and I are having this affair at the moment with a girl called Cherry (short for Cheryl) and tonight we are staging a sexual diversion with this guy, Roger. The four of us, you know, are planning to screw the arse off each other. I thought I might play the role of Madame in a house of ill-repute and pleasurable delights of the flesh, introducing the "new girl" to her gentlemen clients – that's to be Cherry. So what I'm looking for is something innocently enticing. Not anything white – too virginal' – (can't test the credibility that far, not with Cherry's pair of know-it-all eyes!).

'Were you looking for something white for your daughter?'

'Hardly, these days!' We'd both laughed.

'It surprises me that she is getting married at all. Are the young still doing that in England? I can tell that's where you're from by your accent.'

When I presented her with what I'd chosen she complimented me. 'These are some of the cutest things I have here. What colouring is your daughter – she must be a blonde, yeah?'

I looked at my purchases, imagining Cherry in them.

Her small pointed breasts half-revealed in the peach-coloured silk kimono. The smooth curve of her stomach sloping beneath the satin sheen of the wide-legged French knickers, or were these called cami-knickers? I was always confused about that. Either way, wide-legged enough to allow entry of fingers, fists and erections.

'What I'm looking for now,' I watched the exquisite slithers of fabric being folded between layers of fine white tissue paper, 'are some matching silk stockings, a pair of garters, lacy ones with perhaps something like a small rosette on each. Oh, and some lace gloves. And a length of fine satin ribbon to be tied around the neck. All in shades of pale apricot and primrose, if that's possible.'

'Whew, the guy your daughter is marrying sure is fortunate. I could have done with a Ma-in-Law like you!'

'So could I,' I said, wondering if I had just the right shade of apricot lipstick for Cherry's lips and nipples, the proper dawn-pink powder to put on her cheeks and between her breasts. And in the round of her inner thighs.

One thing I didn't have to concern myself with was perfume. Amazingly enough, Cherry and I wear the same perfume. Not *Bal A Versailles*, which I reserve for special occasions (like that first time the three of us went to bed together – seems like years ago now). Not that one, but my other favourite, *Shalimar* by Guerlain. 'Handy that the two of us should wear this perfume. Anyone planning to be unfaithful to his wife should check on that first, so never to be found out. Never to be betrayed by the different perfume of his mistress. He should just keep giving the both of them the same one!' I'd thought I was clever to work that one out, to say it to Adam.

'What on earth makes you think that men haven't thought of that already?' That's what his answer had been.

But I wasn't able to buy the stockings or the lace gloves at *Lovely Legends*, excellent though their service had been in every other respect. Though they sweetly pointed me in the right direction to a place further along the same street where I did manage to find them. Looking at the slender width of the salmon-blush stocking-top I doubted whether Cherry's healthy thighs would squeeze into them. Then I realised that they wouldn't necesarily need to reach up that far. These stockings were purely (impurely) for decoration, erotic symbols of undress. To achieve the desired effect they merely needed to dribble down the leg – at any point above or beneath the knee. It would be miraculous if they survived the first thirty seconds without laddering anyway. The whole point of this exercise was the initial impact, I cared little what happened after that to any of the garments I had bought.

But passing over my American Express card, totting up that I had spent something like seventy dollars already (and so what!), my eyes fell upon a silky black smoking-jacket. Man-size. I bought it for Adam. Beneath it I imagined his long legs (and the tip of his cock when extended), and his tight buttocks. I'd have to ask him to bend over, Cherry and I together. He'd like that. We could fondle his private parts, both of us from behind . . .

For the first time I could feel myself getting sexually aroused by the adventure ahead. For the very first time I felt myself warming erotically towards Cherry. I couldn't wait to start dressing her up.

When we arrived at the loft, Roger was already there with Cherry. The atmosphere relaxed perceptibly with our entrance and with the opening of the first bottle of champagne.

'Cheers!' We all toasted each other, after kissing chastely on the cheeks. Then I took Cherry up to the sleeping quarters above, designed as a superior modern equivalent of a minstrel's gallery. The minute we were alone she embraced me, holding me tightly to her, pressing her fleshy pussy hard up against my own. This was before she had taken any clothes off, before I had even begun to excite her (and myself) with the strange delights of her new image.

'Hold on,' I said, drawing back, despite myself. Perhaps I could sense the recklessness of her mood and was afraid of getting involved in it too soon. For now she was trying to kiss me properly on the lips, her tongue sliding in and teasing my teeth, laying upon my own tongue like a trout making love to another. And I liked it too, something quivered in my clitoris. If I were male I could have boasted an incipient erection.

'You're getting me going, Cherry,' I tore my mouth away from her eagerness. Her mouth, looking at it now at such smudged close quarters, is one of Cherry's best facial points. A little like Jane Fonda's mouth, swollen at all times like a child's. Bee-stung lips, we used to call them. That's one of the things about getting older, you lose that pouting fullness. The lips become thinner with tension, altogether tighter and meaner compared with how they once were. It makes you immediately less enticing to kiss. Especially women who have attempted to recapture the former outline of their earlier mouths by painting new ones over the edges of what's there now. Lately I have taken to looking at mouths, having started to study just what it is in the faces of people my age that ages some more than others. And I have come to the conclusion that above all it is the expression, in the eyes first and foremost and then around the mouth. Sexual dissatisfaction wreaks havoc all round!

'It's you, Eve, you look so, so – in command tonight. Like some wonderful dominatrix – ooh, I'd just like you to tie me up and do cruel things to me. I would, really!'

I looked at her and then beyond her at my reflection in the mirror. This lush loft apartment was disappointingly short on mirrors, unlike our rooms back in the Eden. Cherry wouldn't appreciate that when it came to looking at herself in all my finery. I must take it out of its wrappings in a minute, watch the expression of thrilled delight on her dear little face – perhaps pretend that I have decided not to go ahead with my plans for the transformation. Just to enjoy her childish disappointment.

'You'd like that, would you? You'd like me to be cruel?' My reflection shimmered back at me, dark and dramatic like the wicked witch out of Snow White. The one that I had always been drawn to as a child, the image that had haunted my dreams back in bed for nights after, turning them into nightmares of the most deliciously terrifying kind. So much more fun than Snow White herself, that mealy-mouthed goody-goody, that household drudge content to clean house for her seven midgets!

'Have you ever played Snow White, Cherry?' I said cunningly, running my hands through her bonded hair. 'You'd be perfect for the part. Adam could be your Prince Charming.'

390

'And you could be the wicked witch, the beautiful step-mother . . .' Her blue eyes were shining.

'Right in one,' I said softly – and then I yanked harshly on her hair.

'Christ, you bitch!' She cried out before she could stop herself, raising her hand towards my face as if to strike me. But I was too quick for her, I caught the hand and forced it down.

'Slaves are not allowed to strike back at their mistresses,' I spoke coldly. 'Now get all your clothes off, you slut!' And I struck her as hard as I could across her cheek. Minutes later I was pleased to note that the red mark was still there, shiny in places where her tears has smeared over her face. When the time came, in a short while, I would tenderly wipe her skin clean, smoothing cologne to tone down the evidence of my unwarranted violence. But before that, young Cherry was going to have to apologise. It was to be clearly understood who was in control here from now on.

Adam would enjoy this fresh turn of events. Of late he has made the complaint that the affair with Cherry seemed to be heading into an unexciting cul-de-sac. Perhaps I had stumbled on the right solution. At least it provided me with some sort of role in this new sex life of ours. A way of including me in the action.

It was from that moment that I began to feel better. From then on I started to take a more active part in things. After all it was me who arranged our first real orgy. Me who collected the gang of participants together, me who picked up these 'perfect strangers'. I seem to have developed an enviable knack for this sort of thing.

But first I must dwell a little on the memorable evening with Roger and Cherry and Adam and myself. It was a kind of perfect one in its way. A little gem. And it presented me with the valued sight of Adam with another man's penis in his mouth. It was a first in all sorts of ways. Without that evening with Roger and Cherry none of the others would have taken place. I consider it as the starting point.

When we descended the stairs, I went ahead. 'Gentlemen clients,' I announced, 'I would like to introduce our new girl to you!' Cherry was waiting a few steps behind the bend in the stairs as I made this pronouncement. When she appeared, both Roger and Adam gasped. I was proud of my handiwork and turned myself to survey the results.

Cherry had never looked so entrancing. Who could have guessed that only minutes before she had licked the entire length of my snatch and intruded her tongue into my anus . . .

'I trust, gentlemen,' I spoke sternly, 'that you will be gentle with this child.' I held out my hand, which Cherry took with suddenly shy, timid fingers. Her eyes were downcast, her shoulders drooped gently, even the sturdy limbs appeared fragile and juvenile.

'You must stand like this,' I had told her, as I painted her face. And I'd pointed my toes deliberately inwards, with my knees inclined together. As my daughters used to stand through adolescence. She had reminded me of them, so trusting, so seemingly innocent. But far from giving me any twinges of conscience over this sexual charade, this apparent bespoiling of a young girl, I felt exhilarated. Wickedly and enjoyably sinful. We mothers can't remain responsible parents all our lives. There has to be a time when we're let out to play too, before we die.

It was the painting of the softly plump cheeks that had taken me back. My own cheeks are hard, so angular by comparison. My own eyes are so much deeper, set closer now to the skull, whilst Cherry's still sit on the surface – two fried eggs resting on the outer slopes of the shell. I watched my childrens' eyes gradually recede into their countenances. Newborn, they were as pop-eyed as lunatic people. Wild and vacantly staring.

I had changed into a Madame figure myself by this time.

'Oh,' Cherry had breathed, pouting, 'I like what you're wearing more than my own. You look better than me now. I should have been in black too.'

'Nonsense!' I'd been suitably sharp. Admittedly I did look pretty sensational, but I had planned it this way to provide a contrast between us – and a choice for the men. And I pointed this out to her, adjusting my black lacy waist cincher into place, deepening the swooping cleavage caused by the Merry Widow. Checking that my six-inch stilettos were not in danger of tearing the flouncing hemline of my negligee. Time then to make our grand entrance.

In the bedroom we took turns at using the actual bed – though we none of us really minded the floor, which made a perfectly good working surface too. The thing that surprised me most, and perhaps it surprised the others too, was the way that we ended up as two distinct couples. Adam and Roger, and Cherry and me. But there were moments before this that I now choose not to remember.

The most poignant was after Roger had rogered (cheap joke) me and I had watched over his heaving shoulder at Adam and Cherry making love. Strange that I should make this distinction. That the others 'made love' whilst I viewed what Roger and I was doing as mere lust. The execrable romantic streak in myself, no doubt. The element that I am going to have to cancel out if I am to make a success of this casual sex thing. The streak of false sentimentality that occasions my searing (and painful, to me) bouts of prudery.

I can't remember who shouted, 'All change now.' Perhaps nobody did. Perhaps it just happened on its own accord. Anyway, Adam and I found ourselves kissing each other, preparing to get going, gazing at Roger's huge shoulders hovering over Cherry.

'Hello, my darling,' I'd whispered tenderly into Adam's ear. 'Nice to be back.' He had kissed me gently on the lips and positioned himself alongside me on the floor. His prick was as limp as a pork sausage.

'Shall I get it in,' I'd said good-humouredly. We often did it like that, not waiting until he had an erection before entry, but easing it inside me like pliable dough. We both enjoyed the sensation of its stiffening inside. Expanding to fill the vacuum. 'Shall I?' I'd whispered, preparing to do it.

But he hadn't answered. He was gazing over at Cherry and Roger. And before I had fully grasped all the implications of what and why he was doing it, he had left my side and was joining in with what those other two were doing.

I was left on my own again. But I was getting used to this. It must be my own fault somewhere along the line. Wasn't there always some reason why some kids in the school playground always stood on their own? Couldn't one just see why it was that they were left out of everyone's games? Didn't one just ache to tell them how to join in, how to ensure that they would always be included.

The trick was in laughter. Make everyone laugh – then they will all love you. Won't be able to get enough of you.

I went to the drinks over by the dressing-table, by the sole mirror in the bedroom. And I looked hard at myself, at my striking sophistication. At the lush curve of my large mouth. At the challenging light in my dark eyes. At the hourglass enticements of my curving body. 'This is not enough, old girl!' I mouthed to myself, already a little drunk by the headiness of the occasion (and the swig from the bottle that I'd stolen, ahead of the others, before we had started). And I meant it. My siren days were coming to an end. Though the glamour of my appearance may be even stronger than in those early years when I still hadn't mastered the expertise I now flaunted, I was still the sex object. This was no longer true. 'You have changed from a sex object into a sexual predator, Eve!' I mouthed again to myself. But now voices were calling me from the bed. When would *that* ever end, the need to have my participation! I filled my mouth with champagne, carrying the bottle with me.

When I reached the trio I found them to be in a state of pall, the action had slackened off noticeably. So, taking Cherry's face in my hands I kissed her lovingly on the mouth – and deposited the contents of my own onto her tongue. She gagged in surprise, allowing a trickle of champagne to dribble down over her chin and onto her breast.

'Oh, allow me,' I leaned over and licked up the dribble. But not before I had coaxed a drop right down to her nipple.

'More for anyone else? Gentlemen?' I filled up again, drinking straight from the neck of the bottle.

'Perhaps this little chap might appreciate a drop or two!' I swooped down upon Adam and Roger, gathering their genitals together in my cupped hands before drenching them with the fizzing contents of my mouth.

'Nice,' Adam exclaimed, surveying his dripping pubic

hair. 'Just what a person needs. Now who is going to lick it dry?' He is looking at Roger. They are looking at each other. That's how their cock-sucking came about, it was then that they really got started.

There has never been any doubt in my mind over which I would prefer, or rather, which I would least mind – my husband being unfaithful to me with a member of his own sex, or with a member of mine. Any male lover he may choose constitutes, in my mind, far less of a threat than another woman. And homosexuality, which is present in every one of us, has always intrigued and excited me. I have become increasingly drawn to the idea of it over the years, both for myself and for Adam. Sometimes I have fantasised aloud during our fucks that he is being caressed by certain boys or men that we have noticed because of their beauty. And Adam has always played along with the notion. 'Anything,' he's said, 'except dick up my bum. I prefer to reserve that particular portion of my person for proper evacuation of my bowels. Everyone is entitled to idiosyncracies regarding their own bodies and I prefer to keep my back passage private. It is my property as I see it.'

I think that my reply was, 'Quite so, you pompous fart!' Something suitably witty like that.

But watching Adam and Roger playing so gently with each other I would very much have liked some buggery to take place. There was, somewhere, a sneaking sense of incompleteness to what they were doing. Neither of them even came off in each other's mouth, though both were groaning with pleasure at what the other was doing. More than anything I felt that they knew so much more than a woman about just how to arouse each other. Cherry and I were transfixed.

'They are bloody good at it, aren't they,' I whispered to her. 'Look at the sly way they are licking each other's bollocks and giving butterfly kisses around the bum.'

'Done it before, bet your bottom dollar on it.'

'Darling!' I was appallingly excited.

'Not necessarily with each other,' she said hastily in case I should get upset. 'But in the past with other people. You can spot experience when you see it. I can, anyway, having been around more than you, Evie.'

I let that one pass, cheeky little bitch. Besides I wanted to concentrate on the sight of my husband practising sixty-nine on our good pal, Roger. He had never professed a sexual interest in old Roger before, but perhaps this present (delightful) excess was taking place simply because it was all so handy. There, so to speak. To do with not looking a gift-horse in the gob.

Looking at the two bodies thrashing away at each other I felt afresh a surge of lustful desire for the man I was married to. His leanness, the width of his shoulders, tapering to those narrow flanks, the lovely, lovely length of his legs, the smoothness of his biscuit-brown skin. All of it was turning me on. And not only me. Cherry was clearly getting just as aroused, pressing herself closely against me, guiding my fingers over her wonderfully stiff nipples and down onto her clitoris.

'Shall we start?' She bit the lobe of my ear between words, placing fluttering kisses over my cheeks until she reached my wet mouth. Then she darted her tongue right in past my teeth and made a devastating assault on my tonsils. I feared I might never take breath again but merely choke on our mutual pleasure. My final view of my husband before I closed my eyes was of Roger ejaculating all over his face. And then of him doing the same over Roger. I thought what great fun it was, now being married to a gay.

Three

Puck (to rhyme with fuck, right!) has failed to come again. He was due here in our bed at around about noon and now it is one o'clock.

I am posing in front of the full-length mirror, impatiently playing with myself. Pinching each nipple so hard that it really hurts, interested to see them instantly stiffen. Placing my fingertips first daintily upon my tongue to get a spot of moisture going, then directing them down there. Down there between my legs. It isn't cock, but it can get me started at least. I am preparing myself in case Puck should come storming through the door, seizing me in his arms, tearing the seductive black lace from my body, forcing the bulging contents of his flies into me. Not even waiting until Adam gets back to help me empty his hard-on. And shouting, shouting that his lust for me has become so uncontrollable since our first meeting two weeks ago that he ejaculates each time he thinks of me. And of the three of us fucking together. I don't wish to be demurely dry when he arrives, should he be in that mood.

This morning, to celebrate our intended act of troilism, I took a cab to Saks on Fifth Avenue and purchased the delectable garment that I am wearing now. It's called a teddy, a term we don't use in England. Our teddies are bears, soft toys for small children to take to bed with them. And this confused me for some while when we came to take up residence here in New York, back in the autumn. I would read the start of a torrid passage in some hot porn or other: 'She sprawled back on the bed enticingly, clutching her pink teddy to her huge tits . . .' Regressive behaviour, I'd thought, or rather kinky. Sex and soft toys. Not a combination I'd ever sampled.

But then I'd caught the Saks advertisement in the *New*

York Times. 'Look,' I'd said to Adam, 'this girl's wearing what's called a teddy.' And I'd pointed to the ravishing creature on the left-hand side of the page, in her boudoir version of a barely-there swimsuit.

'Mm,' Adam had said, salivating, 'you should get one of those, Eve, and wear it in bed. I could screw the arse off you in that.' In those days it was still just the two of us . . .

Eleven years we've been together. In just two weeks' time it'll be our eleventh wedding anniversary. The present plan is to have Puck and his rock group perform at the party. And since this is to be a combination gathering, celebrating darling Cherry's thirtieth birthday (we join in her commiserations), I think of that as being the height of chic.

'It's not bad is it,' I said to Adam the other day, 'our lover, Puck, playing for our lover, Cherry, and for us on our wedding anniversary. And all of us so nicely there together.' And I wondered as I said it whether or not any of our other guests would even begin to guess at the situation.

'Not bad at all.' Adam's voice had a dry edge to it. 'Except that we haven't managed to pull Puck yet.'

'Oh, don't you worry about that. By the time of the party I'll have managed to nail him. It's getting him to understand that without you he can't have me, that we go together as a team – that's what's taking the time. But it'll be all right, I promise.' And kissing his mouth I'd cupped his cock and balls in my two hands, holding them securely through his corduroy trousers.

'I love you, Adam.'

'I love you, Eve.'

We love each other. This new sex thing is simply a game.

Yes, time is passing, things are happening. We have been here in New York for almost five months, I see in my diary, in which the fabric of our marriage has completely changed. But the stitching remains as strong as ever.

In retrospect, it helps to see the actual dates of our dizzy doings in the diary, though it is an enthusiasm not shared by Adam. He refuses to acknowledge his past, can hardly bear to talk about things that happened as far back as yesterday. It's frustrating for somebody like me who adores to gossip, it means that I've had to adjust to speculation instead. Forever looking ahead to the future, instead of comfortably mulling over the 'might-have-beens' long since passed.

Yesterday a Welsh newspaper came to interview me, wanting to know how the move to America was working out, whether I'd started on a new novel, wondering what my impact on the American public had been. And how much this skyscraper landscape had influenced Adam's recent paintings.

I gave routine replies to these mechanical questions, more interested in sussing out whether or not either the interviewer or his photographer might do for our bed. Positioning myself cleverly with my profile to the light, I was better able to guess how well each of them was hung. Whether it was worth a subtle seduction on my part. But I must stop viewing the male species in this sort of way, I know that. As Adam so vehemently maintains, it's not the size of the thing that's important (he speaks from the safe base of seven inches).

Then, as he was closing his notebook the shy reporter asks idly, 'Any, hm, social chit-chat, Eve? Any hot item that might interest our readers, now?'

'As to who's fucking who, you mean? That sort of thing?' I whammed him, as he flinched, with one of my brilliant ball-emptying grins. Then before he had any chance to reply I came in with the scorcher. 'A leading politician is rogering one of these new child stars – that any good? She's sixteen. Some say that if it gets out it could lose him his job, but I think the other way around. The sensualists would vote for him, thinking that if he gets in there'd be a chance that he'd lower the age of consent. But they'd have had to have Errol Flynn as President to make that a certainty. He was very keen on the young ones, you know, like Charlie Chaplin.'

This is what I'm really good at, salacious gossip of the most slanderous sort. The reporter's jaw slackened, but only for a second.

'Am I to write that all down, Eve?'

'Well, it's your pen, not mine.' It's never clear in my mind who's liable to be sued in these cases. The Welsh press has a bigger purse than me.

It wasn't very good, the interview I gave him (except for this last bit). I think that I may have lost the magical knack of tossing shimmering *bon mots*, and highly quotable extravagances of witty wisdom. New York has desensitised those eccentricities for which I am so celebrated in Europe. They like sharp shit-shooters here. Fey lady-novelists, however funny, get short shrift even when they're from Britain (though they are batty about the British).

So this is my new American persona – raunchier, ruder, rough enough to cause a wince. The only thing is, that image needs some polishing round the edges to make it perfect. And the success of it rests with revealing all about myself and my current preoccupation with group sex – with 'swinging', as they call it over here. Something in me shrank back from showering the shy Welshman with the full extent of my American excesses. I didn't feel that the Welsh were the right audience for this first spilling of the beans. To do myself full justice I require a more sophisticated readership, the sort who've gone in for a diet of De Sade and Bataille, who take Al Goldstein's *Screw*, the sex review magazine, every week. Those adventurers of the wilder shores of sensuality.

When the sweet lad posed the question as to whether I considered New York to be the sexiest city that I had ever lived in, I unhesitatingly said that yes it was. But further than that I kept mum. 'Sex is thrumming in the air,' I paused, pleased with that flash of my former poetic streak. And I watched him writing the quote down carefully, seeing, instead of him, Adam's seven inches disappearing into Cherry's beautifully formed mouth. That Jane Fonda upper lip smudging into his scrotum, whilst I manoeuvred myself across to his face so he could start chewing on my clitoris – and I could start chewing on Cherry's.

'Final question, Eve. You and Adam are living and working here together in the Eden. After eleven years of togetherness, never a single night spent apart, would you say that your famed romance is still going as strong as it ever was, eh now? And the sex side of things – no falling off in that direction?' Some of these shy buggers really push themselves to the hilt.

'The whole thing is better than it's ever been. We're more in love now than we were at the start and as to the

400

sex – it gets sexier and sexier. What more can I say?' And I blinked ingenuously as I said that, concluding the interview, squeezing my eyelids swiftly together to induce that special shine on my dark green eyes. The eyes that Beauty Editors of glossy magazines praise so breathily in informative articles for the over-forties. The shy Welshman clearly got the message. Another poor besotted sod to buy my books.

But right now I'm not pleased with myself. My confidence has taken another blow from that gorgeous little shit, Puck. That dashing Adonis, that doll of a boy, the swaggering rock-singer has stood me up again. And I am seething with sexual frustration. Ugly! But I am as determined now to sample his body as I was when I set eyes upon him seven days ago.

I shall never forget that first sight of him. I thought then and I still do, and probably shall forever, that he was the most *beautiful* creature I had ever seen. A Greek god up on stage posturing for his public, preening and parading as purposefully as a peacock. Pouting those perfectly chiselled lips as prettily as a girl. Flaring the finely proportioned nostrils as fiercely as a wild stallion. Striking the arresting poses of a trained dancer with a body resembling that of Rudolph Nureyev, who I had first seen perform in his early twenties. The age of this vision. My stomach lurched over my heart.

He was singing a song, snarling some lyrics, the words of which it was impossible to decipher. You couldn't hear them for one thing, the accompanying band was too loud. But it made no difference, it didn't matter, the impact was there. Though we had already risen to leave, having caught the previous act, the one we had come to see, there was no question of going once Puck was on.

'Hot shit, eh!' I gasped to Adam. His own jaw had dropped. We seldom disagree over our quarry, only rarely do we fall out as to the suitability of our prey. For we have become sexual predators *par excellence* over these last months, we work as a closely co-ordinated team.

'What d'you think?' I ask cunningly. My mind is made up already. 'This kid's one for us, isn't he?' Only polite to check first with one's partner in crime.

'Doesn't look bad,' Adam answered with some caution.

'The question is though, which one of us is he going to be interested in?'

'I shall enquire in my usual fashion when the time comes. He's probably on for another forty-five minutes. Then he's going to ask me to dance.'

'You're pretty confident, my angel.' Adam leaned forward to kiss my cheek. It took me a second to wonder whether or not I was pleased that he was doing so. I had already exchanged smouldering glances with the singer on stage, I'd captured his interest, I was sure of that. But Adam's proprietry gesture of affection could have thrown things off-balance at this early stage of the game. On the other hand, when the sexual object is given to understand that there is somebody else in the running, one with a prior claim to the sexual attention of the sexual predator, then more often than not it can make him more eager than before to become involved. Or so I've found from our recent experiences. I learn something new every time.

So I say, 'Yes,' to my husband. Meaning, 'Yes, I am pretty confident that I will catch this one as our bed-fellow.' But I also am not quite certain in which direction his preferences lie. His appeal is androgynous. The halo of golden curls, so becoming with this expert back-lighting, is nevertheless in the process of growing out the frazzled results of a rather poor perm. The blatant message of straining blue jeans, threadbare at the crotch to lend extra titillation to the obvious left-hand dressing, is diverted by the theatrical campness of the torn lurex tee-shirt. Though the face could belong to a spectacularly handsome girl with possible Sapphic tendencies, the coarse-grained complexion could only belong to a boy.

The sole flaw in the perfection – the pocked remains of past acne from adolescence. That and the undeniable lack of inches. This Adonis is shortish, shorter than Adam by some five, or so, inches.

'Shame, that he's shortish,' I mouth sideways to Adam. The singer is now singing almost exclusively to me. All I can hope is that he doesn't lip-read. 'Pity about the pockmarks.'

'That's average, not shortish. I'm tall. That's the trouble, you can't go judging everyone else by what you're used to, Eve. If I started comparing all the girls to you

402

we'd never take any single one of them to bed, just because they wouldn't come up to scratch. You can't impose these impossible standards. This one looks good "n" healthy to me.'

I am silent for a while, reflecting on the compliment that he's just given me. I must be hellishly more insecure than I ever thought I'd be to feel so ridiculously pleased by his praise. I look at him, lounging elegantly beside me. Black shirt, black trousers, white shoes, white fifties tuxedo (from a fashionable antique clothes shop in Greenwich Village).

Beneath his trousers, his big penis and scrotum are contained in a pair of brief hipster underpants. Black and silky. Sexy ones, specially aimed at a specifically sexy market. I bought them for him myself, just last week in Macys. I was the only female in the men's underwear department. The rest were all gay males.

'How did you know that they were all gay?' Adam had demanded to know when I reported back. He loathes shopping for his own clothes, especially stuff like underwear. He used to consider underware pedestrian, until I pointed out the importance of the right underwear at the undressing stage, the stage of bedroom seduction. Important to us these days, with our massed orgies. Before he thought of underpants as a purely practical means of mopping up drips and soaking in skid-marks (caused by a carelessly wiped bum).

'I've learned to recognise gays. I'm married to one, aren't I?' I put my arms around his flat belly, but he wasn't pleased.

'I wish you'd get it into your head that I am *bi-sexual*, not as you would have it. *I am bi-sexual*, just as everyone else is bi-sexual, those with any sensitivity and any sense. I consider it short-sighted and stupid to be exclusively homosexual. It's cutting out an entire area of excitement and pleasure. It's best to be both. You agree with that, don't you?'

He wasn't really expecting an answer to that hypothetical question. And I was relieved. My feelings were not as clear and as uncomplicated as Adam's. There were still times when I thought we had made a mistake in embarking on this life of 'swinging'.

403

I had taken to reading magazines such as *Penthouse*, to compare my feelings with those of interviewed 'swinging' wives. I still had childish trouble controlling my jealousy. And I was ashamed of that, yet at the same time afraid that when I didn't experience jealousy any more at the sight of Adam fucking another female, that would mean that I no longer cared for him in the way that I had done for all these years.

I knew that I didn't want to lose the intensity of what I felt for him. In my heart I think I was afraid that if he wasn't jealous of me, as I was of him, his love for me must have lessened. That's what I couldn't bear. But when I confronted him with this possibility he hugged me – and laughed it off. He meant that to be reassuring, but it wasn't enough.

And yet, perversely, I enjoy (*very* much enjoy!) actually *pulling* the people. That part I *love*. Spotting the likely ones. Propositioning them. Popping them into taxi cabs at the end of the parties, and whisking them back to the Eden with us.

But several nights ago it went sour. A tall, dark, and handsome lawyer, a lad who had known me in a previous existence in London (though I had a hard job remembering him), had turned sexual predator. I was his goal for the evening, he made that pretty clear during the round of clubs and venues that we visited with our crowd.

'What the hell does he think he's hanging around you for?' Adam was showing me his irritable side. Cherry, who was with us was getting the charm. It was not much to my liking, I must say, this new thing of his. This devoting his light-hearted geniality towards Cherry whenever she accompanied us on social occasions, whilst more or less ignoring me. At one time it was never possible for me to move without bumping into him at my side, devoting himself to my every need. The contrast between now and the past was more than unflattering, it hurt. But how could one put that into words without whining?

'What the hell does he think he's hanging around me for, Adam?' I'd repeated his question, whilst ignoring his frown. 'Perfectly obvious, I should have thought – hoping for a fuck, wouldn't you say?'

'It's not on, Eve.'

'That reply is both hostile and, in my view, rather rude. I happen to quite fancy Tall, Dark and Handsome in case you're interested.'

But all he did was turn his back on me, spinning around to face me again only because I'd jabbed him so viciously on the shoulder.

'Is there any particular reason for your unpleasant behaviour?' I smiled icily, pleased to see that Cherry was drifting away now, having lost Adam's undivided attention.

Things between her and me have deteriorated over the past few months. When she rings up it is Adam she is really only interested in talking to. If I pick up the telephone now, I automatically hand it over to him, after a friendly but perfunctory exchange of polite hellos. When we fuck, the three of us together, I feel more like a voyeur than an active participant. This, despite the fact that I appear to be performing with my usual enthusiasm. But afterwards if I try to explain this sense of detachment that I suffer, Adam pooh-poohs it away. 'That same old prudery,' he mocks. 'You'd think that you would have managed to shake off the puritanical chapel up-bringing by your age.' He's lucky, he doesn't get dragged down by a conscience himself.

My 'prudery' is causing problems between us.

'The only unpleasant behaviour here, Eve, is your own. You haven't so much as given a civil word to Cherry all evening. You can hardly be bothered to acknowledge her even. I've had to talk all evening with her to make up for you.'

'What hardship!' I'm snarling. How distant he seems from his great height. How coldly he scrutinises me behind his smart spectacles.

'Your flashy admirer is a thug, Eve. I happen to know that he is carrying a gun on him at this very moment. It is not what we want in our bed tonight, do you understand?'

I am speechless. Adam has won again. Of course we do not want a gun-toting sharp-shooter sharing slumber and sex with us. What if he took exception to some mistimed remark, my tendency to whoop with glee at the point of orgasmic rapture, my million eccentricities between the sheets . . .

405

Cherry came back with us instead.

The singer, Puck, is coming to the end of his final song. Adam is re-ordering drinks up at the bar. I see that a brunette and her girlfriend, seated on two of the barstools have managed to engage him in conversation. It will be because they have heard his British accent. Everyone talks to you in these sort of places when they know you are from Britain. The broad-shouldered boy, Zack, on the next table has already asked me to dance once he overheard me speak. His mother was born in Manchester, he tells me. He is a good-looking guy, an actor, a pal of Puck's. I am relying on him now for a formal introduction to my goal, though our eyes – Puck's and mine – have been inter-twined even whilst I was dancing. We have reached the stage now of openly smiling between songs.

I am feeling as horny as hell.

'How's things? Here's your drink.' Adam has returned, but I notice that he has left his own glass back at the bar. The two girls are waiting for him to return.

'Things are fine.' I wink at him, inclining my head in the direction of the stage to indicate that everything with the singer is under control.

'I'll leave you to it, then.' He grins and makes his way back to the two girls. I wonder whether they are lovers, or not. It wouldn't necessarily cancel out anything with Adam, even if they were lovers. In New York everyone does everything with anyone.

The singer leaves the stage and goes through the swing doors leading to the dressing-rooms. A gaggle of fans follow him, clamouring for a word, some recognition from him. For the first time it now occurs to me that he may have made a previous arrangement with one of these kids, and that this might be my final sight of him. I prepare to rise from my seat and follow on too. When my blood is up, when the excitement of the chase is coursing through my nervous system there is no place for pride.

But something stops me, some instinct of self-preserva-tion. I feel sure enough of myself to play it cool this time. Puck will return to me.

I glance over at Adam. He catches my eye and beckons for me to join him and the two girls, but I don't want to do this. I must be seated in the same spot for the re-emergence of my prey. Besides I must keep up a relationship with Zack on the next table. He is already drawing his chair closer to mine, preparing to chat me up again. So I shake my head at Adam and remain where I am, despite his frown. It is interesting that I am not experiencing my usual pangs of possessive jealousy to see his flirtatious teasing of these two girls. For he is enthralling them both, I can tell by the way they are squirming against him, one on each side now. And he is leaning nonchalantly with his back against the crowded bar, taller, more arrestingly distinguished than anyone else there. His dimples winking in and out, twenty to the dozen, working overtime for maximum seductive effect. And the girls are laughing, he is amusing them with his sardonic humour. They find him sophisticated, like a film star. They probably believe him to be some sort of English lord, they will have seen *My Fair Lady* on their television screens, as a late-night movie, and wish to play Eliza Doolittle to Adam's Professor Higgins. Or they have been brought up by mothers who still care for Cary Grant and his smooth veneer, and here out of the blue they are experiencing it first-hand, in the flesh. The sauveness of the older man. Someone who knows how to spend his money.

We are by far the oldest pair in the place. It is a somewhat seedy venue, this one. Not as swish a joint as those that we have been in the habit of patronising. But we were bent on catching a certain performer. An ex-superstar from the Andy Warhol stable, who is attempting a comeback.

Consequently we, me in particular, are somewhat over-dressed. Surrounded by a sea of tattered and taut denim, with a sprinkling of mildly menacing sub-punks in black leather, we must seem from another world. As if slumming. But I no longer feel self-conscious – everyone is so friendly it would be impossible not to feel at home. Eyes swivelled as we entered, at Adam's white tuxedo, and at me in my slinky cerise sequin slash of a dress, with my veiled matching pillbox on my head. 'Love the style, honey,' someone murmured as we passed, ushered by the effusive proprietor to the best seats at the front. We look as if we are made of money, which compared to these kids we are. Yet so far not a single one has attempted to bum a drink from us, no one has rushed us for a handout. Quite the reverse – at this very moment sweet Zack is offering to top up my drink. And I graciously allow him to do so. I am drinking spritzers, a gentle mix of dry white wine and soda banked up by a mound of ice. The kind of concoction will keep me going far longer I have found than the strong liquor that I used to indulge in before coming to the States. It means that by five in the morning, when our nights mostly end, I am still able to stand up. And Adam can still perform in bed. Too many of our past nights of passion with people we've picked up have been marred by alcoholic impotence on the part of the males.

It is interesting that coming from a generation in which alcohol is the socially accepted drug, it seemed natural to lure would-be lovers back to our lair with the offer of a nightcap. 'Would you care to come back to our place for champagne?' We would whisper disarmingly, in our very best British accent. But when the disinterested responses began to occur with a dispiriting regularity we deduced that champagne in itself was not enticement enough, so we sat down to review the situation.

'Perhaps we could just suggest coming back to see our etchings, and shove the champagne,' I suggested to Adam. 'Or are etchings a purely Anglo-Saxon lure started off by the cave-men? Did they have cave-men in America?'

Adam approached the problem more studiously. 'We are employing the wrong drug, that's all it is. We must get in some dope. That's more what these kids understand. Though,' he spoke thoughtfully, 'I don't think that offering a joint is actually going to be enough. We shall probably have to invest in a stock of coke.'

'Cocaine!' I was shocked. 'Purveyors of hard drugs! Next thing you'll be suggesting a tray of needles and heroin, with me dressed up like a cinema usherette strolling around dispensing my ungodly wares. Be reasonable, Adam, we don't want to get into all that drug scene. I had enough of that at the Garbage Club, I never want to have another snort again in my life!'

'You'd best leave New York tomorrow, then!' That had been his cryptic reply.

And he was perfectly right. The Garbage Club was the

first dive we'd been to where a guy was actually strolling around with his tray of delights on sale.

'Listen to what he's shouting,' Adam had said to me. I listened. 'Pharmaceuticals! Pharmaceuticals! Get your pharmaceuticals here ... treat yourself right tonight, Thunderbuns!'

Thunderbuns was a passing boy of not more than sixteen, if that. He could more appropriately have been called Bambi, but wouldn't have appreciated it as much. We watched him stop in his tracks and return to the vendor. He purchased a small phial of something called Locker Room. I had some thrust under my own nose just a week before by the gay I'd been dancing with at the club, Mirage. The effect was immediate, an onrush of instant energy. I could only imagine that they are called Locker Rooms because sportsmen might have recourse to them before an important game. But this is merely a supposition, I must remember to test the theory out on Adam. He knows all these associations of terms. He will doubtless tell me I'm completely wrong. He's been decrying me rather a lot lately. I have the feeling that, for him, the sun no longer shines out of my eyes. Not as it used to.

I was less than honest in my answers to the Welsh newspaper reporter, but I am not yet capable of formulating these unsettling fears. My experience of problems in the past has been that it is best to leave them to find the light of day on their own. Confrontation takes courage, and though I have the courage of David faced with Goliath, I now consider that only fools rush in too quickly. I am no longer the fool that I once was.

Though I was fool enough on the night of the visit to the Garbage Club. Everyone agreed on that afterwards, though I waited a few days to tell the full story. Even waited till the morning to relate the truth to Adam.

We had gone with an ill-assorted group, most of whom were strangers to us. The invitation was to attend a party being given for Bubbles and her group, Liquid. At some point in the evening she would be performing. It was our first time at the Garbage Club, since it had become the fashionable spot with the avant-garde. When we had been to it before it had only been open a week and hadn't then found its feet. Now it has become glamorously notorious. I was looking forward to the evening, and had dressed in a suitably outlandish fashion. Not unlike a cockroach from outer space, almost entirely in delicate plastic tubing applied to a base of pliable mesh webbing. Rather tiresome to get in and out of, this particular structure. But stunning, for effect, in dense greys and transparent polythene. It was the creation of an inspired designer who I had recently become acquainted with here in New York. A poverty-stricken artist who one day will have been heard of by everyone. But who for now is having to sit back and wait for his just recognition. We are meeting more and more like that in this savage city.

But what induced me to start drinking Budweiser beers, whilst wearing such difficult garb I cannot imagine. For within twenty minutes of arrival at the Garbage Club, I naturally needed to relieve the insistent pressure on my bladder.

When I had been to the club before, the lavatories were on the ground floor, behind the bandstand. But now I was directed up the steep stairs to the ones on the floor above. Bubbles and other performers that evening were being given the exclusive use of those downstairs.

Upstairs it was all action around the other bar. At one end people were watching video; instant video of themselves drinking and dancing, some stretched out on scattered cushions on the floor about to embark (or having embarked already) on pretty serious fornication. Boys with boys, girls with girls. Others were simply playing idly with themselves. Disconsolate with their own dreams.

But this was an ill-lit alcove, no more. The air was charged with the smell of dope, many of these young people looked as if they were on the point of death. I felt cheerfully healthy, but I needed to pee.

'Can you tell me which way the ladies' rest room is please,' I smiled pleasantly at a passing girl with a dyed purple pompadour. She scowled right back at me and pointed.

'Unisex, honey. There ain't no difference here.'

I thanked her effusively, hoping she wasn't thinking what an old fart I was. Unisex. Of course, Unisex. What else would I expect! I hurried the way that she'd pointed, to the other end of the long bar. And then I stepped over the threshold.

It was like being back in kindergarten, in the babies' class at school where the lavatories are arranged in a row with no surrounding closet walls – so that small children would be prevented from shutting themselves in. There were eight of them here, solitary white toilets set along the side of the room, opposite the reflecting mirrors. Enabling one a good view of oneself sitting down, in the case of ladies. Or, as in the case of the two guys having a pee at this very moment, a satisfying view of themselves standing up (if they craned around to look over their shoulders).

But nobody was interested in looking either at themselves or at anyone else in here. The big activity at the mirrors and in the four corners of the room was the snorting of the white stuff, cocaine. Sniff, sniff . . . sniff, sniff. It was going on all around me. Heads held high and then back so that not a speck of the precious coke should be wasted. Not a single snowflake should escape. Girls teetered on steep stilettos, steadying themselves against each other. Boys braced themselves before taking breath then flung the potent magic up high into their flaring nostrils, blinking as if blinded by the sudden bounce in their brain. Not a single one of them turned in my direction, no one so much as glanced at me as I stepped so cautiously amongst them. They couldn't have cared less if I had taken every article of my clothing off. They were carrying themselves off on their own cloud nine.

Which was just as well, because in the garment I had on, I was all but forced into removing most of it before I could clear a passage for urine to escape in a straight line to anywhere. But eventually I managed the relief that I so urgently sought, and sitting there with my plastic drapes around my ankles, viewing the jolly goings-on all about me, I really began to feel that I was enjoying myself hugely. What very pretty examples of American youth were represented here!

Returning less than an hour later (my bladder was behaving gruesomely this evening!) I was quite disappointed to be greeted this time with the unusual sight of a completely deserted rest room. Not a girl or a boy in sight, not a single snorter in view! Relieved that I had the place

411

to myself, however, for the grotesque disrobing procedure. I completed my near-strip and sat down on one of the vacant toilets. No sooner had I done so that a hairy ape, a colossus – half animal, half human – stumbled in. And to my dismay decided to ensure complete privacy on behalf of us both by securing the door firmly behind him. Then he shambled over to where I sat.

This is it, I thought, I am about to die! I have always been plagued with the notion that my eventual end would occur under bizarre circumstances. Now it seemed that I would be proved right! Pinioned with my pants pathetically at half-mast. Haloed in the most humiliating position. Pissing my final precious moments away. My soul siphoned off into the New York sewers of SoHo . . .

I raised my head and smiled bravely up at him, for now he/it was towering immediately above me with his huge sneakered toes trampling my delicate garment into the ground.

'Good evening,' I fluted charmingly in my best Deborah Kerr fashion, thinking desperately that this might avert the aggression I was certain was due my way any second. I waited for the flick-knife to fillet my throat, to slice into my heart which was settling there in a sea of saliva.

But all I got was a gutteral grunt and a groan of pleasure as the giant plunged his nose into the palm of his bunched hand. Then he tried to speak. 'Coke – you wanna snort?' And he thrust the same fist towards my nose. I understood immediately.

'Oh, how very sweet of you,' I gushed up at him. 'But no, thank you very much all the same. I am actually on Budweiser beer, myself, this evening. But you go ahead by all means with your snort.' And I attempted to twinkle up at his non-comprehending face. The sound of my tinkling piddle filled the silence between us, my entire innards had turned to water.

He was zonked out of his head but there wasn't much to criticise in the speed of his next action. His cock was out of his trousers and jammed into my mouth within seconds.

'Cock or coke? Wassit to be?' He'd taken the decision for me. I remained where I was, gagged by gargantuan dick, my eyes swivelling wildly over the closed-circuit

412

sagging of his muscled stomach. My trembling chin bearded by his balls. Forced fellatio, frightened out of my wits, but at least relieved to know that the pocket bulge wasn't a pistol!

Then I'd finished. 'I've finished!' I tentatively tugged on his trousers. 'I've finished . . .' There was no way with my mouthful, with my choking delivery, that any English-speaking person could have understood what I was saying. I was meaning to convey that my business was up, that my seemingly inexhaustable supply of piss had suddenly dried up. I wanted to be up and off, my facial muscles were stretched to buggery. I'd need surgery to stitch my mouth back into shape, several seams taken in at both sides.

But the zombie knew what I was saying, he was swaying above me with a seraphic smile on his lips. In different circumstances I might have managed to become quite fond of him. I could see that, but at this moment I terribly badly wanted to get away. I was aware of the light at the end of the tunnel, my escape route. Though I knew that at any given moment it could disappear, that senseless aggression could erupt without warning. This chap wasn't absolutely 'all there'. That was what saved me, the fact that he didn't really know what was going on, what was happening to other parts of his body besides his big nostrils. For he had barely ceased sniffing coke throughout our encounter.

I can only think he believed that I had brought him to climax already, that when I was indicating I had finished, it meant he had shot off. His look of gratitude was childishly touching.

'Was that the big oaf who kept leering at you all evening?' Adam had demanded to know when I related the incident.

'He wanted a date, he wanted to come home with me. He wouldn't have been that much out of place with some of the nutters we bring back to bed anyway.' In retrospect I had become affectionately disposed toward my brute, I couldn't help feeling grateful to him that I had escaped unharmed. Except that there was this uneasiness, this sense of disloyalty that I was suffering. Having a sexual escapade in Adam's absence, the first time that it had ever

413

happened. The only other occasions when I had sucked some other man's cock, Adam had been there (sucking it too, as often as not – taking it in turns). But this had been, so I comforted myself with thinking, a matter of necessity. A question of life and death. I hoped that Adam, or indeed anyone with the right priorities, would have done the same in the circumstances. I have never believed in defending one's honour to the death. I certainly am sure that I would prefer Adam with the scent of cunt on his cock or the taste of pussy over his tongue, than discover him dead. Strange pussy has got to be preferable any day to a pistol-shot through the head.

Puck is sauntering towards me! Every pore of my person is exploding (I can hear them – can he?) with a dirisible combination of nerves and desire. If he speaks to me I shall shit myself.

He greets Zack, the hovering Zack, but his eyes are on me. I know this in the same way that I know Adam is following the scene from the bar. I am the centre of both their attentions, the knowledge encourages me to *flaunt* myself. I prepare to behave outrageously (I can be rather good at that when I put my mind to it).

'Congratulations,' I challenge him with coquettishly narrowed eyes, 'on a splendid performance.' And I insolently allow my gaze to caress his body, lingering deliberately at crotch level, before coming finally to rest on his mouth. At close quarters his lack of height is more apparent, but that is because I am so used to looking up at Adam. And I am relived that I don't find it as disappointing as I might have expected, for I have never been attracted before by any men other than tall ones.

But the beauty is breathtaking. I cannot imagine how this boy has escaped discovery by some enterprising agent. If I were an agent I'd snap him up, even now I am searching in my mind for the names among my contacts here who might conceivably advance this kid's career. I consciously wish to impress him, I want to lay him on my casting couch. Oh, depravity!

He is surprised, not to say startled, by the formality of my greeting, by the exaggerated English accent. More than by my sexual come-on, he must have got used to those in his life by now. But he smiles with what seems like delighted pleasure even so. The smile of a small child confronted with a present, or the prospect of a party. Unselfconsciously cute, lovable, trusting. Fresh feelings, indefinable ones, begin flooding through me displacing the other animal emotions. Now I want to hold him tenderly in my arms, to cradle him, take care of him, to kiss him very gently on that marvellous mouth.

I am falling in love.

We are dancing together and talking, talking twenty-to-the-dozen as if making up for all those years when we didn't know each other, when we hadn't yet met. Adam and I were the same at our first meeting, mesmerised by each other. The only difference being that, with Adam and me, it was he who had made the first sexual approach. Within moments of being introduced he'd leaned forward and said, 'I like the look of you very much, but I can't fit you in until Wednesday – how about it?' Bloody cheek, but it had worked.

With Puck I'd employed the same brutal technique. 'Before we waste any more time, I'd like to know which way your tendencies lead you. Who would you be more interested in screwing? Him or me?' And I'd indicated Adam up at the bar.

There had been no hesitation. 'You. I go with girls, I'm not gay.'

'Just checking. Another thing – we come as a team, Adam and Eve. We don't split up to screw.'

No flinching. 'OK, Eve. I guess we can get it together.'

'That's that out of the way then. Best to say it right at the start.'

'No problem, Eve.' Then he'd led me onto the tiny dance floor. I wished Adam would stop staring, that was all.

The telephone rings, 'Any sign of your recalcitrant rock-star?' It's Adam, I swallow my disappointment. Standing in my lace teddy, spring sun mercilessly spot-lighting my winter-pale skin, I reflect on what a ridicu-lously pathetic situation I have got myself into.

'Oh, hi, Adam,' I say brightly. 'Nope, no sign. Looks like yet another rejection.' I am struggling to keep the break out of my voice, when what I really want to do is burst into tears. Have my husband comfort me as he has comforted me over the last eleven years. But I dare not do that, show weakness to add strength to his insistence that I should stop making a fool of myself over Puck.

There is an exasperated sigh at the other end of the line. 'Honestly Eve', when is this going to stop! How many times has he stood you up now? This, this, super-acned, singing twerp!'

I remain silent. My throat is clogging up with the unshed tears, an unsightly red blotchiness has broken out between my breasts. Tension.

'I mean, who needs it, Eve – eh, this hanging around? How much work did you get done this morning? How many words of this new novel did you write?'

'Oh, I did – a fair whack.' I cross guilty fingers to cancel out the effects of the lie. I'd have to pretend that this teddy I'm wearing was purchased in the past, a secret to bring out as a pleasurable surprise on one of our spontaneous fucks. The ones that Adam and I have on our own, for those still continue despite the events of our recent orgiastic nights. In fact, if anything, our sex-life together has a sharper edge now than it his ever done. I don't know how much of that is due to an underlying current of desperation, a heightened intensity, like that of two rats clinging to an imperilled raft.

'A fair whack – I bet, you bloody liar!'

'That's nice. What a lovely way to talk to one's wife.'

Now he is silent. When he does speak his voice is low, but the words tear into me. 'Hard to remember that you are my wife, Eve, in the midst of this latest madness. Do you really think that this singer is worth it, surely you can see that he's just a second-rate joke. You must do in your saner moments.'

'Saner moments, Adam?' I make my voice cold, cold and nasty. He's struck a stubborn streak and a resentful one. 'Perhaps I don't allow myself the indulgence of saner moments any more. Perhaps madness is my natural milieu. Yours too. I wouldn't have said that either of us has been behaving with much sanity since our arrival in the States, would you? Hardly your stereotype marriage any more, is it.'

'Our marriage, Eve, is as strong now as it has ever been.

Stronger. More passionate. More difficult. More demanding. No deceptions. Absolute loyalty.' A pause. 'I *adore* you.' Another pause. 'I love *you*. Forever. Eve?'

The sunlight is shimmering through my swimming eyes. I blink and salt water splashes onto my blotched breasts. Liquid snot is streaming into my mouth.

'Eve, angel . . .' There is a special pleading tenderness that Adam has always used to get through to the core of me. It never fails. I can see his warm eyes now, as if he were in front of me. It is the first time in a week that I have seen anything in my mind's eye other than Puck's face.

'Darling, Eve, are you listening?' The huskiness has reduced his deep voice down to a whisper.

I sniff loudly, running the back of my hand under my wet nostrils to dry them off. 'I'm listening, you bastard. I know just what you're going to say. All right, I'll forget him. I'll put him out of my mind.' As I speak, the image of Puck re-asserts itself, the memory of our dancing, the talking together . . .

'Time for the off, old girl. We go now.' Adam had tapped me briskly on the shoulder. Behind him the two girls were giggling together, clearly we would be all departing together. But I was so surprised by the abruptness of the decision that I just stood where I was, encircled in Puck's embrace. He remained perfectly still, too, through the pounding disco sounds, just standing there, all of him close up against me. So close that I could feel his erect cock gradually dwindling, dying at the sight of my husband standing over us. Killed by the command in the British voice.

I'd cleared my throat, but otherwise had made no move towards leaving, towards doing as I'd been told. 'You two haven't properly met, have you – this is my husband, Adam (the cock shrivelled instantly). This is Puck, Adam.'

They had exchanged cordialities, Adam complimenting Puck on his performance. 'You have a magnificent stage presence. Extraordinary magnetism. Yes, really! Well, you've managed to magnetise my wife!'

I'd seethed all the way in the taxi, clutching Puck's telephone number in my trembling fingers. He hadn't

417

been able to leave the club with us, he had another set to sing at two in the morning. After that he might be able to come on and join us at the party, but usually what he liked to do after performing was go and eat, then gradually wind down before collapsing into bed. His collapse was what I'd been looking forward to sharing. There was obviously going to be no chance of that now. But I managed satisfactorily to fuck up Adam's finely-laid plans with the two giggling girls. I casually mentioned, when we three were fixing our faces in front of the mirror, that Adam was suffering from a social disease. That's how New Yorkers describe VD.

'Oh, where have your charming girlfriends vanished to?' I'd enquired sweetly after their prolonged non-appearance. My expression was one of solicitous innocence, after all it was an unspoken pact that neither of us would allow likely prey to break loose.

He'd shrugged, put a commendably brave face on it. But I knew every nuance, every change of light in those twinkling eyes, every taut muscle around that familiar mouth. *Inside* it was seething, malevolent frustration.

Four

'But what I can't understand here, Eve, looking at your medical file, your gynaecological history, is why you should be seeking a contraceptive device at all. From what I understand, your husband has had a vasectomy. So you

418

are highly unlikely to conceive . . .'

'Yes, doctor, but we, my husband and I, are now having an affair with someone – he's a rock star who hasn't had a vasectomy, you understand.'

'I understand completely, Eve. That puts a different light on the circumstances. Now, knees a little higher and wider apart, please. It would seem to me that if you have a husband and lover waiting impatiently back home, you'll be wanting to get this over as quickly as possible and rush back to them.'

'Puck.'

'Er – what's that, Eve? I didn't quite catch . . .'

'Sorry, doctor. I said Puck.' (Not fuck as you probably imagined. Christ, could one ever have talked like this to one's GP back home!) 'Puck is his name. The name of our lover. He's gorgeous.' I say it dreamily, with reverence. But now I am being admonished for chattering. It's difficult taking a cervical smear, checking that cancer is not present, in preparation for my new contraceptive coil. The patient must lie still, which is not so easy for someone in my euphoric state.

'What about the pill, doctor?' I'd asked at the start of my appointment, some ten minutes ago. But he'd checked on my date of birth which I'd had to fill in on my form whilst waiting, and he'd shaken his head. Violently.

'I take it that you are not suicidally inclined? Never been drawn to voluntarily put an end to your life, Eve?' He'd started off calling me by my first name the moment I'd stepped into his office. Friendly, familiar in the American fashion. None of the pompous formality of the British medical profession. This young gynaecologist (young and bewilderingly attractive – swarthy, with the swimming eyes of a spaniel) speaks to me as casually as the guy who serves at the local Deli. Conversely, the Deli counterhand holds a conversation with me with as much social confidence as this highly qualified physician. The British class structure has failed to cross the Atlantic. Mercifully.

'Because,' the doctor had continued, faced with my sagging jaw and wide eyes, 'that is what you would be doing if we gave a person your age the pill now. Experience has taught us this much.'

419

'Well,' I'd answered jauntily (this, though, was before I'd explained about our lover, Puck), 'I'm not prepared to die for love, so I'll by-pass the pill. I'll take whatever you suggest, doctor.' But, having mentioned love as early as this in our professional relationship, I really needed this young man to understand that I wasn't just another wife looking to cheat on her unsuspecting husband. I would never do a thing like that to Adam. Never! I have, as he does, an absolute abhorrence of shabbiness, of hole-in-the-corner affairs taking place behind the other one's back. Even so, I hadn't expected this instant acceptance. This, 'I understand completely, Eve,' stuff. It made me wonder just how many of his other patients were indulging in a *ménage-à-trois*. Were all the rest of them bloody perverts too? Like me. And like Adam.

'Eve?' I wince now as something is removed from my cunt. Some sort of wrench, the kind used by car mechanics to jack up the back axle. Why didn't I notice that instrument when it was on its way in? Must have been thinking about Puck. And about his boyish embarrassment when I had emerged from the bathroom on his very first visit, clad only in my lace teddy. He claimed never to have seen a teddy before.

'What, not even on your mother?' I'd teased, flinging myself provocatively across the bed.

And that had made him grin. 'Sure as hell would have liked to have seen mother in one of those!' But he'd stayed where he was, over on the other side of the room. Too shy to cross over to me. Anxious to talk first, to get to know each other a little more. To tell me all about his mother and how he'd never known who she was, being a foundling, just dumped on the doorstep of an orphanage in somewhere like Dallas – or was it Detroit?

I'd sat perfectly still, not wanting to break the spell, not wishing to kill the unexpected intimacy that was linking us together despite the distance of the room. I was uncomfortable and cold. I felt silly in my ridiculously flimsy garment. Fat and ungainly, mutton dressed up as lamb. The gusset was cutting in between my buttocks at the back, getting soaked with the expectant sexual juices in the front. An expectancy which was now gradually dying by the second, with each faltering sentence that this anxious child was stammering.

420

And a child was how I saw him now, with tenderness and a growing compassion. I wanted to hold him, but in a different way. I wanted to comfort him and let him cry against me, and stroke him very gently. With a rocking to-and-fro, as I'd done with my own babies when they were very young, and even when they were older and seemed to need me.

Then Adam had come in. 'How's it going in here, eh? What, not in bed yet, you two. There was I in the other room letting you get started – was hoping to join in the orgy by now!'

I couldn't look at Puck. I couldn't look at Adam either. No one spoke until I did. 'Puck,' I cleared my throat of the clogging emotion, 'Puck was just telling me how he's a foundling. He's never known who his mother is . . .' And then I'd jumped up, no longer embarrassed by my mode of undress, aware only of the desire in Adam's eyes as his gaze travelled over my body. And conscious now too of the sensual drooping of Puck's eyelids. As if Adam's entry has lifted us all onto another plane.

That's when I'd taken each of them by the hand and led them into the bed. That was our first time of making love.

I can't say that it was entirely successful.

It may have been that I had over-anticipated the great event, that my disappointment over Puck's non-appearance and my promise over the telephone to Adam to give Puck up, had ruined it all. The situation was fraught before it even started. But all I could remember afterwards was my spiralling heart when Puck had rung moments later to say that he was downstairs in the lobby of the Eden, apologising for being so late.

I'd had to ring Adam back, quick. 'He's here! Puck's arrived! He's on his way up in the elevator!'

'Be right over – don't do anything until I get there, Eve.' And Adam had slammed the phone down. I was still holding it, stunned, perspiring with the shock of it all, when Puck rang the doorbell in the corridor outside. My knees buckled as I drew a colourful kimono over my lace teddy. The moment I let him in I knew my louche clothing was a big mistake. I ought to have greeted him in a demure dress, suitable for taking afternoon tea. That would have put him more at his ease, instead of this

421

hungry whore's get-up. I felt like a greedy spider luring an innocent fly into her web, with my mate winging his way across town to join eagerly in the devouring.

It struck me, not for the first time, that this life we were leading of debauched depravity might be having a coarsening effect on our sensitivity. That we had begun to see human beings in terms of their youth and beauty, only rating them as worth bothering with if there was sex in it for us.

This boy, Puck, deserved better than me.

'Sorry about that, Eve . . .' Back in the doctor's surgery the swimming brown eyes of the spaniel are smiling at me, whilst their owner proceeds to peel fine rubber gloves from each hand. Nice nails, I now notice. The attendant nurse, a baby Doris Day, twinkles beside him. I watch her dispose of the mechanic's wrench into a sterilised metallic tray. But I am incapable of action, myself, in this hive of sudden efficiency. I might decide to remain here like this all morning, in the Female Protection clinic. On my back, completely naked from the waist down, my knees high in the air like a trusting babe waiting to be swaddled up in clean nappies and small woollie garments.

But my doctor, Dr Leventine, is not having any of it. There is a line of patients waiting for him outside in the swanky reception area. At this moment they sit there, perusing American *Harpers*, studying fey shots of teenage Brooke Shields in her new movie, reading the reviews of Nancy Friday's latest offering, *Men in Love*. Though all the time their brains are really lodged in the base of their bellies. Every nerve, every thought, every twinge, every tremor is concentrated on their reproductive tracts. That smooth, glossy brunette – is she suffering from thrush? The savoury blonde – has she a dose of syphilis? The razor-thin red-head – does she require a quick abortion?

We are all of us at Female Protection for reasons such as these. We haven't left our well-paid desks for the fun of it.

'Sorry about that, Eve.' Dr Leventine is repeating himself, or else I am having a time-lapse again. This keeps on happening to me these days. My mind is unhinged by mad, middle-aged love for a ludicrously younger man. Classic case. And, too, for the first time I am having to question how deep my commitment is to my husband.

422

How can I feel so drawn to Puck if I am still desperately devoted to Adam? Or has this devotion now deteriorated into mere dependency?

'Afraid you're going to suffer a spot of cramp for a short while, nothing to worry about. What I'd like to establish now is when you had your last period, Eve?'

'Sorry, doctor, I nearly dozed off then.' I laugh flirtatiously back at him. The nurse has retreated from the room now and my legs are in a more decorous position, feet on the floor. I am deliberately putting on my poshest English accent, to intrigue. The way that I do all the time with Puck.

My challenge is being met, though. This doctor must have seen it all, every come-on in the business. Stands to reason that if you love women, the female sex, and want to be in medicine anyway, then the branch you would be bound to choose (if you've any sense at all) would be gynaecology. Fiddling around with female privates all day. Plunging your fist up their plumbing. Forcing them open with mechanical aids (like the apparatus I've just dispelled from my orifice).

So I back down – why do I? And instead I answer the question.

'My period? I've just finished one three days ago.'

But now he is shaking his head. 'Shame about that. We like to insert the coil just before or during a period. This means that you will have to wait a few more weeks until the time is right, Eve.' And he turns away to write something in my notes.

'Oh, no, no, no, no . . .' I'm wailing at his back (*great* muscles beneath his white coat!). 'But I can't wait that long – I want the coil in *today*, this minute, oh, please. DOCTOR!

He is laughing, chuckling as he turns to face me. 'My, my, Eve – you're *so* hot. But . . .' then he looks grave, it wouldn't be possible to have the coil inserted today anyway. We have to await the results of this cancer smear first. That will take a few days to come through – unless I mark it urgent.' His spaniel eyes are becoming more liquid by the minute. Tom Conti, the actor, that's who he reminds me of. We went to see him on Broadway several weeks ago in, *Whose Life is it Anyway?* A British play which has managed to make the successful transition from London's West End over to here. But we didn't enjoy it one bit. We find more fun in spots like The Comic Strip, or Improv, where young comedians (up and coming Woody Allens) stand up and improvise hilarious routines – involving unfortunate members of the audience in the process. The last time we went, they picked on us and made huge fun of our accents, mimicking them in the manner of Winston Churchill. Everyone enjoyed it immensely, taking the piss out of the pompous limeys.

'Oh, please, do mark it urgent, doctor. And when does that mean I can have the coil in?' My voice drops to a pleading whisper. I am really grovelling now. 'By the weekend, do you think? It means an awful lot . . .'

'To the three of you?' He is laughing again, but nodding too. 'Come in Saturday morning, I'll fix you up – that's if your cancer smear is clear. And as long as you promise me you won't get pregnant in the meantime.'

My turn to laugh at that one. 'I think I may be relied upon to harness my passions until then, doctor. It's only three days to go.'

'And four nights.' He spoke cryptically, obviously having a far wider knowledge of female sexuality than myself.

'Well, at my age I should think that . . .'

'At your age and in exactly the same situation as yourself with a husband and lover, though not necessarily all three in the bed altogether, a patient of fifty became pregnant last year. I performed an abortion and sterilised her. You mustn't underestimate how intense your emotions are or how far they can carry you, despite firm resolves, Eve.' He spoke so kindly I almost cried.

Half an hour later, walking along Lexington Avenue in the direction of Bloomingdales (one of my favourite stores in the whole world), I reflected on how wise his words were. Ignoring all the men who were staring hard at me as they passed, I concentrated on trying to walk in an upright position. Almost impossible to straighten the spine, I find, following an internal examination. So that one is forced into the humiliating stance of a person attempting to contain a full bladder and not spill tell-tale drips upon the ground. Bum jutting.

424

But this isn't why the men are fascinated by me. They are drawn by the powerful aura of sex that I emanate. I'm on heat. And they sense it. I vibrate in the air and their tentacles are picking up these strong tremors.

It has become much more noticeable since Puck. He has unleashed hidden passions. But all is not well with Puck and Adam. I am having immense difficulty with the two of them.

The first fuck was not a success. Puck was overconscious of Adam being in bed with us. He explained it, haltingly but with greater articulacy than I would have expected. He is vehemently anti-homosexual (he protesteth too much, Adam said to me afterwards).

'You mean you've never had a gay experience?' I put it to him with certain undisguised astonishment.

'I'm not saying that, Eve, but –' he appealed to Adam, 'I am interested in your wife. I want to be in bed with just her. I want her all to myself.'

'We all want that, Puck.' There was a new note of harshness in Adam's voice that I couldn't recall noticing before. I thought, Adam dislikes Puck. He doesn't want him here. What started as a joke is going all wrong. Neither one of them needs or wants the other to be around. The last thing they want is to have to be in the same bed and the only reason they are sticking it out is because of me.

The situation is impossible. Adam wouldn't agree to me having Puck on my own, even if such a thought had entered my head. And it hasn't. And since these are the rules by which Puck entered the game in the first place, he has no right to complain now. Except that now he is falling in love with me. And I am falling in love with him. If it were not for Adam we probably would be content not even to go to bed at all, just moon around holding hands. Looking soulfully and with intense feeling into each others' eyes.

But this is not allowable, it's breaking the rules of so called 'swinging'. There's no sex involved. And it excludes Adam. As he points out to me, coldly, now. He and Cherry don't indulge themselves with such romantic twaddle. They are perfectly open and demonstrative and sexual in their regard for each other and for me. A perfect triangle. Whilst this one with Puck is decidedly imperfect.

And yet we managed somehow to fuck. They both got

erections. Adam's, fortunately or unfortunately, was longer lasting and more impressive. But then, as he pointed out afterwards in the inevitable postmortem (after Puck had departed), he felt more at home. He was in his own bed.

In fact Adam was more than generous in his judgement of Puck's difficulties. He thought the sexual performance was commendable under the circumstances (safe in the knowledge that I had found it sadly lacking myself!).

But they both got their cocks in, Puck's went in first. Smaller than Adam's, but then he is smaller all over so I might have expected that. Then, when he'd shot off and it didn't take long, he rolled over and said to Adam, 'D'you wanna get in there now?' And they both laughed at that, as if it was a male joke between them. As if they were treating me as some cheap piece of meat that they'd dragged home off the street, instead of the woman with whom they were both very much in love.

I understood all that. More than even they did themselves.

So it was, 'Why not, old chap! May as well get in there, give it a going over . . .' That from Adam, my beloved husband of eleven years' standing. I think it excited him no end.

But in my heart I was uneasy. Trouble was brewing, it was just a question of time. And of the timing.

Bent double on my way to Bloomingdales, glancing into a shiny window and wondering who the interestingly-dressed hunchbacked dwarf was (then realising it was me), I thought about the evening. The evening following the first afternoon fuck with Puck.

It had been established early on in our relationship what his movements were, where one might expect to find him at any time of the day or night. From what I could gather he was a most dedicated performer who spent all the time, when he wasn't onstage performing his act with his band, rehearsing that act. Polishing it up and trying out new numbers. He wrote all his own songs, all his own music. Which seemed to me particularly miraculous.

'Most groups do now, Eve,' Adam had coolly explained. 'There is a greater profit margin if they don't have to pay royalties. Got it?' He speaks increasingly as if

426

I am some sort of idiot. I'm not. It's just that Puck moves in a world about which I know very little. All that Adam knows about it comes from reading.

So evenings were out, unless Puck was performing somewhere and had a gig on, which we could attend. 'Oh, we'd love to come and see you, wouldn't we, Adam,' I'd enthused. Adam remained silent.

'I promise to tell you, Eve, next time there's a gig, and get your names put on my guest list. Then you won't have to pay.'

'Oh, we'd come anyway. We don't mind paying, do we, Adam!' But I hadn't looked at Adam's face as I said it, knowing what the expression would be. Adam has always decided where, or not, we should go. Up until now, that is.

That evening (after the fuck) we went to a swish party in a sumptuously converted loft, somewhere eminently fashionable around West Broadway. We arrived to find a crowd of easily 500 people, being attended to by waiters with trays of glasses brimming with champagne.

Andy Warhol was there and insisted on photographing me, and then being photographed with me. We got into conversation, so that when we gradually became separated I was still being sought out by media people wanting to know who I was, taking further photographs.

I met Tom Wolfe, though I had met him before. He couldn't remember, but he said he could. Engaging his attention on some top topic of trivia which amused us both. I prided myself on my social expertise. On judging exactly just when I would bore him and make him restless to leave if I continued talking to him any longer. So before that point loomed up (and with mere seconds to go) I excused myself. I made it easy for him, I escaped before giving him a chance to leave me stranded on my own.

All the social observers who were noting these things like vultures, made a note of this second victory. From then on I lacked no companions. They were thronging around me until Adam said it was time to leave, to go on elsewhere.

But throughout it all, throughout the social triumphs I could think of only one thing. Puck. Puck and his vulnerability. Mine too.

Two nights later Puck and his group were playing out in Brooklyn. It was my intention to go.

427

'But Brooklyn is *miles*!' Adam had protested, sulking already.

'I've asked Cherry,' I said cunningly. 'And Zack and Puck have got a car in which they will collect us. All we have to do is sit here and wait.' I regretted those words as soon as I'd said them.

'That could take all night knowing our lad's record for punctuality!'

'Cherry is really keen to meet Puck, she's dying to go.' This was perfectly true. Cherry was dying to go solely in order to set her cap at Puck. I knew this and though it should have caused me at least a twinge of anxiety, it didn't. I was completely confident of my young lover's loyalty to me. But there is always the element of risk, especially where a greedy little pussy-cat like Cherry is concerned. Perhaps I was using her as a testing ground, though I was absolutely conscious of it at the time.

She had heard all about Puck, in detail, the previous afternoon. We had taken her to bed following Sunday brunch – English muffins and marmalade, eggs over-easy, home-fries, endless coffee to make the heart go . . . then a languid session of love-making with Cherry. Just the three of us.

There was a fourth person present, but he was only in my mind. I ached for him all the way through. I had never felt lonelier or more alienated, nor had I ever put a jollier face on things. Adam and Cherry agreed how much more relaxed I was in bed with them now. If writing ever failed me I could always take up acting.

'Any chance of getting this dreamboat in bed with us, then, Eve?' Cherry, brushing her hair and dimpling. Licking my husband's spunk around her strong, white teeth. Picking one of his pubic hairs from the corner of her mouth.

'Every chance, I should say,' I answered evenly. 'What do you think, Adam?'

'Perhaps that's just what he needs, neurotic bugger, to loosen him up – another girl in the bed. Terrified of being thought a poof, Cherry. He's a bloody poof if ever I saw one. More of a poof than me.'

'That's saying something!' Cherry and I chorused. But Adam can take any amount of teasing. He is sure enough

428

of himself – of his masculinity, he says – to be able to enjoy such cheap verbal slurs as these.

So we go out to Brooklyn, Zack collects us in the car and I sit in front with him. Cherry and Adam sit at the back with a girl called Carly. I assume that she's a girlfriend of Zack, but we are on our way to pick up Puck from some reheasal studio. It transpires that he is working on other material with an altogether separate group. I can't wait for him to get in the car beside me. When he does my insides begin to melt.

He kisses me hard on the mouth, barely turning to acknowledge the rest of them in the car. When I try to introduce him to Cherry in the back seat, he simply nods, 'Hi, Cherry!'

Then he returns his sole, and burning attention to me. 'How've you been? Say, you look *so beautiful*! I've *missed* you.' But my pleasure is spoiled by the awareness of Adam in the back seat. I can feel his disapproval. And his pain. I only pray that young Cherry is making up for things. I bear her no resentment now whatsoever, I have my own love-object, that's why.

We do very little kissing on the journey, which is a relief, in a way, as far as the atmosphere is concerned – though I ache continually for the feel of his mouth on mine. But Puck is tense, pre-performance nerves (though he protests that this isn't the case). He claims to be more concerned at the appalling venue. A place called Zappas, where great performers like Brian Eno are meant to have played in their time. But this is a Wednesday, not a promising night. He is having doubts about the wisdom of inviting us out this far. He fears that the night will turn out a flop and that we may be the only ones in the audience.

We are.

'Jesus Christ!' Adam looks at the decor, at the deserted bar, at the empty dance floor. 'You're going to have to do some personality-projection to make believe this place is full of fans for your precious Puck, Eve. What a following he pulls, they've come out in droves. Which guys are the record producers, do you suppose.'

'Don't be bitchy.' My retort is curt. I am as secretly as appalled as he is, but I have no intention of showing it.

429

'What are you drinking, Cherry? I have money. Others seem a little slow with theirs.' I cast a withering glance in Adam's direction as I seat myself up at the nearest barstool.

Cherry climbs eagerly onto the one next to mine. 'He's *divine*, isn't he!' Her eyes are on Puck, as he confers with his group up on the darkened stage.

As if suddenly aware that we are looking at him, he turns around. And blows a kiss in my direction. Cherry sighs. 'How romantic.'

Adam is listening sardonically. 'I'm sure he's yours for the asking, Cherry darling.' And he drops a kiss on her forehead. If I'd had a drink in my hand I'd have drenched him.

But the drinks were not quite so easy to locate. 'This place must be noted for its music rather than for the service,' I say to Zack, now that he's joined us after parking the car. He grimaces back, sympathetically, but in no time has organised a round of spritzers. They prove undrinkable, the white wine being far too sweet. We all decide to switch to beer and consequently get far drunker – far sooner than any of us had intended.

The show, Puck's singing, seemed absolutely superlative. We were the only people there, but it didn't matter. What we lacked in numbers we made up for in enthusiasm. Cherry and I danced together close to the stage. Adam stood mid-floor swaying, always just off the beat of the music in his usual way. Adam has trouble with the beat, he can't understand when and where it comes. He has a blockage, which is what makes him an awkward dancing partner on the floor. One of the difficulties between us, always a bone of contention, a source of near-disagreement in the past. Tonight I feel particularly ill-disposed towards Adam, his dancing skills seem more than usually pathetic. Perhaps in comparison with Puck's agility onstage. But my irritability affords me no pleasure, only a sneaking underfeeling of guilt. A self-loathing for the obvious disloyalty.

'How's the beat over here in Alaska?' I can't stop myself from smoothly gyrating over to him, hopping ineptly from one foot to another. 'Got the hang of it yet?' And I catch hold of him by the waist, skilfully swerving and swooping in perfect time and rhythm. Showing off to my idol up there.

Then I lose patience with the clumsiness of my partner and leave him spinning helplessly again on his own. It has never been explained to me how such a superb lover, instinctive and sensitive as Adam is, could be such a bad mover in front of a band. I'd been brought up to believe that the two skills went hand in hand. But then I'd been brought up in the tradition of going to a Saturday night dance every weekend throughout my adolescence. Adam claimed to have spent his Saturday evenings at amateur offerings by the local repertory company. Or listening to plays and serious discussions on the wireless. Or simply reading an intellectual book at home. But this is the man that I chose to love, honour and obey. To cherish till the end of my days. I can't start complaining now because he's not a disco dude. There must be many more disappointing factors about me, for him, but he doesn't treat me with contempt.

Or do I feel that he has begun to do exactly that. Are we becoming eventually disillusioned with each other? Is that why I'm drawn to this new admirer? Will Puck start replacing Adam in my life? A month ago the likelihood of anyone doing that would have been unthinkable. Now it's not unthinkable at all!

I return to the edge of the stage. Cherry is dancing with Zack and the girl, Carly, now. But all the time she is gazing adoringly up at Puck. My throat constricts, I dare not look at him myself to see just how much of his attention she commands. *But I must.* He is looking at me with such passionate appeal that I am weak at the knees again, just as I was when he arrived at the apartment that first time. I want to climb up on-stage and embrace him, with all my heart I want to. Was there ever such a love as emotional as this . . .

After the performance, cheered wildly by us at the front, and mildly by several stragglers who have convened at the back, we sit down at a table for a further beer. Soon we are joined by Puck and several members of the group. Puck heads straight into the chair that I have been saving for him next to me. Cherry sits opposite with her arm around Adam's neck. I think to myself how fortunate it is for me

431

that I now have Puck. Otherwise wouldn't it look as if I were the cuckolded wife – if wives can ever be described as being cuckolded! Cherry is always extremely demonstrative in public, much to Adam's embarrassment – or so he claims (though not tonight, tonight he actually appears to be encouraging her show of obvious affection for him). I think that he is *furious* over something.

We decide to go on somewhere to eat. Puck mentions, One Fifth, a fashionable spot on Fifth Avenue. Adam does not want to go there.

I say, 'What about Elaine's?' And everyone looks at me with awe, except Adam. We go there quite often, Elaine knows me and always gives me a very good table.

'Isn't that a very exclusive place, Elaine's? Doesn't it require a tie?' Puck says nervously. To Adam's delight.

'Great idea, Eve! We go to Elaine's . . .' Adam is up and ready for off, he seems to be enjoying himself for the first time this evening.

The journey back into town is far jollier than the trip out. It is just after midnight but we have an exciting destination. And Adam has decided to be his usual witty and amusing self. He keeps the others in fits of laughter all the way back.

I am silent. I have begun to dread our arrival at Elaine's Restaurant. What if she cannot – genuinely cannot – fit us in. What if she really is full up, and I am placed in the awkward situation of having to be turned away. A failure in the eyes of my worshipper, who believes that I can perform miracles . . .

'You're very quiet, Eve. Isn't Eve quiet, everyone? Puck – what sort of spell have you placed on my wife now?' I loathed the way Adam referred to me as *his wife* to Puck.

I retaliated. 'And you're very garrulous, Adam. What have you been doing to my husband, Cherry?'

Everyone laughed. Only Adam and I knew exactly what we were doing, but the terrain was treacherously unfamiliar. We were plumbing new depths of hostility. It was a case of the survival of the fittest.

Elaine, mercifully, has a table for us, one in a highly-prized position. It is next to Woody Allen's usually reserved place. But he is not here tonight, he must have eaten and gone already. Because we usually see him here,

432

I usually have a word with him. Though we have never arrived quite as late as this before. But Puck is hugely impressed. 'Say,' he whispers excitedly, 'isn't that Lauren Bacall sitting here on the next table?' It is. 'And isn't that Diane Keaton on the right of her?' I nod, though I can't even be sure of this myself. But I want him to believe that it is Diane Keaton, if that is what particularly thrills him. It occurs to me how small a chance there would be of impressing him in this way in a London restaurant, the equivalent of Elaine's. He wouldn't know who anyone was. The names wouldn't impress him. We come from culturally different backgrounds. Besides being from different generations.

During the course of the dinner Puck gets up to go to the men's room. I am interested to see how many heads turn to study him in this restaurant, so used to wealth, fame and excessive good looks. Every head turns. I notice Adam watching me watching. There is an unpleasant lift to one eyebrow. Cherry has given up completely on trying to captivate Puck. She sees that it is useless, he is too involved in me. She's making my husband the goal for the night.

But now, making use of Puck's absence, she leans forward. 'Have you got it fixed up for tonight, Eve? The foursome?'

The foursome! The foursome? When was it decided that we should have a foursome? And was it meant to be taking place tonight? Adam has overheard and is nodding. 'Leave it to Eve,' he is saying reassuringly to Cherry, his hand covering hers. 'You'll be fixing it, won't you, my darling.' This is not a question, there is a hard gleam in the eyes. It has been issued as more of a command.

But I avoid answering. I can't trust myself to speak, that's why. I just nod, as if abstracted, as if thinking about something else. As Puck approaches on his return to the table I think how young, and how tired he looks. And how I would like to tuck him up in bed beside me, just the two of us, and go to sleep without having to have any kind of sexual antics before dropping off. None at all. But I am conscious of Adam staring at me, and of Cherry licking her lips in sexual anticipation of this beautiful creature, this lovely boy. And I am filled with self-disgust. Sexual predators. My puritan background, Adam would have explained it away dismissively. All at once I feel unaccountably depressed.

When Puck sat down beside me, he took my hand in his and covered the back of it with kisses. Then he turned it over and did the same with the centre of the palm. Finally he leaned forward and kissed me lightly on the lips. I felt myself brought back to life. With a boldness that I knew would probably horrify him, put him off me forever (but I had to test him yet again, I had to), I whispered in his ear. 'I have been asked whether you would be interested in a foursome tonight. You, me, Adam and Cherry. You might feel happier in the bed if there was another girl. Less troubled by Adam being there . . .'

I waited for his reaction. It wasn't what I expected.

A small frown appeared first of all between his eyes. A perplexed crease, almost of disbelief in what he had heard. And a miniscule tightening of the muscles around the fullness of that mouth. Then he started shaking his head, imperceptibly and then more and more urgently. It seemed ages before he uttered a word. When he did it came out in a torrent that everyone on the table could hear. It was very much the outpouring of a young man. A young man in love.

'What you don't understand, Eve, is that I'm not looking for there to be *more* in the bed. I'm looking for there to be less. I'm looking for it to be just you and me – don't you understand that? Don't you believe me when I say that I'm in love with you? Don't you know that I want you to come and live with me? That I'm hoping that one day you will marry me . . .'

That's when I stopped listening, just as his voice was rising, just as other people on other tables were beginning to become as engrossed in the proceedings as everyone on our own table was.

I got up and left. I ran all the way out of Elaine's, past the famous diners, past the thronged bar of gawpers, straight out into the street. My brain was bursting. It was bubbling with happiness. HE WANTED TO MARRY ME!!!!

I laughed up at the sky, at the skyscrapers, at the silhouette of Manhattan – this magical city, where the one

434

that I had fallen in love with had fallen in love with me. And then I felt his arms around me, hugging me to him, laughing with me up into the stars . . .

That night we slept together. As usual. The three of us. How could I marry Puck? I was married already, to Adam.

I am looking forward to Saturday, when I get my coil in. I'm sitting at my typewriter trying to work, trying to place some sort of structure on this new novel of mine. But all the time I'm thinking of how much better the sex will be with Puck when I get my coil in and don't have to worry about getting pregnant. Perhaps it will make all the difference to the three of us in bed, me being more relaxed. But I don't think so.

That morning, following the scene at Elaine's, Adam sucked Puck's cock for the first time. He said it was lovely feeling it come up so big and thick under his practised tongue. But Puck did not reciprocate in any way at all, except right at the end he did lay his hand on Adam's head. As if to say that it was all right, he didn't mind too much. I couldn't really look either of them in the eye. It was just too uneasy for words. Nothing nice, nothing really loving passing between them. Just Adam trying to prove something to himself. And Puck not allowing him to prove it.

So I interrupted. I slid down in the bed, right to the bottom so that my breasts rested on both sets of their knees. And I took both of their cocks into my mouth, one in each cheek. It was lovely! And I sucked as hard as I could on both of them, now and then rolling them together in my mouth with my tongue until the tips of each of them was rubbing against the other. Just like that! They both, both men, began groaning with pleasure. From the ecstatic noises they were making, they were driven wild by it. And it was fun for me too because I could caress their cocks actually *through* my own cheeks. Running my finger-tips over my face I could trace the outline of their glands inside my mouth, but on the other side.

They both came off in my mouth, more or less at the same time. I have never had to cope with so much spunk before, slipping down my throat. I feared that I might drown in the stuff!

And then in the morning Puck came with us swimming,

435

over at the Y. It almost felt as if he and I were married already. But we weren't. It was playing at being a *ménage-à-trois*. Nearly all right, but not quite. Neither one thing nor the other.

It is the evening after my visit to the Female Protection clinic. Puck is rehearsing tonight with his secondary group. Adam and I are meant to be seeing a preview of a film on witchcraft directed by a friend of ours. We are taking a date along with us. The girlfriend of a guy we know. A girl who claims to have been frigid for almost a year. It is, or was, our plan to de-freeze her. But I have little enthusiasm for the project. I am going along with it for Adam's sake. I have to be careful, very careful with Adam these days. He is behaving irrationally it seems to me. But then I, myself, am so emotional that it is difficult really to judge which of the two of us is behaving rationally. I think that it's this city, it is affecting us.

Five

There is a small Renoir painting on the wall, spotlit, with security guards scattered amongst the party guests pretending to merge with the crowds. They stand out like aliens from some other planet, a place where the standards of physical perfection fall far short of the requirements of this crowd. These guards are too plain to belong to the beautiful people. Their conversation is not camp enough. Their way with words will never qualify them as recognised wits. Their style of dress is altogether too suburban. Yet their presence puts everyone else at some sort of ease. They represent safety and the stamp of a certain creamy layer of life. To be in a party with security guards watchfully surveying the scene means that one has made it to the top.

This is the top. It's the top two, or is it three, floors of one of the most expensive and exclusive apartment blocks in New York. The host is Paul Simon, and this may be the most opulent gathering I'm ever likely to attend. I sip champagne with Adam making suitably facile social interchange.

'Oh,' I say, fingering a roll of granary bread at the groaning buffet, 'this bread looks jolly good – the same texture as mine. Do you remember, Adam the homemade bread I used to bake? That sticky wholemeal which used to come out of the oven like cake? Wasn't it gorgeous . . .'

'Yes, it was gorgeous. I still have the stretch marks on the top of my thighs. The signs of a mis-spent youth!'

But we are not concentrating on each other. We are not connecting at all.

'Oh, look – there's Teddy and Kenneth.' I wave with barely disguised relief at the prospect of being joined by these gay acquaintances of ours. Both are from London, both are in the fashion business. They have taken to the gay world of Manhattan with exuberant delight, there are not enough hours in the day and night for them to do justice to their pleasurable pursuits. They are no longer lovers, if indeed they ever were – but they hunt as a team. And meet up immediately afterwards to compare results. A bit like Adam and myself, except that we never separate. And we are not on such intimate terms of easy friendship as they are. They would put the blame on that for being married.

'Hello, Teddy – hello Kenneth! How divine you both look!' We kiss each other on the cheek, first the left then the right. They embrace Adam, kissing him directly (and enthusiastically) on the mouth. Nobody in the room finds this odd. If only Puck could be this uninhibited with Adam. Puck is on my mind all the time, my wrists tingle whenever I think of him. I have to blink his face out of my eyes.

437

'You're looking pretty dreamy yourself, darling,' Teddy is murmuring. 'Isn't Eve looking sensational, Kenneth?'

'*Sensational*, Eve! You're looking sensational – cock sandwich? Can we put it down to that, Adam?' Kenneth nudges Adam playfully, at the same time as he runs a suggestive tongue around his own bunched lips.

'Something like that, boys,' I answer quickly for Adam. Though his own homosexuality is burgeoning so satisfactorily, he usually complains about this level of conversation. He regards it as being exclusively to do with 'queens', 'old queens'. A world he regards as far removed from himself. Already his gaze is wandering across the room. I discreetly follow it and discover it resting upon a young couple, nubile, gauche. They look as if they badly need to be rescued, lost in this sophisticated gathering. But I am not prepared to offer to proposition them at this moment, I don't feel like playing pimp, I'm enjoying myself with Teddy and Kenneth. My pals. Adam begins to drift away as we three start our usual banter. He drains his glass and waving it in the air he offers to re-fill ours. There is no need for this, the party is awash with waiters and waitresses there expressly to satisfy the thirst of the guests. But I understand his restlessness and actually would prefer him to go, instead of standing there inhibiting the repartee between the boys and me.

So I nod. 'Love another.' And I hand him my glass, glancing at my watch as I do so. This is a new watch, one that I bought for myself. A tiny cocktail watch, the sort that was more popular in the forties, covered in glittery diamanté. I expect Teddy and Kenneth to comment on it and they do.

'Adore the jewel, angel. *Too* much! Payment for services rendered?'

'Of *course*, my darlings,' I gush back. 'How about your good selves – have you earned some small trinkets this week?'

Both raise their eyebrows heavenwards. 'Would that we had, Eve! The trade that we find couldn't raise the price of a cigarette pack!'

'I expect they raise other more interesting things though,' I speak in my reassuringly Earth Mother voice, insinuating it with sniggering overtones. 'What have you found on the park benches lately – or rather *under* them?' I sweep my eyes in the direction of Central Park. There is a magnificent view of it from these immense windows. Adam, I see, is engaged in conversation with the young couple. His glass is significantly empty. 'Plenty of rogering, eh?' My eyes tease Teddy first, and then Kenneth. I can remember the time when Adam and I used to stand together all through a party such as this, teasing each other till it was time to go home. Not having spoken to another person for the entire evening. And so hot for each other that we would start making love the minute we got into the lift, lurching along the street together locked in each others arms. Me limp with desire. And yet emboldened enough by my lust for him that I would undo his pants, and take his swollen penis in the palms of both hands. And walk backwards all the way home, just holding onto him like that. Stopping, when I couldn't help myself, to suck on it there in the lamp-lit streets. Daring the passing traffic sparse though it was at that hour, to stop and complain of our obscene behaviour . . .

'*Plenty* of rogering, Eve!' Kenneth explodes and points derisively at Teddy. 'Whew – that's just what she could do with, couldn't you, Teddy dear – a really good rogering!'

Teddy draws himself up to an elegant height and shrugs petulantly. 'We'd all like a good rogering, Eve darling.' He examines an immaculate thumbnail. 'Kenneth and I spent the whole of last evening looking for a good rogering, didn't we, Kenneth?'

Kenneth nods. 'Oh, *what* a performance! We both of us deserved to get the Oscar! Let's hope this evening reaps greater rewards.'

Teddy is already on the alert. 'Jagger's meant to be here tonight. And David Bowie – oh, yes – all the greats. Look, you know who that is over there! Thingummy-what's-is-name. You know, he was in whatever-it-was-called?' But I leave them, I'm getting concerned over the time. It's my plan to go and see Puck perform. He's due on at midnight and again at one-thirty, and although there is no way we can make the midnight set, I am determined to get to the next one. I promised that I would today when he rang me. But Adam is going to prove resistant to leaving this party, I am well aware of that. When I mentioned it earlier on he said he would prefer not to commit himself, that we were to wait and see how the party panned out. I don't see the difficulty, I'd replied to that. After all, if there is anything that we madly fancy, we can take it along with us to see Puck. But he'd stared at me, coldly. And he'd enquired (like a stranger) whether I was being serious in suggesting that anybody in their right mind would consider leaving a party of Paul Simon's, with the music celebrities who would be bound to be present, to go to a tin-pot performance of a fifth-rate pop group, fronted by such a person as Puck.

'I'm in my right mind, Adam. And I am certainly considering it.' I felt courageous in the face of his scorn.

'That, Eve, is not a foregone conclusion.' He'd returned to reading a philosophical tome, one with an absolutely incomprehensible title, which was meant to pinpoint the vast gap in the judgments of his right mind and mine.

My blood began boiling, as much at his tone of voice as at what it was he was trying to convey to me. 'What's not a foregone conclusion, Adam? Whether I'm in my right mind? Or whether I am considering going to see Puck?'

He didn't raise his eyes from the page. 'Both, if you like.'

I'd left the room. In case I did him a damage.

Now I am summoning up the correct degree of casual insouciance to approach him and the young couple he's chatting to. The boy is very dark and skinny, his skin is smooth, his hair is short. He is listening to what Adam is saying with an unusual intensity, leaning forward from the shoulders. His neck is long and immensely moving for some unknown reason. If I were in love with him I should want to fondle that neck, to kiss it constantly, all around. The straining angle of the neck puts me in mind of what his penis must look like, when terribly aroused. Also straining, straining to make contact with the flesh of the person next to it. Looking down at the boy's jeans I see that the flies are bulging, that maybe this kid is excited to be in conversation with this English intellectual. That the mind is actually influencing the fleshly matter. And I recall one of Adam's favourite dictums. That the tongue is the most powerful sexual weapon. I think that he has talked his way into this kid's affection. And not only the

440

boy, but the girl with him is entranced too. She, if anything, is more beautiful than her companion. But also more conventional, she doesn't command the attention in the same way. She hasn't the smile that he has. He is smiling now, his eyes shining in my direction as Adam beckons me over. And the smile transforms his seriousness into a dancing-eyed vivacity, like a young gypsy child. The girl's welcoming blondeness doesn't hold the same warmth. There is a clearness in her, a Nordic coolness, a goddess quality which other women would distrust. But not me. I like them both. Adam, my husband has fallen on his feet with these two. Easy fodder for our bed. Except not for tonight. We have just over half-an-hour in which to get to Puck. Nothing in this world would stop me getting to that rendezvous.

I am lying in bed next to Adam with my arms clenched over my face to protect it from further blows. Though it is over an hour since the final furious bout was delivered, and I understand from the steady breathing that Adam is now asleep, I am too frightened to risk it starting up again. And so I have remained rigidly in this position and will continue to do so until I am able to relax sufficiently to fall asleep myself.

But I may not be capable of slumber tonight. Too much rage and hatred has passed between the two of us. I marvel at how he has so easily fallen asleep himself. But now I see that he has done so as a form of retreat, knowing that I shall not be able to follow him.

'*You fucker*!!' I mouth this silently into the darkness. My vehemence energises my pounding heart. I am almost frightened by the fierceness of my loathing for this recumbent form alongside me. I would like to hammer him with vicious blows, just as he has so recently done to me. It is years since this had happened. 'You mustn't,' warned a sound woman friend of mine during the early years of our coming together – Adam and myself – 'you mustn't confuse violence with passion.' That was the week I was walking around with one of my front teeth missing. And a black eye which reached down into my mouth. I looked hideous, absolutely awful. Small children shrank away from the sight of me approaching in the street.

441

Taxi-drivers refused my fare. I'd had to stay away from the journalistic job I had at the time; the paper was running a lead article on the spreading prevalence of battered wives and I was afraid that they might ask me to pose for the *Review* front photograph. Staff members were expected to make themselves available at all times for such acts of unselfishness in the service of the newspaper. And even the grocery delivery-boy, well known for his denseness, had looked disbelieving when I'd explained that I'd run unthinkingly into a door.

I was ashamed that somebody of my intelligence and independence should remain with a man who would strike a woman with such violence. And yet I had remained, despite the grieving resentment in my soul. I reasoned, as many women have reasoned before me and will continue to reason long after I am dead (hopefully not through husband-inflicted blows), that this violence must harbour a deep-seated aggression towards women as a whole. That this had been triggered off in childhood, that it was to do with the mother. And that I must, above all, be understanding and tolerant. And try my utmost not to unleash it.

It wasn't even as if this violence was in any way new to me either. Hadn't my first husband almost beaten me to a pulp too? Many times. Hadn't my own father punished me, for what I regarded now as minor misdemeanours, by hitting me so hard and so repeatedly, in such inexplicable fury, that I was unable to attend school for the following week in case I should bring disgrace on the family by occasioning an enquiry as to the source of my bruises.

So perhaps it was I who craved this unspeakably vile excitement. The guilt of this self-knowledge has never been easy to live with!

But, as I lie here now, gingerly feeling my face for those tender swellings with which I have learned to become so familiar, I can't help but regard this latest physical attack as being unjustified. I am disinclined to accept the heartfelt apologies which I know will follow in the morning. I want to withhold my forgiveness this time. I intend to harbour the same resentment that triggered this assault. I am feeling indignantly sorry for myself and one of the two of us is going to have to pay.

442

That person is not going to be me.

This time my life has been threatened. I regard that as a serious matter.

'You are going to have to bloody choose between us, Eve!' Wham! Bang! Wallop! One to the nose. Two to the teeth. My arms dodge around, protecting both areas. I have become very adept at doing this over the years. Ten out of ten in the ring for defence tactics. As agile as Mohammed Ali. 'Do you – or do you not understand, you fucking cunt . . .' Vroom! Thump! Slam! 'Fucking CUNT! CUNT! CUNT! CUNT!' Hair pulling now. And blows to the back of the head. Dangerous, those. But I know how to duck. I AM NOT A CUNT. I say this secretly to myself, hugging the knowledge to me. I *have* a cunt but I am *not* a cunt . . . and if I am a cunt how come my cunt is something which you have so praised to the skies at other times . . . meaning to say that OK if I am a cunt, as you now accuse me of being, then this must be a term of praise . . . not of abuse . . . get my meaning Adam . . . because I do . . . I see it clearly now . . . you have resented that about me which gives you so much pleasure . . . I have never scathingly called you a cock. I could never imagine shouting at you, 'You PENIS! You!' Genital terms are merely medical titles, anatomical labels, that's all.

'Fucking cunt! You are only fit to be thrown over the balcony . . . cunt.'

I withdraw. I shrink back. I make myself smaller. So small that I evade his outstretched and enraged grasp. Over the balcony, this seventh floor balcony, is somewhere that I do not want to go.

Another time, in a balloon, on a long fireman's ladder, in the arms of a more loving human than Adam, maybe then . . . but now now. Human beings have the same instinct for survival as other animals and I sense real danger now. If I can avert it for a few seconds longer, until this brainstorm abates, then I shall be safe. So now as he shouts at me, 'What are you?' I answer quietly that I am a cunt, that I always have been, but that of late I have been even more of a cunt than before . . . And each time I answer correctly I receive a further blow for my fine efforts. THWACK! THWACK! THWACK! But each blow loses the power of the one that has preceded it, until gradually they cease. There are no more threats. My Lord and Master slumbereth tenderly by my side.

I am safe from my balcony sacrifice tonight. My skull shall not be shattered to pieces on the pavement, the sidewalk – not this time. All saved up for the future . . .

Bitterness is an uneasy bedfellow. It creates bile in the belly. Which in turn leads to burping. And burping is something that I dare not do now. So I suppress this ill-wind and it festers inside and poisons my thoughts. It creates a seething insomnia, something from which I have not suffered before.

But it is not altogether unrewarding. I don't know why insomniacs complain. I am getting a lot of thinking done. I am planning my future and reviewing my past, my immediate past. I lie thus until the light of the cold dawn starts to shiver into the room. I have never spent such a night as this in my entire life. I like it, I shall endeavour to do it again each time I sense a crisis looming into my life. For this is a crisis now, I am pretty sure of that.

I am determined not to be made to choose between Adam and Puck. If there is any decision to be taken it is that I shall choose to survive on my own. I shall leave Adam. But not in order to join Puck. I am better off by myself. Until I can sort out what I want.

I rise early. Why not, I am awake anyway. And I shower and dress as stealthily as I can, managing to leave the apartment before Adam awakes. I have a dental appointment this morning, uptown, and I walk to it. It takes me almost three-quarters of an hour. I stop on the way for a coffee, nothing to eat – out of regard for the dentist. Who would wish to forage through a mouth full of doughnut droppings, gums waxed up with surgery gunge? In any case I am not hungry, I'm angry instead and this is combining with my sleepless night to make me marvellously light-headed. I feel as if I am on some incredible drug, the elixir of life itself.

But when I come out of the dental appointment all this has evaporated. Now I need a close friend in whom I can confide. My marriage is breaking up, I want to talk it over with someone, a best friend. But the irony of the situation is that my husband has become my best friend. I haven't another. I am not even back home in Britain where at

444

least I have half a dozen female intimates who would sympathise with my predicament now. The only intimate that I have here in the States is someone who I have come to regard as a rival for my husband's affection – Cherry. Or do I really regard her thus? Haven't I got over all that jealousy business? And wouldn't it be rather pleasant, a nice gesture, to be able to say that she can have him now, that I hand him over on a silver platter.

'Have you a telephone in this building, please?' I ask the smiling attendant as I emerge from the elevator on the ground floor of the dentist's building. His pleasant, 'Have a good day now,' seems a bright omen for the rest of the morning. I shall invite Cherry to a brunch somewhere. I shall be civilised and charming, woman-of-the-worldish. I shall end up feeling very proud of myself and they will both think considerably more of me than they do at the moment. Adam and Cherry, I mean. Having had to put up with my petty reactions over the past months . . .

As I think these magnanimous thoughts, as I luxuriate in these finer feelings, Cherry's telephone continues to ring. It gradually occurs to me that she is not at home. I am to be denied the luxury of my generous gesture after all. Fate is possibly conspiring against me. I dissolve into near tears. It is ten-thirty in the morning and I have nowhere to go, no pal to turn to. I think of Teddy and Kenneth, but they aren't the right ones. They'll invite me to drink away what, to them, will seem a superficial sorrow. Their relationships last little more than five minutes, they expect that things should break up. They will say that there are plenty more fish in the sea. They will try to comfort me with a string of tired clichés, when what I require is wisdom of the soul, a degree of compassionate understanding for the suffering which is becoming more acute with every minute.

There must be somebody who can understand this. There must be at least one person who will treat me with a serious regard . . . Puck. Of course!

I telephone Puck, praying that he will answer the call himself. So often when I ring his number, Zack responds at the other end. They are sharing an apartment together in the Village, close to Christopher Street, the gay ghetto. I haven't been to it yet. Puck prefers that I don't, he says that it is not as he would like it to be. I don't press him, why should I? It's not his apartment I'm interested in, and anyway I will never be in a position to visit it alone. Adam would always be with me and he doesn't enjoy visiting other people's homes. He prefers the European manner of meeting on neutral territory, in restaurants and cafés, or bars and clubs.

The voice at the other end of the line is guarded – before it hears mine. Then the love spills all over me. 'Eve!' It is Puck. We are meeting for brunch in forty-five minutes' time, downtown, close to him. 'I need to talk to a friend, Puck.' I said it straight out to him, I blurted it like a bashful schoolgirl.

'*I'm* a friend, Eve. I'm *your* friend.'

I think of my husband, as the monster who wanted to chuck me over the balcony like a potful of slops . . .

'Darling Puck.' I choke on my own emotion, so moved by the infinite tenderness in his husky drawl. I would fall for that voice, for the quality of the kindness in it, without even a glimpse of the extraordinary face. He is a sweet boy, this one. As sweet as a nut. Can I be such a fucking cunt if this child has learned to love me . . . I walk towards Lexington Avenue on foam-rubber feet. How very soft the sidewalks are this morning, as if the skies have fallen down and are now settled there like snow. I am now feeling very hungry indeed.

He is sitting at the table when I arrive at the appointed place, Puck is. I realise with something of a surprise that I haven't seen him very much in the actual light of day. Apart from the time that he came swimming with us at the Y, and I don't count that time because we had spent the night together, all three of us. It wasn't too easy to look each other casually in the eye. We were over-conscious of what had taken place in the night.

But this, this meeting, is like a normal date. He feels this too. 'Our first real date,' he laughs delightedly, reaching forward to draw me to him. He won't let go of me, despite the interested regard of the rest of the clientele. This place is typically New York, a glamorous cross between a bistro, bar and a restaurant. Somewhere the pretty people go to talk over a cup of coffee, or a beer, or a brunch such as we are ordering now. But there is nobody here half as pretty as Puck, I am proud to see. No one who commands the attention of all the other tables as he is doing. I watch him walk away from me towards the coat-stand as he goes to take something from his coat pocket. The childishly slim hips taper down from the wide shoulders into a set of enviably slim thighs. Yet the whole impression is one of steely strength. He has a great shape, there is little doubt of that. But when he returns towards me, smiling, his eyes warm on my own, I have the same sensation as I did the first time I saw him. I am drowning in delight for he is a feast to behold. A god amongst men. Me – me, who has claimed not to be affected by physical perfection, by the extremely beautiful! And here I am swooning before it like a silly schoolgirl. Pathetic! I blush with ridiculous pleasure at his next words.

'You are so beautiful today, Eve.' And suddenly I feel beautiful. I glow with the most inexplicable radiance, as if someone has poured molten gold through a hole in my head.

'Thank you, Puck,' I say. And even my voice sounds thrilling. Seductive and soft as cotton wool, with a surface of raw silk to take off the sickly sugariness. And Puck is sitting opposite me there, gazing humbly at me. Waiting. And then I remember why it is I have rung him up for this altogether illicit assignation. For I am still a married woman, though for how much longer it is not so easy to tell. And I spill it out, all of it, about the balcony threat and everything. And he laughs about that bit. He finds it rather thrillingly melodramatic, but I can see that he doesn't really believe that a person could do such a thing. And then I understand that such violence is something completely alien to the nature of this boy, and that in the culture and generation to which he subscribes, or the laid-back Californian background from which he springs, such threats would be considered laughable. Where he comes from they are more likely to kill with emotional lethargy and the left-over indulgence of flower-power. I am thinking this and then I remember Charles Manson. But I say nothing, instead I cry as I start to talk of my marriage and the sadness which has been creeping into it. And I try to tell Puck that none of that is his fault, for he is looking troubled. And I don't like to see that smooth brow furrowed with problems of mine.

Then, 'Will you marry me, Eve? Please say yes . . .'

447

I try to laugh it off. Now why should I do that, why should I react in such a bloody awful British way! I take his hands in mine.

'Oh, Puck,' I say, my eyes filling. 'You don't want to marry somebody my age. Don't be silly.' And I smile, quiveringly at him, touching his curved mouth. 'I want to kiss you so much,' I whisper.

He stands up tall from the table and comes around to my side. And he crushes me to his chest, hard until I gasp. Then he lifts my chin up and kisses me long and lingeringly on the lips, until I go giddy from lack of oxygen. And the feelings flow powerfully along and up my cunt and he takes my hand down between his legs in this crowded restaurant with everyone looking at us instead of at each other.

'I'm horny as hell for you, Eve, honey.'

'I'm horny as hell for you, Puck – honey. Too.'

'Let's go back to my place. What d'you say, Eve?' His voice is so pleading that I melt, everywhere. I am leaking emotion, there is no stemming the flow of me. What a fuck this will be – if I can only say yes.

But I can't. I am too indoctrinated by my own code of loyalty. It won't allow me to. And yet when I explain this to Puck he is hurt. He thinks that I don't love and desire him as strongly as he desires me. I have never desired anyone more in my entire life – at least not for a long time. Not since Adam and I started kissing on that train from Stoke-on-Trent to . . . where was it? We missed our destination, I remember that. We overshot the mark as we were shooting our load at each other in the locked lavatory at the end of the first class compartments. No one's fault. It cost a fortune in taxi fares trying to reach the right station in time to catch a right connection. 'If you had not got contraception,' Adam had said afterwards to me, 'that one would have scored a bullseye, I know it. The force of the hurtling train speeding the spunk to the certain spot . . .' So I know all about floods of uncontrollable desire in public places. I once got stung on the bum by a bumble-bee, doing it under a bridge in Florence, with a blizzard of promenading Italian bourgoisie mere feet above us. Bloody painful it was too, the size of the bee-sting swelling up in direct relation to the size of

Adam's penis dwindling away (if such an analogy can be said to exist).

'I can't come with you, Puck. Not like this, not behind Adam's back. I want it to be perfect for the first time on our own together.' And he understands, he says that he understands. So we talk about when that possibility may come to pass, for now it is something that we have both acknowledged must happen sooner or later. We can't go on like this, with three of us in a bed. And nobody getting any real satisfaction out of it.

'After all,' reasons Puck, 'Adam has Cherry as his girlfriend, so why shouldn't you have me as your boy-friend?' And he smiles at the simplicity of what seems to him a logical argument.

I don't want him to know the truth of that particular set-up. I don't want to have to go into a long explanation of how Cherry is the girlfriend of both Adam and myself. Putting it into actual words will make it (make me) sound so dreadfully depraved. Though I would prefer him to know me as I actually am, I have no desire to besmirch whatever image of me he holds dear to his heart. What would be the point of doing that, spreading disillusionment all around?

So he boyishly continues with heated indignation. 'After all it is hardly fair, is it! If Adam persists with Cherry, then you surely deserve to have me . . .' He is glaring now, his lower lip thrust stubbornly forward. I suppress the desire to laugh at him, it wouldn't do to laugh. He would think that I am making fun of him, not taking him seriously. When what I long to do is exactly that, take him and his youthful passion and press it hard to my withering heart.

But it is wrong. He is *far* too young for me – this is a *twenty*-year gap! Spring and winter, not even spring and autumn like Adam and me . . .

So I try to look at it objectively. 'Puck, darling,' I start to say. And because I have called him darling, because he hears his own name on my lips, he smothers my hands with ardent kisses.

'Eve, Eve, Eve . . .'

'No. Puck. This should stop now. I . . . I . . . am much, much, too old for you. It is ridiculous, don't you see. Surely your friends must see that.'

His expression changes to one of incredulity. Then he starts blushing like a very young boy. 'My friends,' he says it gruffly, 'my friends don't mention your name in connection with age. They are only shocked that I am having an affair with a married couple. They say, "Gee, Puck – you must be really going down the tubes!" It is when I say that the three of us go to bed together. But, Eve,' now he looks appealing at me, 'you know that I only go along with that because of you, because that is the only way that I get to hold you tight and to make love to you. That was your rule from the start. I knew what I was getting into.'

I look at his earnest face, his innocent eyes and his quivering mouth. And I am terribly ashamed of myself. We have wronged him, this kid. Adam and I have been playing our own games and we have abused the trusting innocence of this love-sick young person. I have deliberately enslaved him, enchanted him, simply to gratify my sexual appetite . . . Except that in so doing I have become enslaved myself. Cupid has paid me out in my own kind.

I look at the time – habits die hard – the daily swim is almost upon me. But how can I leave this beautiful boy, gazing so imploringly into my face.

'I ought to go, Puck,' I whisper.

'Don't go, Eve,' he whispers back. 'We haven't resolved anything at all. You are no better off now than when you rang me up this morning. I have been of no help at all . . .' He looks absolutely broken. He looks as I felt when I arrived, whereas I have gathered myself together sufficiently to be thinking of our daily swimming schedule. Adam's and mine. That realisation pulls me up with a sudden shock. Are the habits of marriage to dominate the rest of my days. Am I to sacrifice love for a swimming schedule?

But even so I rise to go. Puck follows my example. We have not paid the bill yet, we have not been given 'the cheque', as they call the bill in the States. I wonder whether to point the difference out to Puck. I wonder whether he would find it interesting that in Britain we require the restaurant bill in order to pay it with a cheque, whereas over in this country it is exactly the opposite. I decide that it is not interesting enough a topic to mention

450

again – to anybody. It is one of Adam's oft-repeated observations. A particularly dull one, I now think sourly to myself. My blood starts racing unpleasantly at the thought of a confrontation with Adam. But it has to be got over and done with, sooner or later.

'I have to return to the Eden, Puck.' I say it calmly in the face of his now obvious anguish.

He catches my hand and presses it between his fingers. 'Eve,' he hesitates then, but bravely continues. 'If you decide to leave Adam, will you come and live with me . . . please?'

His *please* reverberates around my brain as we walk along the street together. I mean to think 'along the sidewalk', not street, but in my upset I can't remember all the American expressions that I have garnered since our arrival in New York.

Then I stop short in my tracks. 'He may decide that we must return to England, away from this trouble. Away from you and temptation, Puck.' Putting this thought into words has suddenly made it into a very real possibility indeed.

Puck moans softly beside me. He is wearing a long, shaggy fur coat, which reaches practically to the ground. His head is protected against the cold weather by some sort of peaked cap. And his eyes are invisible behind glamorous, film-star dark glasses. Everyone stares at us as we pass by, especially at Puck. Only his full mouth is really visible and yet that still proves mesmerising. It is a fact that I can't get over, the physical charisma that he possesses. It makes me proud and privileged to be beside him – or am I over-humbling myself? Isn't he just another very good-looking boy, like thousands of others? What is it that draws me irresistibly to him, and what is it that draws so many others as well? Yet I feel no shred of possessiveness over him, no unreasoning bursts of jealousy, as I have with Adam and Cherry, for instance.

Of course, Puck has not yet given me cause to. I have always had his undivided attention whilst Adam's has quite definitely been wandering for some time. Perhaps my falling in love with Puck is simply my way of punishing Adam. Except that, unfortunately, my love for Puck is genuine.

451

'You promise that if you need me you will call me, Eve.' Puck's troubled face is close to the cab window, still trying to give me another kiss goodbye.

'Promise, Puck,' I reply. My throat is bursting with tears but I try to hold them in check. I want to look good for this small goodbye. I want him to take away a pleasant memory of my face, not someone snivelling into their sleeve.

'And you remember that I am playing at The Space Age tonight, and that I'm putting your name, Eve, on my guest list.'

I nod back at him. 'If things go badly with Adam, I shall see you tonight. If I don't then you will know that I am trying to work it out. It is very unhappy for everyone.' A tear rolls unbidden down my left cheek. Puck leans over the cab window to lick it away.

'If you decide to leave Adam and come and live with me it will be the happiest day of my life, Eve.'

We have been swimming in silence, neither one daring to look at the other, Adam and I. And we have returned to our studio where he is now trying to paint and I am pretending to write. But it's no good.

'We'd better have it out, Adam.' There, I've said it.

He raises his head. 'There is nothing to have out as far as I am concerned, Eve. Either you give up this ridiculous infatuation that is making a fool of you and everyone concerned with you, which quite obviously includes me – or else . . .'

'Or else what, Adam?' My voice is very controlled and quiet. There is no hysteria.

'Well – it's obvious, Eve, isn't it. You and I can't continue together. I won't have it.'

'We won't then.'

'What!'

'I said, we won't then. Continue.'

There is a short silence, then he speaks. 'My god, you must have taken leave of your senses.'

I allow another silence. 'Or found them.'

'You can't be serious?'

'I am not prepared to give him up, Adam. And if you say that this has to be the end of us because of that, then it will have to be the end of us.'

452

'You must be joking.'

'If I'm joking, then it isn't very amusing. Not to me, maybe to you.'

'Well, if I were not in shock then I might be able to laugh. I am just waiting for you to tell me that you don't mean any of this.'

'Why should I not mean it any more than you, Adam? You have given me an ultimatum. I have accepted the ultimatum. Just because I have not decided in your favour doesn't mean that I haven't seriously considered the far-reaching results of my decision. It is actually as painful to me,' my voice is trembling dangerously now and I struggle to keep it sounding normal, 'as it must be for you.' There, I have managed to complete the sentence. But I dare not trust myself to look at his face. That dear face. That face that I have kissed, every inch of it, so many countless times over so many countless years. That face which has lain beside me 'in sickness and in health'. That I have admired, bronzed in summer, and warmed (red-nosed as Rudolph the reindeer) in winter. Seen perspiring, and parched, nervous and triumphant. Bitter, and infinitely tender and kind.

Then I think of last night. Of the balcony. Of the beating. And my heart re-hardens. 'I take it,' I say, quite coldly and well in control again, 'that you will be wanting me to move out of your studio. I can as easily work in the apartment next door. Until we get sorted out as to future plans that is probably the best solution. I shall move next door. I'll start right away, gathering my things together.' I stand up briskly, it feels better to be on the move. Not having to see that sudden slump to his shoulders, not catching sight of his sagging jaw. Not having to register the unfamiliar pallor of his profile. *Sod it – we all have to suffer! Fuck the bugger!* Bloody well serves him right!

Six

'You don't mind if I keep this?' I am pointing to my
Valentine card, which has been pinned to the wall behind
my desk. Or rather behind where my desk used to be up
until two hours ago. My side of the studio is now
completely bare. I have heaved, dragged, pushed, rolled,
humped, every item of furniture that occupied my half
into the apartment next door. Now I am clearing the wall
space. I'm removing all the photographs of mens' dicks,
all the bums (male and female), all the cunt shots cut out
from girlie mags, all the torso shots from gay literature . . .
'Oh, do you want to hang onto STEVE, by the way?' I am
referring to a photograph of a leering youth, captioned
STEVE, with a penis that stretches (on the slack!)
straight down to his knee-joints.

But all I get in response to these perfectly civil questions
is a tragic shaking of the head. No real, spoken answer at
all. What an over-reaction, that's what I want to say.
After all, married couples are splitting up every single
second of the day and night. Somewhere on the globe. At
this very moment a pair of eskimos are probably slicing
the contents of their igloo in two, 'You take the white
polar-bear fur rug and I'll have the ice-making tray . . .'

It's no big deal. I prise my Valentine card carefully
from the wall. This is an original work of art, a card, an
image that Adam painted especially for me as he has
always painted such greetings. All my previous birthday
and Valentine cards are stored back in Britain, but this
one was painted since we arrived here. It portrays a large
penis, plus bollocks (rather resembling Adam's own set),
but the shape of the pale pink glans is in the shape of a
heart. I told him when he presented it to me on
Valentine's Day that he could make a fortune from this

one, if he sold it as an idea for a commercial greetings card. The gays would go out and buy it in absolute droves. But Adam is not interested in these obvious ideas for wildly commercial success. He just likes creating the image that's all. The true artist. He has wasted masses of opportunities in this way. But I like being married to someone who lives in an ivory tower of idealism. At least I used to . . .

'No. You can have STEVE.' The voice is heartbreaking to hear. A voice that I have never heard from Adam before. Like someone with an inner turmoil so intense that it seems removed from that person altogether. Disembodied.

I study STEVE. Do I really want him either? Will he seem such a joke on my own wall without Adam there in the room to laugh with; without Adam there to pinpoint STEVE to all our visitors; without me rushing with mock horror to cover him up when the Eden staff have to call in on us to mend the fridge or to exterminate the occasional cockroach . . .

'I think I'll give STEVE a miss too,' I say, tearing him up and dropping his pieces into the waste-bin. 'What about Raquel? You will probably want her, won't you? I hold up the famous *Playboy* cover of Raquel Welch from last Christmas, wearing her tantalising micro bikini. Knocking forty and still looking bloody fabulous, lucky cow.

But Adam is shaking his head, from side to side like a wounded beast. Dumb and vulnerable. Something rips through my innards.

'I hope,' I say callously, 'that you haven't completely lost the use of your tongue. It's going to make our necessary social arrangements from now on pretty awkward if I am having to communicate with a deaf mute.'

In answer, he plunges his head in his hands, dislodging his spectacles in so doing. And he buries his head down upon his big desk and quietly, almost soundlessly, he begins sobbing.

I noisily let him know that I am leaving the room. I drop a heavy metal ashtray and an enamel mug, and kick a plastic container before my feet full of loose change and precious coins and seashells from the beach. Anything to cancel out the keening in the corner.

'Right,' I sound as if I am shouting at the wind, 'see you around. See you sometime. It's been a lovely eleven years.'

And I make sure to bang the door behind me as brutally as possible.

I don't recognise the striken figure in the full-length mirror of the next apartment. I try to find familiar features in the ancient reflection of the face. 'This is you, you stupid shit –just look what you've gone and done now . . .' But the reflection stares, wild-eyed back at me, opening its mouth in an agonised wail that cannot even escape from the throat.

I look like the victim of an emotional holocaust. Only a ferret could fancy me now. I'll take a job as a cleaner at St Dunstans, an establishment for the blind, out of consideration for humanity. My future lies with the blind. I can't inflict this suffering countenance on my friends or on my fellow humans, forcing them to look at me, pitying what they see. I have just made myself redundant from the rest of the human race.

I cannot imagine how long I have sat here staring out of the window, down onto West Twenty-third Street. Three derelicts, who have maybe moved up from the Bowery or even just around the corner, are sleeping their vinous sleep in one dark, sheltering doorway opposite. Tomorrow morning, whilst the rest of the world goes to work, they will sprawl dazedly on the steps of shops not yet open, with sticky bottles tilted upwards while they drain the final drops. It won't be long before the pimps and the whores, junkies and pushers will start plying their pathetic trade along the sidewalk. Lone Puerto Ricans pass by, making love cheek-to-cheek with the ubiquitous transistor radio. Roller-skating teenagers cruise the streets in twos and threes. The solitary ones skate in the opposite direction to the oncoming traffic, challenging hysterical drivers of cars, ignoring the threat of the large lorries. The wide street is a-roar with the gasp and thunder of trucks, the scream of police cars and fire engines, the death-winge of speeding ambulances. And the grinding whine of the big, slow, moving garbage truck, which seems to take forever to get from Eighth to Seventh Avenue. Peering immediately beneath me I can see a constant group of ever-changing tourists standing in front of the Victorian Gothic splendour of the Eden, looking at the bronze tablets on either side of the wide entrance. Three separate

456

groups of musicians have unloaded their gear in front of this building. All are young. All are wildly romantic in appearance. One or two resemble Puck in their manner of dress and the confidence and set of their shoulders. All are thin, very thin. They live their lives on the stimulus of the music they create. And the amount of stuff that they snort to revivify their senses and send their spirits soaring up to the skies.

Is this the sort of life that I am preparing to live with Puck? Do I relish the prospect of 'going on the road' with him as he's asked me to do? Do I look forward to being the oldest groupie in the business? A pathetic hanger-on of Puck's, albeit his love-object, his mother-figure, his inspiration and his guide. His reason for living . . .

Perhaps I do.

There is a knock at my door. Someone has come to interrupt my reverie. For a wild moment I expect to see Puck standing there, he was so clearly in my mind a moment ago.

It is Adam. My heart leaps. Now why should it do that? In the hours, minutes, days, seconds, that have elapsed since I last saw Adam he has become a complete stranger to me.

'Can I, may I, come in – please?' He is humility itself. A model of unfamiliar politeness.

'Do come in.' I step aside to allow him to enter. It is as if we have never even been introduced. As if we have never set eyes on each other, as if he were merely a stranger occupying the room next door, along the corridor.

'Thank you. Do you think that I could sit down?'

I motion him to a chair.

He clears his throat. 'What I am wanting to know is whether, or not, you have made any plans for this evening? Have you a date? Because if you have then that leaves me free to pursue my own plans. If you haven't, then perhaps you would care to have dinner with me. You may have forgotten, but we do happen to have tickets for Brenda Bergman. She is that performer that you have been looking forward to seeing . . .' There is no hint of appeal now in his impassive face. Just the ticking of a small muscle near his right eye. I notice that he is not wearing his spectacles, that he is bearing the discomfort of his contact lenses. He only wears them in the evening, when he wishes to make a desperately special effort. When he fears the masculine competition. When we two go out together, just the two of us, he *never* bothers to put them in. I am being honoured. Is it meant to be a subtle form of flattery, or the start of a wooing campaign?

'Well, to tell you the truth, Puck is playing at the Space Age this evening . . .'

'And he wants you to attend. He has put you on his guest list . . .'

'Yes, but . . .'

'That is all I wanted to clear up. Do you mind if I use the telephone in here, there is a fault on the line next door. Thank you.'

'But . . .' The word dies on my lips as I watch him dial Cherry's number. I know that number by heart. Haven't I seen him dial it a thousand times?

'Hello, Cherry – it's me, Adam. Look, Eve is leaving me. We are splitting up. When? Well now. We've done it already, we're separated. The thing is that I've got tickets for Brenda Bergman and I was wondering if you'd like to come with me tonight. About ten o'clock. I see, you're off to dinner. Well, what time will your dinner end? Then you are off to a party – well what time will your party end? Doesn't matter about the tickets, she'll be singing another time. Do you think that whatever time your party ends you could come over here to have a drink with me? Or I could come to wherever it is you're likely to be. You don't know yet. Could you give me a ring? The thing is, Cherry darling – I, I, I think that by tonight I'm going to be in awful need of a spot of human comfort. Someone to hold me tight – that sort of thing. Naturally I thought of you first . . . but, yes, oh, don't worry. I understand, yes. I'll be all right. Yes, honestly. Yes, I was thinking that, a good idea, a stiff drink. You suggest a large Scotch? I'm sure you're right . . . time will heal. Yes, of course I'll ring you tomorrow. Oh, I see . . . well, after the weekend.'

He replaces the receiver and looks at me, attempting a haggard, lopsided, and *terrible* smile. 'That was my date.'

'Little bitch! She always has been a selfish turd, an absolute arsehole . . . I could never imagine what you saw in her, Adam.'

'I could never imagine what *you* saw in her, Eve.'

I stare at him. 'What do you mean – *me*, Adam? Cherry wasn't my idea, she was always there for you.'

We stare at each other. 'Yes, but . . .' he speaks eventually. 'She was introduced into the marriage, wasn't she as an extension of it for both of us. We were specifically in it together, weren't we.'

'I wasn't, Adam.' I speak flatly, not prepared to give way on what I know now is a supremely important point between us. 'I think that you may have persuaded yourself to think that but from my point of view, all I can see is that this is a way of having a spot of nubile young flesh in the bed, with my smile of approval. It's called having your crumpet and eating it. Men have always managed to do that.'

'So this is your way of paying me back is it – this so called "falling in love" with Puck.'

'I don't like the way this conversation is developing, Adam. I specifically vacated your premises in order to avoid this sort of scene and now you have invaded my home and . . .'

But I am not allowed to continue. His head is in my lap and his long arms are wrapped tightly around me and my skirt is dampening beneath the welter of his tears. 'Don't leave me, Eve. Please don't do it . . . I couldn't live without you . . . how could I possibly exist in a world with you no longer by my side. We have so much together . . . we are so strong with each other. I adore you. I adore your mind and your spirit and everything that is so funny and dear about you. And your little feet and your tiny hands and your false teeth and your dirty laugh. I worship your body. I have always worshipped it. Nobody else could ever excite me or stimulate me or enthrall me the way you do . . .'

When he finally finishes the room is in darkness. He lies against me on the bed, both of us naked, both of us warm. His cock is still in me, though long since grown soft. And his open mouth is breathing moist air into the corner of my mouth.

But my heart is heavy. This has not been the answer and we both know it. Puck still hangs between us. This is a temporary reprieve. The road ahead is emotional. There are no survivors.

Seven

Puck arrives in our bed at three o'clock in the morning. He's been rehearsing and is exhausted, he creeps in at my side, kisses me on the mouth and falls asleep immediately. Adam has awoken at the sound of his entry, although Puck makes sure not to switch the lights on so as not to disturb him.

Adam sits up. 'That's nice,' he hisses at me. 'We wait for the little shit since Christ knows what hour, and then when he gets here he has the bloody gall to go straight off to sleep. Where, pray tell me, is the sexual satisfaction in that?'

'Shush,' I whisper back. 'The poor boy is exhausted, let him sleep. There's still the morning. He needs to get a good night's rest.'

'Why should he get a good night's rest when he's ruined everyone else's? Tell me that! Explain that to me, Eve. Why is his sleep more important than everyone else's around here?'

I sigh deep inside myself, feeling sick in my stomach. 'Don't be silly, my darling. It isn't more important. I love you both, you know that. Very much.'

'Huh, funny way of showing it! Some have greater priorities, that's all I'm complaining about.' And he turns his back on me, won't even hold my hand. In moments he is snoring. Loudly, purposefully loudly, or is that my imagination – that he is trying hard to disturb Puck . . . I lie between the two of them, sleeplessly. The fifth night in a row that I have failed to maintain harmony. I am feeling about a hundred years old. A successful *ménage-à-trois* requires a younger constitution than mine, I reflect. If I was bent on doing it, I should have had the first shot at it years ago. This dog is too old in the tooth for these new

460

tricks . . .

The first light is creeping through the shutters when I feel Adam's thumb on my clitoris. He is superbly good at this early morning seduction. Sometimes I wake up thinking that I have just been dreaming that a man has seduced me. Or raped me against my will, but that I end up enjoying it, actually adoring what he is doing to me even though it is rape. And it always turns out that it is Adam who has been playing with me. Amusing himself with my body whilst I have been unconscious. I tell him that he must have a special penchant for fucking inert bodies. That he should make it his business to get friendly with an obliging undertaker. That he may find that necrophilia is his particular bag after all.

Now I am dripping wet in my cunt and absolutely raring to go. He must have been eating me for at least ten minutes without my really realising it. He heaves the length of himself right up to the pillow and inserts his huge penis into my mouth. I would have liked to have cleaned my teeth first. My mouth is full of early-morning mustiness. We have an unspoken code of behaviour in this bed of three bodies early in the morning. Before we embark on our pleasurable sessions, if any one of us wishes to evacuate our bowels, that person must use the lavatory in the adjoining apartment, in the bathroom adjoining the studio. Offensive odours have no part in our idyll, none at all.

But Adam has the hots this morning. He will not be put off. He suffered sexual frustration last night, waiting for Puck. Despite my warning that the lad might be very late indeed. He allowed himself to get disastrously over-excited. Consequently his disappointment at Puck's non-appearance was as bitter as that of a very small child. He can be childish when crossed, Adam. Very childish and petty when he doesn't get all his own way.

Now he is really agitated. I glance over at Puck. He is still deep in sleep. It would be tragic to awaken him just to play games at this hour. 'What's the time, Adam?' I whisper.

'What the hell has that to do with anything,' he whispers back. It is time for all this. And he holds my chin in his hand and forces me to kiss Puck's sleeping face, full

461

on the lips. I tug my head away, the sharp movement causes Puck to stir in his sleep. He gives a low moan, but he doesn't look as if he is about to wake up.

I put my finger warningly to my lips at Adam, as if to reprimand him. As if to say go easy, there is plenty of time. But it is obviously not the thing to do. I think the gesture has incensed him. Now he mounts me roughly, pushing his stiff cock into my vagina without any foreplay at all. It is intended to be, and is tantamount to, the roughest rape technique. It is a good job that I am already so wet otherwise it could have hurt me considerably. I stare at him. He stares at me. There is a game going on. It is an unpleasant one. Violent. There is acute hostility in this bed. Not for the first time in this past month, I am aware of a terrible weariness and a dread of something unspecific. As if a tragedy could take place. Something that we three would live to regret all our lives. I feel I should put a stop to the whole situation. But I seem caught in a trap of my own making, from which for the time being there is no escape. I have to be borne along on this disaster course. There is no other way for the present.

'I intend fucking you, Eve.' There is menace in the voice.

'I know that Adam.' I keep my voice as light as I possibly can.

'And I intend for you to fuck the child.' We have taken to calling Puck The Child, it is a little joke between the three of us. One that we use over and over again.

'The child is asleep, Adam. Leave him alone.' I use a reasonable mother's voice to say this. I appeal to the decent father in him. It doesn't work though.

'He's had enough sleep, the child.' Adam pulls my hand and places it on Puck's sleeping prick. 'I command you to bring that back to life.'

'I am not a Genie,' I say. I have been commanded to rub it. 'And this is not a magic lantern, it is an ordinary prick. Its owner has no intention of awakening either.'

'Oh, you can do it, Eve, if anyone can. You little cock teaser . . . Go on tease it into action, go on. I've had enough of a quiet time here. Where are we meant to be living anyway – in a fucking morgue? Come on, let's play with the child.'

462

I watch in horror whilst Adam pulls back the sheet and plunges his mouth onto Puck's inert parts. He takes not only the cock into his mouth but the balls too. This is an act of callous aggression, but I am powerless to prevent it.

And so I kiss Puck myself, as gently as I know how, cradling his lovely head in the crook of my arm as if to protect him from the violation down below. Though I am being violated too. Adam is managing to ride me at the same time, in-and-out, in-and-out of my cunt. The bed rocks with the feverish motion, it is nightmarish perversity on Adam's part. As if he is taking his revenge.

Despair settles over me, bleak as a damp blanket.

Now Puck is waking up. He turns to look at me, imploringly, his eyes opening·with confused alarm. And from my hopeless resignation his gaze travels down my naked body to the spectacle of Adam and his bold mouthful. A frown gathers between his handsome eyebrows. It is impossible to define the exact nature of his reaction. Horror and disgust are too strong as definitions, yet weary revulsion is certainly present. I am embarrassed by what is taking place and long to be anywhere but here. I think of the fountains in London's Trafalgar Square. Of the fierce Cornish seas lashing that rocky coastline. Of the polka-dotted shoes, pink over white, that I noticed in the window of Maud Frisson's shoe shop uptown. Of the bright violet brassiere that I shall purchase down in SoHo this Saturday. Of the letter I will write to my dear ageing mother over in Wales. Of the postcards I've received from my daughters.

Whilst I concentrate on other things in this manner, with my eyes tightly shut, Adam shoots off up my snatch. I whimper with delight to please him, though I have felt no pleasure at all – only irritation and relief that it is all over.

Except that it isn't. Adam continues to suck frantically on Puck's penis – to no avail now, I see. And I watch with sickly fascination and a deep dread of the outcome as Puck, with great dignity and admirable self-control, firmly places his hands each side of Adam's head and eases it off. He places the head to one side, like an ornament on the shelf. The released penis lolls over, retrieved, still glistening with my husband's saliva. Silly little thing.

Then Puck turns briefly to kiss me. 'I'll ring you, Eve,' he whispers. 'I'm tired. I need to rest.'

Before I can think what to say, humbly in reply, he has dressed and departed for his own home.

'Fucking hell! How d'you like that for a bloody cool customer!' Adam is thoroughly aggrieved. More, he is not prepared to drop the matter. This is my fault. I didn't try hard enough. I am spoiling the child. I should have put down my foot and forced him to have sex. Shows how very much the child actually fancies me . . . must be my age that just fails to turn him on . . . if I were a young girl he wouldn't have been so interested in sleep . . . oh, dear, no . . .

These are deliberately cruel taunts. But I understand the terrible emotion that prompts their utterance. Adam is suffering from searing jealousy. I can remember that painful erosion myself.

So I hold him in my arms (like a suffering madonna, eyes turned heavenward, praying for patience) and I say nothing. My silence calms him eventually, but as the violent ranting recedes, its place is taken by a wheedling whine. More childishness.

'He's never going to be interested in me, is he, Puck? It's all you, you, you, Eve. I'd be a bloody fool if I didn't recognise that fact. So what's the use of going on with it? Eh, tell me that!'

I hug him closer, heartbroken, yet relieved that at least the situation is about to be resolved. One way or the other.

'The best thing, I think, is for me to go back to England. I'm known there. I'm respected. I am sure of my own presence. New York is too disorientating for me and my work. And emotionally I feel an encumbrance to you and the child. I should be able to say to you that I'd understand if you wanted to go off with him and have an affair on your own. But I'm not big enough to be able to do that, and the knowledge that I'm not is too uncomfortable to live with as well. I am in pieces. I can't go on. It is incomprehensible to me how you could even entertain thoughts of love towards this intellectual pigmy when you already have me. I would never, could never, fall for any of the foolish girls that we have taken into our bed. But then I abide by the rules, the swingers' rule, of not confusing sex with sentiment. You have committed the cardinal sin, it seems to me. And I don't think that I can ever recover from your callous disloyalty. But I shall continue to worship you. I want you to return to London with me. I say this, knowing that if you decide not to come with me then I will probably kill myself, since my life would be pointless without you. But I don't intend that as any form of moral blackmail. You deserve to be happy, you never put your needs first. You have always sacrificed your own happiness for the happiness of others. But I don't want you to do that this time, Eve. I give you the rest of this week to make up your mind. I thought about catching the plane this coming weekend. If we go by Laker we can buy the ticket on the same day as the flight.'

I am on my way to Puck's apartment, all alone in the back of the taxi-cab. My new, pleated chiffon negligée is nestling at the bottom of my black leather tote-bag. I am wearing a long, black leather trench-coat, a black fox-fur hat, shiny black patent-leather ankle boots, and lashings of perfume. I am going to Puck's apartment on my own for a pre-arranged fuck, organised by Adam, my loving husband. It is his present to me, an afternoon of private passion with the boy of my dreams in exchange for spending the rest of my life back in London with him, Adam.

I am suffused with gratitude. So is Puck. We can hardly believe our luck at this magnanimous gesture on the part of Adam. He has even been out and bought the champagne for us, the bottle is resting in my bag next to the negligée. Chilled to just the right temperature.

'How is Adam?' Puck answers the door wearing only a kimono and a pair of loose lounging trousers – like someone in a Japanese film. His feet are bare and his chest appears bronzed in this light, beneath the turquoise silk of the open garment.

Desire clutches me sinfully by the throat.

'How is he?' There is anxiety in the question. I realise that it is not an empty one, I am really expected to answer. And so this longed-for assignation starts off with a concerned discussion on the state of mind of my husband. But it's best to get the topic out of the way.

465

Then we get down to sipping the champagne.

'Mm, this is good stuff. We used to drink a lot of this Californian champagne in California.' Puck nuzzles my neck.

'That would seem to be sensible – when in Rome do as the Romans do.' I let him nuzzle my neck.

'Where did you get it from, this particular brand?'

'Adam bought it, I don't know where from.'

'Adam bought it? That was pretty decent of him – especially for us today, you mean?'

'Mm. Yes.' Miserable guilt leaks through my subsiding desire. 'Shall we go into the bedroom, Puck?' I glanced at my watch. 'I promised him faithfully that I'd be back by five. That only gives us three hours or so.'

'How will he be spending this afternoon?' We have just finished our first fuck (on the floor – we never even made it as far as the bed).

'Adam?'

'Yeah. Adam. What a great guy to let you come here like this. How will he be spending the time till you get back?'

'Be in the New York Public Library I should imagine. He has always claimed books to be better company than people, you know.'

'And do you agree with him, Eve?'

I squint across at the sensational face on the fur rug there beside me, and I trace caressing fingers around the curling upper lip. 'Well, I know that you have a greater effect on me here, in the flesh, than if I was reading you. Or reading about you, Puck. Or even looking at a photograph of you. But I also understand what Adam means.'

'He's a bright guy, isn't he. Adam.'

'Oh, yes, he's bright all right.' Brighter than you think, a bloody sight brighter than either of us, I think savagely. He has managed successfully to torpedo this little tryst. He's here with us in the room . . . the third figure at the feast . . . the invisible voyeur. Him and his generous gesture.

We buy a tie for my husband whilst trying to pick up a taxi-cab to take me home to him. My snatch smiles with approval as Puck signs the small package. He has chosen

466

the tie from the shop window next to the Private Parts
Sexual Aid Centre. I am reminded of the final words from
my evil, Eve!' And I have followed his advice, haven't I
just? With frantic abandon, I should have said!

Tears stream down Puck's face as he sobs out my
destination to the astonished cab-driver.

'Is that right, Ms? *The* Eden? That where y'wanna go?'
I nod back at him, tears streaming down my own cheeks
too.

He shakes his shaggy head in bewilderment as he
returns to his wheel. 'What the hell is this – some kinda
fuckin' wake! Co'mon buddy, let's move it. Let's get this
show on the fuckin' road . . .' He addresses this last
remark to Puck, who is hanging half in and half out of the
back window, smothering my wet face with final kisses.
Our idyllic assignation has failed, thanks to Adam. His
Machiavellian largesse has lopsided the fine balance of
our grand passion, reducing it to a sordid spot of
'something on the side'. Limiting its leaping inner life.
Puck understands this as well as I do, that is the reason for
our tears. The divisive death-blow to our love dangles
between us. We clutch hands through the window until
the cab glides into the traffic of Sixth Avenue and we are
forced to let go. I watch Puck growing smaller and smaller
in the distance, his beautifully broad shoulders shrunken
by misery. The god-like head, the golden curls, the
curving mouth continue to glow in my mind though he is
now invisible. I begin to wonder whether he isn't simply a
fantasy, a figment of my imagination. But the sweet taste
of him still on my tongue tells me otherwise . . .

Eight

'So what have you got lined up for me tonight, Eve?'

'What would you like me to line up for you, Adam?' My answer has a mechanical ring to it. A robot receiving instructions from the master.

We are standing in the shallow end of the swimming pool in Chelsea Baths, off London's Kings Road. A scattering of schoolchildren, being instructed by their swimming teacher, hinders the progress from one end of the pool to the other. We have already spoken nostalgically of the YMCA pool back in New York, and the ordered regimentation of the swimming lanes over there. Though I secretly enjoy the haphazard nature of our daily swims here. They seem to epitomise the difference between life in Britain (no longer Great) and life in the States. At least – to fine it to a further point – the attitude to success and ambition in London and New York City. And the attitude towards sexual opportunity.

Over there it is all so much more clearly defined, all laid on for you, like swimming lanes. So that you see more clearly where you are going. If you want to go there. Chance doesn't really enter into it, only your own will and decision. Here it is all so much more a hit and miss affair, with obstacles on the way to sidetrack you in your aim. Ambivalence prevails, replacing rigid purpose. Adam prefers New York now and is already making firm plans for our return in the spring. I prefer life in London, though it doesn't have Puck. But then he is in my heart, wherever I reside. It isn't necessary to have his physical presence.

'Well, I think a change from last night, don't you?' Adam looks meaningfully up at the Spectators' Gallery above us. The two young people up there wave excitedly back.

The girl shouts something encouraging to me in French and I wave in acknowledgement, though I have no idea what it is she may have said. She is a nineteen-year-old student from the Sorbonne, but waitressing for a while in a wine bar off Leicester Square to familiarise herself with the English language. My left armpit bears the small scar left by the lighted cigarette which fell from her lips last night, in her eagerness to suck my nipple. I would have appreciated some warning. The burn, though small, is still painful. It must have successfully killed off the life-growth of at least four follicles of under-arm hair. Still, saves shaving I suppose. I like to look on the bright side.

Adam's admirer is rather more effeminate than mine. Though it is not yet nine in the morning he is wearing full evening make-up. His petunia lips pout down prettily in our direction. His veridian-green shadowed eyelids shimmer like exotic butterfly wings. He is infinitely more beautiful than my little French friend, but each has something that the other longs for. Stubble. And the lack of stubble.

My French friend is taking male hormones in order, eventually, to shave her chin. This is her obsessive desire. Already her voice has deepened several octaves and her arms have developed flexing muscles (which she commands me to feel every five minutes). But she has yet to achieve a satisfactory five o'clock shadow, it is the constant disappointment of her young life.

Adam's art student despairs of his dark chin. It takes three coats of Max Factor Pancake Foundation to cancel it out, to perfect the pearly prettiness so that it matches up with the porcelain appearance of the forehead and cheek-bones. He is forced to wear this make-up, even in bed (as Adam's pillow-case proves), in order to preserve the illusion.

'You want a change do you? OK, I'll fix it.' It will be my job to ease these two youngsters off Adam's back. His exhibition is almost due to start, the exhibition of all the paintings that he did in New York. The last thing he needs now is any sort of emotional tension – or any degree of sexual frustration. My role is to see to everything down to the smallest whim or shallow requirement. I play the traditional part of the Artist's Wife. It has been played by

469

better women than me throughout the pages of creative history. The price paid for basking in the reflected glory of the Great Man.

'You just tell me what you want, my darling.' I speak confidently, my eyes bright, my gaze watchful of his possible displeasure. Already I have made a mental note to go on a diet for this next month because of the remark which has just been made to me as I lowered myself into the pool.

'How's your weight, Eve?' There was criticism, implied criticism in the question. But I was off-guard, thinking of other things, so I had answered absently. 'Fine. Why, how's yours?'

But the coldness of the returned glance, lingering over my swimsuit, spoke more eloquently than any further comment. I didn't continue the conversation.

Nor had I continued the conversation the previous week regarding a face-lift. Instead I have begun to worry about raising the money.

'I do wish that you wouldn't sit like that, Eve.' The irritability had brought instant tears to my eyes, like the reaction of an infant to the unexpected parental reprimand. But we are dining in a discreetly candle-lit restaurant where shining eyes can pass as merely the small reflections of the dancing flames.

'Like what, Adam?' I had straightened my back, fearing that I may have slumped into a middle-aged (therefore unattractive to Adam) splodge. Though, throughout my life, striving to appear taller than my five foot two inches I have carried myself with the upright stance of a tin soldier.

'Like that, with your chin cupped up on either side by your hands. What do you imagine that you are achieving – an instant face-lift?'

Only the memory of Puck's words from the past had seen me through the rest of the meal. 'Eve, honey, when the time comes please don't start messing around with face-lifts and things like American women. Remember that beauty is in the eye of the beholder. And you are and will always be beautiful to me. I'll just have one more wrinkle to love . . . promise me . . .'

But Adam has been as edgy as this in the previous

470

weeks prior to each of his exhibitions. All ten of them during our time together. And I have always managed to make allowances. Except that this time my own work, my writing of the latest novel, is going so badly that my patience is ragged around the edges. I only hope that I can hold on. For though on the surface I seem so sunnily in control, so loving, so affectionate, so all-forgiving, something lies dead at the centre of me.

I no longer have any feeling for Adam.

Adam no longer has any feeling for me.

It only requires one of us to say this to the other and we both of us can be released.

Nine

The Studio at Tea time, Tuesday
Devon

Dearest Adam

First of all – I love you, terribly. I do. And what's more I can never envisage that coming to an end, ever. I have just arrived in the studio and all around are photographs of us together. To my right is the snap of us on our wedding day, looking so happy. I shall turn its face to the wall until I am able to look at it without crying.

Life without you is indescribably numb.

I couldn't have said goodbye, I would have found it unbearable. But the longer we are apart I gradually begin to see the sense of it. We were undermining each other in a

471

particularly insidious way, without even realising it, thinking that we would be together forever. Thinking that this was just a bad patch which would get better again.

And it might have got better – I mean I know that it can only get better from now on. We shall see each other, I shall ask you out, we will be able to date one another. But not for a while, I am too emotional about it all to do much except break down. A fucking bore as a dinner companion. Besides which my nose is permanently red from snuffling into tissue hankies. I look positively hideous. You wouldn't care for that, I know.

In a moment I shall shop along High Street for a hot-water bottle to cuddle in bed tonight. Perhaps two of them. One for between my legs and the other for my tits. I am horrified to realise that I am without sexual aids. I *need* a large steel penis and my favourite Angel's Delight. Do you think that you could send me these? Be easier for you to buy up in London, there is not to my knowledge a sex shop in these parts. Thank you, my darling. I shall go on missing you until I die. In the meantime I'll make do with a cucumber.

Kiss your beautiful cock for me, will you please (mind your back whilst you are doing it). Write soon . . .

Eve

Friday. Tea time. The Studio.

Darling Adam,

I still love you. I am still bruised inside. I still carry an unmeltable permanent pebble inside my throat. Buying records just now in the record shop I suddenly burst into streaming tears. The poor, shy punk behind the counter was shocked into asking if I was all right. 'Terrible cold,' I sobbed back at him. But he backed away suspiciously as if I was a leper, incapable of even advising me what bloody awful records I was choosing. And they are bloody awful too. I have them here beside me but may well throw them away without even playing a single track.

The titles alone should tell you the sort of thing. All about LOVE: 'You've lost that lovin' feeling.' 'I'll never fall in love again.' 'When will I see you again.' 'I only

want to be with you.' 'Stay with me Baby' . . . got the
idea? And a particularly trite compilation LP marked
down to a pound because no one in their right mind would
buy it, called 'I Am Woman', leading off with Gloria
Gaynor singing 'I Will Survive'.

Still I seem to need this sentimental sop. I listen to the
radio a lot. I go to sleep with the radio perched on my chest,
hot-water bottle soothing down my starved erogenous
zones. Then I wake at two o'clock in the morning to
crackling wires, cold-water bottles, the light still on beside
the bed. The little orange light, remember that we made so
much lyrical love to . . . even scored our marathon fucks to
. . . what did the record number of times stand at by the
end? Was it ever the round dozen? Or was it just ten?

Oh, I miss your body, my angel! What a fine fit. And
your silky skin. And the way you have always known how
to kiss me. There can never be such a lover again for me,
not like you, Adam . . .

Writing this, I have turned your photographs around
on the desk to face me – but only for a second because I
am not yet enough on the mend to bear seeing that lovely,
passionate face of yours . . . But every day I grow a little
bit stronger. I am thankful that you are not telephoning
me. Later on I shall be able to talk to you and keep the
break out of my voice and the terrible ache out of my
heart. Heartache is the right description. Who thought of
it first? Though mine is more broken – clean down the
middle. I may have to have surgery when I save the
money. More pressing than a face (or stomach) lift. For
what do I care who sees me looking old and ugly if you are
not around . . . I might, at last, turn into a proper
bag-lady!

I rush now to catch the post, hoping this reaches you
tomorrow, Saturday. Your letter this morning seemed to
save my life, though re-opened fatal wounds again. Will
the bleeding ever stop?

We have had a special magic together. These threads
now are worth fighting very hard for.

Please miss me,
I love you *so* much . . .
Eve

473

Adam, my darling,

I awoke to your sexual aids – that is to say that the
postman delivered them this morning. Neither works, not
the steel and plastic penis, nor the little Angel's Delight.
On inspection, gulping back tears of love at your thought-
fulness and thrusting down my sexual frustration, I found
that the batteries in both were exuding an ominous
transparent stickiness. Had you wanked into each prior to
dispatch, by chance?

In a moment I shall take an envelope containing these
seeping batteries along to Warner's the electrician in High
Street. I hesitate to flourish the actual sexual aids before
his startled eyes, but shall say that the batteries are for
torches if he should ask. Though I suppose I could
truthfully explain them as being for adult toys.

So I still haven't engaged in sexual pleasure with myself
yet. This is the longest that either of us has 'gone without'
in our entire lifetime, isn't it. And yet I have no
hankerings whatsoever. I can easily imagine never fucking
ever again. How for instance, if one ever found oneself in
bed with another, would one cope with farting and
halitosis and post-coital sadness . . . And in whatever
fashion would one learn to fall asleep with a stranger . . .
Could it be cuddling, as you and I did with such
cherishing of each other for eleven such passionate years?
Do other people laugh with each other as we have done –
and will do again when this terrible pain of parting
becomes more liveable with? For you will once again
become my best friend, and I yours. I know that. No, we
won't live with one another any more or ever again. But
inextricable bonds remain and I take pleasure and pride
in their existence. I have nearly finished this new novel
though you are not with me to help with the spelling, my
dearest Adam. You have been my inspiration and my
creative driving force and for that I am eternally grateful.
Knowing that you exist in the world is a profound help
and will always be to me. If you had died whilst we were
still together I would not have been able to see the point of
continuing my own life without you. This way we are
granting each other fresh options, the freedom to flourish

independently of the other. When we are able to do so, when we are emotionally stronger, we shall be able to rejoice (tearfully probably) together.

I salute your sensitivity. I kiss your inviting lips. I smile bravely (though brokenly) into your shining eyes. I think of the dimple that forms when you laugh, and of your white, well-taken-care-of, slightly crooked teeth. I long for the feel of your lean flanks. And the profoundly moving sight of your sleeping face on the pillow next to mine . . .

It may be possible, who knows yet, to take a dirty weekend away together in future times. A secret treat for just the two of us to hug in our wounded hearts. I never would have imagined that two such loving humans such as us could cause each other this terrible anguish.

And yet it is a necessary period, a purifying process to wipe out the pettiness and creeping indifference (sometimes cruelty) which had entered our love for each other. Sometimes, fleetingly, I catch glimpses of a future without you by my side in which I am able to mention your name without howling inside. For now I live only to reach the end of each day still intact in my sanity (though shakily so). I love you, sweet Adam . . . I am here with support whenever you need it. Even if only to strengthen our decision to remain apart. Irony. Take special care of yourself, my baby . . .

Eve

Ten

Chelsea, London, SW3

Dear Puck,

I am writing to say that today Adam and I were divorced . . .